Whiskey Tango Foxtrot

Walking in the Shadow of Death

By W. J. Lundy

05.01.2014

**Whiskey Tango Foxtrot
Walking in the Shadow of Death**

© 2014 W. J. Lundy

This book is a work of fiction. The names, characters, places and incidents are products of the writer's imagination or have been used fictitiously and are not to be construed as real. Any resemblance to persons, living or dead, actual events, locales or organizations is entirely coincidental. All Rights Are Reserved. No part of this book may be used or reproduced in any manner whatsoever without written permission from the author.

* * *

Edited by Monique Happy Editorial Services
www.indiebookauthors.com

Cover Art by
André Vazquez Jr.

1.

The aircraft dropped and shuddered against the strain of the storm. Brad felt himself being thrown against the seatbelt; he felt weightless as the plane dropped, followed by the heaviness against the seat as the aircraft climbed, fighting gravity. The Antonov creaked and rattled hard before leveling out. Brad looked at Brooks still sleeping soundly in the seat next to him. Across the aisle, Sean was strapped into a row of jump seats that ran along the side of the aircraft, his head arched back and his mouth wide open, snoring. The two men were consummate experts at conserving energy.

The rest of the group were strapped into the removable rows of seats farther up the bay. Brad could see Chelsea in her ragged Russian-issue flight suit standing near the entrance to the cockpit. He looked up at her but she appeared to be lost in thought and didn't notice his gaze. Brad shook his head and unsnapped the lap belt as he pulled himself to his feet. It had been nearly a week since they'd left Yemen.

His leg still bothered him some, but Brooks assured him it was healing nicely. At least there were no signs of infection. On his feet, Brad stretched his shoulders and back before moving towards the rear cargo compartment of the aircraft, carefully holding the seats to maintain his balance as the aircraft rattled through another patch of turbulence.

He moved past the last row and found what he was looking for. The team had removed several of the unused rows of seating to make room for pallets of goods that were now stored in the cargo bay. Most of it had come from the airbase on Crete. Kelli wanted to make it to Italy on the first leg of the trip, but once airborne it was decided that the Greek island would be a safer bet. They studied maps and recalculated the expected range of the AN-12. A route of island hopping was finally settled on. Crete, The Isle of Man, and finally Hanscom Air Force Base near Boston.

Crete had been easy. They'd landed there in the middle of the night, finding the airbase on the north of the island virtually abandoned. Surveying from the cockpit, they'd observed evidence of a massive military evacuation. Dumped luggage was scattered about and in piles. Civilian clothing mixed with military items were strewn against a long chain-link fence where the wind had dropped them. The runway was void of aircraft, as if anything that could take flight left long ago. They'd waited until morning before leaving the safety of the plane, spending the night huddled in silence.

The next morning they'd had their run of the airbase and used the time to gather supplies and to get better acquainted with the aircraft.

What few primals they'd found were easily dispatched with suppressed rifles. Crete looked to have survived much of the fall; things were not destroyed or burnt out as they had seen in the past. The base was enclosed by a series of high security fences. As they'd approached the outer entrance to the base, they'd found the remains of bodies outside the gates and piles of spent brass near the guard shacks.

Far off in the distance on the opposite side of the airfield, a group of Primals had taken interest in the lone aircraft sitting against the back of the runway. Hundreds of meters out, the creatures were nearly invisible to the naked human eye, but through the scopes they'd seen them slowly gathering against the outer perimeter fences. The noise of the landing aircraft must have drawn them to the fences.

Over several days the men had filled the cargo bay of the aircraft with pallets of water and rations, always keeping a nervous eye on the distant fences as the mass of primals grew. With no slowdown in the growth, they'd decided they had worn out their welcome and prepared to leave. All of the tanks were topped off and they'd readied themselves for departure on the morning of the fifth day. As they'd taxied down the runway, they had seen the enormity of the growing mass against the security fence. Hundreds, maybe thousands had gathered and pressed against it. Any more time on the ground and the primals would have surely breached and quickly overwhelmed them.

Brad reached into the pallet of water and twisted a bottle free from the shrink warp. Suddenly the plane jumped again and slid out from under him. Brad grabbed tightly to the seat back and spun himself down into the cushioned row. The storm seemed to be getting worse. He strained to look out of a port window and could clearly see that the number two engine was still dead. The props were sitting idle at an odd and twisted angle. Kelli had convinced them she could still get the Antonov home on three engines. Brad hoped she was right. He twisted the cap off the bottle and took a long drink of the cold water.

Crete was a Greek vacation compared to what they'd found on the Isle of Man. It was a short four-hour flight to the small airport on the British island. They'd been hoping for just a quick stop that time. Gather fuel, top off the tanks and then get going again on the long haul to the States. They'd arrived at just past noon with the sun planted high in the sky. As soon as Kelli put the Antonov on the ground and spun it around, they'd known things wouldn't be so simple. Before she could even idle the engines, she'd seen the primals rushing in from the nearby towns and colliding against the security fencing.

Unlike Crete, the Man airport was littered

with wreckage. The main terminal was burnt out, and destroyed hulks of aircraft sat parked against it. Kelli navigated the aircraft through wreckage and along the runway until she was alongside a large tanker truck. The AN-12 came to rest awkwardly parked across a corner of the tarmac. She was taking extra risks to get the plane as close to the refueling vehicles as possible.

Gunner had drilled the team on a quick refueling mission and they were ready to accomplish it. They'd trained extensively on supporting the aircraft during the downtime in Crete. With the airfield in disrepair and surrounded by hostiles, they would need to move quickly. As soon as Kelli applied the brakes, the rear ramp dropped and the support Marines flanked by the rest of Charlie Group rushed towards the tanker truck. They dispatched the support Marines, then moved out to set up a hasty perimeter.

Corporal Swanson took command of the Marine techs, Nelson and Craig, who were dragging a large two-wheeled cart of stacked 12-volt batteries they had collected in Crete. They connected the cart to the fuel truck and quickly had the tanker's engine up and running. Swanson talked them through connecting grounding wires and fuel lines for a hot refueling. Even though more dangerous, this allowed Kelli to keep the engines running. The rest of Charlie Group moved further out, creating a bubble of 360-degree security.

Brad was with the security element on the right side of the aircraft beyond the nose. He could barely make out the screams of the mobs pressing against the fences over the roar of the engines. Without any verbal warning, the Villegas brothers, the group's only Marine riflemen, opened fire at the back of the perimeter. Brad twisted his position and observed a mob of over fifty primals pouring out of a large hanger bay located far behind them. Sergeant Hahn barked orders and one of the soldiers ran towards the Villegases' position. He quickly dropped prone and lay down a wall of protective fire with his M249 squad automatic weapon.

The SAW gunner cut left and right through the charging mass. With quick bursts and hundreds of rounds per minute, the primals were knocked back. The few remaining on their feet were cut down by the Villegases' rifles. The noise of the aircraft and firing had drawn more attention. All around the weak perimeter came shouts of contact along with ranges and directions. They were already surrounded and the enemy was closing in on them quickly. Brad was taking aimed shots all along his line of sight, but they were moving on them fast and they were losing ground.

Gunner ordered the refueling party to

wrap it up. Kelli screamed back from the cockpit that they still needed more fuel to make it to the continent. Frustrated, Gunner collapsed the perimeter to just around the body of the aircraft. Brad backed up and took a knee just to the right of the landing gear. The men continued to fire as the masses closed in around them. Brad cut down a small group of primals that ran directly at him. Aiming center mass, he hoped to knock them off their feet, hitting a moving target in the head at over a hundred meters being nearly impossible.

A section of the outer fence suddenly failed with a screech of metal that could be heard over the aircraft's engines; a stream of primals started to break through. Gunner lost all patience and ordered everyone back onboard. The perimeter team fell back to the rear ramp of the aircraft, shooting as they moved. Sean and Brooks quickly took up positions in the cockpit using their rifles to try and slow the approaching mass. Panicking, Swanson disconnected the main fuel line while it was still under pressure, a back wash of fuel spitting out of the nozzle and across the deck.

Swanson lost control of the high pressure hose and was knocked to the ground with the line dumping fuel across her and the runway. Nelson was quickly at her side. He grabbed her by the back of the uniform and dragged her to her feet. With the aircraft disconnected, Kelli released the brakes and the plane slowly started to move away.

As the plane crawled towards the runway, Brad noticed that the Marine techs were still outside. He yelled to the rest of the team asking about their location. Gunner ran past the men firing on the ramp and saw Nelson and Swanson running towards them as the plane slowly moved onto the runway. A mass of hundreds were just behind them and closing. Gunner ordered the ramp to be raised just as Swanson and Nelson came aboard.

"Where is Craig?" Swanson screamed. Craig had been positioned on the truck running the pumps. As the ramp closed, the mass collided with it just seconds later. They could hear them swarming all around the slowly moving AN-12.

"Where is Craig?" Swanson screamed again.

Brad moved into the body of the aircraft searching for a window. He could see Craig perched in the driver's seat of the large tanker truck. The primals had it surrounded, they had them all surrounded; hundreds of them had gotten through and were pressing against the aircraft and tanker truck. Craig looked up towards the cockpit and flashed a thumbs up. He put the truck in gear and it lurched forward, crunching through the tangled mob of primals. He drove it forward and ahead of the AN-12, using the large truck as an ice breaker to plow a path through the sea of primals massed in front of the aircraft. As the tanker truck crashed through the primals and debris and began building speed, Kelli pushed on the throttles, following closely in the wake of the vehicle.

The tanker truck collided with a small luggage carrier and pushed it out of the way. A large piece of debris shot into the air and crashed into the side of the Antonov, hitting one of the large engines and destroying its blades. Kelli had no choice but to commit to the takeoff. She killed the damaged engine and forced the remaining throttles to max; the plane raced on, crashing through the crowd of primals as it slowly climbed into the air.

Once airborne she banked hard and made a pass back around the airfield. They saw Craig in the truck running laps up and down the tarmac, crushing primals in his path.

"We have to go back for him, we have to find a way to get him," Swanson sobbed just as a flame swallowed the cab of the truck. The tanker exploded and wrapped everything around it in a yellow and orange ball of flame. The truck had been dragging the open fuel line behind it, and Craig had tossed a flare from the window, igniting the runway and everything else covered in fuel. Brad moved away from the window and fell into a row of seats.

Another large round of turbulence

knocked Brad out of his day dream and back to the present. He was tossed up and back against the seat he had fallen into. The remaining water in the bottle poured down the front of his uniform shirt. The plane bucked hard again, this time twisting in the air and seeming to free fall before the engines strained and righted the aircraft. Brad reached down for the restraints and strapped himself in. Looking up, he could see that everyone was now awake.

The bays lights came on and he could hear Kelli's strained voice over the intercom. *"Folks, we're not doing so well up here. The dead engine and the extra drag are really hurting us."*

The PA died as they battled through another rough patch of turbulence. Lights flickered on and off; the plane rattled and creaked. Brad looked around the bay and could see that everyone was now sitting upright and strapping in. Chelsea had disappeared into the cockpit. Sean moved away from the jump seats and took a spot just in front of Brad near the center of the row.

The intercom popped back on. *"This storm is beating us up, we won't have fuel to make Boston in these conditions. We are approaching the coastal islands of Canada – "*

Another particular harsh batch of turbulence cut her off. The change in air pressure caused the plane to almost completely roll to the left side; the nose dropped and Brad felt himself lose his stomach. He could hear the plane rattle and vibrate as Kelli fought the controls. Brad stretched to look out of a window but now could see nothing but blackness.

"Prepare for hard landing ... I don't know what's out there ... folks we will be on the ground shortly ... If you believe in something now would be a good time to ask for favors."

2.

When Brad regained consciousness he found himself suspended in the air and in the dark. The seat restraint was cutting into his abdomen. He wasn't quite upside down, but more at a right angle to the ground. Lights began to flash on, and he could hear people shouting back and forth. Brad's ears were still popping from the quick descent and the sounds were coming through muffled. He could hear voices but couldn't put names to the clouded shouts for help.

He swallowed hard and his ears popped, finally letting in the orchestra of sounds. He could hear metal being ripped away, men struggling to move about the fuselage of the aircraft. He saw movement below him and he waved his arm, drawing the figure's attention. Sean looked up at him, smiling. "Come on Brad, this is no time to be hanging out. We have work to do."

"Thanks smartass, now how about giving me a hand," Brad said back in protest.

Brooks moved up from behind Brad, slowly clapping his hands. "Good job buddy," Brooks said grinning as he reached up and pushed on Brad's shoulders to take the weight off his seatbelt. At the same time Brad undid the buckle and dropped out of the seat. With the help of Brooks he managed to land on his feet.

"Seriously, now are you—" Sean began to ask before he was cut off by calls for help coming from the front of the aircraft. They heard a muffled cry and Gunner shouting. Quickly the trio worked their way forward, stepping over bags and pieces of the aircraft that had come loose. They had to step high over objects then duck low to make it up the body of the aircraft. Near the front they could see the illumination of lights.

As they moved closer to the light they could see Gunner and Hahn pulling against the door to the cockpit. They could hear Nelson on the other side shouting for help. The door was creased and deformed due to the shifting of the walls of the fuselage causing the door frame to buckle in on itself. Hahn was frantically pulling and punching the door, pausing only long enough to step back and throw his shoulder against it. Gunner had found a fire axe and was preparing to swing it.

Sean quickly stepped forward and gripped Gunner's shoulder with his gloved hand. "Stop! Come on now guys, let's calm down for a moment."

Brad could still hear Nelson yelling from inside the cockpit. Gunner looked back at Sean. His uniform blouse was streaked with blood; he had a gash going down the sleeve of his shirt, and bright red blood was dripping from an open wound. Gunner stared at Sean with glassy eyes. "Why don't you take a break, Gunner, we can take care of this. Brooks, can you help my friend out with his arm?" Gunner nodded in recognition and took a step back before leaning against a battered console that had come loose and fallen across the floor.

Brooks stepped around them and quickly got to work tearing away Gunner's uniform, exposing a deep cut across his bicep. There was another crash as Hahn again launched himself at the door. Brad called out to Hahn, "Sergeant, give me a SITREP."

"Huh? What? Situation report?" Hahn stopped what he was doing and spun around on his feet. He looked back at Brad with a dazed expression. His head was scraped open and bleeding and his nose looked broken; thick blood and mucus covered his upper lip.

"What is the situation here Sergeant!" Brad asked again.

"Ahh we're ahh ... Sergeant ... they are trapped in the cockpit. Nelson says Kelli is hurt and bleeding badly. We need to get to them," Hahn answered, finally calming down.

"Okay, thank you Sergeant, where are the rest of the men?"

"Oh ... ahh, Theo is dead," Hahn said matter-of-factly, directing his flashlight at the seats suspended above them. A broken and crumpled figure hung lifelessly. Specialist Theo's neck was broken and twisted at an off angle. "Joe took his brother and Parker outside. They're setting up security."

"Okay, so the Vilegases are in charge outside. Good. Let's see about this door."

"Yeah … the door, we have to get it open," Hahn mumbled back, his voice becoming slurred.

They could hear Nelson yelling again from inside.

"Nelson! This is Sergeant Thompson, can you tell me what's going on in there," Brad yelled at the door.

"It's Kelli, Sergeant, she's hurt bad, she's bleeding. Swanson too, she's out and won't wake up."

"Okay Nelson, I need you to stand away from this door. We're gonna be coming in. Get pressure on those wounds okay?"

"Roger, Sergeant," responded a muffled but more calm Nelson.

Brad saw that Hahn was still carrying his tomahawk strapped to his thigh. He reached down for it and Hahn quickly undid the straps and handed it over. Brad swung the hawk in a powerful two-handed swing, catching the door above the top hinge. Applying his weight to the handle, the hinges popped and broke free. Brad repeated this with the remaining two hinges, then used the face of the 'hawk to break the door free of the frame.

With the door removed, Brad and Sean pulled it out of the way and stepped into the cockpit. Nelson had a light focused on Kelli. Part of the nose of the aircraft had imploded inward and her lower body was trapped between the seat and the consoles. Nelson was struggling to free her from the wreckage. Sean moved forward using the handle of Gunner's axe to apply leverage to the frame of the pilot's seat. He pushed hard. They could hear the wood of the axe strain and pop as if the handle was about to break. With some of the tension removed from the seat, Nelson and Brad were able to pull Kelli's limp body out and away from the wreckage.

They positioned her on the floor. Both of her legs were broken; the right leg had an open fracture and was bleeding. Brad tried to straighten her legs as Brooks walked into the space holding a bright light. He looked down and shook his head. He motioned for Brad to move out of the way as he kneeled beside his patient and went to work.

Brad took a step back and moved towards Chelsea. She was strapped into a smaller jump seat near the bulkhead. With the angle of the aircraft she was almost lying flat on her back now. Brad moved towards her and removed the seat restraints. He checked that she was breathing and had a strong pulse. She was wearing a flight helmet, but there was an obvious crack going along the top of it. Brad looked down at her and could see the cloud of condensation around her mouth every time she exhaled. It was the first time Brad had noticed how cold it was.

"How is she?" Brooks called out, looking over his shoulder to Brad.

"I can't tell. She's unconscious. From the break on her helmet, something must have knocked her out."

"Okay Brad, let's just assume for now it's a concussion. I need you to run your hands along her body and check for any broken bones or bleeding, okay? I'm pretty tied up over here."

"Okay," Brad said back softly. Quickly he began the process of moving his palms down Chelsea's arms and legs. When he completed that, he checked her torso as well as he could. Finding no breaks or blood, he reported back to Brooks, "Everything looks okay, what do I do now to help her?"

"Just let her rest. Why don't you check on the men outside?" Brooks said while he continued to work on Kelli.

"Are you sure there's nothing else that can be done for her?"

"Brad, go!" Brooks said, annoyed.

Brad found one of Chelsea's bags pushed up tight between the seat and the wall. There was a small blanket rolled tightly and fastened to the top of it. He unrolled the blanket and laid it out over Chelsea, tucking in the edges. Nelson came up behind him looking on.

"She'll be okay, Sergeant, I'll keep an eye on her," Nelson said in a low voice.

Brad turned to look at Nelson. His face was white and he had blood on his hands and uniform from helping Kelli.

"How are you holding up, Nelson?" Brad asked.

"I'm okay, just scared me. I thought I was the only one left for a bit there."

"Yeah we're good now. Take care of Chelsea, and help Brooks, I'll be right back," Brad said.

Brad looked up and saw that Sean had left the cockpit. He saw him and Gunner standing in the doorway. They turned away and Brad followed them back into the body of the aircraft. Gunner was now wearing a sling on his bandaged right arm. He was holding a Sig 1911 in his left hand. Sergeant Hahn was sitting farther away, now with his head heavily bandaged. Brad shook his head and looked at the floor.

"We're pretty beat up here, Chief," Brad reported.

Sean reached down and picked up a M203 that was lying awkwardly on the ground. This caused Brad to look across the plane to the now covered body of Specialist Theo.

Sean walked across the room and laid the weapon near Theo's body. "Things could be a lot worse Brad, considering we were just in a plane crash."

Just then they saw a light come from the open door behind them. Daniel Villegas pulled himself up and into the cover of the AN-12. "It's cold as fuck out there man," he gasped.

Villegas moved towards the huddled group of men and looked to Gunner. "We got a couple guards posted, Pops. But it's damn cold out there, and I forgot to pack my coat."

Gunner looked back at the shivering Marine. "You see anything out there?"

"Nothing Boss, it's dark and the snow is coming down hard. Can't see shit in that mess."

"There ain't no sense in us posting up outside. Bring the guys back in, let's try and secure the interior of the aircraft as much as possible until first light. We can strip the fabric off of these seats and try and insulate our clothing," Gunner ordered.

Brad was reassured to see that Gunner had regained his composure and was back on the job. "Let's go Daniel, I'll help you gather the guys," Brad said, moving towards the door.

Villegas looked up at him and nodded. Together they climbed out of the aircraft and into the darkness. Brad lowered himself out of the door and let go, dropping to the ground with a thud. Daniel dropped just beside him, then stepped off, leading the way.

Brad took in their surroundings. Just as Daniel had said, the snow was coming down hard; it was nearly blizzard conditions. There was surprisingly a lot of light. Brad looked into the sky and could just barely make out a full moon through the blowing clouds. He'd grown up in Michigan's northern peninsula, so a heavy snow fall was nothing new to him. He followed Daniel out and away from the aircraft, the snow making a dry crunch under his boots. Brad knew that dry snow was a clear indication of below freezing temperatures. He would have to find a source of heat for the men or they risked hypothermia. They moved farther from the aircraft and near a crumpled section of the AN-12's lost wing.

Corporal Parker was beside it with his M249 set up on its bipod resting across the wreckage. He had his arms crossed tightly across his body, shivering. Parker looked at the men uncomfortably as they approached. "Let's go Parker, Gunner wants us to hold up inside," Daniel whispered.

"Thank God, bro, it's so cold out here I think my nuts have retracted up inside of my body," Parker stuttered in response. He rubbed his gloved hands together before reaching down and securing his SAW. He indicated he was ready and followed Daniel and Brad down towards the tail of the aircraft. They stepped off, staying close to each other, the close proximity giving them a false sense of security.

Brad could see that the plane appeared to have crashed in a somewhat open field. Not the farm fields or pastures he recognized from home, but rather a large open break in a tall, old-growth forest. Kelli had done well putting them down in the clearing and avoiding the trees. There were no signs of any structures or manmade lights. They were surrounded by high ridgelines on both sides. A scattering of trees lined the tops of the ridges.

Brad searched as far as the limited visibility would allow as they crunched through the falling snow. The wind was picking up, swirling snow pushing into his face, the biting cold causing his eyes to tear up. They needed to get back into cover; it was too cold to be outside exposed to the elements.

They found Joseph Villegas just a few feet out from the tail of the aircraft. He was standing silently with his rifle at the low ready. Daniel let out a low whistle to warn his brother that they were coming up behind him. Joseph turned and nodded to them. "Where the hell are we, Hermano?" he said, looking to Daniel.

"No idea, brother. You see anything out here?" Daniel answered.

"No, just wind and snow, even the wildlife is too cold to be out in this. What kind of frozen hell did we end up in?"

"Kelli had said something about Canadian Islands before we went down? I don't know what that means, but Canada has always reminded me of cold. Maybe this is good, maybe the primals will freeze solid in this shit," Brad added.

Parker stomped his feet and rubbed his gloved hands together. "I don't know fellas, but can we talk about this somewhere else?"

"You're right, let's get back inside," Brad said.

3.

When Brad returned to the plane, he found that they had moved Kelli out of the cockpit. Brooks had her positioned in a makeshift hammock. She was attached to one of the emergency backboards that were stowed aboard the aircraft. They had tightly fastened Kelli to the board, then suspended it a few feet off the ground so they could keep her feet elevated. Most of her uniform pant legs had been cut away, and her legs were covered in improvised bandages. On her chest lay an IV solution bag with a line leading directly to her arm. Brooks was standing over her closely monitoring her vitals.

Behind Kelli, Brad saw that Chelsea was now awake and sitting in one of the low side jump seats. She was covered in blankets and shivering. Nelson and Hahn were sitting next to her bundled under a similar pile of blankets. Brad moved near Brooks who was taking inventory of his aid bag. "What are you thinking?" Brad said barely above a whisper.

"Fortunately she hasn't regained consciousness. When … or if she does, she is going to be in a lot of pain. I'll have to give her morphine, but right now … with those injuries … shit man, I just don't know.," Brooks said, not looking up from the bag.

"And Chelsea?"

"She's fine bro, just got her bell rung. Nelson has orders to get her to eat something, but she looks okay. Gunner's arm is jacked up pretty bad. I'm gonna have to get some sutures in it pretty soon. Hahn took a pretty good whack to the head. He's seeing double; I'm worried about him. He hasn't been right since we landed."

"What can I do to help?"

"You can find a way to heat this place up. If we don't get some warmth we're all gonna freeze. You notice those water bottles back there? Most of them are already froze solid," Brooks said, motioning towards a half case of water.

"Okay, I'll see what I can do," Brad said.

He moved towards the back of the aircraft. The cargo they had carefully stacked earlier had come loose and was piled up against the walls of the plane. Looking at the mess, Brad was surprised any of them had survived the crash. He dug through the pile and found what he was looking for. The large wooden pallets were buried deep under the scattered piles of goods. Brad called over his shoulder for Parker to help him. Quickly they started the job of digging out and cutting away the wooden pallets.

They managed to free the wood from four large pallets. Still Brad wasn't confident about lighting a fire inside the body of the aircraft. The strong fumes of jet fuel were in the air. Brad didn't know if a small fire would be enough to ignite them, but he wasn't ready to take a chance. They ripped down heavy insulation blankets from the inside of the plane and built a makeshift shelter within the plane and surrounding Kelli.

It wasn't enough. Brooks said her core temperature was still dropping; they would need to do more or they would lose her. Sean had moved near the sheltered area and joined Brooks and Brad in their discussion. Brooks looked to Sean. "If we can't warm her up she won't see morning."

"What do you suggest, Brooks?" Sean asked.

"I hate to say it, but I think we're gonna have to make camp outside. We need to get a fire going. I'm willing to stay in here and burn one. I'll take my chances on blowing up." Brooks said.

Brad shook his head. "What if I can take a couple guys out and get those pallets burning? Maybe we can heat some blankets and drape those over Kelli. Could heat up some stones or metal too. Shit, anything to warm her."

Sean stared at Kelli. "I don't know. If we draw attention … If we draw in any infected we're fucked. None of us are up for a sustained battle right now."

Brad nodded. "Honestly, if we don't get some real shelter I think we're all fucked anyhow. It's too damn cold. And those primals still have human DNA. I'm willing to gamble they can't operate in this storm any better than we can."

Brooks reached down into his bag and pulled out a block of C4. He held it in his hand for a minute before handing it to Brad along with his Zippo lighter. "Here, take this Brad. It's gonna be hell getting a fire started out there. Break off some small chunks of this. They'll burn pretty hot, should help getting that wood to burn."

Brad took the C4 and placed it and the Zippo into his assault bag. He turned back and saw Parker and the Villegases get to their feet and begin to strap on their gear. Brad was relieved they had overheard his conversation and he wouldn't have to convince them to go with him. They still had no cold weather gear. The thin Multicam uniforms and body armor wouldn't do much to keep them warm outside.

Brad saw more of the heavy blankets they had managed to gather from the cargo bay. They were made of a heavy material and normally used to put over and protect cargo, but they would work. Brad grabbed a stack of them and turned to the Villegases and Parker. "Let's cut these into squares. We can turn them into ponchos, then wrap the rest around our legs and tape them in place."

Joseph shook his head. "Oh, so because we're Mexicans, you assume we want to wear ponchos and shit?"

Brad looked at Joseph, confused. "Okay, suit yourself," he said, handing a blanket to Parker.

Daniel pushed his brother out of the way. "Man, ignore this fool, I love ponchos," he said, pulling a large Ka-Bar knife and using it to start cutting away on the heavy cargo blankets.

Quickly the four of them broke down the pallets into shards of boards and splinters. They loaded these into their now empty sea bags. They draped the cargo blanket ponchos over their bodies, tying them at the waist. Their legs were bundled and taped so that they looked like hockey goalies from the bulky insulation. After gathering their bags and gear, they stood in the door of the aircraft. The Villegas brothers lowered themselves down and back into the dark night. Brad and Parker quickly followed them out the door.

Once on the ground, Brad led the way into the darkness. Daniel had spotted a piece of the tail on the far side of the aircraft and in an outcropping of rocks. The team had already decided that would make the best place to build a shelter. Their primary concern was getting clear of the jet fuel-soaked snow. Brad moved in close to the broken tail section of the AN-12. It was nothing more than twisted sheet metal wrapped between the large stones, but it would work.

Brad moved towards a dead space in the boulders and dumped the wooden contents of his sea bag. He made a loose stack of the broken pallet parts, then used his knife to cut a long sliver from the nearly frozen block of C4. When the shard was free of the block, he carefully pushed it against a portion of the wood and, using his hands to shield the wind, ignited the plastic explosive. It lit quickly and began burning with a bright yellow flame. Brad added additional wood to the small flame until the dried bits of pallet began to take hold.

Soon they had a large fire going. The men dug away the snow and used the metal from the tail to build a wind screen and also to reflect the heat of the fire back towards the rocks. With the fire going strong, Brad positioned one of the sea bags filled with blankets as near the fire as he dared. The flames were just out of reach of the bag and Brad saw steam rising off the edges of the green fabric. As soon as the bag and its contents were hot to the touch, Parker quickly ran the bag back to the aircraft's door and tossed it up to Brooks. Brooks removed the heated blankets and laid them out over Kelli, then tossed the sea bag back down, now filled with replacement blankets to be heated by the fire.

All through the night the men took turns

standing watch, maintaining the fire and running the heated blankets back to the plane. As their supply of wood ran short they began burning parts of the aircraft and down wood from the tree line, using anything to keep their heat source going. They were surprised that they didn't see any signs of primals. They were even beginning to hope that they had crashed in an area where the infection might not have spread. Eventually Sean, Gunner, Hahn, and Chelsea found themselves down by the fire, while Brooks and Nelson took turns keeping vigil over Kelli.

The daylight came to the men as a dull gray. Slowly spreading over the tops of the high ridges, the cloud cover blocked out the sun, and the thick snowflakes dropping on the ground covered any sounds of nature. Brad had stayed awake all night helping to increase the watch. He stood now and searched the horizon as far out as he could see in all directions. He could clearly see that the plane had crashed in a valley, eating up earth as it had cut a path down through the snow-covered ground. Brad couldn't see any structures or buildings, and no other signs of life, just the tall forests ringing the clearing.

He reached down and dropped another bundle of branches on the fire before stepping off towards where Daniel and Joseph had taken up positions away from the makeshift campsite.

As soon as daybreak approached they had moved out to set up observation posts. He held his rifle at the ready as he walked in the direction where he knew the brothers would be. The snow had come down fast the previous night, but had begun to let up over the last couple of hours. The snow covered the sound of his movements but he still wasn't able to sneak up on the brothers. As Brad stepped closer to the tree line, Daniel stepped out of cover to greet him.

Brad walked closer then leaned against a tall pine looking back towards the makeshift campsite. "Where's your brother?"

"Two hundred meters out that way. Watching over the far side of the plane."

"You see anything?"

Daniel shook his head and looked out over the campsite. "Nothing. How's Kelli?"

"Brooks is keeping her drugged up. He says she's going to need a doctor."

"Doctor? Hell, where we gonna find us one of them?" Daniel grouched.

"Yeah ... I don't know."

"Psst, get back in the trees," Daniel whispered as he stepped back in to the cover of the tree line.

Brad took a knee next to the tall pine he had been leaning against. "What is it?"

"Joey just signaled," Daniel whispered, pointing far off. "There, see it?"

Brad followed his finger to the far off patch of trees. He spotted the flash of a signal mirror.

"What does it mean?"

"It ain't exactly a radio, Sergeant … he sees something, so get your eyes open."

"There, off the nose of the aircraft above that ridgeline," Daniel whispered.

Brad lifted his rifle and used the optics to search the area. He spotted them: three figures walking slowly, two out front, and another trailing farther behind. "What do you make of it?" he whispered.

"Well they ain't primal. The two out front are carrying long guns."

"I have to get down to the campsite and warn the others, you stay here. If things go bad, meet up with your brother and flank from his direction," Brad whispered.

He stepped off, ducking low. He tried to stay in the shadow of the trees as he wound his way back down into the valley and towards the campsite. As he moved he felt the wound in his leg tighten up. The pain reminded him that he still hadn't fully recovered from the fall in Yemen, the fall that had nearly cost him his life. Brad slowed his pace and took a knee in the snow. He lifted his rifle and searched the far off ridge line. He could no longer see the three strangers.

Brad slowly got back on his feet and

continued his move towards the others. As he approached, Sergeant Hahn took notice of him and lifted his head in Brad's direction. Brad quickly held up three fingers and pointed to the far off ridgeline. Hahn nodded before turning on the balls of his feet and quietly began waking the others. Brad moved into the enclosed campsite and kicked out the low-burning fire. He was careful to spread the ashes instead of smothering it, to prevent extra smoke.

Chelsea was awake and cradling her rifle. Gunner and Sean had already gotten to their feet and had moved off towards the aircraft to warn Brooks and Nelson who were caring for Kelli. Parker and Hahn, with weapons in their arms, moved into the outcropping of rocks and took up a concealed position just ahead of them. Parker had swapped his SAW for Theo's suppressed M203. He didn't want to make more noise than necessary. Chelsea looked back at Brad as the men moved out. She looked confused as if she wasn't sure what to do. "What did you see, Brad?"

"There's three people on the ridge moving in this direction," he answered.

"Primals?" she gasped, fear in her voice.

"No. Not unless the primals are carrying rifles now ... They looked like civilians, but they're armed."

"Should I be worried?"

"I don't even know where we are at. We

have no idea who is out here."

"We're in Canada," Chelsea said.

"That's a pretty big place."

"I know ... Kelli said she was going to put us down on an island near the coast. Well, that was the plan before we started losing altitude."

"Okay, stay quiet, either way we have them out gunned and outnumbered. Are you okay to move forward?" Brad asked, not wanting to leave her alone at the campsite.

"Yeah, I'm feeling better," Chelsea answered.

"Good, stay behind me and stay as quiet as possible," Brad ordered.

He checked his rifle and headed into the rocks towards Hahn and Parker. He found them prone with their rifles pointed towards the tail of the aircraft. There was a muddy path in the snow that led down and around to the aircraft's door. They had used the path all night to ferry heated stones and blankets to Kelli. Brad wanted to get into a better position. If their visitors spotted the tracks in the snow, they would know the team was outside of the aircraft. Brad didn't want to give up that information.

He slapped Hahn on the shoulder and pointed towards the tail of the plane. "Leave Parker here in over watch. I want to move up ahead and get an angle on the far side," Brad whispered.

Hahn nodded back and the three of them

moved out quietly in a wedge formation with Chelsea falling in just behind them. As they stealthily moved towards the tail, Brad spotted Gunner kneeling near a blind corner. Just to the other side of him would be the back ramp to the AN-12. Brad moved his people farther out from the tail. He dropped to the prone and crawled through the cold snow.

Brad stopped when he could see the right side of the aircraft and the hillside where the approaching strangers should come from. He watched cautiously, slowly pushing and packing snow in front of him to try and conceal his position. Chelsea was in a similar spot off his right heel; Hahn was behind him and to the left. He took a quick peek at both of them and saw they had also built small piles of snow to their fronts in an attempt to conceal themselves. On the snow-covered ground and wrapped in the grey blankets, they should be nearly invisible from a distance.

Brad moved his M4 up and slid the tip of the barrel over the small mound of snow to his front. He watched the strangers approach just off the nose of the aircraft and on the high ground. Looking though his optics, he could identify them as three males. One looked to be barely in his teens. Another was a large stocky man; the other was possibly a young adult. Brad watched them closely. He had a better view of them now than he had back up in the tree line. From their dress and arms, they appeared to be farmers, maybe hunters.

The two younger males were carrying long guns, not military weapons. The older male was covered in heavy furs and wasn't visibly armed. Brad watched the older man stop and speak to the other two. He pointed to an embankment that overlooked the approach to the downed aircraft. The two younger men turned and walked towards the higher ground. The man dressed in furs began moving down the slope and towards the aircraft.

He watched the demeanor of the man change as he got closer. Instead of the casual gait, he began to get lower in his stride. He hunched his shoulders, his arms were spread, and his head slowly pivoted from side to side. This man obviously had some military training, or at the least was experienced in the woods. The man stopped and looked intently at the aircraft. Brad watched as he removed a small handgun from his pocket. The man looked back to the two younger males then continued moving towards the tail.

Brad felt his heart rate begin to quicken with the pre-ambush surge of adrenaline. His sights were locked on the man; he could easily pull the trigger and end this. He closely watched the man's movements, trying to decide if he posed a threat.

"Maybe they're just locals," he heard

Chelsea whisper.

"Maybe, but the way he hunkered down and pulled his piece don't make him look like a search and rescue," Hahn whispered back.

Brad began to speak, to give instructions to his team, but he was cut off by the sound of a bird's call. Brad took his focus off the old man and put his sights to the two on the embankment. He saw that the Vilegas brothers had closed on the two and quickly disarmed them, but not before one of them had given a warning to the older man. Brad quickly moved his rifle down and saw the man step back. Out of nowhere Sean popped up beside him. Startled, the man turned and began to raise the pistol just as Brooks grabbed him under the left arm and gripped the pistol in his hand, disarming him.

Relieved, Brad let out an audible sigh before taking his eye off of his optics. Slowly he climbed to his feet.

"Let's go," he said to the others barely above a whisper.

They moved towards the tail and joined up with Gunner before rounding the corner. They came up just short of where Sean and Brooks had confronted the stranger. The man had his hands in the air and was speaking excitedly to Sean. Sean motioned for the man to lower his hands as he spoke. "You can lower your arms, friend, we don't want any trouble."

The man smiled and looked up at Brad

and the others moving in from around the tail of the aircraft. "Excuse my poor manners. We haven't seen many folks round here. Much less a downed plane."

Sean raised his hand to the Villegas, signaling for them to bring down the others. "Yes sir, I understand that. This was a bit of an unscheduled stop."

"Americans, are ya? I served with Americans, been nearly a decade, but I'm still familiar with yer uniforms."

"You a soldier?" Brad asked, moving closer.

"Not any more, my wars are over," the man answered.

Brooks laughed. "Hate to be the bringer of bad news, old man, but I think we've all been recalled to active duty."

The old man shook his head. "Aye, you may be correct in thinking that."

"So it's here then?" Chelsea asked.

"Oh yes, young lady, it's here," the man said, not needing clarification of the question.

They paused their conversation as the Vilegases walked into the group herding the two young men in front of them. They could see they were just boys with a strong resemblance to the old man. Daniel was carrying their weapons; they were light but not crude: a well-maintained double barrel shotgun and a semi auto rifle. Daniel carefully leaned them against the aircraft.

The old man motioned towards the young men. "These be my boys, William and Michael, and ya can call me Jeremiah. My wife and oldest boy are tending to the farm."

"Good to meet you all. Jeremiah, we have a wounded pilot, is there a hospital open? Or an aid station?" Sean asked.

"No, nothing like that. We can bring her back to the farm, my wife has some training, but the city isn't safe."

"The city?" Sean asked.

The older boy William nodded and spoke. "It's no good sir, my brother Thomas was in the city when it started. He told of the killing. He just barely made it home."

"How far is this farm? And is it secure?" Brooks asked.

"It's a few kilometers, and so far it's been safe. We are up high and away from the main roads. We have only had a couple incidents. Most of them have stayed clear of us. We have been careful to avoid them and not lead them up the valley."

"It won't be easy moving her, Chief, she is hurt bad," Brooks said.

A suppressed gunshot broke the conversation. It came from behind the aircraft where Corporal Parker had been standing watch. "They're in the trees!" Parker yelled.

More shots continued to pour out from a suppressed rifle. Hahn followed by the Villegas took off towards Parker's position. "We aren't going to have a choice. Brooks, get her ready to move," Sean said.

"On it, Chief," Brooks answered as he turned to run towards the aircraft.

Sean looked to the old man. "I'm sorry to inconvenience you like this, but could you and your boys assist in getting my wounded pilot on the ground? We will be moving out immediately ... and collect your arms," he said, pointing at the long guns leaning against the aircraft where Daniel had left them. "Gunner, you go with them, and take Swanson," Sean ordered.

"Hell with that Chief, I'm still in this fight," Gunner contested.

"Not with your shooting arm in that sling, and besides I'll need you and Swanson to provide security while they carry Kelli," Sean spit back.

Gunner nodded his head. "Okay, I'll keep them safe. Swanson, let's move."

Chelsea hesitated, looking at Brad, "I can fight, I'll stay here."

Sean smiled, looking at her. "Chelsea, I know you can fight, but that wasn't a request it was an order. Now move out and help with the wounded." Chelsea gave Sean a discouraged look, then watched as Brad turned his back and walked away. "Okay Chief, keep an eye on him for me," Chelsea said dejectedly as she left to join the others near the aircraft's door.

"You got it," Sean said.

Quickly he turned and jogged to catch up with Brad. "That girl is sweet on you. If you haven't seen it yet, you're a damn fool," he said as he joined Brad's side.

Brad stopped walking and turned to face Sean. "Not the time or the place, Chief."

Sean laughed. "Okay buddy, keep telling yourself that," he said before heading out towards Parker's position in the rocks. Brad quickly followed him with his rifle at the ready. When they turned the corner, they could see the bodies of three individuals high up the far slope. They were all face down in the snow. One of them still had its arms flailing about and moaning. Parker took another aimed shot and they saw a red splash paint the snow above its skull.

The men were on line searching in all directions. "Was it just the three of them?" Sean asked to no one in particular.

"Yes Chief, they came staggering out of the woods, walking all crazy-like. Not like the others; they were moving all slow and awkward. Maybe the colds got 'em fucked up?" Parker answered.

Joseph raised his rifle. "Shit, multiple contacts in the trees."

Brad squinted and looked towards the tree line above the far slope. They were breaking out of the trees, but just like Parker had said, they were moving slower. It wasn't a stagger; they looked more like speed walkers with bad posture. "What the hell is wrong with them?" Brad gasped.

"I told you, I think it's the cold. Maybe they're frozen," Parker answered.

"Anyhow, guess it makes them easier to kill. Let them get into range, take good shots, conserve your ammo," Sean ordered as he raised his weapon.

Brad watched them continue to move out of the trees. He counted seventeen of them before they stopped coming out of the darkness of the forest. The mass of primals moved at them in a mottled cluster. There was no organization to their movements, they were just headed towards the plane. Brad looked through his rifle at them. They looked malnourished, the same as the primals in the desert. Their skin was stretched tightly over their bones. Some of them were barely dressed, ashen and frost bitten skin showing through torn clothing. Others had frozen clumps of blood and gore stuck to their open wounds.

He watched the primals move closer and closer; they were one hundred and fifty meters out now. He took a knee and steadied his rifle. Hahn was the first to fire, hitting a tall man high in the chest. The shot failed to kill the man, spinning him backwards and knocking him to the ground. Brad watched as the thing struggled in the snow, fighting back to his feet before Hahn placed a second shot to the top of its head. The other walking primals didn't seem to be bothered by their fallen comrade; they continued the march forward.

Brad placed his sight on a well-dressed male. He put the reticle just below the man's chin, eased back on the trigger with the tip of his finger, and felt the rifle respond as he watched the man's head kick back in a confirmed hit. He shifted to the left and continued the motion on the next target. Aiming below the chin, pressure on the trigger, another hit. Soon the mass of them were on the ground. The team quickly replaced magazines and topped off empty ones before calling out to each other that they were up.

Sean brought the team online and they slowly approached the cluster of dead primals in the snow. As they got closer they noticed one thing right off. The first three that Parker had taken down were dressed in heavy coats, similarly to the strangers they had encountered. This new group was well dressed and in city clothing: suits and skirts, leather jackets, street clothes. Sean walked close to one of them, kicking it to make sure it was dead before searching him for identification. He found a wallet in the man's jacket pocket.

"This fella is dressed nice, bus tickets in his wallet," Sean said.

Hahn had done the same on one farther back. "This one too. Business card says he was a lawyer."

"They are from the city," a voice called from behind them. It was William. He had wandered down to the group. "The plane crash must have drawn them in, we usually don't see city ones this far out."

"Well that is unfortunate," Sean said.

"Mister Brooks wanted me to tell you that we are ready to move," William said.

"Okay, tell him to get going, we will be right behind you."

William stood there, giving Sean a concerned stare.

"Is there something else, son?" Sean asked.

"You can't follow us. You will lead them to us," William explained. "They will follow you right back to the farm."

"How exactly will you get away without being followed?" Sean asked.

"We know a way, but if they are coming in from the city like this … They can't find the farm," the boy said with a look of fear in his eyes.

"Okay, quick then, draw me a map to your home. I will lead them away. If I can distance myself from them I'll make my way to the farm," Sean said, handing the boy a small brown notebook and pencil.

"I cannot give you directions to the farm, Dad wouldn't allow it. But here ... This is a path to a hunter's cabin, my uncle's place. It's not well known and not too far from here. If you can lose them and make it to the cabin, we will come for you in two to three days."

The boy quickly began to sketch the map and point out different landmarks as he explained the route to Sean. Just as he finished the drawing, a new batch of primals emerged from the tree line. This group was thicker and twice the number of the previous group. The boy handed the paper back as the first shots opened up on the mob. Sean grabbed the boy's arm and leaned in close to him. "William, please hurry and get my people to safety. Ask the men to ready my bag and leave it outside of the aircraft. I have a feeling I'll be moving fast when I stop to pick it up."

Brad was close by and overhead Sean's words to the boy. "Chief, you're full of shit if you think we're leaving you out here on your own!" Brad yelled over the gunfire. "Go boy, get out of here, tell the others we'll meet up with you later," Brad yelled as the boy ran back towards the aircraft.

"Suit yourself," Sean said with a grin as he raised his MP5 towards the closing mass.

4.

Brad watched as Chelsea and the others lowered Kelli to the ground on the makeshift stretcher. From a distance, Sean waved goodbye to the group, then ordered the rest of them to go loud with their rifles. They watched the others move off to the northeast until they lost sight of them. Brad removed his suppressor as did the others. Parker slung the M203 over his back and lifted his SAW. At once they opened fire on the mass of primals that were slowly moving down and out of the trees.

With the loud report of the rifles, the entire mob put its focus on Sean and his team. They continued firing until the last of the third wave had been put down. Then quickly they ran back towards the aircraft. As Sean had requested, all of their bags had been dropped on the ground. Sean found his familiar ruck with his large scoped rifle strapped to the top. Sean hoisted the bag onto his shoulders then turned to help the others.

"Quickly! Let's get ready to move. As soon as the next wave breaks the trees we'll lead them away and into the far side of the clearing," Sean instructed.

Brad found his bag, grabbed the straps, and made some adjustments so that they would still fit his shoulders over his heavy poncho. He removed the leggings and strapped those to the top of the ruck. Cold wouldn't be as much of a factor with them moving on the trail. The bag was heavy with supplies. They had decided long ago to always keep their rucks stuffed with rations and ammo in case they had to bug out in a hurry. Brad lifted the bag up and onto his back. He looked and saw the rest of the men appeared ready to move. He walked away from the plane and found Sean farther out, facing the tree line where the waves had been appearing.

"We're ready to roll," Brad said.

Sean turned to face the men waiting in the cold. "Daniel, I want you and your brother to run point. Let's hold our fire and avoid shooting unless we have to. The plan is to get them to follow us, then we will try and lose them in the trees. Parker, you stay back by me with that SAW. If things go sideways we will be counting on you to cut an exit hole."

"How far we got to go, Chief?" asked Daniel.

"I figure if we move west for a good few hours that should do it. Then we can break north and loop back around. The boy showed me the location of a cabin, looks like maybe a day and a half's walk. There should be a river north of here, the map says if we follow it we should see the cabin."

"Day and a half? Shit, then we got to spend another night outside?" Parker asked.

Daniel nodded and pointed at the far tree line, "Here they come, Chief."

"Okay. Devil dogs, lead the way. Stay west until I say otherwise. As long as these things keep that slow pace we should be able to stay ahead of them. Keep your eyes sharp boys; if we wander into another mob and get surrounded, it could really mess up our day."

"Ha!" Hahn laughed. "My day is already ruined."

The brothers moved out, slowly scouting a path into the western tree line. Hahn walked behind them, then Brad, with Sean and Parker taking up the rear. It was in their nature to move quickly, but Sean had to remind them to slow their pace. They wanted to keep the mob in sight to ensure they led them away from the other team.

As they entered the tall pine forest the temperatures dropped even more. Most of the sunlight was blocked out from reaching the ground by the tall canopy of pine trees. There was also less snow. In several areas the ground was covered in large beds of pine needles and broken branches. Brad could see the Villegases out ahead; they were walking on line with each other about ten meters apart. Hahn was just ahead of him. Every few minutes Hahn would turn and look back at Brad with a worried expression.

As they moved deeper into the forest,

they could hear the primals behind them, crashing through the trees. There must have been hundreds of them now. Their moans carried over the wind and they seemed to reverberate and echo back against the pines all around them. Brad had to consciously will his legs not to run. He wanted nothing more than to distance himself from the mob behind them.

Sean had allowed the primals to close to within two hundred yards. Every time Brad looked back he could see the expanse of the mob. Occasionally one would break out of the mass and move at them quicker than the others. The first time this happened, Parker let out a frightened yelp. They all stopped to look back. A previously young male had broken away from the pack. He still wasn't running but his stagger was less pronounced and was definitely faster than the others.

Sean watched the thing with concern for a moment or two before raising his scoped rifle and knocking it down with a single shot.

"Nothing to worry about guys, fast ones seem to be the exception today and not the rule. But keep an eye on our six, Parker," Sean said as he slapped the young soldier on the back.

They had moved a good five miles into the woods when the terrain began to change. The ground got rougher and started to slope up. As they struggled to work their way up the incline their pace began to slow. Brad noticed that the primals didn't seem to be bothered as much by the extra effort in moving uphill. Even though they were clumsy and awkward they didn't tire out, and the mass had an efficient fluid motion. The things in the back would push the others forward. Yes, they would sometimes fall, but they would get right back to their feet, or another would replace its spot in the formation. It was like a wall closing on them at a constant speed.

Brad started to worry about what would happen if they couldn't lose the pursuing mob. He thought back to his time in the desert, when the nearly mile-wide mob had surprised them on the Hairatan road. That time they'd taken shelter and hid in the MRAP until they had passed. That wouldn't work today. There was no MRAP, and they would have to break contact with them before their pace fell below what they needed to keep their distance.

The men were growing tired. The pace was slow but it was still a long time to constantly keep moving, not being able to stop for more than a few moments before the mob would close on them. They had to eat and drink on their feet, always moving forward, even finding it necessary to relieve themselves on the move. They were all professional military men and long ruck marches were nothing new, but combined with the stress of the closing enemy they began to quickly feel the fatigue.

Sean finally decided enough was enough. He ordered them all to get ready to make a break at the next natural opportunity they came across. It didn't take long. Soon the terrain turned to broken shale and began to quickly slope away from them. The trees thinned out and they saw a long gravel road at the bottom of the hill. Sean instructed the Villegas to quicken their pace.

They moved down the slope at a fast walk, losing visual on the mob behind them. They moved as quickly as they dared without risking a fall on the loose ground. When they reached the road, Sean ordered them to follow it north and move up to a jog. They ran down the road, moving parallel to the face of the mass. Brad looked to his right up into the forest where he knew they would be. He couldn't see them but the sounds of the primals crashing through the woods was frightening.

They continued their jog down the road until it began to curve back towards where they knew the mob would be. Again Sean directed them back into the woods on the left side of the road. They continued the quick pace for another mile or so until they could no longer hear the mob. Sean signaled for the Villegases to move northwest and at an angle away from where he projected the primals to be. They continued to move until they started to lose the light.

Brad checked his watch. It was

approaching 1700, or was it? He didn't really know what time zone they were in, but 1700 still felt correct. Either way, they had been on the move for over eight hours. He couldn't locate the sun. When they could see the sky through the thick canopy of trees it was dark and overcast. Brad's legs were heavy and the wound on his quad burned with every step.

The forest grew thicker with underbrush and it became more difficult to navigate. Further to the north, Sean pointed out some high ground. They could see were the trees climbed up and away from the forest floor. Sean directed them to the higher elevation and told the brothers to look for a suitable campsite. They came upon a slow moving stream that was flowing down from the high ground. The men turned to follow it up towards its source, finding where it disappeared into a large formation of rocks.

Even though the road and stream had not been on William's roughly drawn map, this rock face was. Sean guided them along it until they found a game trail that led to a spot that was reasonable to climb. He moved them up the trail and to a large, step-type ledge. As they turned to walk along the step, the ground widened enough to where they could make a camp. Quickly they dropped their bags and collapsed onto the ground. All of them were breathing heavily and were well beaten from the day's march.

Brad laid back against his pack and stretched out his legs. He could see the steam rising from the sweat around his calves. He was hot now, but he knew they would soon chill as their activity levels dropped. Their clothing was soaked with sweat and they would be at risk for hypothermia as they cooled off. As the men made camp they removed the sweat-soaked clothing and changed into dry layers from their packs. Parker set up the SAW across a downed tree trunk that covered the approach up to where they were positioned.

Brad and Hahn used their tomahawks to dig a deep hole in the frozen earth a few feet away from the rock face, then they circled the hole with stones. They positioned pieces of timber into the shape of a lean-to and finally covering that with broken lengths of pine boughs. When they were confident they had sufficiently concealed the shelter, Brad gathered wood for a fire. Normally they would never build a fire out in such close proximity to the enemy, but in the artic conditions they didn't have a choice.

Splitting small logs with their tomahawks, they were able to get to the dry bits inside. Just enough to start a fire. Brad used a small chunk of the C4 to get the kindling going and slowly he added more wood until they had a warm glowing bed of coals. As darkness came the snow again began to fall. They used the fresh snow to patch any light leaks in the shelter and to build more walls around them. Soon they were all huddled under the shelter of the lean-to.

Sean had decided on a thirty percent watch; two of them would be awake at all times. One would tend the fire while the other remained outside listening and watching for anything that intended to cause them harm. Brad and Sean elected to take the last watch, with Daniel and Joseph taking the first. Brad moved against the rock face and let the radiant heat of the fire warm him. He pulled his legs up and wrapped the blanket around him. After the long day's march, sleep was easy to find.

Brad felt the cold on his face. A hole had formed in the canopy above him. He lifted his hand to plug the gap but it only got worse. More snow fell in, landing on him. He rolled out of the way as more and more snow filled the shelter. Brad kicked and pushed at the snow. His attempt to avoid the dropping snow caused him to kick his foot into the fire, inadvertently kicking glowing embers amongst the pine boughs.

Soon the entire shelter was engulfed in flames. Brad tried to look around him to warn the others to escape, but he couldn't find them. He dropped to his belly and low crawled out of the shelter, coughing and gagging on the smoke. Once he was clear, he rolled to his back before lifting himself to a sitting position. Brad looked around. The fire was already out, the shelter gone. "Where are the others?" he thought to himself before seeing a lifeless form in the snow next to him.

Brad rolled and crawled close to the uniformed soldier. He grabbed at his shirt and pulled him closer. The body was warm; he was alive. Brad grabbed him and rolled his head into his lap, yelling for him to wake up, shaking the man's shoulders. "Ryan, Ryan wake up!" Brad screamed, no longer worried about being quiet.

Private First Class Ryan opened his eyes. They were milky and glassy. Ryan's lips rolled back, exposing bloody and broken teeth. He screamed and moaned before lunging up at Brad, snapping his jaws as he attacked. Brad kicked his feet and pushed down on the man's face, forcing himself back, pushing away. Brad fell to his side face down in the snow.

Startled by the cold, Brad sat straight up. He was awake now, his heart still pounding from the dream. He looked around the shelter. He could see the brothers at the far end sleeping soundly. He pulled the blanket up around his shoulders and leaned back against the rock face.

5.

"Psst," Parker whispered.

"Huh?" Brad murmured as he looked around the enclosure. The fire had died down but the coals were still glowing and putting out a bit of radiant warmth. The Villegases were asleep at the far end of the lean-to; Hahn and Sean were missing. Parker was at the entrance leaning low on a knee.

"Come on Sergeant, get with it, something's happening," Parker said in a low voice.

Brad reached beyond him and slapped Joey's boot. The Marine looked out from the blanket that was tightly wrapped around his head. He stared at Brad, confused, then saw Parker in the entrance and his eyes went to alert. He reached over and gently shook his brother awake.

"What is it?" Brad whispered to Parker.

"The primals, they're here."

"The mob, how the ... how did they find us?"

"It's not the mob, it's something different. Come on, Chief wants you," Parker answered.

Brad removed himself from out of the warm blankets. He tightened the laces on his boots and crawled on his hands and knees towards the entrance, carrying his rifle in his left hand. Once he exited, the cold air hit him in the face, quickly waking him. Brad moved his back against the rock face and closed his eyes tightly, trying to adjust them to the darkness. Parker was beside him and anxious to move. Brad overheard him whisper to the Villegases to stay put but be ready.

Ready? Ready for what? Brad thought to himself as he got to his feet and stood, bending low at the waist.

Brad followed Parker away from the shelter and farther along the flat ledge they had built their camp on. Parker dropped to his belly and began to crawl through the soft snow and pine needles. *"Great, not only does he wake me up, but now I have to get wet,"* Brad thought as he dropped to his belly and silently crawled through the wet musty leaves, following Parker to the edge of the rock face's ledge. He spotted Sean and Hahn ahead of him and in the prone.

He moved next to Sean as quietly as he could. Sean had his night vision device lying in the snow next to him, but a similar device was mounted to his rifle. He motioned for Brad to move over and to look though the scope. The rifle was on a bipod looking out over the ledge and down the path that the team had followed earlier to reach the rock face. Brad quietly shifted his position so that he could see through the rifle's night vision optics. At the same time Sean picked up his goggles from the snow and put them to his eye.

Brad watched the terrain appear in visions of green and black, almost like looking at an old black and white TV set with green filter. Brad saw flat trees. He could see the river and almost make out the game trail they had followed to get to the current position. "What am I looking at?" Brad asked in the lowest whisper he could achieve.

"Aim down the center of the stream about two hundred meters, then go left a few degrees," Sean answered.

Brad followed his instructions. It was hard for him to judge two hundred meters looking though the optics, but he just followed the stream then panned to the left. He froze when he saw them: A small group of primals standing still in the snow and looking directly at the rock face. Brad put the cross hair of the scope over one of their heads and could almost see its cold dark eyes looking back at him.

"How long?"

"Hahn spotted them about thirty minutes ago. They're just standing there."

"What are they doing?"

"I think they're stalking us. These are different than others, they must have broken from the pack and somehow tracked us."

"Alphas?" Brad said with shock in his voice.

"Yeah, it's your white buffalo in the flesh.

The smart ones."

"What the fuck. Let's kill them!"

"We have to assume the mob is close by. If they call out we don't want to get trapped against the rocks. I don't think they have locked on our position, but they know we are close. I'm going to stay on the glass while you get the guys ready to move out. Keep moving up the rock face. Not the original plan, but we certainly can't go down there."

"No, we stay together," Brad said, still watching the group through the scope. He counted nine of them. The primals made small, quiet movements as they milled around an assumed leader. There was a bulky male in the center of the pack. He moved normally and looked healthier than the others. The rest of them watched him as if they were a pack of wolves waiting for a signal to continue the hunt.

"This is not up for discussion. Gather the men and gear and move out. Stay quiet and follow the game trail. If they make a go at us, I'll start shooting. But just keep moving, I'll be right behind you. We have to assume these are the fast ones so don't stop."

Brad shook his head and crawled away from the rifle and back to the lean-to, knowing it would be useless to argue. Hahn was already there and had moved the packs outside. The Villegases were suited up and ready to move out. Daniel removed a claymore from his pack and set it up so that it would blast down the game trail that led to their elevated position. He rigged it for a trip wire and backed away from it.

"It's my last mine, but hell, seems as good a time to use it as any," Daniel whispered.

Brad nodded his agreement then whispered for them to break a trail farther up the rock face, stay quiet and keep moving, using stealth ahead of speed. Daniel nodded and stepped off silently back towards Sean's direction. Brad stuffed his blankets back into his ruck and hoisted it to his shoulders. Then he reached down and lifted Sean's pack and followed after the others.

They moved close to the rock face and away from the edge to conceal themselves. As Brad neared Sean's position, he quietly sat the chief's ruck on the ground and crawled closer to his friend behind the rifle. "Sean, we are ready to move. You sure about this?" he whispered.

"Make it quick, their numbers have already doubled," Sean answered, ignoring the question.

"How are you going to find us?"

"Trust me, I can track you. Do me a favor and take my bag. I have a feeling I'll be in a hurry when I leave," Sean whispered.

"Can do, and just to let you know, Danny booby-trapped the campsite with an M18."

Sean let out a soft chuckle. "Marines and their party favors. Thanks for the heads up."

"Good luck, Chief," Brad whispered.

"Luck's got nothing to do with it. Now get moving, I'll be right behind you."

Brad crawled back towards the rock face and lifted Sean's bag with his free hand. Before he stepped off, he looked out toward the edge and could see his friend's outline and the soft glow of the night vision scope's eyepiece. He silently wished his friend well as he moved out after the others, still feeling uneasy about the plan.

He quickly found the rest of them as they continued to move along the ledge where the game trail eventually turned hard and moved farther up the rock face. Brad pulled an infrared chem light from his pocket; he snapped and mixed the liquids before cutting it open with his knife. He poured some of the liquid out onto a tree branch to mark the entrance to the new trail head. The IR fluid was invisible to the naked eye, but with NVG devices it would glow brightly like invisible ink under a black light. It would show Sean the way they had traveled.

Before moving up the new trail after the others, Brad paused one more time to look back in Sean's direction. The snow was still coming down in large sticky flakes. The moon was bright tonight. It reminded him of the hunters moons back home, when a full moon in the sky made it possible to walk the forest trails without a flashlight. Everything in the white-painted forest was glowing with a blue hue. Brad searched the distant trail, but there was no sign of Sean. He turned and rushed to catch up with the rest of the team.

Brad came up to the others ahead of him, walking in column on the game trail. The trail had actually widened a bit and twisted up again before starting to level out. When Brad turned to look into the distance he could just make out parts of the night sky and the tops of trees. They must be near the top of whatever high ground they had been climbing. A loud explosion in the distance instinctively made him stop and duck, bending low at the knees.

Parker and Hahn were ahead of him on the trail; they stopped and looked back at him. Brad turned to look back down the trail. They could hear the loud report of an unsuppressed weapon: two quick shots followed by a rapid fire burst. The sound echoed off the trees and up the trail. Hahn stepped back towards Brad and took a knee, aiming back down the path. "That's his submachine gun, they must'a got inside the rifle and popped the claymore," Hahn whispered. "It's your call, Sergeant. You want to go back for him, I'm with you."

Another long burst of shots followed by the single explosion of a frag grenade echoed over the forest.

Brad looked down the trail before finally answering. "No." He shook his head. "We stick to the plan. Besides, if we go back now Chief will kick both of our asses."

"Fair enough, then let's create some distance. We'll find a good spot to wait for Chief."

Brad nodded in agreement as Hahn got back to his feet and moved out on the trail, passing the word to the others as he went.

6.

They followed the game trail through the remainder of the night and into the dawn. Morning came in with a heavy blanket of fog. It was impossible to see more than ten feet in front of them. The Villegases were exhausted from the pressure of being on point. On full alert for hours on end walking a strange trail can take a toll on the mind and body. They had no idea what was in front of them, or behind them. The others began to rotate the point position to help them keep their wits.

Brad had moved up front and was walking the trail alone. He could hear Hahn's footfalls just behind him. They had tightened up the spacing because of the dense fog. Even though the game trail was well marked, they didn't want to lose anyone in the woods. The weather had changed with the fog. The temperatures had risen significantly. It was still extremely cold, but no longer below freezing; the snow had become wet and in places there was runoff causing water to pool on the trail. Brad's desert boots were becoming caked in mud and his toes were wet and painful.

They needed to find a hide. The men had been going non-stop since the predawn contact on the ridge. Brad found a place where the trail ducked into heavy brush and was skirted by high ground; it wasn't the best site defensively because of the limited lines of sight, but it would have to do. He halted the small column and called the rest of them ahead to his position. He watched as the Villegas brothers moved forward just behind Parker and Hahn. The men looked physically beat. Wet clothing and mud-packed boots made them a sorry sight.

"We're gonna rest here and wait for Sean," Brad said to them in a low voice.

Sergeant Hahn removed his pack and set it on the edge of the trail. "You sure Brad? I mean, you know it might be primals following us and not Chief."

"You know Hahn, right now the only thing I'm sure of is I don't want to fucking walk anymore. By my watch we have been in the bush for close to twenty-four hours. My feet are rotting in these wet boots. Yeah, we can keep pushing, but where the hell are we going? We don't know if it's two miles or two hundred miles to the next town," Brad answered.

"What about the cabin, the one the boy told us about?" Parker asked.

Brad nodded. "It should be close, but Chief has the map."

Joseph chuckled. "That wasn't very smart, was it."

Daniel gave his brother a disapproving glare. "Alright Brad. This is as good a place as any. Why don't you all set up on the ridge, my

Bro and I will park down here. It'll give us a nice L-shaped ambush. If Chief is on the run, we will see him. If it's the other things, we will lay low and let them go by."

"Thanks Daniel. Okay guys, let's spread out in this high ground. Go ahead and get comfy, get dry socks on and try to get some chow, get some rest but let's keep one eye open," Brad said, not wanting to assign a watch.

"How long?" asked Hahn.

"Let's give it some time man, not like we have anyplace to be."

***

Brad had found a position halfway up the hillside. He was tucked in under a large bush. There was evidence everywhere of small game. The spot was nearly void of snow and covered with damp leaves and pine needles. He placed his sack on his low side of the hill, and Sean's rucksack next to it. He put the heavy insulated blanket on the ground and plopped on top of it.

He looked off far to his right. If he concentrated hard he could just barely make out the position of Parker; Hahn was to his left and a bit higher up the hill. He couldn't see the Villegases but he knew they would be farther up the trail and in the bush on the opposite side of the path. The brush was thick; he was pretty confident he could dig in and conceal himself if he had to. Yet there were still numerous lanes where he could peek though and see bits of the muddy game trail.

With his ground cover in place, Brad carefully removed his boots and set the open side of them over a couple of long branches he had managed to stick into the ground. He was hoping they would somehow dry out in the moist cold air. He peeled the wet socks from his water-saturated feet, then used a dry towel to swab away the moisture before applying a bit of lotion to his wrinkled skin. After again patting them dry, he rubbed them down with powder before putting on a pair of dry socks. Instantly he felt the relief of the dry fabric. *What will we do when we run out of foot powder and lotion?* Brad thought to himself.

Brad took a few minutes to sit and listen. He was starting to hear the birds chirp and he could hear squirrels rustling though some far off leaves. As a hunter he knew these were all good signs; things tended to go quiet when an apex predator was in the neighborhood. If the wildlife was relaxing, he felt a lot more comfortable.

He searched through his rucksack until he found a stack of foil packets he had stashed in the bottom of his bag. MRE packages were large and bulky, big brown plastic packages with lots of goodies, but most of them were useless or redundant to things he already carried on his kit. So Brad tended to break them down into what was important. Usually nothing more than the main entrée in its foil packet made the cut. The rest of it was just filler and the weight was not worth the investment.

Brad flipped through the stack of foil packets until he found one that was the least unpleasant. He peeled back the top opening the foil container. *Good ol' number nineteen: beef roast with vegetables,* he thought. The food was cold and greasy. Brad did have a couple of the self-contained meal heaters but they put off a strong odor, and he didn't want to take any more risks than they already had. He slowly consumed the meal, telling himself that *food is fuel* to get past the taste.

When he'd finished, he dug a small hole and buried the waste. As his activity level dropped he began to feel a chill, so he pulled a small blanket-like poncho liner from his pack. The thin liner had a woodland green camouflage color pattern. Brad crossed his legs and cradled his rifle in his lap with the poncho liner draped over his shoulders.

He tried to remain as still as possible. The better part of concealment is not moving; the eye can pick up on motion easier than anything else in nature. Brad sat silently on the ground blanket. Occasionally he would slowly pivot his head from side to side. He had lost visual contact with both Hahn and Parker. They must have dropped down into their own ninja modes and disappeared. Brad got as comfortable as he could and parked his eyes on the muddy trail, watching for any movement.

It wasn't long until they heard the sounds of a suppressed rifle. It was muffled and way quieter than a loud gun, but they could still clearly make it out. That meant it was close. Brad looked to his left and right and detected movement in the brush. He knew that Parker and Hahn had also heard it and were back on alert.

Quietly and with as little movement as possible, Brad put his boots back on. They were still wet, but far less so than they had been. He heard more shots. It was definitely Sean's rifle and this last salvo was closer. He was on the move and headed this way. Brad had discussed this possibility with the men. If the enemy came in hot, they would take advantage of their formation and go on the offensive.

The L-shaped position would slow and catch the primals in the cross-fire. Hopefully it would do enough to end the chase. Brad undid the snaps for his magazine carrier and readied his rifle, watching the trail. Two more shots, this time very close and coming from Sean's suppressed .45 pistol, the pitch of the weapon far quieter than the rifle. Brad lifted his M4 with his own suppressor attached and waited.

He saw Sean come around the corner; he was moving fast with his rifle slung across his back and his MP5 attached to his chest. After a few quick steps he sharply turned, took a knee and took two quick shots before turning to run down the trail again. Sean ran past Brad and was flagged down by the Villegas, who quickly pulled him off the trail and into the tree line. Brad watched back down the trail as two primals came into view.

They were moving faster than the ones they had seen a day earlier. Still not like the ones in the desert, but these guys were pretty quick. Brad let them go past him. The entire point of their ambush was to let as many of them as possible get into their kill zone. They wanted to disorient the primals so that they could take them down quickly without giving away their position. Two more came into view just as he heard suppressed rifles from the Marines' position engaging the others.

Brad aimed for the one closest to him: a young man dressed in flannels. He had ripped jeans and bare feet. Obviously he wasn't too concerned with the muddy trail. Brad ended his worries with a quick round through his forehead. Brad watched as the thing's head snapped back and sprayed red mist onto the primal that was following close behind it. Before Brad could adjust his site picture, Hahn to his left dropped the runner-up.

More came moving down the trial. Now they sensed the proximity of the soldiers and began their screaming and howling. The ambush was holding; the creatures were running past Brad and towards the Marines and Sean further up the trail. This allowed Brad and the other soldiers to kill off the rushing primals from the flank. For the most part they seem to have remained completely undiscovered where they were hiding on the hillside, firing through small lanes in the brush.

Another group of five came crashing up the trail. But unlike the last two groups, instead of running past the dead on the ground and charging at the Marines, one of them, dressed in jeans and a torn T-shirt, howled and stopped in place, the others quickly stopping beside him. The apparent leader looked at the dead on the ground and again put his head back and howled. Brad waited to see what they would do, not wanting to break his cover.

Brad watched as one of the primals went to move forward down the trail towards the Marines. The leader lashed out at him. They looked at the dead on the ground. This was the first time they had ever seemed to take notice of their own fallen. Brad watched intently as the leader knelt on the trail and touched the muddy soil. He lifted his nose as if to smell the air, then got back to his feet.

Brad watched as the Alpha in the T-shirt turned towards his position. The thing seemed to lock eyes with Brad as it put its head back and howled. The others became frenzied and charged up the hill in Brad's direction. He got to his feet and, with the rifle in his shoulder, took aim as the Alpha primal lunged at him, baring its teeth and screaming. Brad aimed center mass and screamed "Fuck you!" as he pulled the trigger, hitting the leader several times and knocking it off its feet.

Brad saw the mass of them still charging his position, rushing up the hillside. To his left and right Hahn and Parker had also gotten to their feet and were firing and yelling back as they moved in Brad's direction. One of the primals broke the brush just in front of Brad. Brad fired two quick shots, hitting the thing high in the neck and chest. Wounded, the primal continued its charge and was almost on top of him. Brad swung out with the collapsed buttock of his rifle and caught the thing in the chin, knocking it to the ground.

Quickly Brad shuffled his feet and stomped on the downed primal's head while he continued to direct his rifle down the hill at the remains of the mass. Another primal exposed itself on his right, but was quickly dispatched by Parker's rifle. Now fueled with adrenalin, Brad started to move down the hill, closing the distance on the trail. He caught movement on the left. Once identified as primal, Brad let loose with three rapid fire shots, hitting it in the sides before Hahn clipped its head, killing it.

Brad broke out of the heavy underbrush

and landed on the trail. There were several dead primals positioned all around him. He looked far to his right, where he saw the Marines and Sean headed in his direction. Parker came out of the brush just behind him followed by Hahn. Brad found what he was looking for on the ground on the far side of the trail.

With its arms flailing about, the Alpha lay bleeding on the ground. It was looking up at Brad with hate in its eyes. Hahn raised his rifle and covered the open end of the trail as Brad approached the Alpha. There were two dark reds spots on the center of its ripped T-shirt. The rounds should have destroyed the thing's heart; one of the shots must have severed its spine. Brad watched as it struggled on the ground, trying to drag itself closer to Brad, its legs useless.

Brad moved closer with the others slowly gathering behind him. "So what makes you not like the others?" Brad asked the creature in a low voice.

The primal responded to Brad's query with a low gurgling growl. Blood and foam were forming on the creature's lips. Daniel had moved up beside Brad. The primal took notice of the Marine and looked him in the eyes. "No matter how many times I see these things they still freak me out. This is some shit you can't get used to, man," Daniel said.

"Did you see how he stopped looking at

me to look at you?" Brad said. "I'm telling you man, something is still clicking inside of this one."

"Yeah, but they're still stupid," Joseph interjected.

"No," Hahn said, looking back over his shoulder. "Brad is right, this thing somehow halted them on the trail, and he pointed out our position. This one was smart."

Sean finally came up beside the rest of them. He was covered in grime. His uniform top was ripped and blood ran down his arms; his face was scratched and bleeding. Brad looked up at him. "Hell Chief, you okay?"

"I've been better. Come on, suit up guys, we need to get moving."

"Wait Chief, don't ya think you need some rest? You look like shit," Brad said.

"No, we need to get moving again, get off this trail and into the bush. According to the map, the cabin should only be another couple hours. I'll rest when we get there."

"You're bleeding, Chief … Did they scratch you?" Parker said hesitantly.

"No. I messed myself up running through the brush. If you boys really want to help, I need ammo. My 7.62 is dried up. I need nine mil, I burnt though a lot of rounds last night. I was down to half a mag on the MP5 and a couple mags for the sidearm when I found you."

"I have two boxes of nine in my pack.

Let's beat feet. I'll help you reload on the trail," Daniel said.

"What do we do about this?" Brad said, pointing at the Alpha who was still bleeding out.

Joseph stepped forward with his tomahawk and with a quick swing he split the Alpha's skull. "That thing ain't nothing to worry about ... not anymore. Come on, I'll meet you at the top of the hill," he said, walking away with his brother following him.

7.

They followed Joseph up the hill and moved quickly across the top of it. According to Sean's map, the cabin was located across a saddle from their current position. The men kept a quick pace. Even though exhausted, they had no intentions of spending another night outside. That and they wanted to separate themselves from the pursuing primals.

They moved through unbroken brush now, avoiding trails, taking the path of most resistance. They found a small stream, and even though it caused them to soak their cold feet, they waded through the water as they followed it down the hill. The men were doing everything they could to become hard to follow. Walking the streambed paved with polished stones would help them avoid boot prints on the trail. The tradeoff was cold and miserable feet. They tracked the stream for over five hundred meters before moving back to the shore on the far side.

Sean broke some pine boughs to try and brush away the tracks in the snow, concealing the spot where they exited the water. Farther from the stream they spotted the old gravel road that the map showed them would lead to the cabin. A burnt-out stone foundation near a plank bridge was the final landmark. A small drive would be located just past it; it would be covered. The team continued to move in line, meters from the road, trying to remain hidden while they searched for the drive.

Hahn spotted it first, broken and rutted as if a heavy truck had used it often, probably in the spring or early fall when the ground was soft, using four wheel drive to battle its way up the muddy drive. The entrance was halfheartedly blocked by a long pole and two cut pine trees. Brad had seen similar things done around the hunting lodges in northern Michigan. These remote deer camps were often rustic and seldom used, so the owners would block or conceal the drives when they left them at the end of the season, hoping to deter thieves or vandals.

The men approached the drive tactically, posting on the opposite side of the road and providing cover as they ran across it two at a time. Not knowing if there were still roaming primals about, they didn't want to be exposed and in the open. They set back up in three groups of two, now just off the head of the driveway. Sean nodded to the Marines providing point; they stood slowly and began to patrol up the approach to the cabin.

As they followed the drive it widened into a small, open field. The trees there had been cut back and the cabin sat in the middle of a snow-covered meadow. There was a pond behind it and a pair of out buildings. Brad recognized one as an outhouse; the other looked to be a tool shed. The cabin itself wasn't the pioneer housing folks would expect when they heard "cabin." It was a meager one-story structure sheathed in painted plywood and roofed with shabby cedar shingles. The door was made of heavy planks and the windows were covered with heavy shutters. There was a large stack of firewood under the covered front porch.

The men grouped together in some high grass and observed the structure from a distance. They watched for several minutes without detecting any movement. Brad volunteered to check it out, and Hahn followed close behind him for support. The rest of the men covered the driveway and the field behind the building. Brad ran across the open ground and ducked behind the firewood on the porch.

Looking at the front door, he could easily see a hasp and padlock on it. The shutters on the two front windows were also padlocked shut. Brad walked along the outside wall of the cabin, staying low to the ground with his body close to the building. Every window they passed had similar locks. He moved slowly with Hahn following until they had completely circumnavigated the building and returned to the front.

"Unless the owner did some magic trick where he locked the door, then teleported himself inside, the cabin must be empty," Brad whispered.

"You want me to pop the door?" Hahn whispered, unfastening his tomahawk from his belt.

"Okay, let's do it, but try not to damage it, I'd like to be able to use it later."

"Piece of cake," Hahn answered.

The two of them left their position by the woodpile and quickly moved up on opposite sides of the plank door. Hahn inserted the spike of the hawk into the ring of the lock and applied pressure. The lever arm of the hawk worked flawlessly and with a small sound of splitting wood the hasp separated itself from the door. With the hasp removed, Hahn slid his hand down to the knob. He twisted and felt resistance. Hahn returned the hawk to his belt and drew his knife. Forcing the blade between the door and its frame, Hahn pushed the blade forward and the door popped.

He let go of the handle and let the door swing open and into the structure. The door opened with a loud squeak, allowing daylight to bleed into the room. Brad slowly crept into the opening with Hahn beside him. They moved shoulder to shoulder, looking into the dark interior of the cabin. Brad clicked on the light at the end of his M4 and probed the interior of the structure. He swept the beam around the room quickly; finding nothing that looked threatening, they moved inside.

The cabin was sparsely furnished with a set of commercial bunk beds against one wall, a wood stove in a corner with a cook plate on top. On the opposite side of the room was a small kitchen and a long counter top. Mounted above the counter were long rough cut board shelves stocked with canned goods. A small sofa and a kitchen table with four chairs around it sat in the center of the room.

Brad moved in and stood near the table. He swept his hand across the surface and swiped a trail of dust. "This place is empty, has been for a while. Go ahead and signal for the rest of them to move in," Brad said to Hahn.

As Hahn moved outside, Brad walked over to the kitchen area. A small sink was cut out into the counter with a hand pump for water sitting over it. The pump looked rusted and unserviceable. Brad lifted the handle and forced it down; he heard the screech of the gear as it broke free of the rust. He pumped it again and again before he was rewarded by resistance followed by a gush of brown water. Brad let it rest there. He knew from experience that if he continued to pump the water would most likely clear. For now it wasn't a priority with a foot of snow outside available for melting.

He looked at the shelves and the canned goods. This place was obviously stocked by men, probably hunters. He found cans of roast beef, salmon, and corned beef hash. There were very few vegetables or fruits. *Better than nothing*, he thought as he walked to the far wall and dropped his pack on the floor. Brad moved to the small dining table and lit a candle that was sitting near the center of it. By now the rest of the men had entered the cabin and they shut the door, blocking off the sunlight.

The cabin's door was antique and had a wooden latch with a small length of 2x4 lumber to lock it shut. They put the board in place and locked themselves in. The men checked the windows; they were locked shut and the boards outside prevented them from seeing out. They dropped their gear and gathered around the table.

"Fire or no?" Parker asked, pointing to the woodstove.

"Let's see if we can go without. We had a hard time breaking contact with those things. If they creep up on us in here we might not get another chance," Sean said.

Brad walked over to the bunk beds and found a pile of folded blankets stacked on the top rack. "Chief, why don't you get some sleep? We can set up a watch rotation and get settled in. It may still be a while before the kid shows up."

Sean nodded in agreement as he walked across to the bunks. The Villegases agreed to take the first watch, but first they wanted to inspect the out buildings. After they went outside, Parker found a small ceiling access ladder leading to the attic. The attic wasn't finished and the space was narrow with small vents in both gable ends that allowed them to see outside. These would make good watch positions if they elected to keep the windows shuttered.

As Brad helped Parker leave the attic, Daniel came back into the doorway, excited. "Hey Sergeant, check out what we found in the shed."

Brad grabbed his M4 and followed Daniel out of the house and around back to the small out building. The shed door was slid open, and a small padlock lay on the ground. Joey was inside pulling a canvas cover off of a snow mobile; another sat right next to it. They were very sleek racing models.

"Damn, someone had some sick toys!" Joey exclaimed.

Brad moved in and looked closer at the sleds. One was a high end Polaris, the other was an older pull start Artic Cat. From outward appearances they looked to be very well maintained.

"You see any fuel?" Brad asked.

"Oh yeah, we got close to two five-gallon cans along the back wall. Might be stale. There's a jug of stabilizer here also, I bet it will fire these up," Joey said.

"Nice find, anything else?"

"Decent splitting axe and a chainsaw," Joey answered.

"Very good, bring them in the cabin. Might as well get these topped off with fuel, maybe we will have to use them in a hurry. You never know."

Brad stepped out of the shed and took a look at the far tree lines. He sat and observed while he listened to the Villegases fuel the snow mobiles. He scanned the area where they had come up the driveway. He could see the wind blowing some of the high grass that reached above the snow fall, but other than that, there was nothing to be seen. The sun had disappeared back behind the heavy gray clouds. Brad knew it would grow cold again tonight. He hoped they would be able to keep warm enough in the shade of the cabin without a fire.

When the Villegases finished fueling the snow mobiles, Brad helped them secure the doors to the shed, then followed them to the small outhouse. Unlike the other building, this one was unlocked. They pulled the door open and found nothing out of the ordinary. It was just a rustic plank building with a shitter in the center. They closed the door and moved back to the cabin's porch.

"You think we should poke some view ports in these shutters?" Daniel asked.

Brad looked out at the opposing tree lines and the far off area where the driveway disappeared into the tall pines. Even with the vents they'd found in the attic, their view would still be limited. "Yeah, let's do it, but make them small, and let's finish quick. We need to get back inside and button up before we're seen."

"Understood," Daniel said as he unsheathed his Ka-Bar and started working a hole into the wooden shutter.

Brad left the brothers on the porch and moved back into the small cabin. Sean was already snoring away on the bottom bunk. Hahn and Parker were sorting through the various food stores that were in the cabin. Hahn pulled down a rusty old biscuit tin and smiled when he heard the metallic rattle. He popped the top off of the tin and poured the contents onto the table. A little over a half dozen loose rounds and a small paper box landed on the wooden surface.

Brad walked over and picked up the box. "Looks like we're in the home of a big game hunter. A bit over fifty rounds of .308."

"You think the gun is in here somewhere?" Hahn asked.

"Maybe, but I know for a fact Sean will be happy to add these to his kit."

Brad took the box of ammo and piled the rounds close around it. He saw a flash of light enter the cabin where the Villegases outside had successfully carved a peek hole into the shutter. Brad walked across the room to the wood stove. An old mercury thermometer embedded into an old tin beer sign hung on the wall. The sign was advocating some unknown lager, but the thermometer was already twenty-eight degrees Fahrenheit, or negative two degrees Celsius.

Brad stood staring at the thermometer as Parker walked up behind him. "Twenty-eight! Damn, Sergeant, you sure we can't build a fire?"

"Not tonight, we can't risk detection again."

"How we gonna keep from freezing?" Hahn asked as he walked from across the room.

Before Brad could answer, the Villegases came in and bolted the door shut. "We got small spy holes in the front and back, we can see the flanks from the attic. I think we should cover them from the inside so we don't leak any light after dark," Joseph said.

"Sounds good," Brad replied.

"So what were ya all talking about?" Joseph asked.

Parker turned towards the rest of them. "I was telling the sergeant we're gonna need a fire in the stove. It's already below freezing with the sun still up; we're gonna freeze tonight."

Joseph smiled. "Damn Parker, you always belly aching. We'll be okay, we can just double up in them bunks. The body heat will keep you cozy, you can rack with me if ya want."

"Man, fuck you," Parker mumbled, shaking his head.

"It's actually a good idea," Hahn said.

"Four sleeping with two on watch."

"You all are stupid," Parker protested.

"Fine with me, you can have first watch," Joseph said. "I get top bunk with Danny, you all can fight over who gets to sleep with the chief," he said, laughing as he started stripping off his gear.

8.

The first night in the cabin went without incident. The men huddled together for warmth as the guards, bundled heavily with blankets and clothing, took shifts and watched though the peep holes. The night as predicted grew very cold. Brad was amazed to see the temperature drop far into the negative numbers. He knew it was cold the previous night, but actually watching the mercury drop made him realize just how lucky they had been to survive the arctic temperatures.

They stuck to the rotation of two on watch while four rested. It had been decided that they would limit their activity while they holed up in the cabin. It wasn't a tough decision. The men were exhausted from the day and night they had spent on the run through the forest. Snow fell hard through the day and all night. Soon there was no evidence of the road or the tracks they had left the day before. With four walls and a roof over their head, sleep came easy, and with their brothers on watch they slept soundly.

On the third afternoon they reached a compromise; Parker was allowed to use some of the driest and smallest cuts of barkless wood on the porch to build a small fire in the stove. Dry wood tended to smoke less, and by feeding in the small pieces slowly they could build a hot, fast-burning fire with little to no visible smoke. It was still very cold outside so the smoke that was produced rose away from the cabin quickly. They hoped it would be enough so that their position was not given away.

They used the stove to prepare meals from the canned goods. As always, they left the easy to carry MREs packed away and ate what was readily available first. As Brad had surmised, the water from the hand pump in the kitchen cleared after the rust buildup was flushed out. They had found a small can of coffee that they happily brewed and enjoyed while it lasted. The men were feeling good about their situation, even though they didn't know about the rest of their party or the whereabouts of the boy that was supposed to come for them.

They spent their time cleaning weapons, redistributing ammo, and repairing their equipment. When it was necessary they would leave the confines of the cabin to use the outhouse in pairs. They were careful to skirt the perimeter of the buildings and cross as little open ground as possible to avoid silhouetting themselves against the bright snow. They began to develop a routine, and with the routine came boredom. Cabin fever set in and they began to discuss their next move.

Brad was sitting at the kitchen table using

some heavy cord he had found to stitch together a heavy coat. Joseph had made the first one and the others were impressed with the design, so Brad had taken a turn working at the table. He made large, uneven stitches, but it would be enough to hold the coat together, and would help to keep them warm when the time came to travel again. He had just finished attaching the sleeves to the coat when Sean gave a warning call from the attic. Sean had been on watch, using his rifle's scope to keep an eye on the snow-covered fields.

"Movement in the west tree line, ten meters inside the trees," Sean said in a low voice that could easily be heard below.

Brad stopped what he was doing and ran to one of the windows in the side of the cabin. Over the past few days they had improved their peep holes to make them large enough to use their binoculars. Brad spotted them right away: two figures standing side by side inside the trees. They seemed to be observing the cabin.

"Should we snuff the fire?" Hahn asked.

"No, let it burn. If they haven't already seen it, putting it out won't help, it'll just make a cloud of smoke," Sean answered from the attic.

Brad watched as the two figures began approaching the cabin. As they broke the tree line, Brad could see that both of them carried heavy packs. One held a walking stick and the other had a rifle slung over his shoulder. Brad let out an audible sigh of relief as he identified the man with the pack as Private Nelson. The other figure in front he didn't recognize.

"It's Nelson plus one," Brad said in a jovial voice as Sean dropped out of the attic entrance.

"Holy shit, they finally came for us," Daniel said with a laugh as he walked to unbolt the door.

They met the men on the porch and quickly rushed them inside, locking the door behind them. They removed the men's heavy packs and brought them close to the fire to warm up. They wore heavy coats and heavy boots; quickly they were stripped of the clothing and handed cups of warm water.

"Sorry we don't seem to have any tea or coffee, but the water will still help to warm you," Parker said with a smile.

"Most grateful for it, and by the way my name is Thomas," the new man said as he happily took the cup, sipping while the others made introductions.

Nelson stood by the stove warming himself and smiling. "Boy am I glad to see you all, we were really worried you might not have made it. Jeremiah said that was the first time they had seen so many of them so far from town."

"We're sure it was the plane that drew them into the country," Thomas added. "We have been lucky out in the high ground, they don't never seem to venture this far out. Well at least they hadn't."

Sean moved from behind them and leaned against the wall. "Shit, I apologize for stirring up the neighbors, and I promise it wasn't our intent."

Thomas nodded. "Aye, we understand, but still it complicates things ... Mom packed you all some goods. There are a couple loaves of bread and fresh butter in the packs. As well as some thermal underwear, heavy socks and flannel shirts. I know it's not a lot but it's all we got."

Nelson opened a pack and started handing out the goods. Brad took a heavy shirt, grinning. "No, this is all great, we really do appreciate it. So how long before you will be ready to move out? I think I speak for everyone when I say we are ready to get out of here," Brad said.

Thomas's expression changed and he broke eye contact and looked down and into the fire. "What ... what is it?" Sean asked.

Thomas looked up at Nelson. Nelson stood silent for a moment before moving away from the stove and sitting in a chair near Thomas. "Gosh, we drew straws on how to tell you all this. I won but looks like Thomas ain't got it in him to tell ya," Nelson said in a low voice.

"Tell us what?" Brad asked.

"It's Kelli, Sergeant."

"What about her?" Brad asked.

"She ain't doing so well … She is really bad, Brooks says she needs antibiotics. He gave her everything we had, but he says she needs the good stuff, and other things too. He made a list," Nelson said as he reached into his pocket and handed Brad a folded sheet of paper.

Brad unfolded the paper and read down the long list of items and the names of drugs. He folded it back and handed it off to Sean who studied the note.

"So is this stuff hidden away in here somewhere?" Brad asked, already guessing at the answer.

Nelson turned towards Thomas instead of answering. Thomas slowly looked up at Brad and shook his head.

"Okay, then where do we get it?" Sean asked.

Thomas took a long sip from his cup before finally speaking. "There's a town … Well, more of a village really, but they got a drug store and a clinic. Mom says this stuff should be there."

"Mom says, huh?" Sean asked.

"Mom was a nurse before she had us boys. She used to work there."

"Okay, and where is this town?" Sean said.

"Ten kilometers up the road, north, easy to find … The road will take you right to it."

"Primals?" Brad asked.

"Yes sir, lots of 'em."

Sean moved away from the group and went to sit at the kitchen table. Brad followed and joined him along with Hahn and Joseph. Joseph had brought a loaf of bread and the butter with him. He began to cut it into slices and stacked the pieces in a wooden bowl. The men grabbed at the bread and ate hungrily. Hahn was the first to break the silence.

"How do we even know Kelli will make it with the drugs?" Hahn said.

Sean wiped his mouth with his sleeve and took a long drink of water before speaking. "Brooks wrote that if she doesn't get the meds she will die. And without Kelli we won't be flying off this rock."

Joseph grunted. "Shit, Chief, you saw Kelli, she was messed up. She won't be flying anything anytime soon."

Sean took another pull off his bottle of water and grunted before speaking. "If I know Brooks, he is just laying out the facts for us … He would expect us to make the tactical decision, pilot or not, the choice is still ours."

"You are all probably right, but she is the best shot we got. I volunteer … I'll go," Brad said.

Sean shook his head. "Now hold on a

minute, you can't go making this decision on your own. Every member of this team is a critical component right now. What you do, Brad, will affect the rest of us."

"Are you suggesting we ignore the note?" Brad asked, his frustration beginning to show.

Sean took the note and tossed it on the table. "What I am suggesting is that pilot or no pilot, if we die filling this wish list, she still dies. How many of us do we risk to save Kelli? What do you think is acceptable ... Are you willing to risk Parker or Danny to get some drugs that may or may not save her?"

"So that's it then? We just don't go?" Brad asked.

Sean gave Brad an impatient look. "Will you just listen for a minute? I just want everyone to know the score before we decide."

Hahn reached across the table and picked up the note. He read it slowly before asking, "And what is the score, Chief?"

"It's like this: We go after these meds and we save Kelli, or we get the meds and she still dies. Or we fail to get the meds altogether, or half of us die trying and she still dies, or maybe she lives. Hell, maybe we say screw this shopping trip and go back to the farm, then find us a fishing boat and finish our trip home," Sean said.

"What the fuck, Chief!" Brad said, getting up from the table. "Are you trying to talk us out of it?"

"I'm not going to tell you guys what to do, I'm just putting it all out there, and it's already too late in the day to head out and do anything anyhow. So let's decide first thing in the morning. I hate to suggest it, but I think we should vote on it," Sean said as he picked up the paper and stuck it back in his pocket.

9.

Brad walked onto the porch to gather more wood. He looked out at the far tree lines and watched the wind blow the pines. They calmly swayed back and forth in the wind. It was easy for him to imagine that they were not on the run. *This must have been a pleasant place to be at one time. A small cabin on a pond in the middle of the forest,* Brad thought, enjoying the view. *The owner must have been proud of this place. Thomas said his uncle owned the house.*

I wonder what happened to him, I wonder if he died trying to get to this place? Maybe he is out there right now, watching me from the woods, Brad said to himself. The door opened, jarring Brad from his thoughts. Joseph walked out onto the porch.

"Here, let me grab some of that, load me up," Joseph said, holding out his arms.

Brad stacked Joseph's arms full of wood, then they moved back inside and dumped the load next to the stove. Thomas and Nelson were still sitting next to the fire. Parker and Hahn were in the kitchen opening canned goods and preparing the evening meal. The rest of the men still sat around the table. Brad opened the stove door and tossed in pieces of wood. He moved to the wall and sat on the bottom bunk.

"So Thomas, your brother said you

escaped the city?" Brad asked.

"Yea, that's true, but in the first days, before everything shut down," Thomas answered.

"What do you know about it? The infection I mean?" Brad queried.

The other men, hearing the question, moved the chairs from the kitchen and placed them around the stove. Hahn carried a teapot of hot water and refilled Thomas's cup. "I found some sugar. I put it into the water, it'll add calories ... at least make it taste better," Hahn said as he poured.

"Thank you," Thomas answered.

He took a sip, then looked at the fire. The sun was beginning to set, but the fire still cast a dim light in the cabin. "I was a student, I went to the University. We had heard tell of the sickness on the radios and the newscasts. It was an attack, we were told. They intended to hit the United States, but when the borders were closed, they hit us instead. The biggest outbreak we had heard of was in Quebec. The government shut most things down soon after, stopped travel, shut down airports and the shipping.

"It wasn't enough. A lot of the men from here work out west on the mainland. Of course they wanted to come home. Some boats began smuggling them back. Shady fisherman decided to cash in on the need for smugglers. We guess that's how the infection made it to the island. No one knows for sure," Thomas said.

"How fast did it spread?" Sean asked.

"Fast. I was already preparing to go back home. Dad had sent for me before the travel restrictions had started. I hesitated only because school stayed in session. A number of the students are from the mainland with nowhere to go, so they kept classes going. We all hoped this would be over soon. Still, I kept a bag packed. I intended to finish out the week, then I would leave.

"I woke up in my dorm to the sounds of screaming and fighting. I went into the hallway, where a number of people were fighting, and men I didn't recognize were attacking my dorm mates ... more than fighting, they were mauling them, trying to get up the stairs and into the hallway. My roommate was in the mix. He looked at me, then ran past me towards the far end of the hall. He told me to run with him. I wasn't dressed, so I went back into my room and locked the door. I could hear them in the hall, the screaming.

"They pounded and clawed at my door, scratching and howling ... screaming." Thomas paused before looking back down at his cup. "But I hid, I stayed quiet and hid. I think I fell asleep, I'm not sure. The next thing I remember it was dark. The power had gone out, but I could hear sirens in the distance, sometimes a gunshot. The streetlights came on. They shone through my curtains. I knew this must be the infection, that it must be here.

"We had seen the television reports from the mainland ... At first they told us they were riots. Because of the border shutdowns and the movement restrictions. But we all knew better, you could see it in the telecast, the people filled with madness, attacking everything, killing everything. I knew this was it ... It had to be. I packed a few more things into my backpack, just essentials, some clothes and what little food and water I kept in the room. I listened by the door. I didn't hear anything so I slowly opened it and went into the hallway. They were all dead ... my dorm mates, torn apart. All of them dead," Thomas said before burying his face in his hands.

"I'm sorry Thomas, many of us have experienced the same thing. You don't have to continue if you don't want to, we understand," Brad said in a low voice.

"No, it's okay, I want to talk about it. I haven't told Mom and Dad, not all of it, not how bad it was, not really," Thomas said. "You all," he said, looking at the hardened faces around the room, "I can talk to you."

"Okay ... well it's up to you," Brad acknowledged.

"After I saw them ... the dead ... I went back in my room and locked the door. I hid again, listening to the sirens and the screams outside. We had a phone in our room, I tried it but the line was busy, my mobile wouldn't connect either. I listened to the sirens and screaming through the night. The next time I opened my eyes the sun was shining into my room. And I could smell smoke. I went into the hallway. The smoke was thicker there.

"I didn't dare go to the stairway, the way those things had come up, so I ran down the far hall to the back exit. The door was locked from the outside. So I went to the common area, it's like a TV room, but there is a fire escape there. I tried to open the window but it was stuck. I remembered that in the hallway there was a case on the wall; it held an axe. I guess so firefighters could get into our rooms if they ever had to. I ran through the smoke and broke the glass. The axe was heavier than I thought it would be, but it felt good in my hands.

"I ran back into the lounge. I swung the axe and the window shattered. The smoke was thick now and I was coughing. I went through the window and onto the fire escape. I ran down the stairs as fast as I could, all the way down to the ground, then ran across the yard and hid in the shadows of some tall bushes. I watched the dorm burn. No one came. Nobody, no firefighters, not the police ... nobody. I watched, until I was sure I was alone.

"I could still hear the sirens, and the screams, but they were far to the south of me. I could hear more gunshots now also, automatic weapons, the military I guess. All to the south, so I headed north. I tried to find a car, but there were no keys in any of them. I don't know how to hotwire or steal cars. Maybe I should have learnt that instead of studying to be an engineer. A lot of good that will do me now."

"You might be surprised," Nelson said, smiling. "I'm an engineer of sorts, and it has worked out pretty well for me lately."

Thomas nodded and returned the smile before continuing. "I found a bike rack. The bikes were all locked, but the axe made simple work of it. I slung the axe across my back, now I was able to move faster. I wanted to get to the outskirts of the city and into the woods as fast as I could. I figured I could hide better in the forest. I'm not a townie, I grew up in the woods, I feel safe there. I rode across campus and cut through the park. It sits on the edge of the forest.

"I figured if I could make the forest trails, I could follow a path to the main road. The road was the way home. That's when I saw him. Or he saw me ... He was screaming and running right at me. I pedaled hard, but he never slowed, I couldn't lose him. I rode the trail and would slow to catch my breath and he'd be right behind me. I hit a corner too fast and lost it on the bike. I tumbled into the bushes. I hurried to my feet and grabbed the bike, but I had knocked the chain off. I scrambled to fix it but I could hear him screaming and running down the trail.

"I readied the axe and choked up on the handle. The thing rounded the corner, still screaming. I screamed back at him but he didn't stop. I swung as hard as I could. I caught him in the jaw. I saw the splash of blood, I watched his jaw twist and break away from the rest of his head. The man's speed and the blow from the axe carried him past me. He tumbled into a roll, falling into the brush along the trail. My swing carried me forward and I hit the ground and lost control of the axe.

"I climbed to my feet. I was so tired. My lungs were burning, my heart was beating out of my chest. I found the axe near my feet and I picked it up just as the man turned to face me. His jaw was hanging from his face. He was still screaming. Foam and blood were coming from the wound. He snarled and started to get to his feet. I ran at him and smashed him in the top of the head, swinging like I had been taught to split fire wood.

"I stayed in that spot for a long time. I thought more would come. You know, attracted to the screams. But no one came. I stayed there for what seemed like hours. I went through the man's pockets and found his wallet. He was an employee of the University, a custodian. He had pictures in his wallet, a family. What makes a man behave this way? I have killed others since then, but it's that one that I cannot forget."

Hahn stood and used a spoon to stir the contents of a kettle on top of the stove before he sat in a chair. "You won't forget Thomas, but it will be easier to remember with time. How did you manage to get home then? "Hahn asked.

"After that," Thomas continued, "I decided to leave the bike. It was faster but I didn't want to be surprised by one of them again. I stalked the forest trail. Moving slowly, staying hidden. I made it to the road. It was bad there, cars backed up in both directions. Survivors, police, military. They were all there. The military were forming road blocks and checkpoints. People were trying to get out of the city, and others were trying to get in. Everyone was confused. Nobody seemed to know what was going on or what to do.

"I met a family there, they were trying to get into the city to find some family members. But when they were stopped by the roadblocks and told to turn back ... I asked if I could join them. I didn't know them personally, but they live far to the north of here, and my parents' place was on the way. They agreed and I was grateful for the ride. We didn't get far; the road going north was congested with traffic. We sat still more than we moved.

"We saw them running in the distance. People left their cars and ran up the road. We could hear the gunshots from the road blocks. People were panicking. We left the vehicle and joined the chaos on the road. I tried to stay with them but we were soon separated. The infected came over us quickly, mixing in with the crowd. Everyone was lashing out, running, trampling each other.

"I climbed onto a large shipping truck. I laid on the roof and watched the insanity below. Police were firing into the crowds, I watched a panicked officer empty his gun into an infected before being dragged to the ground by a mob of them. I moved to the center of the roof and laid on my back quietly. I listened to them fighting below me. I could hear glass breaking and people screaming in fear, and the infected moans.

"I stayed up there until the sun went down. I looked over the side of the truck. I could still see them, the crowds of the infected moving about on the road. In large groups, they were walking back south, back towards the city. I waited for a break, when I thought they were far enough away. I dropped to the ground and ran back to the woods. I climbed a tree and I slept there until dawn.

"When the sun came up they were gone. In the beginning … When it first started we didn't see them much during the day. They don't seem to like the heat or maybe it's the bright light. It was early fall then and still unseasonably warm. Anyway, when I came out of the tree they were all gone, infected and survivors. I followed the highway from inside the forest, being careful to stay hidden.

"I traveled that way until I got home. Moving during the day and sleeping in trees at night. The farther I got from the city and the road the less of them I saw. When I finally got to the farm, Mom and Dad were sure happy to see me. They didn't really have a clue as to what was happening. The farm lost its phone connection and power about the same time as I did at the University. They had been warned to stay home, of course they'd heard there were riots in the city, but nothing to the level of what I described to them.

"I'm still not sure that Mom totally comprehends our situation. Even after ... Well, even after Dad and I had to put down Mister Emerson and his family. They were neighbors that were infected, they came at us. But we been really lucky, we haven't seen many of them around the farm since then. Usually we find them in ones or twos out around the pastures. Or closer to the villages," Thomas said.

"I guess we messed that all up for ya," Hahn said.

"Yeah, we seen far more of them in recent days. I have never seen groups of them this far north or into the hills. Dad still figures they will make their way back into the city eventually."

Sean moved his chair so that he sat closer to them. "Thomas, what do you know about them?"

"The infected? Not much, the news called it rabies or a virus, but you already know that, your man Brooks explained where you all came from, and how you got here."

"More than that," Sean said, "when did they get so slow?"

"Yeah, Dad's been watching them. They seem to be changing. Some of 'em started moving real slow as the weather turned cold, and others don't seem to be so much bothered by it. Dad thinks maybe it's the freeze, or maybe it's how they feed, maybe the slow ones are starving."

"Have you heard anything about smart ones?" Sean asked.

"What? No, I heard about what happened on the oil rig. But no, we ain't seen that. But we stay out here hidden. I can't say they aren't smart ones but we haven't seen them."

"Well I don't want to burst your bubble kid, but there are smart ones here. We have put a few of them down since we landed on your island," Hahn said.

Parker got to his feet and stirred the contents of a pot resting atop the stove. "Yup it's done," he said, lightening the mood. Quickly, bowls full of the hot stew were passed around. Someone had cut up the rest of the bread and added it to their plates.

"Eat up tonight, gentlemen, I have a

feeling tomorrow will be a long day," Sean said.

10.

Brad woke to a bright light shining in his face. He turned his head and shielded his eyes. "It's your watch, Sergeant," he heard Parker whisper.

Brad grunted as he looked at the glowing dial on his wrist. "It's already 4 a.m.?"

"Yup, you awake? I want to grab a couple more hours before the sun comes up," Parker whispered.

"Yeah I'm awake, you are relieved," Brad said as he sat up. He had taken a spot on the floor next to the stove. With the fire going and the temperature more bearable, the men had spread out in the cabin. Brad slowly got to his feet and sat in a chair while he pulled on his boots. He could hear the creaking up in the attic. He knew it would be Hahn. They were still pulling two man, hour-long shifts, but they alternated the start times by thirty minutes to keep them sharp. At the top of each man's watch, a new man would be rotated in.

Brad moved towards the kitchen area and poured himself a glass of water from a pitcher sitting on the counter. He quietly walked towards one of the front windows and moved the cloth away from the spy hole so that he could see outside. The moon was still nearly full and reflected brightly off of the snow. Brad checked the view in front of the house. He waited patiently for several minutes watching for movement. Observing nothing, he moved to the back of the house and looked through the window that overlooked the pond, again finding nothing.

Brad continued rotating between the front and back of the house. He looked at his watch and saw that enough time had passed that he should relieve Hahn in the attic. Brad went to the ladder and climbed up and into the space above. He found Hahn sitting cross-legged and looking out of the vent. Brad quietly crawled towards him, careful to keep his weight on the beams. Hahn looked back at him as he got closer.

"Anything?" Brad whispered.

"Saw a nice moose earlier," Hahn answered.

"Moose? No shit."

"Yeah, out there moving towards the pond. That's gotta be a good sign, I figure moose wouldn't hang around if primals were out there."

"Good point," Brad said, straining to look out of the vent.

"What are you going to do tomorrow, Brad?" Hahn asked.

"You mean about Kelli?" Brad responded.

"Yeah. I get where Chief is going, but I wouldn't feel right not making the run for her."

"I know. Chief is a tough one to figure

out. I can't tell if he is trying to talk us out of it, or just making sure we understand the risks."

"Shit Brad, everything we do out here is a risk … Did you know we talked Kelli into joining Charlie Group? She had it made out in the fleet," Hahn asked.

"Gunner told us he brought her on because she could fly. And because she is also one hell of a shot," Brad replied.

"Yeah, girl flew transports. But most of the big birds were grounded. There wasn't much work for her. And being an officer and all, she was on full time sham duty. Gunner found out about her one day during one of the briefs. He's the one who got her assigned to us."

"She's handy with that rifle. Too bad she ain't here with us now," Brad said.

"She *is* one of us Brad, remember that. I'd go back for you, this is the same thing."

"I know that, she has proven that to all of us; she handled herself well on the flights here," Brad said.

"See Brad, you ain't getting it. Gunner went and drafted her into Charlie Group. If it wasn't for Gunner, she would be sitting pretty back there on that island. I feel we are responsible for her now. Regardless of how the vote goes, I'll be going after those drugs," Hahn said before getting up and crawling down the ladder.

Brad sat there alone, quietly watching out

the vent, looking across the snow-covered field and into the trees. The sky was beginning to grey; dawn would be coming soon. He could hear Hahn moving around below. He heard him wake Sean to relieve him from his shift. After a while Sean climbed the ladder and moved into position next to Brad.

Sean leaned forward and looked through the vent. "Anything to turn over?" he whispered.

"No, it's been quiet. Hahn said he saw a moose."

"Really, a moose? Hmm, wonder if they are good eating, might have to ask Thomas about that."

"Chief … about Kelli."

"Save it Brad, there will be time enough for that in the morning. Why don't you let Joey sleep in, I'll cover the end of the watch," Sean said in a serious voice.

Brad nodded and turned to make his way down the ladder. When he reached the bottom he walked towards the bunks and grabbed his bag. He separated his assault pack from the back of his ruck and started moving gear around, putting things in the bag he thought he might need for his trip into the village. He had already decided he would be going on the mission.

He knew they would be moving fast and would want to travel light. He grabbed his stack of MRE entrees and put them in the bottom of the bag. He added the boxes of 9mm rounds and all of the 5.56mm he had left, along with the rest of his spare magazines. He stuffed in his poncho liner, several dry T-shirts and pairs of socks along with most of his first aid kit. The rest of his essentials would be worn on his gear.

Brad zipped and closed the pouches on his assault pack and the rucksack and placed them back by the bunks. He added more wood to the fire and placed a fresh pot of water on top of the stove. The sun was breaking the horizon now and he could see the light begin to filter in through the vents in the attic. Brad moved into the kitchen and opened cans of hash and dumped them into a skillet. Joey heard the noise and jumped out of the bed. He looked at his watch. "Damn man, why didn't you wake me, I was supposed to relieve Chief!" Joey said agitatedly as he quickly dressed and put on his boots.

"Don't sweat it Joey, you had the last watch. Chief will be fine," Brad said.

"Man I hope so, I don't want to be on Chief's bad side," Joey said.

"Bro! I said don't worry about it, why don't you make yourself useful and take this skillet over to the stove."

As the hash began to sizzle, the rest of the men started to wake up. Sean came down from the attic and sat at the table. Thomas got up and moved towards the stove. "Looks like you found

Uncle Darrin's stash of corned beef. He does love his hash. We used to eat it for breakfast every time I stayed here," Thomas said, smiling.

"Where is your uncle now?" Sean asked.

"Oh … not really sure, he doesn't stay on the rock much anymore. When the fishing dried up he took a job in the oil business. He only comes home a couple times a year now. But he still loves this place. We spend a lot of time here when he visits."

"It is a nice spot, I imagine the hunting is good," Brad said.

"Oh yeah, great hunting, plenty of game about," Thomas said.

Joey came back to the table with the skillet of sizzling hash. He sat the skillet in the center and the men divided it amongst themselves and scattered about the room to eat. Thomas was still sitting at the table with Brad and Sean; Hahn had pulled up a chair across from them.

"So Thomas, tell me more about this town. The one with the clinic," Brad asked.

Sean shot Brad a disapproving stare, then grabbed for his glass and took a long drink of water. The tension did not go unnoticed by Thomas who looked away and shied back towards his plate of hash.

"No, it's okay, Thomas, you can answer the sergeant's question," Sean said.

"Sir, the town isn't much to look at, small

place, nowhere near the size of the city on the coast. Used to be a quarry there. But that work is mostly gone now."

"How many people live ... lived there?" Brad asked.

"Ahh, I'm not sure. They have a school, and a nice lake, people go there in the summers on holiday. I had a friend that stayed up that way. He lived in a trailer park outside of town, and I'd say at least a thousand folks lived out that way."

"But you say there are lots of infected there? That's what you said yesterday," Sean asked.

"Yes sir. Dad and I tried to get to the town weeks back, thought maybe the constable would have answers, but we only got a few kilometers from the town center before we started spotting them and we turned back."

"So if the town is overrun with infected, how do you think we can just get in and out with what we need?" Sean asked.

"Well ... Brooks, he said you all were experts at sneaking into places you are not supposed to be. And they be moving slower now. I think if you go in during the daylight you could do it. I'll go with you Chief, if you are worried," Thomas said.

Sean smiled and finished the last bite on his plate. He looked up and saw that the others had gathered around the table and were looking at him. Sean drank the rest of his water and refilled his glass from the pitcher. "Hmm ... I guess we might as well get this out of the way," he said.

Sean took the note out of his shirt pocket and opened it up and placed it on the table. "As we all know, Brooks has given us a shopping list. He says without it Kelli may die. This is the sort of thing Charlie Group was known for back in the sand box. So I figure we could possibly make light work of it. But the risks will be high. There is no helicopter to insert or extract us, so we have to go in and out by foot. We have no intel on what's lurking down there, and we can't even be sure if this clinic hasn't already been looted—"

"Now hold on Chief—"Brad started to say before Sean put up his hand to cut him off.

Sean continued, looking at the men around the table. "I will lead a team in by foot. But I need three of you to volunteer to go with me. If we don't get three then the mission is a scratch. I won't force any of you, and I won't look down on you if you elect not to go."

"I'm in," Brad said, looking at Sean, surprised that he was offering to lead the trip.

"Shocker," Sean replied sarcastically before giving Brad a smile.

"Count me in also," Hahn said.

Sean looked around the room at the rest of them. Parker had moved away from the table and was avoiding them near the stove. Nelson was nervously standing next to him. Joey and Daniel were talking to each other in the far corner.

"I'll go, I know the place," Thomas said.

"I'm sure you do, Thomas, but sorry, I won't be taking you. You and Nelson won't be going with me. No offense boys, but I need gunfighters."

Joey moved back to the table with his brother. Daniel stood behind Brad. "We will go, but you have to take both of us. We ain't splitting up," Daniel said.

"It's both of us or none of us," Joey said.

Sean laughed out loud as he looked around the room. "So I have to cut one of you two, to get these two," Sean said, looking at Brad and Hahn. "Do you two want to decide amongst yourselves who will drop out? Both of you going isn't an option, I don't want to cut the teams this much, someone needs to secure the cabin while we are out."

Hahn spoke first. "I'm going. Brad, you don't owe Kelli squat, I'll go."

Brad stood and walked to the counter and grabbed a stack of stick matches. "We both owe Kelli for flying us here, even if she did crash," Brad smiled, "I know neither of us will back down, so let's draw for it."

Brad separated two of the matches from the stack and broke one of them in half. He then held them in his fist and asked Hahn to draw. Hahn selected a match and pulled the short one from Brad's fist. "Damn, you drew the short one, you win, I'm going," Brad said.

"Wait, now that's bullshit, the short stick goes," Hahn argued.

"Hahn, we drew fair and square. I'm not going to argue about this, I'm going. You are in charge until we get back," Brad ordered.

Hahn threw his piece of the match down onto the table and stomped off towards the bunks, cussing under his breath.

"Chief, when do you want to head out?" Brad asked.

"I think we should get prepped and move within the next hour."

Brad looked to the Villegases. "Can you all be ready to move?"

"Shit son, we're always ready," Daniel answered.

11.

The four-man team gathered around the table. Thomas smoothed out an old topographical map, and roughly drew a route from the cabin and the approaches in and out of the town. The rest of the men were outside preparing the snowmobiles for their trip.

"It's easy to get there, just follow the road about ten kilometers, it will take you up the main drive. The clinic is at the first and only stoplight," Thomas said while tracing his finger down the route.

"Well we won't exactly be rolling down Main Street, Thomas," Brad said.

Sean smiled "Why not?"

"What?" Joey said, stepping closer.

"I was thinking, what if I send you and your brother racing down Main, make some noise, lots of noise, draw the primals off after you?" Sean said.

Joey looked down at the sketch and watched where Sean was pointing. "Okay, Chief, I'm listening."

"We will ride together until about two miles out of town. Brad and I can conceal our sled here," Sean said, pointing to a place where the road curved away from the town. "You two will hold up while we will begin to slip in on foot to a spot on the outskirts of town …

hopefully unseen."

"And us?" Joey asked.

"Yeah ... give us some time to move into a nice hide where we can see the streets, two miles through closed terrain ... hmm, let's say two hours max, then you two roll through town hot. Speed in like you own the place, hit the town by surprise. Maybe stop and make sure they pursue you. Once we see them following you and clear out, we will sneak in, do us some quick shoplifting, and then sneak back out," Sean said.

"Sounds good for you, but what we supposed to do with a town load of crazies after us?" Daniel argued.

Sean looked across at Daniel while pointing at the map. "I'm sure you all will figure it out. But if it was me I'd lead them out of the town. Once you get a good group following, haul ass, break contact, then hide up somewhere till it's clear to circle back to the cabin. If you move out and north this road should take you away from the town and back here."

"Not much of a plan, but I like it," Daniel grinned.

"The sleds are topped off with fuel. Thomas says that will give us about a hundred miles. You should be prepped to hide out for a day, maybe two. Just make sure you don't lead them back here," Sean said. "Brad, same with us, make sure you have gear for at least two days, seems simple enough, but the simple ops are typically the most fucked up."

Sean looked down at the map again before folding up the note and placing it in his pocket. "Once again, this is all volunteer, but once we hit the trail consider yourselves fully committed to this. We will all be counting on each other to succeed."

***

They were outside the cabin. Thomas had both sleds up and running; the men were sitting double on each. The Villegases had taken the newer sport model, while Sean and Brad had the older snowmobile. Thomas had gone over the controls and given them a quick rundown on how to keep them running.

Brad had more experience with snowmobiles, living in the north, so he got the driver's seat. After brief goodbyes, Brad squeezed the throttle and the snowmobile jetted forward and away from the shed. He checked his rear view mirror and saw that the Villegases were close behind them. He rode alongside the rutted driveway sticking to the field of snow-covered grass until they hit the gate.

Brad slowed the sled and pulled up just short of the downed pole. Quickly Danny and Sean jumped from the back of the sleds and removed the barricade, allowing the snowmobiles to pass through. Quickly they replaced the barrier and jumped back on. Brad again hit the throttle and they were off at high speed down the gravel road.

They wanted to move fast and avoid staying in one spot for too long, to avoid drawing attention to the location of the cabin. Brad took lead and kept the sled at near full throttle, which was only half that of the newer model behind him. He plowed through high snow drifts and around downed trees and other obstacles that tended to occur when road maintenance stops. Brad could feel the chill on his face and the cold air biting against his neck and forehead.

They had taken the thermals and flannels that Thomas had brought with him, but it still was not the correct gear for a winter snowmobile trip. Brad continued to race down the road until he spotted a landmark that Thomas had mentioned to them: a large wooden sign notating the direction to a national forest. Thomas had said the sign would be close to the entrance into the town.

As they drew closer they began to spot homes on both sides of the road. Some were burnt down or had broken windows. Others were shuttered with no signs of life, as if the owners had left them and would one day return. There were cars in driveways covered with large drifts of snow. Brad knew he was close to the town now, close to the planned stop. He passed a large brown ranch house with boarded-up and shuttered windows. As he cleared the empty driveway, he eased off the throttle and pulled the sled off the side of the road and into some heavy brush.

The Villegases slowed and continued to idle the engine until Sean directed them into cover farther ahead. They killed the engines and sat quietly listening. All that could be heard was the wind and the sounds of branches clicking together. Sean slowly stepped onto the trail with Brad following close behind. The Villegases stepped out of the trees to meet them.

"Okay, you two get cozy, give us a couple hours to move into position before you move out," Sean said.

Joseph nodded back to Sean. "We got it Chief, see you back at the cabin," he whispered as he followed his brother back into the thick underbrush.

Sean looked to Brad and patted him on the back. "The road loops around here then down into the town. We should be able to follow the compass east."

Brad acknowledged the comment with a nod as he checked the straps on his pack and stepped off into the woods in the direction Sean had pointed. They moved quietly through the heavy snow without speaking. The last few days had been warm and the snow had gotten damp and sticky. In some places the drifts were nearly knee deep, which made movement more difficult. They were finding it hard to keep a quick pace.

They climbed a slowly rising hill for over an hour, staying away from trails and sticking to the thicker trees of the forest. The deeper in the trees they got the more the drifts and snow pack began to lighten. Brad found it easier to move and he quickened his pace. Several times Sean would stop him to take their bearings with his compass, then give Brad a new heading. As they summited the top of the hill they could just begin to make out the town below them.

It was still some distance off, but they could see where the main street ran through the center of town. The town rested below them with an X-shaped set of streets intersecting in the center of it. Most of the buildings sat along the main street running north and south. From their high vantage point and with binoculars, they could barely make out the road that traveled east from the intersection and into the trailer park Thomas had mentioned.

Sean pointed to a small outcropping of hills farther down. "We should try and make it to that point before the boys roll out."

"On it," Brad whispered back as he stepped off in the direction of the point.

Moving downhill they found travel easier, yet still they had to move slowly to keep themselves concealed. Especially now that they were on the slope facing the town. The two men were careful to keep themselves in the shadows of the tree lines. When they had to cross into the open they would crouch lower and sometimes even bear crawl to avoid silhouetting themselves.

As Brad approached the small point, he could see that a home rested within two hundred meters of the hill's crest. Brad dropped to his belly and broke the tree line, crawling towards the observation point. Odds were the home was empty of any living thing, but there was no point in taking chances. He crawled across the damp ground until he reached a comfortable position on the top of the hill overlooking the town.

They were lower now and could no longer see the entire town, but they had a good over watch on the length of the main road. Sean crawled up alongside Brad. He removed the scoped rifle from his back and set it up on its bipod, then handed Brad a compact spotting scope. Brad unscrewed the lens caps and began to glass the buildings below.

He started near, looking down at the house below them. It was well kept and looked to be of newer construction. The grass in the lawn was high and snow covered, the bushes overgrown. It made sense as the fall had happened months ago and at the end of the growing season. Landscaping was probably not a priority with the end of the world approaching. He moved his focal point along the windows and doors. The home appeared to be secure with no obvious points of forced entry. Scanning farther out, he spotted a detached three-car garage. Again all of the doors and windows appeared to be secure.

"Dang, seems quiet enough. Maybe we should have just crept in, place looks empty," Brad said as he continued to scan.

A long driveway cut away from the house and joined the main road. Brad followed it down and continued his left to right scan of the buildings in front of him. He let his eye travel the road deep and to the heavy cluster of buildings at the intersection. "That must be the clinic," he whispered.

"I see it," Sean replied.

There was a single-story white building sitting just where Thomas had said it would be. There were several cars, some law enforcement vehicles, and an ambulance scattered around the building's parking lot, all covered with snow. A small sign in front of the clinic read "Urgent Medical." Looking up and down the street, they could see that many of the store fronts had been broken into. A small mom and pop grocery store had items scattered about and covering the ground in front of it. Then Brad spotted something that alarmed him.

"Sean, what is that? See the line by the row of cars. Is it what I think it is?" Brad whispered.

Both sides of the street were congested with cars, but down the middle of the snow-covered street there was a definite foot path that had been packed down and cut through the snow.

"Looks like a trail. Well, no surprise, right? We expected them to be here," Sean said as he looked up at Brad.

"Yeah, guess you're right, I just didn't expect a trail. Must be a lot of them to cut a path like that—"Brad stopped speaking as he heard the sound of a distant engine.

"Here they come, perfect timing," Sean said, putting his eye back on the scope.

Brad turned on his elbows so he could see more of the road as it approached the town. The sound of the engine got louder and he saw the snowmobile pass through his view at high speed. Brad took his eye from the scope and watched the sled race down the street. It cut down the main drag and ran over top of the foot trail they had spotted moments earlier. Still there was no movement from any of the buildings.

The snowmobile plowed into the intersection in front of the clinic and stopped. Brad watched Daniel jump from the back of the machine with a pistol in his hand. He yelled, "Come on out bitches, it's dinner time up in here." Brad could just barely make out his voice over the idle of the sled's engine. Daniel continued yelling obscenities and dares as he walked to a nearby car and pounded on the hood.

Brad put his eye back on the scope and scanned the buildings; he saw no movement. He looked back in the direction of the brothers and watched as Daniel leveled his handgun towards one of the parked cars. He rapidly fired off several rounds, the gunshots echoing through the town. "What are you waiting for?" Daniel screamed.

The moans started. They seemed to be coming from all directions at once. Joseph revved the engine of the snowmobile as Daniel ran back and jumped on the seat behind his brother. Joseph continued to rev the engine, the sound of the sled joining the moans of the primals. "What are they doing? They need to get the fuck out of there!" Brad whispered to Sean.

Slowly figures began to come out of the buildings. Joseph moved the sled forward at a slow pace; Daniel raised his handgun and began taking shots at the slowly shuffling creatures moving towards them. Soon the sidewalks were filled with them, moving slow, staggering, trying to make it to the brothers' location. Joseph increased his speed as Daniel switched to the rifle, continuing to take shots, dropping several of the primals.

"He's a modern day Pied Piper," Sean said as they watched the buildings' occupants drain into the streets, following the slowly moving sled out of town.

"How many of them do you figure there are? Did you see any fast ones?" Brad asked.

"I don't know, has to be over a thousand. They are still bleeding out of those structures. I think we're gonna have to sit here for a bit."

The snowmobile drove farther up the road and gradually picked up speed. Eventually the numbers pouring from the buildings lessened while the masses moved to the center of the road and joined the march after the vehicle. The brothers had moved out of sight, but Brad could still occasionally hear a shot from their rifle. Brad used the scope to scan the streets. They were clearing out again now as the mass moved beyond the city limits.

They waited nearly an hour after the last one had moved out of sight after the snowmobile. "Looks clear, let's move out," Sean said as he slid to his knees and slung his rifle across his back.

Brad stepped up and screwed the lens caps back onto the spotting scope before stowing it in his pack. He checked his rifle, gripping the suppressor to ensure it was tightly secured. He looked to Sean and nodded before slowly moving down the hill.

They were following an old path now. Connected to the lookout, it snaked its way down the side of the hill and connected with a sidewalk below. Just like any other small town, this trail was probably used by kids on dirt bikes. The thought made Brad smile as he slowly worked his way down the hill, cautiously searching the area in front of him.

The trail dumped them onto the sidewalk still short of the main street and three blocks from the clinic. Brad took two steps onto the approach and kneeled down, looking in both directions. His side of the street was void of structures until the next block. There was a small house across from them, and a side street that looked to be stacked with similar homes.

"What's the call, Chief, stick to the main drag, or roll through the neighborhood?" Brad whispered.

"Stay on this side of the street. Stick to the walls on the left. We will look for a clear place to cross farther up," Sean said.

Brad lifted himself from the damp snow. Even though he could feel the cold through his pants, he was still sweating from the exertion of the day's march. He walked slowly in a low crouch, sticking to the left side of the street. Sean was right behind him, close enough to reach up and grab his shoulder. They continued to move, taking short deliberate steps and scanning the area in front of them. Every few feet, Sean would turn to look at their back trail.

They moved towards the end of the sidewalk and again Brad took a knee. Across the street was the beginning of the downtown. A long row of store fronts lined both sides of the street. Across from them began the chaos of parked and jumbled vehicles. Brad could also make out the beginnings of the primals' footprints in the snow and the heavy path they had created.

Brad felt the tap on his shoulder, the 'go command' from Sean to move forward. Brad crouched down near the very edge of the sidewalk, feeling exposed on the street corner. He quickly looked both ways and ran across the street, looking for cover. Finding it, he quickly moved into a hide near a car fender. Brad quickly scanned left and right then signaled for Sean to move up.

Keeping his eyes up and down the street, he heard Sean coming, then quickly felt his presence next to him. "Okay, we're doing good, keep moving, hug the wall, avoid doors and windows," Sean said as he tapped Brad on the shoulder.

Brad stepped off and moved to the wall next to him. He remembered hearing instructions to never walk close to walls, that bullets could hit a wall, ricochet then follow the wall right into you. But he wasn't fighting insurgents today, so hugging walls and staying in the shadows was the order of battle. As he moved along the building's surface he began to pick up the familiar stench of death and decay.

Even in the crisp cold air, the stench drifted heavily.

He reached into his collar and pulled his shemagh tightly over his nose and mouth. He moved forward, walking low, ducking and even crawling below windows. When they came to a door they would quickly move past it one at a time. Brad was curious what might be inside each building but that wasn't today's mission. They moved under a low storefront. The glass was broken and mannequins lay in the display and on the sidewalk. Brad put his back to the wall, quickly peeked into the building, then ran past the window.

Brad posted up on the far side of the window and waited for Sean. He looked down the street and saw the lumps in the snow. The street in front of him was littered with frozen and twisted bodies. He pressed back against the building as Sean came up beside him. "What is it? You see something," Sean whispered.

Brad pointed at the cluster of bodies in front of them. Sean nodded and signaled for Brad to keep moving. "Come on, only a bit further."

They continued moving the same way down the length of the street. Brad again hugged the corner and looked down the side street when he reached the end of the block. The crosswalk here was littered with bodies and jammed with vehicles. Brad did a quick scan in all directions before stepping off quickly and clearing the danger area. Again he searched for cover and stuck himself to the nearest wall, trying to blend in.

Sean moved up behind Brad; Brad felt the tap and began to step off. They were now one block from the clinic. He could just see it at the end of the street and on the other side. He moved on, still hugging the walls and ducking under windows. He felt Sean grab at his shirt and deliberately tug him, then push him low to the ground. He took the pressure and fell to both knees, hunched over. He let himself slide into the wall in a low kneeling position. Sean crawled up next to him.

"What!" Brad whispered.

"J.D.L.R.," Sean whispered back quickly.

Brad gave Sean a puzzled look.

Sean shook his head, "Just doesn't look right,"

"No shit, it's a city full of dead things!"

"Something's wrong … I can't place it. I'll take point, fall in behind me," Sean said as he began to low crawl forward.

Brad followed in the trail Sean was making in the snow. Now instead of hugging the building, they were slowly making their way to the curbside. Sean dropped between two cars and moved towards the center of the street with Brad close behind. Sean dropped his right arm at an angle and showed Brad his outward turned palm. Brad stopped and looked for cover. Sean had again dropped into the snow and was crawling backwards. He turned and placed his face close to Brad's.

"We have to get inside ... now!" Sean said.

"What is it? What did you see?"

"Alphas," Sean said as he began crawling to the closest building.

12.

The two men moved quickly to a nearby store front. Sean put his shoulder against the doorframe and tried to look inside. It appeared empty. He put his hand on the door and slowly opened it, then moved in and to the right. Brad turned to look behind him. He still didn't see the threat that Sean had mentioned. He followed his friend into the building.

Sean slowly let the door close until the latch caught, then turned his attention back into the depths of the building. They had found themselves in some sort of coffee shop or diner. Booths were along the right wall, while a long counter ran the length of the left wall. Far to the back they could see a restroom sign and an exit door.

Sean pressed his back to the wall and slowly lowered himself into a seating position with his legs in front of him. Brad moved next to him and sat shoulder to shoulder. "You smell that Brad?" Sean whispered.

"Mildew?"

"Exactly. It don't smell like fucking primal. We may be secure in here for the time being. Follow me to the back."

Sean dropped to his hip then slowly rose to his hands and knees as he moved deeper into the coffee shop. Brad did the same and followed him. When they were farther from the front windows and safely concealed in the shadows of the structure, Sean rose to his feet. He walked quietly on the toes of his boots and looked over the counter.

"Clear," Sean whispered.

Brad climbed to his feet and walked beyond Sean, holding his rifle level to the back exit door. As he got closer he could see the door's bolt was latched in the locked position. He moved down the passageway to the restroom door and swung the door in: darkness. Brad held the door for a moment before letting it close. "No need to go in there, if a primal was using the shitter I'm sure he would have come out to say hi."

Sean didn't acknowledge the comment; he had moved behind the counter and was setting up his rifle. He had it up on the bi-pod and was looking out of the window and into the street. He let the rifle rest on the counter before looking down and smiling. He reached into the cooler behind him and pulled out two cans of Coke. "Here," he said to Brad as he tossed one in his direction.

Brad caught the can and moved around the counter to join Sean. He popped the top on the can and heard the all too familiar hiss. He sipped at the soda; it was at a pleasant room temperature of nearly frozen. After weeks without a carbonated beverage and drinking nothing more than water, the soda burned and the sweet liquid made him clench his jaw. Quickly he chugged the Coke and placed the empty can on the counter.

"What did you see out there?" he asked Sean.

Sean was leaning against the cooler; he pointed to the rifle. "Take a look, across the street at the market."

Brad knelt behind the stock. The magnification of the scope quickly picked up the walls of the buildings across the street. He moved the barrel left and down until he could see the broken glass of the market. Just inside the frame of the window stood a single figure. Behind him more were moving through the building. Brad counted five of them total.

"What are they doing?" Brad asked.

"Your guess is as good as mine. Their behavior is no longer predictable, and this is going to make things more difficult for us," Sean said.

"You want to call it off and go back?"

Sean turned to look at Brad before smiling. "No, we aren't calling it off." He moved towards Brad and lifted the rifle off the counter and to his shoulder as he looked through the scope. "I figure we have three choices," he said as he looked at the figures across the street.

"One, go hard in the paint ... violence of action ... rush the fuckers and take them all down. I'm confident we could kill the ones in the market, maybe even hit the clinic, but I don't know if we would ever get away.

"Two, look for high ground, stay quiet and drop them from afar, might work for a while, but we still have to move eventually. Or we wait until dark, see if we can sneak past them in the darkness, and make our way into the clinic," Sean said in a soft voice.

Brad looked down. "This is your expertise Sean ... I'll go with whatever you decide."

Sean took the rifle and collapsed the bipod. "Let's check out the rest of this place, no reason to rush getting ourselves killed."

He slung the rifle across his back and lifted his MP5 to the low ready position. Brad fell in behind him and they moved to a set of doors that led into the kitchen. The doors swung in; the kitchen area was dark and surprisingly clean. Brad had expected to see rotting food, or worse. But the place was spotless. "They musta been closed?" Brad whispered.

"Yeah, looks that way," Sean grunted.

They continued through the kitchen and into a stocked pantry where they saw shelves of dry goods and canned meats and vegetables. Not only that but more than two cases of coffee. Brad used his light to examine the shelves of stocked goods. "Look at this place, it's a fucking gold mine," Brad whispered.

"Too bad we won't have room for it,"

Sean said.

He shined his light deeper into the room. There was a small manager's office with a glass window looking into the kitchen, and a heavy wooden door at the end of the wall. The two men walked towards the door. Sean leaned down and tried the handle. It turned easily in his hand, but there was a heavy bolt lock that prevented the door from opening. Brad took out his tomahawk and prepared to strike the door, when Sean held up his hand.

"Go check the office for keys," Sean said.

Brad turned and headed back to the office. He could see into it through the glass window. The room was small, maybe six foot by six foot. A desk sat directly under the window, a row of filing cabinets on the back wall. Brad entered the room and ran his hand across the desk top, knocking over stacks of paperwork and invoices. On the wall to the right of the desk sat an antique timecard machine.

Brad saw a stack of timecards sitting in a rack, each with a name and photo stapled to the top. Brad grabbed the stack of time cards and sat heavily in the chair positioned behind the desk. He slowly flipped through the cards looking at the photos of the diner's employees. *What happened to you?* Brad said to himself somberly as he stared at the pictures.

"Any luck with those keys?" he heard Sean call out.

Brad woke himself from his mood and tossed the stack of timecards onto the mess covering the desk. He heard a metallic cling as the stack landed. Brad reached over and moved away the paperwork to see a large ring of keys. He scooped them up in his hand and walked back towards the heavy door. He handed the keys off to Sean who grinned.

"We must have a key to everything in this town," he chuckled as he started working his way through the ring. Key after key failed to fit the lock, or refused to turn. "It's always the last one," Sean said just as one of the keys clicked home, then easily turned in the lock. They heard the metallic clunk as the bolt returned to the open position. Sean reached down and tried the door again. He pulled and the door opened in his direction.

They stepped back and saw a set of stairs leading up. "Game face," Sean whispered as he put his shoulder to the door and shined the light up the stairway. Brad acknowledged him and got into position just behind Sean. Together they slowly moved into the staircase. Sean's light lit the top of the stairs and ended on another heavy door. Together they walked the stairs to the top.

Sean slowly got in position on the doorknob side; Brad lined up on the opposite wall. Sean slowly moved his left hand down to the knob while keeping his weapon's barrel elevated. He turned the knob and pressed the door in and it quietly swung into the space. Quickly they were both hit with the smell of death. The old, pungent stench they had both grown accustomed to. Sean let the door continue to open. At the end of its range the door let out an audible squeak before it clicked against the far wall.

Brad stepped into the opening and took a knee with Sean just over his shoulder. Their lights illuminated a small hallway that led into a small apartment. They sat still for several minutes, waiting for a howling and growling beast to come tearing at them. None of that happened. Sean reached down and tapped Brad on the shoulder. Side by side they moved into the apartment, visually clearing every corner.

The home was decorated in a homey style: plaid armchairs and wooden end tables. Brad could see that a small dining room and kitchen connected to the living space. On a far wall were two doors that were hanging open. From their position they could see that one was a small bathroom. Shining the light at the second doorway, they could just make out the corner of a bed.

Together they moved in the direction of the two doors. They opened the bathroom door fully and did a quick scan of the room before moving onto the bedroom. Here the smell got stronger. Brad again pulled the shemagh over his face before they stepped into the bedroom.

The source of the smell was obvious. Lying side by side on the bed was an elderly couple. They were locked together in each other's arms. At the bottom of the bed was a golden Lab, curled up, its eyes closed in death.

Sean moved to a nightstand and found several empty bottles of medication. "Looks like a mix of sleeping pills and pain killers," he said, putting the bottles back on the table.

They walked out of the room and closed the door behind them. "At least they left on their own terms," Brad said as he walked across the room and sat in one of the plaid chairs. Sean followed him and fell onto a sofa covered in hand-knitted blankets.

"What are we doing, Sean?"

Sean leaned back on the sofa. A tall window sat behind him and he carefully pulled back the curtain. He had an expansive view of the street below. From the window he could see the market and the clinic. He let the curtain go and turned back to face Brad.

"You are not going to like what I have to say," Sean said.

"Just give it to me fast, I'd rather have you kick me square in the nuts then squeeze and twist on them all afternoon."

"I'm going to send you down into the clinic by yourself," Sean said.

"What the fuck? Have you lost it Sean?"

"No ... Maybe. I've been bouncing ideas

around in my head and I think that makes the most sense."

Brad sat up in the chair and looked Sean in the eye. "Me going down there alone makes the most sense?"

"Give me a chance here. I've been trying to think this through. How would I have ran this op a year ago? Two men, hostile terrain, we need to fill a shopping list from a semi-secured location, get in and out without being seen," Sean said.

"Me, alone! That's the best you can come up with?"

"Now hold up, you won't be all alone."

"Continue."

"I'll be up here on the rifle. I don't see how else to make this work. We wait till the sun goes down. We already know those things can't see in the dark … that gives us some advantage. We can goggle up; with night vision we should be able to stay a step ahead of them. I'll be up here on the glass. I have a good eighteen to twenty subsonic shots for the long gun and plenty of loud rounds after that. I'll stay silenced and guard you the entire way. If any of them picks up on you, or looks funny, I'll put them to sleep."

"But in the dark? They move around more in the dark!"

"True, but hopefully most of them are still out hunting the brothers. Brad, this is the best plan I got. If I go down there with you, we won't have any over watch. I'd leave you up here, but I'm better on the rifle. Don't worry, if shit goes south, I'll twist free and go loud. That will draw them to me, and free you up to haul ass. Just keep moving, get as far away as you can."

"Bro, your plan fucking sucks," Brad said as he sat back into the chair.

"Yeah, well, sometimes you have to embrace the suck. Let's get some shut eye, it'll be dark in a few hours and I want to be ready to do this."

13.

When Brad opened his eyes he had nearly forgotten where he was. He looked around the small living room and saw a glow of light coming from under the bathroom door. He called out to Sean in as a low a voice as he could muster.

"I'm in here," he heard Sean whisper back.

Brad made his way to the bathroom door. He tapped and the light went out as the door opened.

"Come in, I'm trying to hide the light. This bathroom only had a small window and figured it would be easier to cover."

Brad moved into the room and closed the door behind him. Sean covered the bottom of the door with a rolled towel, then flipped his light back on. He was sitting on the floor and had his gear laid out in front of him. He was replacing batteries in his night vision optics and placing a similar type of scope on his rifle. He looked up to Brad who had taken a seat on the edge of a cast iron bathtub. "How are you doing on batteries?" Sean asked.

"I have a few fresh sets left, but that's gonna become a problem if we can't find more,"

Brad answered.

"Yeah ... problem for another day. Here's the list," Sean said as he handed Brooks' note across to Brad. "You need to pack up like you won't be coming back here. I rummaged through the old folks' hall closet. Found that coat, looks like it will fit you, and some boots and old gloves. Boots were my size so I win there, you can have the gloves. "

"Damn, I'm happy with a coat ... So how am I supposed to find this shit in there?" Brad asked, looking at the paper.

"Just do what you can, give yourself ten to fifteen minutes inside. If you don't find what you are looking for ... get out."

"So just leave empty-handed?"

"That sums it up. Do your best, but if the stuff isn't there, get out," Sean said again.

He handed Brad a small radio set. "This is my backup. We will have two-way communication but there isn't much range to this. Try not to speak to me, I don't want them hearing you. If you swallow hard, I'll be able to pick it up."

"Okay, and where are you going to be?"

"I'll be out there in the living room, which should give me line of sight over your entire approach. This is simple, Brad, move one block, cross the street and enter the clinic. Fill the shopping list and come back the way you came. Last I checked the streets are still empty," Sean said.

"For the record, I hate you and this plan," Brad said.

"Good. Get geared up. Let's be ready to go in the next thirty minutes."

Sean shut off the light so Brad could open the door and step back into the living room. He closed the door behind him and made his way back to his small assault pack. There was enough moonlight entering the picture window so that once his eyes adjusted he was able to go through his kit. Brad tried on the heavy coat. It was a little loose fitting but made of a heavy material, with plenty of pockets in the front and on the sleeves.

"Yeah, this will do," he said to himself as he moved his arms and flexed the material. Brad put on his tactical vest and the rest of his equipment over the coat. He lifted his pack, but before putting it on he strolled over into the apartment's small kitchen. He put his hand on the refrigerator door's handle but thought twice about opening the door, wondering what spoiled mess might be inside. Instead he opened a cupboard door and smiled.

"Peanut butter," Brad said just above a whisper. He took the jar down and opened it. A nearly full jar of creamy goodness. Brad dipped in his finger; the contents were thick from the cold, but not so thick that he wasn't able to gather a heaping mouthful. "Maybe city life isn't so bad," he said to himself, smiling.

Brad looked through the other cupboards, finding cans of vegetables and spices. Some things were worth carrying, but he wouldn't have the room in his pack after gathering the medical supplies. Brad placed the cans on the counter in hopes that maybe Sean would find room. And then there was still the supply store down stairs. "So much stuff, but no way to get it out," Brad said, shaking his head as he placed the peanut butter into his assault pack.

He attached the radio ear piece and throat mic and clicked the small on switch before stuffing the receiver box into his pocket. Brad tapped the small throat mic. "Testing, testing," he said.

"Yeah, I hear ya," came Sean's reply.

Brad smiled in response, not expecting Sean to be on his coms yet.

"I think I'm ready to go here, Chief."

"Okay, I'm almost done on this end."

Brad looked over his rifle and magazines, making sure the suppressor was secured. Then he put on his head harness for his NVGs, still leaving them powered off and in the up position. He put on the assault pack and moved towards the large window. He could see down into the street and to the clinic. From his elevated position it really didn't look that far. The building they had entered was in the center of the block. Another quarter block down the street and on the opposite side sat the market with the broken windows.

At the end of the street and two buildings down from the market sat the clinic. Brad searched the street, finding it empty. He looked across to the market but couldn't see inside the darkened interior. He flipped down his night vision optics, watching the street in front of him illuminate in green. He could see more, but the field of view was narrow. He turned his head from side to side, still finding nothing. Satisfied, he powered down the optics and stepped away from the window.

Sean was just walking out of the bathroom holding his rifle in his arms. He moved across to a window facing the street. He unlatched the locks and, after a brief struggle, he was able to unseat the window and slide it open. Sean moved a small chair and a table in front of the window and readied his rifle. "Brad, take this," Sean whispered, handing Brad his small integrally suppressed MKII, followed by a handful of fully loaded magazines.

"It's a small caliber, but a lot quieter than your M4. Hit them in the grape and they'll go down," Sean whispered. "I mounted my infrared laser, don't be afraid to use it."

Brad nodded and took the pistol, keeping it in his right hand and putting the spare magazines in the coat pocket. He let the M4 hang loose on his tactical sling. Brad checked the straps on his assault pack and turned towards the door.

"Okay, take your time getting outside, use the nods, no white light," he heard Sean say over the radio.

"Got it, I'm stepping off now," Brad said as he flipped down his goggles and opened the apartment door. He could easily see down the stairs and to the heavy door below them. Brad held the MKII tightly in his right hand and placed his gloved left hand on the stairwell's handrail. Even though his NVGs illuminated the space, he had no depth perception and was not in a mood to take a tumble down a flight of stairs.

Walking slowly he made it to the bottom step and quietly opened the door. He carefully counted time in his head, giving anything he might have surprised time to react. Only hearing his heartbeat and his own breathing, he stepped into the kitchen and scanned the space. Still empty the way they had left it. Taking slow, deliberate steps, Brad made his way back to the diner door. Again he slowly opened the door with his free hand while holding the MKII at the ready.

With the door opened he again counted to thirty in his head, waiting for an attack that never came. Brad stepped onto the floor of the diner and swallowed hard.

"Everything okay?" he heard Sean answer.

"Good, I'm in the diner moving to the front."

"Okay, buddy, when you hit the street I need you to get close to the curb before I can cover you. You'll be in my blind spot if you hoover on the wall."

"Got it."

Brad moved to the street entrance and took a knee; he cautiously looked out of the store front window and onto the street, searching for threats or movement. After a few tense minutes, he took a deep breath and put his hand on the door.

"I'm going outside, going silent," Brad whispered.

"Roger, slow and steady."

Brad pulled on the door. He felt the cold air hit his face as he slowly stepped outside and guided the door shut behind him. Brad put his back to the wall and searched left and right, finding nothing. He walked to the edge of the street and kneeled next to the bed of a large pickup truck with flat tires.

"Okay, I see you now, just continue to follow the curb," Sean said.

Brad swallowed hard to acknowledge Sean's message. He got to his feet and walked along the curbside, watching where he placed his feet to avoid tripping. He continued this slow movement until he was almost directly in front of the market. He stopped and looked across the street, still seeing nothing.

The market was positioned farther off the curb than the other buildings. There were several cars stacked in front of it. The market had one large double door; it looked like the motion-activated type, but was currently ripped from its hinges. The entrance was flanked by what used to be two large plate glass windows which were now shattered, allowing easy access into the building.

"I need you to get in the street, cross to the vehicle on the other side. The angle is too steep where you are at."

Brad swallowed hard again and quietly stepped between the parked cars. He was moving very slowly, standing nearly upright now. He was trying to move as quietly as possible, counting on the darkness to conceal him. Brad cut into the street and took two steps into the center before he heard Sean again.

"Hold."

Brad froze and looked in both directions, at first seeing nothing. He slowly dropped to a knee and held his position, trying to control his breathing. Then he saw them. Two of them, walking along the street in his direction. They looked almost normal, walking upright with their eyes straight ahead. Brad estimated their distance at close to a hundred yards and coming from the direction of the clinic.

Brad turned to face them. They seemed oblivious to his presence. They continued to walk in his direction, looking straight ahead. Brad scrunched as low as he could and tried to hide in the shadows of the parked cars. He felt the pistol in his hand and silently clicked the safety with his thumb, then used his pointer finger to activate the laser.

"Take the one closest to you, I'll hit the trailer."

Brad swallowed hard and raised his hand, watching the green dot dance about as his hand shook nervously. He used his left hand to steady his aim and carefully placed the IR dot that was invisible to the naked eye on the primal's forehead. When they closed to within several yards, he exhaled as silently as possible and depressed the trigger until he felt the pistol buck in his hand. He immediately heard a *thhhhpt ... thwack* as a round ripped through the air and hit the other primal. Both creatures dropped heavily to the ground.

"Clear, move up."

Again Brad swallowed hard. He closed his eyes tightly as the strain through the NVGs was already beginning to take a toll on them. He got back to his feet and looked towards the market. From his new position he could just see inside the broken window. The space appeared empty. *Must all be outside,* he thought to himself.

Brad continued to follow the parked cars. He was close to the clinic now; he could see the outline of the first rows of law enforcement vehicles and the entrance to the building. He had to repress the urge to walk faster, not to run. He wanted nothing more than to be back inside.

"*Hold.*"

Brad looked left and right, seeing nothing.

Thhhhpt ... thwack ... thhhhpt ... thwack

Brad heard a dull thud from behind him.

"*Clear, move up.*"

Brad could feel his knees shaking as he turned and looked all around. Just behind him he saw the body of a primal with fresh blood oozing from its head. Farther back lay another one.

He swallowed hard and willed his legs forward. He was moving between the law enforcement vehicles now. Two police cars with shattered windows. A car door was open. Brad looked inside the car and saw a police officer with his throat torn out. He quickly looked away and continued towards the clinic.

"*Hold.*"

Bad, bad idea, Brad thought to himself as he froze in place, trying to make himself invisible.

Thhhhpt ... thwack

"*Clear, move up.*"

Brad moved to the wall beside the clinic door and pressed against it. Just to the left of him was the entrance. It was jammed open. A body lay on the ground preventing it from closing. Brad looked at it, unable to identify it as male or female because of the snow covering it. Brad leaned out away from the wall and looked inside. There was a small lobby littered with objects and bodies. Furniture had been tossed about, and a long drift of snow was piled up just inside the door.

Bad fucking idea, he thought.

"Okay ... once you get inside I won't have eyes on you," Sean said over the radio.

No shit Sherlock, Brad thought angrily as his mood continued to go south.

He took another deep breath, swallowed hard, then stepped over the body and into the clinic. He quickly moved inside and backed against a wall, trying to conceal himself. He thought of trying to close the clinic door so nothing could sneak in behind him. He grabbed the edge of the door with his free hand, but it was completely blocked by the body and frozen in place. Probing the body with his boot, he found that it was frozen to the ground. Brad reached down and gripped its frozen shoulder with his gloved hand and started to tug.

"Stop worrying about the door, I won't let anything in," he heard Sean say.

Brad looked back over his shoulder, trying to focus his vision on the tiny apartment located above the coffee shop. Finding the building but little else, Brad released the cadaver's shoulder and re-entered the tiny lobby of the clinic. He moved through the snow and found an inside wall. He pressed back against it and knelt down into the shadows of the room. Brad sat silently like a statue, only moving his head as he slowly panned his night vision display across the space.

The room had a tile floor that was covered in paperwork and broken furniture. Half the room was filled with snow where it had blown in through the open door. Brad scanned the drift and quickly identified several sets of footprints in the snow. He panned and searched deeper into the room. It ended at a long counter. To the right of the counter was a doorway; its door had long ago been torn from its hinges.

"Are you alone?"

"I don't know," he whispered, breaking his silence.

"Explain?"

"I don't see anything, but there are tracks in the snow."

"Coming or going?"

Brad looked again at the footprints. They did all appear to have the toe pointed towards the doorway. He let out a sigh of relief and shook his head as he reported back over the radio, "Going."

"Good, they were probably with the group pursuing the brothers. Be cautious, get in ... get out."

Brad swallowed hard before getting back to his feet. He searched the room again and moved towards the counter, stepping deliberately to be as silent as possible. Brad pushed up against the cutout of the long counter. He scanned left and right. To the right he could see banks of printers and tall file cabinets. To the right was another door leading back. Brad leaned out over the counter and looked behind it.

He saw the body of a thin woman. She was wearing a long lab coat and loose-fitting pants. Her coat was ripped and an arm was twisted away from her at an odd angle. Brad knew that if he were to remove his goggle and use a flashlight he would probably find blood and gore on her clothing. For a brief moment he was grateful of the sanitized view the night vision device provided.

Brad stepped back and slowly walked towards the open doorway. He posted up next to the entrance and stood silently, again listening intently for anything that might be lurking inside. He could hear the wind whistling through the door. There was the clanging of an object. The beat was random yet rhythmic, probably something that had come loose in the wind, now slapping against the side of the building.

Satisfied, Brad raised his pistol to the ready position and stepped into the doorway. He looked down a long hallway with doors on both sides; the end of the hall turned off and to the left. Brad stepped into the hallway and cautiously made his way to the first door. He looked at a sign above the door. It was labeled *'Patient Room 1.'* Brad wasn't there to clear the building; the door was closed so he moved on. Doors were staggered along the hall, each one labeled with an ascending number. He reached the end of the hall and slowly turned the corner, slicing it with his vision so that he always had his pistol pointed in the correct direction as new objects came into view.

The hallway as it turned left opened into another large space. There was a destroyed coffee table in the middle and an overturned magazine rack. Brad saw a number of sofas and chairs along a wall. He took a step deeper into the space and saw more bodies. Like the woman in the front, they were also dressed as medical workers. Brad made his way towards a wall and again pressed back against it as he recon'd the space.

The room was a large square. Across from him was an exit sign above a door, to the left, a lab, and to the right, a pharmacy. Brad stayed in his position and slowly lifted the goggles from his eyes to check the room for ambient light. As he'd suspected the room was pitch black. Deep in the building he was concealed in complete darkness. He continued to listen, hearing nothing but his own heartbeat, the wind, and the clanging object.

"You have a status? There is more movement out here." Brad jumped as Sean's voice broke the silence.

"I found the pharmacy, I'm about to enter," Brad said as quietly as possible.

"Okay, pick up the pace. The numbers are manageable, but they seem to be waking up, doubling every few minutes. They are all coming from the market."

"Great, thanks for the positive forecast."

"Anytime, buddy."

Brad rolled his shoulders and stepped towards the pharmacy door. Just to the right of the door was a small service window. A large panel had been slid across the window, shutting off the access. Brad reached down and tried the door. He found it locked; the knob turned easily in his hand, but the door wouldn't budge. Sliding his gloved hand along the edges of the door he noticed there were bolts at the top and bottom. Possibly secured from inside or with a key.

Brad pressed on the door again and verified the resistance and the weight of the door. He was certain he wouldn't be able to break into it using the hawk. He moved on to the service window. There was a large pane of Plexiglas with a slot at the bottom. Just beyond that was a large wood panel sealing off the door. Looking closer he could see the wood panel was only held in place by a small locking latch and a track at the top and bottom of the panel. Brad reached his arm down into the slot and pulled on the Plexiglas. It was solid but he was confident he could remove it. Twisting his arm, he pushed against the wood door beyond the glass. He found it to be light and loosely fitted.

"I have a problem," Brad said over the radio.

"Go."

"The door to the pharmacy, it's heavy and secured. I'd need a fire axe or more to get in … There is a small window but it's closed up and blocked on the far side with another door. Looks weak enough to gain entry but it's going to be loud."

"It's your call … I won't lie to you, if you make noise you are probably going to piss off the neighbors."

"How's it looking out there?"

"Just shy of twenty of them. They took notice of the ones I put down. These fuckers aren't acting dumb," Sean said with anxiety in his voice.

"We didn't come all this way to go back empty-handed."

"Got it, I'll keep them outside."

"Okay. There's an exit door right here. If they get in, I'll egress that direction … I'm about to open this can of whoop ass," Brad said.

14.

Brad placed the spike of the tomahawk under the glass and the claw against the wall. He pressed down on the handle and heard the Plexiglas strain before snapping loudly and popping out of the frame. "Oops, that was a lot louder than I expected it to be," Brad whispered.

"I don't think they heard it," Sean answered.

"Good, I'm going to breach the sliding interior door now," Brad whispered.

Brad positioned the tomahawk against the small metal latch. He began to apply his weight to the handle of the hawk. *Boom!* There was an impact against the far side. Brad jumped back, almost tripping over his own feet, yelping in the process. The banging continued and was joined by moaning and the high pitched scream of the primals.

"What was that are you okay?"

"Oh shit ... Something's in there," Brad answered.

"Okay ... Brad, listen to me ... get out, get out now. We're scrubbing this mission."

"No, I got this, they still can't see me."

"Brad ... it's over, get out of there!" Sean yelled.

Brad ignored him and took the tomahawk

in a baseball bat grip and swung at the door. The spike stuck, the thing banging on the other side continuing its assault on the door. Brad ignored the screaming and Sean's instructions over the radio as he pulled out the hawk and swung again. This time the flimsy door began to split. Brad slipped the hawk back into its holster on his hip and leveled his M4. He had already made plenty of noise. *What will a little more hurt?* He thought to himself.

Brad saw the split in the door open as a set of grey fingers reached through the crack. They pulled at the door until a piece of it broke away. Brad raised the rifle just as he recognized an eye staring back at him from the hole. He squeezed the trigger, putting two rounds into the door just right of the eye, the suppressed rifle sounding far louder in the confined space. The fingers lost their grip on the door and he heard a thud on the far side.

Not wasting time, Brad used the collapsed stock of his rifle to knock away the remaining pieces of the sliding door. The pieces fell in, now allowing him to see into the pharmacy. He spied row after row of tall shelves stocked with bottles and boxes of medication. Brad looked left and right and saw no movement.

"I'm going inside," Brad said over the radio.

"You need to hurry, the neighbors are pissed

about the noise; they are moving towards the clinic."

"Got it," Brad said as he pulled himself through the window.

He landed next to the crumpled creature he'd just put down. Unlike the others, this one was wearing a law enforcement uniform. Its arm was wrapped in stained bandages. Brad saw that deeper into the room lay a pump shotgun and a semi auto pistol near the officer's jacket. There were more bodies in the room, these ones torn apart. Brad looked to the heavy entrance door and saw that it had been locked and barricaded from the inside. The surface of the door was covered in deep scratches.

"I see multiple dead in here … Clinic must have fallen … They hid in here together. Until this one turned on them, then folks didn't have a chance," Brad mumbled.

"Yeah, we've seen that before. Are the meds there? Brad, you need to hurry," Sean said, cutting him off.

"Yeah, shelves of them. Okay, let me look."

"Brad, I'm trying to push them back, but they are onto you. They're all moving towards the clinic now."

Brad pulled the sheet of paper from his breast pocket. It listed generic medical items such as gauze bandages, syringes. Brad saw a wall stacked with miscellaneous medical supplies. He opened his pack and began stuffing them in, several of everything, no time to sort in the dark. He came to the drug list. It called for pain killers and antibiotics. Darvocet, Percocet, Oxycodone, Tramadol. Brad read the list but didn't see them on the shelf. He quickly ran up and down the aisles searching until he saw a locked cabinet in the back.

No time to waste. Brad leveled the M4 and shot through the handle. He grabbed the door and twisted the latch until it popped open. The first thing he saw was a box labeled *'Hydrocodone/Vicodin.'* *Shit, close enough,* Brad thought as he grabbed the box and dumped its contents into his pack. Then he grabbed several other bottles from the cabinet and threw them in. *If it's worth locking up it must be good shit, he* thought as he turned to search for the antibiotics.

He looked at the list. They all seemed to end in 'cin'. He was looking, knocking over boxes, when he heard an unsuppressed gunshot. "What was that?" he asked, continuing his search.

"I'm buying you some time, they're at the clinic door," Sean said just as Brad heard another gunshot.

Brad tipped over another box, finding a bottle labeled *'Sisomicin.'* "I don't know what you are, but you're coming with me," Brad whispered as he dumped the bottles and those around it into his pack. He quickly zipped it shut and put it on his back. He turned towards the window as the frequency of gunshots increased.

"Brad, they're inside! You need to find another way out," he heard Sean yell just as a primal crashed against the window.

Brad jumped back, pumping rounds into the creature's head as it attempted to climb into the space. "Fuck, they're at the window!" Brad yelled as he turned and grabbed a shelf behind him. He pulled it sideways and then shoved it against the wall, blocking the window. He took a desk in the corner and slid it across the room and jammed it against the shelf. Now Brad could hear them screaming and beating against the other side of the shelf.

"Brad they're in the coffee shop below me, I have to bug out!" Sean said.

"What the fuck, I'm trapped in here, don't leave me Chief."

"Hey, you're still in the fight, don't quit … I'm moving, back with you in a few."

Brad continued to pile the shelves against the window entrance. He could hear them screaming against the far side, but his barricade was holding. Brad looked around the room, finding it hard to see. He flipped up his night vision and turned on his flashlight. He immediately wished he hadn't; the room's floor was coated with dried blood, the walls streaked with bloody handprints. The white light brought color to the horror of what had happened to the pharmacy workers.

Brad moved the light along the ceiling and walls. He was closed in. There appeared to be no other way out. He moved around the room, yanking shelving from the walls and throwing them against the barricade. He knocked over the cabinet filled with painkillers, searching the wall behind it. Nothing. He was trapped. Brad moved to the wall opposite the barricaded window and dropped to the floor. They were still screaming outside and beating against the shelving. He watched the wall vibrate with every impact.

"Chief? You there? ... Sean?"

There was no response. Brad pushed the magazine release on the M4, quickly replacing the mag with a full one. He took off the assault pack and sat it next to him. He could see his breath. Even though he was still sweating, he knew he would be cold soon. Brad searched the room and saw the police jacket still lying near the shotgun and pistol in the corner. He got to his feet and moved towards it. The jacket was dark blue and of a heavy quilted material. Brad picked it up. There was a large tear and blood marks on the sleeve.

Brad pulled his knife and cut away the bloody part of the jacket. He looked down at the pistol. The slide was locked to the rear and empty. He picked up the shotgun, a standard 12-gauge with iron sights. On closer inspection he found three rounds in the tube and five more attached to the stock. He left the pistol but decided to take the shotgun for now. He moved back to his spot by the wall and sat down, pulled his knees in tight and placed the police jacket over them. All the while the primals continued to scream and press against the barricade.

Brad shut off the light and sat quietly in the dark. The longer he sat, the calmer the primals became. He could still hear them on the other side of the room, snarling and occasionally lashing out at each other. Brad would sometimes drift off, but sharply be woken by the sounds of an attack against the barricade. He forced himself to stay quiet, to avoid using the light. Often he would power on his night vision to reassure himself that he was still alone in the pharmacy. He tried the radio several more times, getting no response.

It was cold and he began to shiver. Brad was tempted to build a fire in the room, but he didn't want to risk burning himself alive or agitate the primals anymore. He removed a stained lab coat from one of the workers and added it to his layers of clothing. He found a newspaper and used the crumpled paper to insulate the layers of his jacket. Brad again sat back against the wall in the dark. The primals were still out there; he could hear them. There was no way he would be able to get out the way he'd come. Brad closed his eyes, trying to formulate a plan. He drifted in and out of sleep in the corner with the shotgun in his lap.

"Knock." There was a noise at the heavy locked door. Brad jumped, shaking his head; he turned on the flashlight and searched the room, finding nothing. He listened intently for the noise that had startled him, finding only silence. "The primals? Where did they go?" he thought. Brad rolled himself to his feet and slowly walked towards the barricaded window. He strained again to listen. Still nothing.

"Knock, Knock." There was another pounding at the door.

"Sean, is that you?" Brad called out as he backed up and leveled the light at the door. He was startled when he saw the handle move up and down. "Sean?" Brad called out, again getting no response. He moved closer to the door and heard an audible click as a key slid into the lock. Brad watched as the bolt lever on his side of the door turned into the open position.

Brad took another step back, shaking now, still holding the light. The handle moved. Brad dropped the flashlight, kicking it away. He heard movement. He fired his rifle, the muzzle flash lighting the space. He could see Ryan entering the room, running at him, screaming. Brad continued to fire, falling backwards. Ryan landed on top of him, clawing at his face. Brad turned and twisted, trying to escape, gasping for air.

15.

Brad's head snapped forward, his heart racing. *Another nightmare,* he thought, taking in big gulps of air to calm his nerves. He glanced around, searching the room. It was quiet, but more than that, there was light. Where was it coming from? Brad searched the walls. High in a corner, a small blade of light filtered into the pharmacy. He got to his feet and moved towards it. There was a round can-type light fixture mounted in the ceiling. At the edge of the fixture a very small ray of light was coming through. Brad took a stool from a corner of the room and stood on it so that he could reach the light. He used his knife and pried away the frame of the cover.

More light bled into the room. Brad reached up and grabbed ahold of the fixture and twisted it hard in his hand; as he pulled, he lost his footing and fell, but he took the light down with him. He crashed to the floor hard, landing on his back and knocking the wind out of himself. The primals had taken notice of the commotion and began to moan and again assault the barricade. Brad lay on his back trying to recover from the fall. He looked up and saw that he had not only yanked out the light fixture but had also broken away a large chunk of the ceiling.

More daylight was now pouring into the room. Brad could see up above the plaster and sheetrock ceiling to another metal roof above it. There was maybe three feet of dead space between the ceiling and the roof. Brad got back on the stool and grabbed the edge of the sheet rock and pulled down. It cracked and gave way, falling to the floor with a crash. The primals became frenzied at the sounds of activity. Brad ignored them and continued to work away at the ceiling until he had a hole that he could easily fit through.

He pulled one of the shelves away from a far wall and braced it so that he could climb it like a ladder. The heavy metal shelving was sturdy and took his weight, but it was loud and the steel screeched in protest as he put his weight on the shelves. Brad was able to get his head and shoulders above the ceiling and into the dead space. He used his light to look in all directions. The entire clinic was covered in the low dropped ceiling; he could see runs of electrical and computer cables, and metal ventilation ducts ran along the walls.

Less than ten feet from his position Brad saw a plank no more than eighteen inches wide that crossed the dead space: an access walkway. He knew that it should lead to an attic access, or maybe even the roof. Brad dropped back into the pharmacy and excitedly began strapping on his gear. He took the shotgun in his hand, debating whether he should keep it or toss it. He shook his head and quickly strapped it to the top of his bag, grabbed his M4 and moved back to the makeshift ladder.

"Chief? Chief, can you hear me?" Brad said. "Chief, are you there? I think I found a way out. I'm going for it."

Brad pulled on the backpack as he waited for a reply. He looked back around the room and at the barricade. The noise from moving the shelves and breaking the ceiling had stirred up the primals, but Brad didn't care anymore. He took his M4 and connected it to the front of his armor and climbed the shelving. He positioned himself as high as he could, then grabbed a bundle of electrical wire with his gloved hands and pulled himself into the dead space.

He had to cross several feet of open ceiling covered with insulation before he would reach the plank walkway. Brad positioned himself on a ceiling joist and slowly shimmied his way towards the planks. As he moved, he felt the ceiling rattle and flex. He moved steadily, making good time and finally reached the edge of the plank. Brad stretched out and again using the wires pulled himself across to the narrow boards and onto the plank.

He used his flashlight to search the space ahead and to try and get his bearings. He estimated he must be directly above the room outside of the pharmacy, directly above the primals. He could hear them below snarling and growing ever more frenzied, attacking the barricade. Brad slowly pulled himself onto his knees. While walking on all fours he would just barely clear the metal roof above him. Brad crawled along the plank towards what he knew was the center of the clinic.

As he moved, he realized the primals below were following him. He felt an impact shudder through him; they must have jumped up against the ceiling, trying to get at him. Brad felt the plank buck under his knees. He crawled fast towards the heart of the building. The primals below stayed with him, jumping and slapping against the ceiling below. Brad found another section of plank that broke off at a right angle. He followed it, hoping it would stop or confuse the primals.

He heard them below screaming and pounding on a closed door. Brad continued to crawl looking for a way out as he heard breaking glass and a door being slammed open. Soon the primals were again below him. *Light!* He could see more light where the end of the plank met an attic vent. A large square panel was set into the block wall. Brad moved quickly towards it and pulled on the louvered vents. It was of a heavy metal design; the vents were made to pivot to allow air to flow out of the attic but prevent outside air from getting in.

Brad flexed the louvers and pried them fully open. He could see outside now. The sun was up, and he saw an empty alley below him. Brad attempt to pull the panel out towards him, but it wouldn't give. He carefully rolled to his back and kicked with both feet, knocking the vent free. He heard it fall and rattle as it hit the ground outside. He felt the plank below him buck again as the primals launched themselves into the ceiling. He saw a crack in the sheetrock to his right and clouds of dust form as the primals worked their way through.

Farther back he saw a hand punch through the sheetrock and rip down an entire section of the ceiling. Brad was beginning to panic as he watched primal arms reach through the ceiling searching for handholds. He launched himself at the vent hole but couldn't get himself through. Pulling back, he took off the pack and tried again. He could get his shoulders through. Brad stretched through the opening and first considered dropping to the ground, but looking up he could see that the roof edge was within reach.

Brad pulled back inside the hole and grabbed his pack. A primal cleared the ceiling and pulled itself onto the plank less than twenty feet from Brad's position. Brad dropped to his side and leveled his rifle, firing several shots, eventually striking the creature through the side of its chest and crippling it. Another primal got to the plank and attempted to jump the crippled primal; it overshot the plank and hit the sheetrock, crashing through and falling below.

Brad grabbed his pack and swung it out of the vent hole and to the roof above. He took another look back and saw the primals scrambling, trying to get into the space. Brad again eased his shoulders through the vent hole, then turned his body so that he was in a sitting position with his chest facing the building. He stretched his arms and grabbed the edge of the roof. Pulling with his arms while his feet searched for traction, he slowly worked himself out of the vent opening and onto the roof. Quickly he rolled onto the roof and lay on his back just above the opening. He lay motionless, remaining as quiet as possible.

He could hear them below fighting and struggling to get into the dead space, then heard them at the vent hole. One stuck its head outside and moaned before leaping out. Brad heard the thing impact the ground with a thud, followed by several others. They didn't seem to know that he was on the roof. One after another, Brad heard them gain entry to the dead space and rush to lunge out of the opening. He didn't know how long it went on. He was afraid to move, even enough to look at his watch.

As their numbers outside grew, their attention shifted. Brad heard them running, screaming in all directions, searching for him.

Making very slow and deliberate motions, Brad turned to his side and tried to put his ear to the roof. He could hear nothing; the space sounded empty. Confident they were no longer below him, Brad rolled back to his belly and slowly crawled towards the center of the building. He spotted a cluster of air-conditioning units stacked side by side. Brad made his way towards them and pulled himself up onto the raised platform they rested upon.

Finally feeling safe, he collapsed face down in exhaustion. He rolled to his back and looked up at the blue sky. His only reprieve was that it appeared the weather had finally broken; the bright sun warmed his face. Brad scooted back into a sitting position, removed his glove and scooped a handful of the fresh snow into his mouth. He knew that eating snow would lower his body temperature, but at the moment he didn't care. Brad pulled his knees into his chest and focused to control his breathing, forcing himself to relax.

"Pssshhhhhh ... Brad — psshhh ... Brad," he heard through his headset.

"Sean? Sean, is that you? I can barely hear you, it's all garbled."

"Pshhhhhh ... get out."

"Where are you? I'm on the roof."

"Pshhhhhhhhh."

"Chief, the radio isn't working, I can't hear you," Brad said, trying to stand to improve the signal. "Chief?" He pulled the receiver from his pocket and pushed the black button below the small display. The low battery indicator was flashing. Brad looked at the back. "Of course I don't have batteries for this shit."

Brad flipped the switch, turning off the radio. "I'll try later," he said to himself before stuffing the radio set into his backpack. Brad strapped the pack back on and slowly got to his feet. He walked cautiously to the edge of the building, towards the main street side. He looked out over the edge, careful to keep his body low and concealed. He could see the coffee shop. The storefront window was shattered and the door broken in.

The windows in the small apartment above the coffee shop were now broken, their curtains blowing in the wind. He could find no trace of Sean. He must have made it back to the overlook. Brad pulled out the small spotting scope that he'd used a day earlier to scout the town. He looked down the main street and towards the far off hill top he had lain on with Sean. There was no sign of anything, no signal, no movement other than the primals on the streets below. Brad carefully moved back to his hide in the air-conditioning units and took a seat on the raised platform.

"It really was a stupid plan." He shook his head and pulled his bag open. It was stuffed with the medical supplies. He dug his hand around the bag until he found what he was searching for. He pulled the peanut butter from the bag. "At least I still have you, peanut butter," he said to himself smiling, almost giddy with despair. "So what now? What do you think we should do?" Brad looked at the child's face on the jar. "What? You think I should quit? Well screw you, peanut butter, and all this time I thought we were friends," he said, scooping a heaping fingerful of peanut butter into his mouth. Brad reached into his pack and pulled out a bottle of water, twisted off the cap and took a long drink before leaning back against the AC units. "I guess I have to make it out of this shithole town on my own." He sighed heavily, then put his head back and closed his eyes. "I never liked the people here anyhow, always yelling at me and trying to kill me. I sure as hell won't get out in the daylight. I'm going to have to wait until dark. Going to be harder though without Sean's rifle."

Brad got to his feet and pulled himself onto one of the AC units and searched the area. Behind him at the end of the alley looked to be a residential area, maybe a block deep; beyond that was the forest. The other side was the main street with blocks of buildings behind it.

"Won't make it down Main Street. I'm gonna have to cut through those backyards." He climbed back down from the AC unit and pulled his blankets from his pack. "Well peanut butter,

I think we should try and get some rest before we move out," Brad said as he stuffed the jar back into his pack.

16.

Brad lay on the edge of the roof as he watched the sun go down. His assault pack and shotgun were strapped to his back and his M4 was clipped to his chest. He was on the opposite side of the building, away from the main street and looking down into the alley. Earlier Brad had walked the entire roof looking for a safe way down. He had come up empty.

The roof was at least fifteen feet off the ground. Because it was a one-story building, he found no fire escapes. The closest thing to it was a set of flimsy downspouts on a corner near the alley. The alley ran from the main street to the rear of the building where there was another large parking lot. Brad could tell that tents had been erected there at one time, even though all that was left of the campsite was torn fabric, collapsed structures, and pedestrian barriers.

The rear parking lot of the clinic must have been tagged as a casualty collection site. A place to take the wounded for triage. Brad spotted a number of ambulances staggered around the rear lot, now buried in the snow drifts. A pair of G-Wagons, armored G-Class Mercedes, the Canadian variant of a Humvee, sat at the parking lot entrance, weapons still mounted on the roof. Brad was tempted to make a break for one and drive it away. He knew from experience that the thing probably wouldn't start, a dead battery after spending all of this time outside in the elements and in the sub-freezing temperatures.

Brad tried to reach Sean on the radio several times during the day with no success. He could find no sign of the primals that had pursued him from the building earlier. *Hopefully they gave up and returned to the market,* he hoped. Brad watched the last slivers of daylight disappear. Even with the sun gone, he still had decent vision in the clear dusk sky. He again looked left and right, using a search pattern, moving from the closest in to the farthest away. Still no signs of the enemy. "Well, it's now or never," he said to himself.

He crawled as close to the edge as possible and grabbed the edge of the roof while slowly lowering his legs off the side. Then reaching hand over hand, he grabbed onto the drain pipe and quickly shimmied towards the ground. Once he felt it was a safe distance, he pushed off from the pipe and hit the pavement with a *plop*. Quickly he moved for cover, hiding between a set of dumpsters. After listening carefully for a moment, Brad slid along the wall until he reached the corner of the alley facing the rear of the building. It was growing darker and he was able to conceal himself in the shadows of the buildings. He pulled his night vision down and turned on the optics. He could easily see the casualty collection area. That would be his first goal. He refused to plan a trip back to the cabin. He told himself not to think so far ahead; he would move in small calculated steps tonight. Every step would only be as far as the situation determined.

He didn't want to get ahead of himself and sacrifice his security for movement. As long as he was safely concealed, he would be satisfied with his progress. He had to assume they were around every corner. Without Sean in over watch he would move accordingly. Around the corner and dead ahead was a large panel truck with a Red Cross symbol on the side. Brad mentally planned all of his actions then quietly stepped off, moving as quietly as possible until he reached the panel truck.

Again he stopped, checking security on all sides, looking for movement and listening for sounds. He plotted his next move. Something close, an object he could hide in or behind, something he could make it to quickly, and a median place he could fall back to if he spotted danger. Taking his time again he stepped off, moving silently, hiding in the shadows. He stopped often, refusing to feel rushed. He moved alongside a collapsed tent, then crawled into the fabric and laid still, making sure nothing had detected his movement.

Brad was planning the next leg when he

saw a group of them. They were moving in a staggered cluster, headed in his direction. Too many to fight. He felt for the fabric of the tent and cautiously rolled underneath it, trying to control his breathing, trying to remain silent. He could hear them now; they were close. He pressed his head close to the ground so he could see them as they walked by. Their feet plodded heavily with the pavement. Some wore remnants of shoes, others were bare footed, but they didn't seem to be bothered by it. They all walked with the same gait, moving past him and back towards the clinic.

Brad looked into the tent. The roof had come down from the heavy snow but there was still a few feet of clearance. The smell of death was all around him. He pushed back the feelings and moved on. He found there was room for him to crawl through to the other side. Brad made his way underneath some sort of table. The further he got under it, the more room he found to maneuver. Now fully inside the concealment of the tent, he began to drive forward, trying to make it to the far side. He could still hear the primals milling around behind him, and he wanted to create separation.

As he crawled on his belly an inch at a time, he ran into an obstacle. He reached out with a gloved hand, pulling at the fabric, trying to find a way around. Baggage? Luggage, packaged materials; his path was blocked. He needed to try and get over the obstructions. He reached out and pulled himself over the pile, keeping his body low and trying to avoid contact with the tent fabric hanging just above his body. In close proximity to everything his NVGs had become useless. He couldn't focus on anything.

He relied on touch and his senses to guide him through the tent. He reached out, again searching for a handhold, then quickly snatched his hand back. His heart racing, he was sure he recognized the sensation that shot through his body, the recognition of what he had grabbed. He tried to remain calm, fighting off the panic. He could hear them outside, snarling at each other, reminding him of their presence. He couldn't go back.

Cautiously Brad again stretched out an arm. He opened his hand and patted with his palm, then cringed. He froze, not wanting to continue, his hand rested on a human face. He could feel the frozen nose and lips. Now focused on his location, he had to use everything in him to control his emotions. He probed with his other arm, pressing beneath him, and his fear was realized. Lifting his head and trying to look around him he nearly convulsed, wanting to vomit. He forced back the fear. He was lying on a mass of frozen bodies.

Most of them had been contained in body bags, some only in sheets. As he got closer to the far side of the tent they were in nothing more than hospital gowns. He had unknowingly crawled into a mortuary tent. He pushed his shemagh tightly over his face and bit down until his lips bled, using the pain to distract himself from his emotions. Slowly he regained his composure, feeling his panic subside. Now that he knew where he was, the smell mentally became worse. Every movement became a horrifying burden. He suddenly could feel everything, every bump below him, every knee, head, or elbow he came in contact with.

He clenched his eyes tightly closed and chewed the shemagh, fighting off the urge to vomit until he had made his way through the corpse pile and to the far side of the tent. He poked his head under the far side. He made a quick sweep, looking all around, and suddenly disregarded his plan and his safety. He bolted away from the tent, running just a short distance before stopping near an ambulance with its rear door open. Brad pushed his back against it. He looked back towards the tent where he could still see the primals on the far side loitering near the pharmacy; fortunately they had not spotted him.

Brad dropped to the ground and rolled under the ambulance, low crawling to the other side. He was almost clear of the parking lot. He could see the street and the row of houses now. Brad rolled from under the ambulance and crawled close to its flattened front tire. He lay there listening, straining to hear sounds of danger before moving on. He quietly lifted himself to a sitting position, leaning back against the tire. He was ready to lift himself to his feet when he saw something move. It was coming from the street. Slowly the object became more defined in his night vision as it drew closer.

As it shambled along, he saw that this one had a bad knee. It moved slower than the others. Maybe that's why it was alone. Brad watched it move; it was on a course to pass Brad, presumably aiming to join the others near the tent. Brad held Sean's MKII in his hand. Slowly he moved his hand to his lap and tried to relax his grip. He knew he was invisible in the darkness, but he had to remain silent and control his breathing if he didn't want to give away his position. He sat motionless, keeping his eyes focused on the gimped primal.

It moved along at a slow, easy pace, stepping forward with its strong leg then dragging the other one ahead. It continued that motion, looking straight ahead, seemingly oblivious to Brad. It moved to within eight feet of him. Brad was sure it would continue on, past the ambulance and out of sight, but suddenly it stopped. It took its one good-legged step then paused before allowing the bad leg to be dragged forward. It froze in that stance. Brad watched it uneasily, waiting for it to make a move. The primal's chin raised and it began to sniff the air like a dog.

He expected to be frozen with fear, but he wasn't. He sat next to the tire watching the thing move about, sniffing, hunting for its prey. Brad watched as it turned its head and looked in his direction. It looked down, staring right at him. It knew something was there, but it still wasn't sure. It pulled its bad leg forward, then twisted and took a step in Brad's direction, leaning into the darkness, searching, probing with its nose, licking the air, trying to see what was out there.

Brad slowly raised the pistol from his lap and activated the laser. He squeezed the grip and put the green dot just under the thing's chin and pulled the trigger twice. *Pop, pop.* The primal froze, resting back on its gimped leg. Brad could see that he had hit it just under the chin and again above its nose. The primal swayed to the left and right before it fell to the ground with a thud. The pistol was a lot louder than Brad had remembered. It seemed to shatter the silence. He was sure the remaining mob would come running at him, but they didn't. Brad sat silently, looking at the primal he had just put down.

He sensed more movement in his goggles. More of them coming from across the street headed in his direction. He had to go. Brad crawled away on all fours, moving as quickly as he could while remaining silent. He reached the G-Wagon at the entrance to the parking lot and got to his feet. He ducked low and looked back towards the ambulance. The primals had spotted the dead gimp. They were looking around, sniffing at the air. *They recognized their dead*, Brad thought.

One of them reached down to touch the dead primal. He stood back up again, searching. Brad had to move, he needed to get away. Ducking low he kept the G-Wagon between him and the primals and entered the street. He made a quick dash onto a snow-covered lawn. Tripping over something, he fell, landing heavily in the snow. Brad lay silently, not wanting to move and make any more noise. He cautiously rolled to his side and looked back towards the ambulance again. More of them had gathered around the dead primal.

"What the fuck is going on?" Brad whispered to himself, remembering Sean's words from last night: They were no longer acting dumb. Brad began to low crawl through the snow towards a house skirted with thick bushes, just as the first of the moans and primal screams began. He moved in close to the house. Pulling himself under the thick vegetation, he stopped and turned. He could see the primals spreading out now, screaming and searching for him. He had to keep moving. Brad turned towards the home and continued to crawl following the wall of the house.

The home had a small basement window.

Brad looked down but was unable to see in. He looked behind him. More primals had joined the mass around the ambulance. He didn't have a choice. He pulled his knife and, using the handle, smacked the glass. It broke and fell into the house. Brad took another look back before pulling himself through the window. He tumbled in head first and fell hard to the floor below.

When he fell, his goggles popped up and off of his head. He quickly struggled to right them just as he heard a creak on the floor above. He knew he had to act fast and eliminate the threat. He undid his hip strap and gripped the tomahawk in his left hand, keeping the pistol in his right. He stood, visually scanning the room. It was a rough, unfinished basement, more of a cellar if anything. He saw the wooden steps in the corner leading up; the door at the top was open.

He heard more footsteps above. There was for sure one of them, maybe two. Brad moved towards them. He needed to take them out before they could sound an alarm. He reached the steps and had begun walking up on the balls of his feet when he saw the door pull back. Brad leaned his right shoulder against the wall and raised his extended arm, pointing the pistol. The primal came around the corner, its head at the length of its neck exploring the darkness. Surprise was still on Brad's side.

The soldier didn't wait. He fired rapidly. *Pop, pop, pop* as he ran up the stairs, closing the distance. The first round went wide, but the other two were true. The primal's head bucked back and it tumbled down the stairs towards him. Brad used his left hand with the 'hawk to hook the creature and throw it by him as he continued to rush up the stairs. He burst through the doorway and into the kitchen, nearly colliding with an overweight woman, her shirt torn and barely hanging from her torso. She looked about, trying to find him in the darkness. Brad leveled the pistol and fired again. *Pop, Pop.*

He heard a crash behind him. He turned sharply and was hit from the side behind the knee. His leg buckled from the impact and he fell hard. Brad dropped the pistol as he lowered his right hand to brace his impact with the tile floor. He just caught the movement from his peripheral as he fell. It moved quickly, darting across the room. He sensed the thing coming at him again from behind; he lashed out heavily with the tomahawk. He felt and heard the sickening crunch as it made contact. Brad rolled to his knees and quickly sat back on his haunches, searching the room. He saw movement on the floor. A small child with the back of its skull hacked away was trying to crawl towards him. Its head was slack against the floor, only its eyes focused on where it thought Brad may be.

Brad quickly located his pistol and got to his feet before stepping back. He searched the space for more threats, finding none. The downed creature moaned weakly as it moved closer towards him. He didn't have it in him to use the hawk a second time on the child. He moved towards it and placed the MKII barrel on its temple and pulled the trigger. *Pop*. The pistol shocked the palm of his hand. Brad fell to his knees before dropping back against the wall. The house was silent now. He could still hear the moans from outside, but they sounded far away.

He could smell the stench in the home, the stink of primal. He could smell the death on his clothing from his crawl through the mortuary tent. No longer having the strength to hold it, exhausted from the fight, he turned his head and vomited hard. He continued until his lungs hurt, his eyes were watering, and he was dry heaving. He had to get out of the room. He crawled out of the kitchen and into a dining room, using a chair to pull himself back to his feet. Brad staggered though the house into a dark living area. Stepping clumsily he fell to the floor.

Brad struggled back to a sitting position before dropping his head. He breathed in and out heavily, trying to calm himself. "Suck it up sergeant! You don't have time for this shit," he scolded himself. Brad breathed in the air hard and blew it out, then put his head back and closed his eyes tightly before opening them again. He looked around the room. It was a large living room. There was a mantle fireplace along a wall with fancy furniture surrounding it. A large plasma television hung above the fireplace. Family photos were carefully placed along the mantle.

Brad recognized the child in a photo, sitting on the knee of a proud father with the mother directly behind them. He quickly looked away, burying his emotions. Brad looked to the left and could see the front door. It had large nails spiking it shut at the top and bottom. The windows had heavy curtains drawn over them. There was a box of water bottles in the corner. Brad could see the kitchen table had canned goods scattered around it. "What happened here? How did they get you?" Brad said as he forced himself back to his feet. He checked the pistol, dropped the magazine, and replaced it with a full one.

He cautiously moved down a long hallway. He found a small child's room and a bathroom. Brad peeked inside, then moved on. At the end of the hall was a large master bedroom. Brad moved into the room. The bed was made and the curtains were drawn. There was an attached master bathroom. The family had filled the bathtub with water; there were pitchers and jugs of water on the floor. A large first aid kid sat on the kitchen counter. Bloody bandages filled the sink. Brad returned to the master bedroom and sat on the bed.

He was exhausted. Brad sat his assault pack on the floor and lay back on the bed looking at the ceiling. He could hear them outside, moving, howling. They no longer seemed to be actively pursuing him. Still Brad got the uneasy feeling that they knew he was close. He pulled off the night vision goggles and laid them on the bed next to him. Slowly his eyes adjusted to the darkness, some moonlight leaking into the room over the top of the curtains. Brad unclipped the M4 from his chest rig and laid it next to him. No longer interested in fighting the fatigue, he closed his eyes and let sleep take him.

17.

When he woke it was still dark. Brad looked at his watch: just after 0400, still a couple hours before dawn. Starving, he grabbed the pack and dug though it until he found his MRE packets and the peanut butter. He sat the stack of MREs next to him. *No*, he thought, shaking his head, he should eat what was on hand first and leave the MREs for last resort. He stuffed everything back into the pack and stood up, stretching. He gathered the rest of his gear and pulled the large comforter off of the bed.

He made his way to the kitchen. With the early morning light he could now see that the child's arms were bandaged. The mother had small bite wounds to her neck and face. "So that's how it happened. They got your baby. Was he at school? Outside? You probably tried to protect him, cleaned and dressed his wounds … until he turned on you," Brad whispered sadly, looking at the mother.

Without debating or thinking about it, he grabbed the woman and gently moved her into the basement. He laid her next to the male, then returned for the child and placed him between his parents. Finally, Brad covered the family with the bedspread. "I don't know who you were, but you didn't deserve this. Your home saved me last night, and I thank you," Brad said before he turned and walked back up the stairs.

He closed the door behind him and looked around the kitchen. To the right was a small foyer with a back door; cardboard was taped to it, covering a window. Brad peeled back a corner of the cardboard. The home's backyard met the tree line. The yard was fenced and looked to be fairly well concealed. It shouldn't be too difficult to sneak through the back and make a break into the woods. But first he needed to feed his hunger.

Brad moved back into the kitchen and began looking through the cupboards. They were empty; most of the food had already been pulled out and placed on the kitchen table. Brad moved towards the kitchen table and sorted through the cans. "Green beans and tuna? Breakfast of survivors," he said as he worked the cans open. He found a plastic bowl and dumped the beans into it, eating them cold as he picked at the tuna fish. "I really do hate this town."

He went back to the living room. Finding the package of bottled water, he drank two bottles immediately before stuffing another two in his pack. Then he moved to the sofa and sat down, pulling the peanut butter from his pack, needing something sweet to get him going. He scraped the last remnants from the jar and sat it on the table. Brad leaned back into the sofa staring at the jar. "Well, I guess I should get ready to sneak out of here. If I'm quick I might make the tree line without being seen.

"Yes, peanut butter it would be nice to just chill here for a couple days, but Kelli needs the dope in my pack. It's time to hit the trail again."

Brad got back to his feet and moved to the front of the house. He found another side door with a key rack next to it. He stood still, thinking. "No ... that would be too easy," he said as he moved towards the window-less door. There was a bolt lock on the door, but it was currently unsecured. He put his hand on the knob, carefully turned the handle and pulled the door in towards him. The adjoining room was dark, but there was enough light to see a small Toyota sedan and a large GMC pickup.

"You got to be fucking kidding me," Brad said, smiling. He moved back to the key rack, grabbing a handful of keys and fumbling through the pile until finding the one he wanted. He went back into the garage, moving quietly to the overhead door and making sure it was closed and secured. He didn't want to be snuck up on. He moved to the large pickup truck and opened the driver's door; the dome light came on brightly. Brad got in the seat behind the wheel, held his breath and turned the key just a click and watched the dash light up.

The gas gauge lit and the arrow shot to the ¾ position. The battery showed fully charged. He smiled as he turned the key back and removed it from the ignition. Some people may think a truck won't start after being stored for a couple of months, but Brad knew better. More than once he had put a car in long term storage during a deployment and returned months later to have it easily start. He looked at the dash; it was a loaded model, with four wheel drive and leather seats. The family must have been well off.

"Yeah I'm not walking today," Brad said as he left the vehicle and moved back into the house. He went to the hall closet and dug around, finally finding what he was looking for: a large duffle bag. He went to the dining room and stuffed all of the canned goods into the bag. Then he went to the living room and grabbed the case of water. He started walking back towards the garage before he stopped. He turned back and grabbed the empty peanut butter jar from the table. He went back to the garage and opened the passenger door on the truck and tossed in the duffle bag and water. He set the jar in the cup holder in the center console.

He went back to the overhead door and pressed close to the tinted windows. The driveway was heavily drifted with snow. The road was heavily snowed in also; weeks of pile up and drifting wouldn't be easy to get through. Brad checked the trucks tires. They had an aggressive tread. Obviously the owner was prepared to deal with long hard winters. "Yeah, I can do this," he said confidently as he moved back to the truck and jumped into the driver's seat. He put the key in the ignition and again held his breath.

He turned the key and the engine cranked and purred to life. He looked in the rearview mirror and saw the closed door. "Yes, it would be fun to just crash through it," Brad said, looking down at the jar. "But I don't want to get hung up on the door, that would suck." He laughed as he got back out of the truck, walked to the center of the door and pulled a handle attached to a red cord hanging from the opener's track. With the opener disengaged, Brad walked to the door, turned the handle, and the torsion spring did the work, easily lifting the door.

With the door opened to the outside, the brisk morning air poured in. The sun was just beginning to shine' the snow sparkled and reflected the morning light back at him. Brad looked left and right. There were no primals in sight, but that wouldn't last long. He knew from experience they would come running once he was detected. Brad hurried back to the cab of the truck. He closed and locked the doors behind him, then flipped the control knob to 4x4 before placing the truck in reverse. "You ready for this, peanut butter? Well hold on because we only got one shot."

Brad gunned the engine and the truck

launched backwards, hitting the first drift heavily. He kept his foot on the gas, maintaining speed down the driveway and turning into the road. He continued in reverse until he cleared the heavy drifts, not wanting to get stuck. When he moved into a clear section of the street, he slowed and smoothly came to a stop, being careful to stay in his tracks, then slapped the selector into drive and eased on the accelerator. The truck's heavy V8 engine roared and launched forward, easily breaking through the drifts. Brad slowly added speed to keep the momentum of the vehicle up so that he could crash through the larger snow banks.

Seeing his turn ahead, he eased up on the accelerator and slowly crept away from the corner, making a wide angle right turn and trying not to lose control of the truck. He felt the rear end fish tail as he finished the turn. Brad steered into the skid and gunned the engine, letting the four wheel drive pull him out of the slide. He was now racing towards the main street. He began to see the first primals running out of buildings, looking at the truck barreling through the snow.

Brad hit the main drag and cut the wheel to the left. He misjudged his speed and skidded a bit before the truck slapped against a parked car. He kept the pedal down and his momentum carried him through another set of heavy drifts. Brad looked in the rearview mirror; the street was now quickly filling with primals. They were running, but still struggling in the heavy snow. Brad put his concentration forward, gripping the wheel tightly as he focused on keeping the truck on the road. He passed by the gated house he had seen on the way into town.

Driving fast, he dared to look up at the hilltops where they'd scouted the approach to the town and watched the brothers pass through on the snowmobile. He slowed the truck, still careful not to get stuck in the heavy snow. Lowering the power window on the passenger side, he strained to search the hilltops for Sean, but there was no sign of his friend. Giving up, he put his attention forward just as he failed to avoid another parked car, hitting it hard but still able to keep the truck's forward movement.

He had cleared the town now. He turned the corner and was moving onto open road, plowing through larger drifts and crashing over downed limbs, cringing as he heard them bang against the underside of the truck. Looking in the rearview mirror, he saw that he had outrun the primals. He knew they were back there, but for now he was alone on the road. The farther he got from town the less stalled cars he found. Less signs of life or primals. He followed the tracks the snowmobile had left in the snow days earlier, racing up the hill and around the long corner that led to the house where they had parted ways with the brothers.

As he drove he turned on the radio and let it scan. He watched the digital tuner scroll constantly without stopping. He switched to AM and observed the same. Nothing was on the air, only static if he manually tuned the dial. He reached into his bag and pulled out the small two-way radio Sean had given him. He fidgeted with it, trying to turn it on but it refused to power up, the batteries now completely dead.

Brad began to pass homes again. He slowed, searching for the house where they had hidden the snowmobile. Spotting it ahead, he slowed and pulled into the driveway of the boarded-up brown ranch house. Brad put the truck in park but left the engine running. "I'll be right back," he said, reaching across the center console and grabbing his M4. "Bro, stop nagging, I said I'll be right back."

Brad opened the truck's door and stepped into the heavy snow. It wasn't deep here. The wind had blown most of the snow to the far side of the yard, creating a large drift against the side of an old woodshed. He closed the truck door and stepped into the road, listening for movement, or the moans. Hearing nothing but the purring of the truck's engine, he moved to the heavy brush where they had ditched the snowmobile. It was gone. Brad stood motionless, thinking, *Maybe it was a different spot*? He walked into the brush and saw where the sled had been parked under the bushes. "No, this was the right place," he muttered to himself, shaking his head. He looked in all directions and searched the snow. He could see where the brothers' sled had returned; there was a wide path in the snow. They hadn't stopped. He could tell by the way the drifts were cut and carried past the house.

Brad went back to the bushes. He knelt in the snow, searching until he found where the sled had been started, and maneuvered deeper into the brush. He followed the path which led away from the road, deeper into the woods, before cutting back towards the house. He followed the trail until he was in the side yard and the trail had been covered by drifting snow. He froze when he heard the faint sounds of moaning. "Damn, they are moving fast today," he said.

He turned and moved back the way he had come. As he got to the road he heard a crash in a house next door. "Looks like the neighbors are up," he said as a primal exploded through the picture window of a home across the street. Brad stood his ground, staring as the creature pulled itself up out of the snow and broken glass. "Now what makes them do that? Why are they so pissed off they would jump through their own window to get me? I just don't get it," he said as he raised the rifle, firing twice and dropping the primal.

Brad heard a door slam behind him. Panicked, he spun on the balls of his feet towards the truck. He held his rifle at the ready, searching for threats as he slowly approached the driver's door. He saw movement in front of the truck and stepped quickly to the left, raising the sights to his eye.

"'Bout time you got here!" he heard Sean say just as his friend appeared in front of his rifle.

"What the fuck, Sean, I almost shot you."

"Yeah, yeah, don't flatter yourself. So what took you so long?" Sean said as he continued around the front of the truck. He had his backpack in his left hand and was carrying his rifle with the right.

"Are you serious? I barely made it out of there!"

"Yeah, looks like you were really roughing it," Sean said as he opened the truck door and tossed in his gear. "Damn, this thing has leather. Man, Brad you're getting soft, buddy. I mean I'm not gonna brag or anything, but I walked here."

"Screw you, just get in."

"Seriously though, good job, brother, I was worried about you when we lost coms. Did you get the stuff?"

"Yeah, I think so, I loaded up pretty good in the pharmacy. Can we just get out of here? I think I have half the town following me."

"Waiting on you, brother," Sean said as he fastened his seat belt.

18.

Brad reversed the truck back onto the road and headed to the cabin. As the road twisted and changed directions, some of the drifts lessened and he found the going easier. He relaxed his grip on the wheel and actually began to enjoy his drift-busting experience.

"You are pretty good at this, driving in the snow I mean," Sean said.

"Yeah, grew up in it. There were days Mom would have to go through worse than this just to get me to school."

"Back in Michigan?"

"Yeah, up north we could easily get four foot a year. I grew up in the middle of nowhere so we couldn't count on the snow plows. Mom had a big ol' Blazer. Dad lifted it and put some big knobby tires on it. My mom wasn't one for station wagons and minivans." Brad laughed.

"Shit, glad I have you behind the wheel then. Your folks sound like resourceful people. I'm sure they'll be okay."

Brad drove quietly for a moment, allowing the last comment to digest. "I try not to think about it. I mean … yeah, Dad's as tough as nails, but stubborn as hell too. I worry that if they found him … the primals … Yeah, he wouldn't be one to leave. I could see Mom in the kitchen fixing up venison burgers while Dad is out chasing primals off the lawn."

Sean grunted with laughter. "Definitely sounds like people I want to meet."

"What about you Sean? You have people back home? Been with you for a couple months and still don't know shit about you," Brad asked, keeping his eyes on the road.

"Yeah, home and family aren't the same uplifting conversation pieces they used to be, are they? Makes it hard to keep your head in the game when you're thinking about everything that could be going wrong at home."

"I guess you're right ... Damn, there you go again, dodging the question!" Brad said, laughing.

"Truth is, Brad, I don't have shit. I did once, but I chose to make the Navy my family, everything else faded away. My folks passed away years ago. I have a few ladies in a few ports but nothing special. Closest thing to home is a shitty apartment back in San Diego."

"Damn Chief, that's some sad shit. End of the world is probably the best thing to ever happen to you!" Brad said, continuing to laugh.

"And you wonder why I don't talk to you!" Sean said, laughing with him. "Hey, take that little side road," he said, pointing at a heavily snowed-over road that branched off the highway.

"That thing, you serious? Shit, I'll get

stuck for sure."

"That's the point. You didn't think we were going to drive this right back to the front door of that cabin, did you?"

"I hear ya," Brad said as he slowed before heaving the truck into a wide turn and onto the narrow side road.

As Brad had warned, the truck made it barely fifty feet before they collided with a drift that reached over the hood of the truck. Brad spun the tires before dropping the truck into park.

"Hmm, that's that," he said, dropping his hands.

Sean reached into the rear cab of his truck and pulled his assault pack forward. "Well it's only a mile or so through those woods. Hopefully this is still far enough to keep them from tracking us back. The way that snow is blowing we should be covered up pretty quick."

Brad grabbed the duffel bag from the back, opened it and stuffed in the remaining bottles of water. He started to zip the bag shut before pausing, then grabbed the peanut butter jar from the console and placed it in the bag, zipping it tight.

"What was that for?" Sean asked.

Brad gave him a puzzled look. "What, the jar? Oh, figured I could use it to keep stuff in."

Sean shrugged then, using his shoulder, forced his passenger door open, pushing back the heavy snow. As soon as the door was opened Brad was hit in the face with the brisk air and blowing snow. He reached down and lifted the handle on his side and shoved but the door refused to move. Brad scowled and tossed the bags out of Sean's door, then climbed over the seats.

"A shame to leave such a fine vehicle," Brad said, shutting the truck door.

Sean had already waded through the snow towards the shoulder of the road. He looked back at the truck and nodded. "I'm sure we will find more if need be. Come on, we need to stay ahead of the party."

Once Brad had backed away from the truck he used the duffle bag to cover their tracks, making long, sweeping motions to try and blend the cut in the snow with the rest of the drift. He did that until they were well within the trees. Sean led off on point, setting a fast pace. Soon they were in the thick cover of the forest again; the thicker the trees got the lighter they found the snow.

They continued in a straight line forty-five degrees away from the cabin. They couldn't risk being followed, even though they had confidence in the snow covering their path. Double redundancy was always good in their line of work. Sean moved on, taking them away from the cabin until he found a spot in the forest thick with tall pines. He used this place to jump from one bed of needles to another, breaking any remnant of a trail. Then they turned and headed directly towards the cabin.

Sean led them onto a heavily-traveled game trail where he knelt down, examining the earth and tracks. "Looks clear, mostly small game, a deer or two. Pretty fresh, I'd say we don't have any crazies out here," he said in a low voice.

Brad nodded his approval and they continued moving, now making better time as they stuck to the well-traveled trail. "Did you hear from the brothers at all, after we separated I mean?" Brad asked as he walked.

Sean grunted, "Haven't seen them since they rode through town. If they stuck to the plan they will be fine."

"I stuck to the plan, look what happened to me," Brad said.

"Yeah, but you're always looking for attention," Sean laughed.

"Screw you. You know I couldn't just leave the clinic empty-handed, I had to try."

"I know, but it was stupid … hopefully it all works out and these meds are enough to save her."

"Hopefully we're on time. How long has it been since we got that note?"

"Three days I think, yeah, she could have really taken a turn for the worse in three days, or she is all healed by now," Sean said, putting his head down.

They walked quietly for several minutes, moving though long sections of heavy brush before climbing a tall hill. Here the pines broke though the canopy and stretched towards the clear sky. Everything on the hill was covered in feet of pristine white snow. Sean moved along the trail and found a large, fallen oak tree, its roots exposed and covered with frozen dirt. Sean moved in close to the tree and dropped his pack.

Brad came up behind him, cautiously watching their back trail. "Something wrong, Sean?"

"No, not particularly. From my notes I figure the cabin should be on the far side of this ridge, just thought now would be a good time for a rest," Sean said as he strapped his MP5 to the top of his rucksack. He removed the long rifle and checked the magazine and slide. Brad saw what Sean was doing so he prepared his own kit and weapons for a fight.

"We expecting trouble Sean?" he asked.

"I'm always expecting trouble, that's how I stay alive."

Brad nodded as he unstrapped the shotgun from his pack and removed all of the rounds, getting a solid count before reloading it. He filled the six-round tube and slid one round into the chamber. That left him one extra 12-gauge round on the stock. He cut a length of cord and fashioned himself a hasty sling. He liked the feel of the shotgun; if he could find more shells it would be worth keeping.

"Nice 870, where'd you pick it up?" Sean asked, watching what Brad had been doing.

"Dead cop inside the pharmacy. Must have been a hell of a battle at that place. His sidearm was empty and his jacket torn up pretty good. He probably saved those civilians, getting them locked inside … before he turned on them."

"I'm sure there are a lot of stories like his that will never be told," Sean said. "You ready to move out?"

"Yeah, let's do this." Brad got to his feet and threw his pack over his shoulders. He let the shotgun hang from its new sling as he carried his M4 cradled in his arms. Sean stood and moved ahead with his rifle held at the low ready.

"Just over the ridge and through the trees," Sean whispered as he went back to a tactical stance.

The duo crept forward at a slow pace, stopping often to listen for danger. As Sean had said, once they cleared the top of the ridge they could just make out the clearing of the cabin. They were approaching directly from the back. Brad could identify the pond's flat icy surface. The wind was blowing in their face and he could just barely pick up the scent of wood smoke. "The fire smoldering," he whispered.

"I smell it too," Sean answered.

As they drew closer the shapes of the structures slowly came into focus, their rough outlines standing stark against the snow. Sean paused and knelt close to the ground; Brad pulled up just behind him and to the left. Sean had the scope to his eye sweeping left to right. "Something's off," he said.

Brad raised his own rifle. Looking, he saw nothing. "What is it?"

"The barn door is open, why would they do that?" Sean asked.

"I don't know, maybe they forgot, maybe the latch failed?"

"Yeah, maybe, stay close," Sean said with a grunt.

They continue their slow patrol towards the buildings, Sean stopping often to glass the structures. He spotted something in the snow in front of them and asked Brad to hold back while he moved ahead. Brad watched Sean move close to the buildings then stop to kneel in the snow. He looked in all directions before calling Brad forward.

Brad ran forward to join Sean who was looking at tracks in the snow. "This isn't good, look," Sean said, pointing.

"What, did they already leave? Without us?" Brad asked.

"Look closer, these tracks here, all wearing boots ... then these scattered around, they're in soft shoes, and this one maybe even barefooted."

"Holy shit, they're on the run!" Brad gasped.

"Yeah, looks like they took off from the cabin in a straight line, headed east. These others must have been trailing, far behind I'd imagine or we'd see battle signs."

"Do we follow them?" Brad asked.

"Yeah, but I want to check out the cabin first. Spread out, give me some distance," Sean said as he slung the rifle over his shoulder and drew his pistol.

Sean kept a direct line headed towards the cabin, and Brad moved off far to his right. They walked straight until Sean was within fifty meters of the cabin's wall. Then Brad pin wheeled, allowing himself to cut the corner of the building far off while Sean stayed concealed. As Brad moved forward and to the right, he began to see the right side of the cabin. One of the shutters had been cut away and removed. The inside window glass was broken and the curtain blew in the breeze.

Brad stopped and pointed it out to Sean, who nodded in reply before ordering Brad forward. Brad kept his rifle at the low ready and continued moving towards the front of the building. Once in position, he paused and watched as Sean now got close to the edge of the cabin, stooped low under the window and proceeded to the front corner. Then, Sean waited for Brad to move back online with him before he stepped off, and once again moved out and away from the cabin, allowing Brad to see around the corner at a distance while keeping Sean concealed.

The first thing that caught Brad's attention was the snowmobile, the one the brothers had ridden into town. It was no more than twenty meters in front of the cabin. As Brad focused on the sled, he looked to the left and saw them – scattered bodies in the snow and all along the front of the cabin. Instantly he brought the rifle up to his eye and took a knee. Sean recognized his change in posture and took a step back while bringing up his own weapon.

Brad took a deep breath and, keeping the rifle at eye level, approached the cabin. He moved a few feet at a time, stopping to sweep everything in front of him for movement. As he got closer he could see that the dead were piled up against the cabin's doors. He could see where the snowmobile had entered the yard, the wide deep track coming from the road. The primals' footprints were embedded in the sled's tracks. The brothers had been followed home.

When Brad got back online with Sean at the cabin's corner he stopped. Sean nodded before stepping out from the blind spot and moved to where he was almost shoulder to shoulder again with Brad. Then the two men stepped off together. The cabin's door was still secured even though several of the planks had been broken. Brad stepped over the bodies, cautiously probing them with his rifle's barrel as he passed them.

Sean slid close to the door and tugged on it. It was still bolted from the inside. They moved past the door, seeing that the front window was shattered, its shutter removed. Brad stepped out away from the building, training his rifle at the opening while Sean peeked inside. He looked in, then quickly pulled his head back. "Yeah, they got in," Sean said.

"Our guys?"

"I couldn't tell. It's a mess."

Suddenly there was a loud crash from inside, and the men jumped back as they brought up their weapons. Sean stepped back to join Brad away from the cabin. They held their sights high on the window as they heard the clattering of objects and furniture being knocked over. There was a thump at the door. The two men pivoted, focusing on the entrance. Brad prepared to fire when he heard the latch click. Sean brought his hand up and put it on Brad's shoulder.

The door opened and Hahn tumbled out onto the porch. Brad ran to him and went to lift him up. He stopped when he saw blood on his shirt. Hahn rolled to the side and looked Brad in the eyes. "It's not my blood, I'm not infected,"

Hahn said in a weak voice.

Brad reached down and grabbed Hahn under the shoulders, attempting to move him. Hahn grimaced in pain. "Just help me up, I can walk dammit," he mumbled.

Brad pulled him to his feet and walked him towards the far side of the porch and away from the primal bodies. Sean dropped his pack and they set Hahn up against it. Hahn collapsed, leaning back against the building. His left arm was hanging limp, his left hand a crumpled mess, his entire torso covered in blood. Most of his body armor had been torn away.

"What happened to you, you sure you're not bit?" Brad asked.

"Yeah, if I was bit I woulda turned by now ... I kept waiting for it to happen, I was ready to off myself if the symptoms started. But it hasn't happened, no fever yet," Hahn whispered.

"You're not bit? Scratched?" Brad asked.

"I'm fucked up. They got ahold of me, then chewed the shit out of my hand and forearm ... but the bite shirts and Kevlar gloves, yeah, they fucking work. "

"No shit," Brad said as he moved to examine Hahn's arms. He could see that there were teeth marks in the leather of the Kevlar gloves, but no punctures. The fingers looked to have been smashed inside the material. Hahn's left forearm had depressions in the material and his uniform shirt was torn away, exposing the bite shirt underneath. The bite shirt was made of tightly woven Kevlar fabric; they had been issued to them back on the island. There were doubts that they would hold up against an attack. A dog would easily rip the material apart, but human teeth are not the same as a dog's. Brad used his gloved hand to feel Hahn's arm. He could feel lumps of torn and mashed flesh underneath, but the compression of the shirt was holding his arm together. To Brad it felt like someone had tenderized a steak inside of a freezer bag.

"I know it's bad. I think they dislocated my elbow too, I can't use my arm," Hahn said.

Sean moved forward and cut away more of the bloody outer uniform shirt, exposing the bite shirt. "Brad, give him some of the painkillers, shit, antibiotics too," he said as he used a bottle from his bag to rinse away the primal blood.

Brad looked through the bag, staring at the bottles of medications. "What do I give him?"

"Make him a cocktail, I don't know but we need to get moving, we can't stay here," Sean said, lifting Hahn's mangled arm so that he could remove the material below it. Hahn gritted his teeth and grunted in protest. "Hahn, I'm not going to remove the bite shirt and risk exposing the wound to the contaminated blood on your uniform. I'm just going to immobilize it for now, okay?"

"Do what you got to do," Hahn said, shaking with pain.

Brad finished clearing the wounded area so that Hahn's arm was now resting tightly against his body. Then Sean rushed into the cabin and came back out with an armful of bedding from one of the bunks. He quickly cut a bed sheet into strips and used it to make a sling that he attached to Hahn's arm. Brad interrupted Sean just long enough to give Hahn several pills.

"I don't know what's what in here, but these were locked up. Must be the good stuff," Brad said skeptically as Hahn took them and swallowed water heavily.

"What happened here, Hahn?" Sean asked as he continued to work.

"Huh." Hahn looked up into Sean's face. "It was those Marines. The Villegases. They came back last night on that snow mobile, rode it right up into the yard."

"Why would they do that, they led them right to ya!" Brad exclaimed.

"Yeah, we argued about it, but they didn't listen. They told us they lost them out there in the woods. They said they were cold and didn't want to freeze. According to them they are experts at evasion, they figured nothing would be able to follow them."

Sean wrapped a long strip of the bed

sheet around Hahn's torso, suspending his arm. "Okay, so they followed the brothers back. Got it, but where did they go?"

Hahn coughed again, spitting more blood onto the plank porch. He paused, then took a long draw of water. "Last night, it was late, everyone had turned in. Somehow they got past Parker on watch. They were in close before he noticed them. Parker was the first to sound the alarm, but too late to do anything. The primals attacked the door right off. Piling against it, moaning and fighting. But these were the fast ones, the strong ones.

"When they could see that the door wasn't going to give they put their attention on the window. They ripped off the shutters and broke the glass. We fired on them, stopped the first attack, used up all of the belted SAW ammo pretty quick, but more came. Lots of them … More fast ones. They hit the front and the sides. We decided to break out of the back, make a run for the tree line. Me and Parker kept them busy at the front while the others slipped out.

"The boy, he and Nelson led the way, the Villegases right behind them. They put down covering fire for us to bail out. Parker and I made a break for the back. I shoved him out of the window but one of those things got my arm, latched onto me like a German shepherd and pulled me to the ground. I gut shot that fucker before Parker killed it. But it bit me, fucked up my arm and fingers. I thought I was done, infected you know, I told the others to get, to leave me.

"I fought my way back into the cabin, just kept shooting and fighting, trying to keep the mob focused on me so the others could escape. The damn things got inside so I made my way to the attic and kicked down the ladder. The smelly bastards kept coming. I killed them till my rifle was dry. I saved me some rounds in the pistol, I figured maybe I'd save one for myself.

"I killed them all, all of 'em. I thought the fever would take me, I waited for it all morning, but I never turned. I guess whatever nasty shit is on their teeth never got through the Kevlar. But they still messed me up, I can't barely move my arm. I know they did me good, I can feel the blood in my glove.

"I musta passed out. When I heard you all talking I tried to get down. Guess I fell, it fucking hurt," Hahn said, chuckling.

Sean squeezed the man's good shoulder. "You did good, Hahn, and looks like our guys got away thanks to you."

When Sean had finished slinging Hahn's arm he leaned him back against the cabin wall and covered him with a heavy blanket, then allowed him to rest while the drugs kicked in. Sean opened a new water bottle and placed it in Hahn's hand. The wounded man took it and began to sip, stopping to cough and spit blood out and onto his chin. Hahn coughed a bit more then gave an exaggerated chuckle. "Maybe I broke a rib or two ... I know I look bad ... but shit, did you see the other guys?" Hahn grinned, indicating the inside of the cabin.

Brad gave Hahn a concerned look as he tucked the blanket in around him. Sean grabbed Brad's elbow. "Brad, can you help me take a look inside? We need to collect our rucksacks and salvage what we can before we move out."

Brad turned to look back at Sean who wore the same concerned expression. He followed Sean into the cabin. The space was turned upside down. The bunks were knocked over, and all of the furniture was destroyed. The floor was littered with mangled and broken bodies. The ladder that led up to the attic was destroyed at the top rungs, and a grotesque pile of bodies lay at the bottom of it. Brad walked to the wood stove and felt the top. "Stove is still warm, let's go. They can't be too far ahead of us. Sean, I don't think there is anything in here worth salvaging. Or anything I would want," Brad whispered.

"Oh yeah, what about those?" Sean said, pointing at a large male primal's feet. "They look to be the right size and toasty warm."

"No, come on man, fuck no, man, that's gross," Brad said, looking at a set of heavy leather boots strapped to the stocky legs of a nearly decapitated body.

"Beats frostbite, and you aren't going to last long with wet and frozen feet," Sean said. "Hey, at least they look broken in, so you won't get blisters."

"I don't think I can do it. No, I'm okay, these boots have served me well. I'll be okay."

Sean grunted before kneeling down to untie the boot laces. "You know what, buddy, I'm gonna help you out and pull these off for you okay? But that's not the real reason I brought you in here."

"Yeah?" Brad said, trying not to look disgusted at the thought of wearing primal boots.

"It's Hahn, he's messed up bad, I don't know that he can travel," Sean said.

Brad reached down on the kitchen floor and picked up a can of roast beef. He looked at the label and tossed the can in the air, catching it with his free hand. "Yeah, but we can't leave him."

"I know, leaving him *alone* isn't an option," Sean said.

"Alone?"

"Someone has to stay with—" Sean was interrupted midsentence by the sounds of moans.

Brad turned and walked towards the open window. Five to six staggering figures were moving up the driveway. "We have company."

Sean tossed the boots at Brad's chest before rushing back out onto the front porch with Brad close behind him. When the creatures spotted them on the porch their moans got louder. Brad started to raise his rifle before Sean stepped in front of him. "Let's save our ammo. We can take these slow ones down the old-fashioned way," Sean said as he reached down and picked up the large splitting axe from the wood pile.

Brad clipped his M4 back to his vest. He returned to the cabin, searching the floor. Finding what he was looking for, he reached down and lifted a long iron fireplace poker. He moved back outside. Sean had removed Hahn's sidearm from his holster and placed it into Hahn's good hand. "We're gonna take care of these guys, we'll be right back," Sean said, looking directly into Hahn's eyes. Hahn nodded. His eyes had grown glassy and his face had lost expression. Apparently whatever drugs Brad had given him were working.

Sean put his hand on Hahn's shoulder before turning to face Brad. "You ready to go to work?"

"Let's do it."

The group of primals that shambled up the snow-covered driveway were slow. They staggered and often fell, being easily tripped up in high drifts of snow. Brad and Sean watched them, almost amused at their behavior. They didn't stick together, even though they seemed to have a common goal: to go after the living. But their plan of attack wasn't coordinated, not like any they had seen with the Alphas, not even like the ones they had fought in the desert.

Brad and Sean moved towards the group of them, then spread apart to the left and right side of the mass. The primals seemed to be confused by this, not knowing which direction to go. Then the pack started to drift to the right towards Sean. Brad yelled and waved his hands, distracting them and drawing them back in his direction.   All six of them liked the invitation; they locked on Brad and staggered towards him, now seemingly uninterested in Sean.

Sean held his position as Brad, who was now walking backwards, began leading them to the center of the field and away from Hahn and the cabin. Brad slapped the poker against his gloved hand, pulled his tomahawk from its sheath with his left, and clanged the metal weapons together, further agitating the slow-moving crazies. Brad began taunting them, yelling obscenities. He planted his feet shoulder-width apart and urged the primals to get him.

The primals now completely engaged on Brad had become oblivious to Sean, who worked his way behind the group. Brad continued to yell obscenities and bang the 'hawk and poker together, infuriating the primals. Brad grinned as he watched Sean move up on one of the trailing primals. With a heavy overhand swing of the axe, he split a primal's head. The thing tumbled and collapsed into the snow without any of his comrades taking notice.

"Damn, Sean, these things are dumb as hell," Brad yelled over the moaning creatures.

Two of the primals had closed to within ten feet of Brad who was still moving backwards at a pace just fast enough to stay ahead of them. "You want to see just how dumb?" Sean yelled.

The sound of Sean's voice stopped the creatures in their tracks; they turned to see Sean standing directly behind them. Brad froze, not moving or making a sound. This was enough to distract the primals. They clumsily twisted in the snow, changing direction and heading back towards Sean. As soon as the two closest to Brad had turned their backs to him, Brad lunged forward. He split the back of the nearest primal's head with his 'hawk, the blade sticking in the back of its skull. Brad let go of the handle and let the creature take the 'hawk with it to the ground.

Brad took three quick steps towards the next primal. Now gripping the poker two-handed he swung hard and slapped the creature in the side of the head. There was a large whack as the iron connected with bone. The primal stopped and fell to a knee but didn't go over. It turned its head to face Brad, a look of recognition hitting its face as it opened its mouth to scream at the nearby prey. Brad lifted the poker over his head and crashed it down onto the primal's skull, silencing it.

His actions and the primal's momentary scream had turned the remainder of the pack back towards him and away from Sean. Brad gripped the poker tight as he casually walked back to the first downed crazy and removed his 'hawk from its skull. He looked over his shoulder to see that the remaining three primals were still following him. "Yeah, they are satisfactorily stupid," Brad yelled out just as Sean swung with the axe and knocked over another primal that had turned his back on him.

With two left, Brad continued to walk back and lead them towards him. Sean closed the distance on the trailing primal. He used the head of the axe to poke it in the back. The primal stopped and turned around just as Sean swung, removing its lower jaw with a baseball swing. With one left, Brad stopped moving away from it. The last primal was shirtless, its skin ashen and frostbitten. Parts of its flesh were torn and bitten away. There were remnants of gauze bandages loosely hanging from its neck.

"Look at this, Sean, how is this guy still on his feet?" Brad said as he thrust the poker into the thing's chest, knocking it into the snow. The primal let out a weak moan as it fell face first into a drift. Sean moved up behind it as it struggled to crawl back to its feet. Sean stepped over and used the heel of his boot to shove it back to the ground.

"Is this a different type? Or a progression of the disease?" Sean said. "Have you noticed we only see these guys in the daylight, and the fast ones at night?"

The creature crawled forward again and slid to its knees. It lifted itself up, locking eyes with Brad before letting out another groan. Brad took the tip of the poker and stabbed it high in the shoulder, pushing the primal to its back as it screamed at him in response. Brad stepped forward and delivered a front kick to the thing's chest, knocking it back into the snow. The creature lay on its back, the fresh puncture in its shoulder filling with blood. Sean stepped into position and dropped the axe heavily, crushing the thing's head and putting it out of its misery.

Brad pointed towards the hole he had created in the creature's shoulder with the poker, seeing the wound begin to fill with blood. "Are they still alive? I mean, before you crushed its head."

"This is crazy shit, I think we have us some zombies?" Sean said.

Brad moved back, examining another of the dead. "Zombies? But what about the ... no ... Zombies, no way, zombies don't have heartbeats, they can't bleed without a pumping heart?"

"Yup, close enough. We've suspected it all along Brad, but it never fit the mold till now.

Let's just get past the elephant in the room, these are fucking zombies. I'm calling it," Sean declared.

"But ... they still bleed?" Brad mumbled.

"I mean yeah, before ... yeah some still run and they're fast, even smart sometimes, and we can kill them, and make em' *bleed*. But I don't know, maybe it's the cold, maybe they get like this the longer they are infected, but look at these things, this guy's fucking skin is frozen and peeling off its bones. That kinda shit ain't right."

Sean nodded, looking down at the things around him in the snow before continuing to voice his thoughts. "Yeah, maybe the virus preserves the organs, keeps the heart pumping when they should lay down and die. We already know it does something to the brain, that's why they are so strong, so hard to put down."

Brad stared at the creatures, shaking his head. "We need to get out of here, like at the crash site, more will follow ... it's not safe here."

"We need to figure out what to do with Hahn ... I was gonna suggest one of us stay with him while the other goes for help, but that won't work, especially if the Alphas show up after dark," Sean said.

Brad shook his head adamantly, "He'll walk, and when he can't walk we carry him."

Sean looked at Brad, nodding his head. "Let's go before another wave shows up." He turned and walked towards the cabin.

While Brad prepared Hahn to move, Sean rummaged through the building, stuffing anything usable into his rucksack. He located Brad's full ruck near the bunks and carried it outside. He rushed back to the porch to see Brad wearing the scavenged boots.

"Primal skin boots, very stylish this time of year," Sean said.

"Fuck you very much, you ready to go poke ass, or you just gonna play in the cabin all day?" Brad retorted.

Within minutes they were loaded up and ready. Hahn was on his feet. The drugs had fully kicked in. He was leaning drunkenly against the woodpile while Sean and Brad finished suiting up. Smiling and staring off into the distance, Hahn lifted his good arm and pointed across the field at the opening near the road. "Ha, look at that would ya, more of them, they just keep on coming," Hahn laughed.

Brad stopped and turned. He could see them, more this time, walking in a tight group and headed his way. He lifted the rifle and prepared to fire. Sean looked at him and shook his head. "Save your ammo, we can lose them in the trees."

"You sure, Sean, there are a lot of them," Brad asked.

"Yeah I'm sure, we don't have enough ammo for a sustained fight. Grab your boy and move out, I'm right behind you."

Brad grabbed Hahn by the good arm and pushed him ahead. Hahn stepped off, sometimes losing his balance in the snow with his one side immobilized. When he slipped or began to trip, Brad steadied him. They followed the cabin around to the back until they found the old tracks leading off into the distance, the tracks the others had used to evade the primals. Hahn was hurting but he was able to keep a good pace. Brad and Sean had split his gear and taken his rifle to help lessen his burden.

Hahn suggested they leave him behind, that he would only slow them down. Brad encouraged him not to quit. They both reassured Hahn that he didn't have to outrun Brad and Sean, only the slow-moving primals. Brad's fear was that more of the fast movers would show up, or even worse, the Alphas. He wanted to push as far away from the cabin as possible before the sun went down.

19.

The men followed the tracks across the field and into the trees. The snow here had grown wet and heavy, making it easy to see their friends' tracks, and also the tracks of the primals that had followed them. Even with Hahn's constant coughing and unsteady feet they were able to move along the trail at a steady pace and break contact with their own batch of following primals. They moved through a band of thick trees and along a high bend. Here the trail broke and ran parallel with the top of the ridgeline.

The top of the hill was slippery, and Brad could see where several of the pursuing primals had lost their footing and fallen down the far side of the ridge. He moved closer to Hahn and kept a close eye on him, worried that he may also fall down the steep slope. Ahead the ridgeline faded and the trail cut sharply to the right. Brad moved ahead of Hahn and rounded the blind spot first.

Brad slowed and raised his rifle as he stepped around the blind corner. Farther down the trail he saw several bodies lying face down in the snow. Brad stopped and probed the scene with his rifle's optics. Hahn and Sean slowly moved up behind him. Sean tapped Brad, signaling for him to patrol forward. As they got closer they could clearly see that the bodies in the snow were all primals dressed in random arrangements of civilian attire.

They moved beyond the bodies and saw patches of packed down snow where the soldiers had hidden. There were small piles of brass along the trail and then more tracks that led away. Only now there were only boot prints; no more primal footprints trailed the path of the fighters.

"Smart. They set an ambush and cut down their pursuers here," Sean said.

"What about us, should we think of doing the same thing?" Brad asked.

"I don't think so, like you said this is like the crash site. I fear we will have these slow movers on our trail until we manage to lose them. Good thing is the slow ones don't seem to be good trackers."

Brad nodded his agreement and began to step forward when he heard Hahn fall to the ground behind him. He reached down to help him to his feet, but Hahn just looked up at him, his face pale and dazed. Brad grabbed him under the shoulders and lifted him up. Hahn grunted and with his head down slowly began marching forward, following the boot prints in the snow. Brad looked down at his hands and could see they were covered in bright red blood.

Brad showed his hands to Sean. Sean nodded, "He's bleeding badly. I don't know what to do."

"Maybe a tourniquet on that arm?" Brad suggested, keeping his voice low as they trailed Hahn.

"I already did that, I tried loosening it earlier but he started bleeding again. I think we're going to have to remove the bite shirt and really get at the wound, I just don't want contaminated clothing touching the wrong thing," Sean said.

"As soon as we can find some shelter we will clean him up and peel off the shirt. We're going to have to risk exposure to the infection. If we don't, he's going to bleed out," Brad whispered.

The trail continued downhill and slowly the terrain opened up. They found themselves walking along a high fence row. Brad had moved out front taking point, keeping Hahn behind him with Sean. The terrain had softened, some of the snow even dissipating, exposing long treks of green grass. Brad continued to patrol forward and spotted a road ahead in the distance. He halted and waited for Sean and Hahn to catch up to his position.

Brad watched Hahn stagger forward. His head was hanging low, and Sean was holding him under his good arm, guiding him forward. When they moved up next to Brad, Sean dropped his pack near a fence post and slowly lowered Hahn into a sitting position. Hahn rested and leaned back deeply against the post, his head swaying side to side.

Sean looked up at Brad and shook his head, his face grim. Then he walked past Brad, stepping towards the road and signaling for Brad to follow him. They moved down towards a tall pair of trees.

"Hand me the spotting scope."

Brad removed it from his pack and handed it over. Sean used it to scout the road. "Hahn is in bad shape, only thing moving him now is raw guts," Sean said. Keeping his eye to the glass.

"I know."

Sean continued to scan the far off road before pausing and turning a dial on the scope to bring some far off object into focus.

"Brad, from here it looks like there may be tire tracks down there on that road."

"No way?" Brad said, surprise in his voice. Sean passed the scope to him.

Brad focused on the twisting line hundreds of yards off in the distance. Much of the road was still covered with snow. There were spots where the wind and drifts had swept the road clean, leaving black patches of exposed asphalt. Brad steadied himself against one of the trees and traced the road with the scope. He could make out a pair of cuts through the snow. It could definitely be tire tracks, or just sets of footprints running side by side.

Sean disagreed on the footprint theory as

the tracks were too uniform, and said they must be from a four-wheeled vehicle. Either way, they agreed that they needed to get Hahn to the road and to shelter quickly. There were only a couple of hours of daylight left. One thing they did know, the primals were still more active at night and they wanted to be secured before then.

When they moved back to Hahn they found him unconscious. Brad felt his neck and checked for a pulse. "It's weak, Sean, we need to treat these wounds."

"Not here, not now," Sean answered. "Let's get moving to the road. We'll follow it north, roads will have structures sooner or later. We'll stop and clear the first thing."

"Hahn might not make it that far."

"Brad, if we start exposing him out here in the open he won't make it anyway. I'm not a fucking doctor, but I'm sure if the hypothermia don't get him the blood loss will."

"Fine then let's move, I'll carry him first."

Brad tightened the straps on his pack, then moved in front of Hahn. Sean lifted the unconscious man to his feet as Brad took his good arm and hoisted him to his back in a modified fireman's carry. "Damn, he's heavier than he looks," Brad said.

"I'll lead the way. I'm going to set a quick pace, I'll trade off with you as soon as you need it."

"Just go," Brad grunted, trying to adjust

the man's weight on his shoulders.

Sean had told the truth, he stepped off fast, leading the way to the road. Brad marched forward, focusing on the ground in front of him and coordinating every step with the heavy load on his back. He began to feel the burning in his quad again. With all of the abuse his body had taken over the last few days he had begun to forget about the old wound. Brad welcomed the pain, it gave him something to think about beside the ache in his back and neck.

Sean made it to the road, scouted ahead, then ran back to help Brad lower Hahn to the ground. They checked his vitals. He was still breathing, and still had the faint pulse. "They are definitely tire tracks, looks like a large truck, and they're fresh too," Sean said.

"What do you think?" Brad asked.

"Doesn't matter at this point. We'll stay north, sticking to the road. You take point, I'll carry for a while."

They traded off Hahn, Brad helping to situate him onto Sean's shoulders. Brad stepped off first, moving out ahead and taking point on the right-hand side of the road. Sean allowed him to get several meters ahead so they could react to any threats. The road traveled through high country. To the right the land sloped up and away into rocky wooded terrain. The left sloped down along a wide open meadow of sorts before being met by the heavy forest.

The road traveled gradually downhill, with the high ground to the right. The way the terrain lined up it allowed for an expansive view of the road ahead and the surrounding countryside. Brad continued marching forward, stopping often to look back and make sure Sean was still behind him. Brad stuck to the right side of the road, trying to stay on the dry pavement to avoid leaving tracks.

Brad saw that Sean was falling behind, so he walked to the center of the road and looked closer at the tire tracks while waiting for Sean to catch up. They were deep treads like you would see on a large truck, possibly military. The vehicle had a wide wheel base, and was probably heavy with the way it cut through the larger drifts. But most importantly the tracks were clear and fresh, probably less than eight hours old.

He stood from the road as he saw Sean approach. "You need to trade off."

"I'm good, keep stepping," Sean said back.

Brad nodded and continued his march down the road. He studied the wide open terrain. It would be hard for a primal to sneak up on them out here, but there would also be no place to hide if the Alphas came after them. The thought gave Brad a shiver as he tried to get his mind back to the road. As he marched he began to take note of his situation. He was no longer moving tactical, his rifle was hanging from its sling, his arms crossing his chest with his fingers tucked into his vest. The days of living on edge had taken a toll on him; his body and mind were ready for a break.

Brad continued to walk the road and began to daydream of marches back at Fort Benning, the drill sergeants yelling at them to keep their rifles up, forcing them to hold the weapon just off of their chests until their arms burned from the strain. No breaks, overstuffed packs, eating MREs on the side of the road, then spending the night in a shallow-dug hole or ranger grave. The long forced marches were a rite of passage back then, a requirement to pass and become a soldier. A feat of mind over matter, putting one foot in front of the other until it was over.

Those marches had taught them not to quit, that they would always eventually cross that finish line. That was then; now he was beginning to lose thought of that finish line, that feeling of accomplishment. This just seemed to be another endless hike down a long, long road. Looking deep in the distance he began to see a glimmer of movement or an object. Brad was unsure if it was a mirage from staring at the same terrain for so long, it could just be a glimmer of sunlight off the melting snow. He hesitated to call a halt, waiting to give warning to Sean.

The road dipped ahead of him and he watched the object fade. It took his fatigued brain a moment too long to register what he was observing. The wasted moment took away his advantage. Quickly Brad turned behind and yelled for Sean to get off the road. Brad spun back forward just as a large blue truck came back into view as it climbed out of the dip. The truck was moving fast down the center of the road. As it got closer, Brad at first considered raising his rifle but fought the temptation. He did not want to appear a threat to people that may be able to help them.

The truck maintained its speed and continued on in the center lane. Brad took a step back towards the shoulder of the road, still staring at the truck. He could make out two figures in the cab and another man in the bed of the truck standing over the cab with a long gun in his hands. The truck continued closing the distance. As it passed Brad, the driver turned his head to look at him. Brad saw the man's eyes go wide with surprise. At the same time the man in the bed of the truck began slapping the roof of the cab.

The tires squealed on bits of dry pavement and the truck skidded to a stop, then backed up until it was even with Brad. He stood, watching the men as the truck's window lowered. The man in the back turned to face Brad. The driver was no more than a teenager, and the one standing guard in the back looked even younger. The driver looked at Brad with a smile and yelled to him. "Wha'dyat? I thought you was a creeper!"

Brad, still puzzled and surprised to see the vehicle, found himself at a loss for words. He took a half step forward and began to mumble.

"Are ya okay, friend?" the boy in the bed of the truck shouted with a thick accent, joining the conversation.

Sean continued walking towards Brad. As he got closer he knelt down and slowly lowered Hahn to the ground. He dropped his pack and used it to prop up Hahn's body. As Sean finished he joined Brad by the side of the road, slapping Brad on the shoulder then looking to the truck. "I think we'll be okay now," he said, smiling.

"You Americans?" the boy in the driver's seat asked.

"Yes sir we are," Sean answered. "Where did you all come from? We haven't seen anyone alive in days."

"Your man ... is he bit? He looks about as bad as a boiled boot," the boy asked, ignoring the question.

Sean shook his head. "No, hurt bad though, do you have a safe place to go?"

The boy began to speak as the other man in the truck's cab grabbed his shoulder. Brad could make out the sharp words of an argument.

The thick accents made it difficult for him to follow the conversation. Brad looked back to the bed of the truck and made eye contact with the guard. He was very young, barely out of his teens. He held a pump shotgun loosely in his hands, the gun old was battered, a stretch of black tape looped around the stock to repair a large split in the wood. He didn't hold the weapon in a threatening way, but where he could still quickly bring it to action. By the way the gun rested in the pocket of his right arm, the boy looked like he had used it before.

Brad smiled and nodded to the boy-guard in the back, who smiled and returned his nod. "Are you soldiers? I never seen uniforms like that, but I have seen them kinds of guns before, on games and such."

Brad considered the question; he was wearing the canvas coat from the old couple's closet and his filthy Multicam uniform trousers; the shemagh had been tied around his head and he was wearing the leather primal skin boots. He no longer looked to be any kind of conventional soldier. *I must look like a real shitbag to these strangers,* he thought as he tried to conceal his laughter.

"I guess we don't look quite the part anymore, but we are soldiers, just trying to make it home," Brad said, finally finding his voice.

The boy-guard smiled. "I thought so, I like your back pack." He laughed.

"Yeah it's heavy and holds a lot—" Brad said as he was cut off by the boy driving the truck.

The boy leaned from the cab again. "We can bring you back, we have a safe place, but you will have to give up your guns," the boy said.

"I'm sorry friends, but for our safety and yours it's important we keep our weapons," Sean said casually.

The second man in the cab obviously didn't like this answer and he again stole the attention of the driver. The boy-guard in the back rolled his eyes and leaned against the cab. "They carry on like this all the time," he said.

The driver leaned back through the window. "You can go with us, but we have to get going now, it's nearly dark and the bad ones come out at night."

Brad looked to Sean. "What about the farm?" he asked in a low voice.

"We can figure it out later, I think we need to go with them for Hahn's sake," Sean said as he moved back towards Hahn.

Brad helped Sean lift Hahn and with the help of the boy-guard they lowered him into the bed of the truck before climbing in themselves. As soon as they were on board the truck's gears grinded back into drive and the truck sped off. Brad was sitting towards the front of the truck with Hahn's head in his lap. He looked at the rest of the bed. The truck was filled with cases of canned good. All of the boxes were identical, and appeared to have come from the same location by the way they were stacked.

The boy-guard in the back looked at Brad and frowned. "My name is Alex, sorry for not introducing myself."

Brad looked to the boy-guard. "I guess proper manners haven't been of much use lately, I'm Brad, and that old man there is Sean."

"Your friend, he is hurt bad?" Alex asked.

Brad looked down at Hahn. "Yeah, he's lost a lot of blood. Do you have a doctor?"

"We will have the means to help you, but I am not allowed to talk about our home to outsiders," Alex said.

Sean took his eyes off of the surroundings and looked to Alex. "Where exactly are we going?"

"Don't worry, it's a safe place," Alex said. "Far safer than being out here after dark."

Brad looked at him. "The dark, that's when the fast ones come?"

"Oh, they are more than fast, they are smart, they can open doors, they organize, my German grandfather calls them the Buhmann. I guess we all kinda do now."

"Bogeyman?" Sean asked.

"Aye, same thing I guess," Alex said.

The truck's horn honked and Alex turned and stood back up, looking over the cab. Brad turned to see the road partially filled with slow-moving primals. The driver slowed and skirted the right side of the road, then accelerated, moving to the left and around the crowd of them. As they passed Brad looked back at them. They were the slow-moving ones with the frostbitten faces and grayed skin.

Alex watched Brad looking at them. "Creepers ... Those ones are nothing to be worried about, they are slow and dumb. It's the Buhmann that will get you," he said seriously.

The sides of the road once again became wooded as the truck climbed to higher terrain. The vehicle made a turn off onto a side road that led them to higher ground before it again slowed and came to a stop. The passenger door opened as Alex jumped from the bed. He and the other man quickly moved to the side of the road and pulled a long downed pine out of the way, revealing a broken concrete road.

The truck pulled through and they quickly put the brush back into place, concealing the entrance. Now the road was rougher and the men found themselves being bounced around as they traveled up the pothole-filled road. The truck wound around and finally ended at a large chain link fence. The truck stopped short of a chained gate. The driver put the truck into neutral and applied the parking brake, then exited the cab. He walked around to the bed and looked at Brad and Sean.

"You need to get out here ... stay over there, and don't make any noise. I have to make sure it's okay to let you in," the boy said, pointing toward an old stone foundation.

Alex looked to Sean and Brad. "We are good people, they'll let you in," he said, smiling.

Sean stood and went to Brad's side to help lift Hahn from the bed of the truck.

"It's okay, your man can stay, we wouldn't turn away an unarmed and injured man," the driver said.

Brad looked to Sean uneasily. He didn't want to lose sight of Hahn, especially when he still didn't know what was inside.

Alex again spoke reassuringly. "I will take care of him, just wait here, we will be back for you."

Sean looked to Brad and put a hand on his shoulder. "We have to trust them, right now we don't have many other options."

Brad nodded his head. He removed his pack and tossed it from the bed of the truck, then jumped out after it. He turned back towards the truck. "Look after him, Alex," he said. The boy nodded.

Sean followed Brad from the truck as the driver got back in and shut the door behind him. "We will be back for you once we drop off the truck, just remember be quiet, don't call out. We will find you."

The young man from the passenger seat

had unlocked and swung the gate open, and Brad and Sean watched the truck pull through. He relocked the gate, entered the truck and they drove away.

20.

Brad carried his pack towards the old stone foundation. He dropped the bag in a corner then sat on the pack leaning back, looking towards the gate. Sean had followed him into the rubble and dropped his pack at the opposite end, settling so that his back rested and was concealed by the rubble wall behind him. It was a habit for the man to always rest where he had rear cover. It would be embarrassing for the old sniper to be shot in the back while lounging around. Sean pulled his boonie cap over his eyes and laid his head back as if he were about to take a nap.

Brad looked at Sean, annoyed. "Do you have any idea what just happened?"

"My best guess is those boys are now talking to their leader who is trying to decide if they should let us in or kill us."

"Damn Sean! Why so positive? Maybe we should walk the fence line and see if we can see something?"

Sean let out a sigh. "Probably not a good idea with them watching us."

"They're watching us?" Brad sat up and started scanning the area beyond the fence.

"Shit, will you calm the fuck down and relax."

"How do you know they are watching us?" Brad asked anxiously.

"Brad, relax bro, what would you do in their shoes? Would you guard the way in and out of your camp?"

Brad leaned back against his pack, clearly agitated. He looked around, suddenly feeling uneasy in their situation. "Yeah, I guess that makes sense."

"Good cause, they are, I saw the flash off of his scope at least twice. Once when we pulled up and just after you sat down. But no worries, I know where he is, and he doesn't know that."

"For real? So they are up there right now watching us?"

Sean raised his arms and stretched before crossing his legs and arms as if tucking himself in. "Brad, just get cozy, and don't look threatening, I'm sure that's all they want to see."

"So you're just going to sleep?"

"Oh no, I've been watching him this entire time. He just moved down closer to us, don't look but he is just inside the fence now. He looks to be a bit older, and heavier," Sean said in a casual voice.

Brad tried to resist the urge to look. He pulled his pack in front of him and rummaged through it, finding a bottle of water. He drank slowly, trying to occupy his time, then opened a can of peas and ate quietly, trying to enjoy the bland flavors. The longer he sat he began to identify more things in the surroundings. The old foundation they were sitting in was resting in front of an old, mostly snow-covered asphalt parking lot.

Brad could see remnants of old light poles mixed in with the brush and woods surrounding them. As he scanned he could see that the fence looked old, but probably not as old as the structures. Maybe erected later to keep out vandals or trespassers. It wasn't a sturdy fence, standing maybe eight foot with a single strand of wire along the top. The gate was rusty and matched the fence, but the chain holding it closed looked new, as did the lock.

Brad pulled himself to his feet and strolled to a spot just behind them. He relieved himself on a bush as he looked out, deeper into the forest. His eyes followed the drive down the hill and to the covered brush where they'd left the road. He couldn't see the road from his current position; the overbrush was thick and concealed it very well. He searched the ground looking for tracks, but instead found something else. Strung between the trees all over the property were tightly strung wires, just about waist high. Possibly set as early warning, or to trip up the slow-moving primals.

Brad moved to his left to try and get a better look at the wires when he heard the low hum of an engine. He looked over his shoulder beyond the gate and spotted a vehicle approaching.

"Someone is coming," he whispered to Sean as he turned to face the gate. An old Volkswagen van was slowly winding down the broken concrete road. Instead of pulling through the gate, the van stopped short of it, then reversed and turned around. The engine was shut off and the boy who had driven the truck earlier exited the driver's side. A side door opened and two older men climbed out from the passenger compartment.

Brad watched the party as they cleared the van and walked to the gate. Instead of opening the gate, the men stood in front of the chain link fence. The boy still appeared to be unarmed, but one of the two men was carrying a shotgun. The boy raised his hand to Brad and waved for him to come forward. Brad heard Sean get to his feet behind him. He lifted his pack and stood next to Brad.

"Keep your rifle slung, let me do the talking," Sean whispered.

"The man on the right has a shotgun," Brad said.

"Yeah, not just any shotgun, looks like the same one Alex was carrying. These fellas must be short of weapons," Sean said as he moved towards the fence. "Follow me."

"Lead the way," Brad answered.

Sean moved out ahead, walking slowly and carrying his pack in his left hand, his rifle slung over his right shoulder with the barrel down. Brad noticed that Sean's coat was closed tight and pulled low, the waist of the jacket concealing the .45 pistol that was always strapped to his hip. Brad put on his heavy rucksack and let his M4 hang from the sling as he followed Sean up the road.

Brad stayed just behind Sean and staggered to the left. He could see the men at the gate clearly now. The boy driver stood to the left, apparently unarmed. There was an older red-bearded man in the center, with another overweight and heavily bearded man standing next to him. The men were dressed in canvas overalls and high rubber boots; their coats were of the same canvas type material. To Brad the men appeared soft, not like hardened criminals or killers, but appearance could be deceiving. The overweight man held the shotgun nervously, unlike the way Alex had carried the gun in a relaxed posture. This man held it with the barrel pointed down at an angle with his finger on the trigger.

When Sean was a good eight paces from the fence the man in the middle held up his hand. "That be close enough, friend," he said.

Sean stopped and casually set his pack on the ground, then looked up to face the men. "Good afternoon sir, my name is Chief Petty Officer Sean Rogers. This is my partner, Staff Sergeant Brad Thompson."

The man looked to Sean with a puzzled expression. "American military men, are ya? What are you doing out here in my woods?"

Sean smiled. "Well, it's a long story, but we are awaiting transportation. I can assure you we want nothing from you or your camp, we have our own supplies."

"Do ya now?" the red-bearded man said as he scratched at his beard.

The boy turned to face the red-bearded man. "Come on David, give them a break. If they wanted something from us they could have easily ambushed the truck and taken our supplies."

"Luke, that be enough!" shouted the fat man with the shotgun.

"Whoa, whoa, hold up all of ya. I'm just trying to read the situation here," the bearded man shouted.

Sean smiled and put his hands in front of him, showing his palms. "Okay, I think we can all calm down just a bit. All we are looking for is some shelter for the night, and a safe place to dress our man's wounds. We will be out of your hair first thing in the morning."

The man with the beard nodded his head. "I feel we had a bad start here, I must apologize. We don't get many visitors. My name is David, this is Luke my nephew, my bodyguard here is Francis. You can call him Frank if you like but it seems to piss him off," he said, smiling.

Sean returned the smile and let his arms relax. "Pleased to meet you, now what would it take to convince you to let us stay?"

David pulled at his beard as if in deep thought. "Luke tells me you refuse to give up your weapons?"

"Out there on the road yes, for all of our protection I choose to be armed. I wouldn't be opposed to putting my rifle under lock and key if you have a safe place for it, but I must insist on keeping my sidearm," Sean said.

David continued to stroke his beard before nodding, "Okay that sounds reasonable. You have given me no reason not to trust you. Luke, open the gate."

Luke smiled and stepped forward and unlocked the gate. He swung it open just enough for Brad and Sean to squeeze though, then locked it behind them. Once inside, Francis opened the hatch on the back of the van and asked the men to place their bags and rifles in the cargo compartment. Sean sat his ruck in the back and laid his rifle on the floor behind it. Brad looked to Sean apprehensively. Sean made eye contact and nodded so Brad took his ruck from his back and also placed it in the back before laying his M4 next to Sean's.

Francis closed the hatch and moved to the side of the van and opened the passenger door. "Sorry, we need to hurry, we usually don't spend this much time down here this late in the day," he said, rushing them to enter the van. Brad moved to the side door and followed David in, Sean got in behind him, and Francis closed the door behind them.

Luke and Francis jumped into the front, slamming the doors behind them. The van started and began moving up the road. The passenger compartment held two bench seats sitting parallel to the cabin walls. Brad had taken a seat across from the door with Sean next to him. David was sitting near the back and directly on the floor of the van. There was carpet on the floor and ceilings, and a set of purple curtains divided the passenger compartment from the front seats. More curtains covered the windows, preventing Brad from seeing where they were headed.

"Nice custom job, is it yours?" Brad asked, smiling at David.

David let out an audible chuckle, "No, no, no, oh boy, no, we found it up on the highway a few weeks ago. We needed something with cargo space."

The van drove up a steep slope and around a bend before stopping. Francis opened his door and stepped out. Brad heard the rumble of what he assumed was a large overhead door being opened. They heard a slap on the side of the van as Luke pulled the vehicle into a dark space and killed the engine. Brad heard the overhead door rumble closed and after a brief pause the side door on the van again opened. Francis indicated for the men to exit, and Sean stepped out with Brad right behind him. They were in a large empty building. The worn brick walls were at least fifteen foot tall, with a row of old windows lining the top. Some of the windows were broken; others were still intact and closed.

Brad moved away from the van curiously looking in all directions. The floor was made of broken concrete. He saw that the truck they had ridden in earlier was parked on the other side of the van. In one corner was a pile of old cardboard boxes and a few broken pallets. There was random furniture and machine parts scattered about the space. Brad moved towards a wall that held a picture frame. The glass was broken and the paper inside was stained and unreadable.

"Where are we, David?" Brad asked.

Francis had moved to the back and opened the hatch on the van. Luke had already picked up Brad's bag and hoisted it to his own back with a grunt. Francis grabbed Sean's rucksack then handed Sean his rifle before handing Brad his own.

"This is the old machine works factory. It has been closed for close to thirty years. Come on, this way please," David said as he began walking to the far end of the room.

Luke and Francis hurried along after

David. Sean looked at Brad before shrugging his shoulders and following the men across the old factory floor. At the end of the room was an old steel door. David rapped on it three times. They stood and waited as the door clunked then opened inward. David moved inside with the others following him, then the door closed behind them.

Brad immediately felt the warmth in the room; a glowing wood stove explained why. They had entered a small office of sorts. The room's floor was made of well-worn hardwood, the walls were a rustic brick and void of any windows, and another steel door was on the opposite wall. Two large wall safes were on each side of the door with a large manager's desk sitting to the right of the door they'd just entered. Brad saw right away that an old .38 revolver was lying near center on the desktop. He turned to look behind him and saw that Alex was the one who had closed the door.

Alex extended his hand and shook Brad's hand. "Good to see ya again, Brad."

"You too friend. Where's my man, Sergeant Hahn?" Brad asked.

"Oh, we mucked him off to the doc," Alex answered.

"You have a doctor?" Sean asked, pleasantly surprised.

David stepped back between the men. "We have many things. Would you feel comfortable storing your weapons here?" He pointed at the safe to the left of the door, a tall blue box with a chain wrapped around it and under the handle, and a large padlock like the one on the front gate which held the chain in place.

Brad started to speak as Sean cut him off. "This room is always under guard?" Sean asked.

"Yes, the safe mechanism no longer works but I alone hold the key to that chain," David answered.

"Very well then," Sean said as he approached the safe. He took the rifle from his shoulder and removed the bolt from the rifle and dropped it into a pocket on his jacket. He did the same with his MP5 and Hahn's M4. Brad followed with what he was doing and dropped the magazine on his M4, then pushed the pin separating the receivers of his own rifle and removed the bolt. He quickly unloaded the shotgun, then placed the M4 bolt and twelve gauge shells into his cargo pocket.

David had unlocked the safe. Brad lifted the M4 and shotgun and handed them to David who sat them near to the back. Then he did the same with Sean's weapons. David pushed the safe door shut then secured the chain around it and latched the lock. He looked up at Sean for approval as he finished the task. Sean forced a smile and nodded.

"I think I would prefer to be armed, but if

this makes you more comfortable, I will go along with it," Sean said.

David laughed and stepped away from the safe. "I think it will make us all feel better. I noticed you removed a part of the weapons."

"Just the bolts. That makes me more comfortable," Sean said, smiling sincerely this time.

"Very good then, we are both satisfied," David laughed. "Would you like some taken up? The kitchen should be open now."

Sean looked at him, puzzled. "The kitchen? I won't turn down a meal if that's what you are asking."

Alex grunted and sat at the desk. "I wouldn't say that, you haven't had it yet."

Luke laughed loudly and slapped Alex. "You are ruining my new friend's surprise."

David interrupted, shaking his head. "Enough, boys. Alex, we are closed for the night, that door stays locked, nobody in or out. Luke will be down to relieve you in a couple hours."

"Yes Uncle," Alex answered.

David walked to the steel door at the back of the room and rapped three times. As before, the door opened and a new face looked out at them. A skinny old man dressed in heavy pants and a turtleneck sweater gave Brad a surprised stare before looking back to David. "Whatta yat?" the man asked with a thick accent.

"This is it," David responded.

"And who are they?" the man said, pointing at the strangers.

"They are guests, thank you, Robbie." David said as he pushed open the door and walked past the guard. "This way."

Sean again shrugged to Brad as he followed David through the doorway. The door opened into a small landing. There was a set of old cast iron stairs going up which David took two at a time, then turned a corner and continued to another steel door. At this door he pulled a latch and the door swung in revealing another long room filled with small living encampments.

David stopped in a large open space and waited for the men to enter the room and fall in beside him. "This is our camp. We took over the entire second floor, we could still move to the third floor if necessary. Right now the third floor is reserved for the single men."

Brad looked around the large room, the size and shape being identical inside to the one below where the vehicles had been parked. "How many families do you have here?" he asked.

"There are ten families, but over a hundred and twenty residents. Many of us here are alone, not everyone was lucky enough to get their families out," David said, placing a hand on Luke's shoulder. "I was lucky enough to get my nephews out, but we couldn't locate my brother and his wife."

"I am sorry for your loss," Brad said.

"Many have lost more," Luke replied solemnly.

"How long have you been here?" Brad asked.

"I'm not much for counting days, but we moved to this place about two weeks after the lights went out. We had held up in our homes for a while, then set up a tiny camp in the woods outside of town. But as the weather turned bad we needed to find something better. My father knew of this place, well, more than that, my father worked here as a young man.

"No one had been here in some time; the fences kept out most people. My father said the place had high brick walls and fenced-in yards. It seemed ideal at the time. I'd say this place has served us well. This factory thrived in a time before technology. Many of the woodstoves are original, there is a boiler in the basement, and water tanks all over the property."

Sean looked around and nodded in agreement. "I tell ya, I'm happy to see folks getting along so well. It brightens my spirits."

"Come now, let me show you to your man, right this way," David said, indicating for them to follow him.

As they walked down the center of the room, Brad looked at the makeshift shelters on either side of the path. The living arrangements reminded him of the warehouse in Hairatan, back where they had built the refugee camp for the locals. The thought of Hairatan depressed him, the impossible task of trying to get his men home still was at the back of his mind. How was he supposed to rescue them when he couldn't even rescue himself?

Brad followed the other men, preoccupied with his thoughts as they passed through the factory floor and through another door. They had entered into another office space. The room was filled with makeshift cots and boxes of personal items. Brad looked around the room and saw Hahn sleeping on a bunk. Brad quickly walked across the room and went to his side.

Hahn was still unconscious. His armor and shirt had been removed, and his damaged left arm was elevated and loosely splinted, resting at an angle going away from his body. Hahn's arm was black and discolored, his fingers a twisted mass of dark blue and purples. Hahn's head was to the side and he was breathing shallowly, sweat beading on his forehead. A door opened at the end of the room causing Brad to turn.

A young man, cleanly shaven, approached the bed. He gave Brad a dirty look as he went to push past him. "Ah, the rest of the brave Americans," he said sarcastically. He moved between Brad and the bed. "Excuse me, I need to treat this man." The young man removed a glass bottle from his pocket, then used a syringe to draw out the fluid which he stuck into an IV bag that was plugged into Hahn's good arm.

"Will he be okay?" Brad asked.

The man continued to work on Hahn as if he hadn't heard the question. After taking a quick check of Hahn's vitals, he pulled the blanket up to Hahn's neck then took a step back to face Brad.

The young man looked Brad in the eye. "Will he be okay? He is most likely going to lose that arm, possibly die of infection or maybe blood poisoning. Have you seen this man's toes? The frostbite, and what the hell happened to his head? Is this how you take care of your friends?"

Sean, having heard enough, moved Brad aside and stepped forward. "How long have you been in here, kid? Do you even remember what it's like outside?" he said in a low, serious voice. "He hurt his head in a plane crash, then probably ruined his feet leading a horde of those things away from the survivors. His arm? Yes, once again he fought off a horde to allow the rest of our team to escape."

David quickly stepped between them. "Easy gentleman, our young doctor has had a rough few days himself. I'm sure if we all take a step back you will find our Doctor Ericson here is highly qualified, his bedside manner just needs some work."

Sean clenched his jaw, then with a thoughtful expression he nodded his head. He turned and walked towards the wall and sat on a long bench, leaning back and stretching his legs before letting out a long sigh. "Thank you Doctor, I appreciate everything you have done for my man," he said.

Brad smiled and took a step back, leaning against the opposite wall, amused by the exchange, knowing Sean would rather beat the man senseless than put up with the doctor's shit. But surprisingly, Sean's new tone appeared to be working. The doctor's demeanor relaxed and he went to the same bench and took a seat next to Sean. "I apologize for my harsh words. As David said, it has been a long week," Ericson said.

"You really think he will lose his arm?" Brad asked.

Ericson put his head down. "I'm afraid so. The shirt we peeled off of him seems to have qualities that prevented the spread of the infection, but there has been excessive tissue damage and too much time lost to try and save the arm. Right now fever and sepsis are the problem. Removing it will be risky, but it may have to be done if we can't break the fever."

"Risky?" Brad asked.

The doctor looked up, making eye contact with Brad. "Yes ... we are short of medical supplies, especially antibiotics."

"Well hell Doc, we have stuff," Brad said,

moving quickly across the room and unsnapping his assault pack from the larger rucksack that Luke had carried into the room. Brad unzipped the top of the bag and spread the bag open, showing Ericson the contents.

Ericson stuck his hand into the bag, digging through the items. "This is quality medicine, more than any soldier would be carrying, why do you have this? Where did you get it?" he asked suspiciously.

"We have more injured friends in our party that needed medical supplies. We made an excursion into a small town near here, and we raided a medical clinic," Brad said.

"The clinic? The one near the evacuation center? Impossible, that place was overrun long ago," Ericson gasped.

"We were told the town would be occupied, but we had no idea how bad." Brad paused, looking down at the ground. "Anyway, none of that matters now, we have medicine ... can you use it?"

The doctor took the bag from Brad and continued to look through it before sitting it next to his feet. "Yes of course, I'd like to get your man started on some of these right away, but you said there were more of you? Who told you about the town and the clinic?"

"Can you save his arm?" Brad asked.

"This will help, but I can't make any promises, now about the clinic?"

Brad looked to Sean, unsure of how much information he should share. Sean acknowledged him with a nod and took over the conversation. He tactfully caught David and Ericson up on where they had come from, and how they became stranded on the island. Sean told the story of the plane crash and their wounded, how they had raided the town and barely made it out. He was very careful to withhold information on the farm and the names of the family that took in his men. He was still unsure who these people were and if they could be trusted.

There was a knock at the door interrupting Sean's story. The door opened and an elderly woman entered, pushing a cart filled with bowls of stew and pieces of hard bread. "Supper is ready, gentlemen, wish I had more for you," the woman said in a joyful voice.

"This will be fine, Mary, just leave the cart. I'll see that Luke brings it back to the kitchen," David said, signaling for the woman to leave.

"Alright, alright, I can see you boys are busy, just make sure you don't keep these gentlemen too long. They look very tired and in need of a bath," Mary said, walking from the room and closing the door behind her.

David handed out bowls of stew. "Well, that explains the increase in activity."

Sean nodded, using a spoon to take a

mouthful of the liquid and smiling at the taste. "Yeah, sorry about that, the plane crash drew several of them in from the city. The stew is very good by the way."

"Thank you, it's lobscouse. Mary will like hearing that. So these friends of yours? Where are they now?"

"I'm not sure," Sean said, not completely lying. "We were separated after the crash. They took shelter on a farm; we were trying to locate them when we ran into your boys."

"On the highway ... yes, the daily supply run," David said, nodding as he sopped up the remainder of his stew with a piece of bread. "My boys go out every day, raiding empty homes mostly, sometimes markets or warehouses. They have become very good at it."

"How do they keep from leading the primals back?" Brad asked.

"Primals?"

"The creepers," Brad said, correcting himself.

"Ah yes ... Primals you say, well the ones that show themselves in the daylight are very slow, and even a bit daft. As long as you don't leave obvious tracks, they are fairly easy to lose when in vehicles. We never stay out past dark, that's when the others come out, the Buhmann ... they are fast and clever ... But I'm sure you know all of this," David said, placing his bowl back on the tray.

Ericson had just finished injecting another round of medication into Hahn's IV bag. "You say you have more injured men? If you take me to them, I will treat them in exchange for the remainder of these medical supplies. You have more than enough."

"Ericson, wait," David said. "You're our only doctor, I can't allow you to make that deal."

Ericson put his hand up. "It's okay David, and the man is right, it has been too long since I have left this place," he said, looking to Sean.

Sean looked at Brad, who shrugged his shoulders in response. "I sure would appreciate the help, but I can't guarantee what meds will be left after treating our injured."

"Well I'll take that risk. Your man won't be mobile for some time. But I assure you, he will be safe here. The rest of us ... we can leave in the morning. The boys can drop us where they picked you up, or give you a ride to the door if you want to give us the names of the family," Ericson answered.

Sean and Brad sat silently searching for the right response.

David smiled. "I appreciate you protecting the family that took in your men. This is a remote area, and we know most everyone in these parts. From the location where Luke picked you up, it could only be a couple places. I'm thinking either Taylor's farm at the end of the valley, or the Emersons'." David walked to a locked cabinet. He took the combination padlock in his hand and began to spin the dial. "The Taylors, now that would be a hell of a walk, way down the valley they be. And being that Luke salvaged goods from their farm not ten days ago, I'd say I can scratch that name."

David made the final turn of the lock and pulled it open. He opened a cabinet door and revealed several bottles of alcohol and a number of glasses. "Brandy be okay for you, Sean?" David asked.

Sean smiled. "Very nice, thank you."

David pulled the bottle from the cabinet and slowly began filling glasses and passing them to the men as they finished their dinner. "So, I heard tell on the fate of the Emersons; seems his wife was attacked. They went to town and the clinic looking for assistance as things fell apart. Nobody has seen them since. Luke went by their farm, but things were torn apart so he let the place be. We try to distance ourselves from danger."

Sean took a sip of the brandy. He closed his eyes, enjoying the warmth of it. "This is very good," he said as he took another sip. "Staying clear of danger is a good policy. I'm sorry friend, but those names do not sound familiar to me."

Luke, having been silent the entire time, finally moved forward to speak. "There is another place uncle. The Murphys' ... You know my pal Thomas's place. They are a bit off the road and up the mountain, but I bet if anyone was to survive, Old Man Murphy and his boys would."

David laughed and refilled his glass. "Good ol' Jeremiah … I nearly forgot about him." As he said the words David caught the look of recognition on Brad's face. David put the top on the bottle and tossed it in Brad's direction, who caught it and refilled his own glass before handing the bottle off to Sean.

"Yeah, Jeremiah is a tough one. Did some time in the Army, a good brood of sons too, and his wife is a nurse even, or was at some point—"

"Now wait a minute!" the doctor interrupted. "So there is a nurse living up the road, and you all neglected to tell me about it? Or to go and get her?"

David laughed as he pulled the glass away from his lips. "Ericson, we have been busy you know, and who knows if the Murphys are even alive."

"Damn, if there is a chance of a nurse living up there, then I think we need to check it out. I have sick and injured children here," Ericson said, barely concealing his frustration.

Sean sat his empty glass on a table before speaking. "I don't know anything about a nurse or these Murphys, but if it's important to you all, I'd be more than happy to patrol up the road with the doctor here and visit their farm. In exchange for treating my man, of course."

"Deal!" Ericson blurted out before David could give an answer.

"And the rest of the medical supplies?" David asked.

Sean smiled again, "Well those have been earmarked for my wounded, but if we happen to find them out there on the road, and we find we have enough for our needs, I'll gladly hand off the remainder to you."

David looked to Ericson and studied his expression. "Doc, if you think it's worth the risk ..."

"Of course it is, we have children dying of simple infections, and we need these antibiotics," Ericson said eagerly.

Sean stood, reaching across to shake David's and Ericson's hands. "It's done then. Now the lady had said something about a bath?"

21.

Luke had relieved Alex from his watch. The younger boy was now giving the men a brief tour of the bachelor's quarters at the top of the building. He led them up to the third floor and showed them a small storage room; it was one of the few empty spaces that had a locking door. The room had random supplies stacked along a wall, items they must have considered valuable, but had no urgent need for.

Alex explained that his uncle thought they may be more comfortable in a private room rather than sleeping in the larger open bay. He gave Sean an old skeleton key to the small storage room door. The men were told they could leave their bags there while they used the wash room. Sean and Brad dropped their heavy rucksacks, but elected to take their smaller assault packs and side arms with them to the bathroom which was located off the back of the larger space.

The room had once been a latrine of sorts, although now badly antiquated and falling apart from decades of neglect. A long rusted steel countertop with embedded sinks ran along a wall. On the opposite wall sat a row of porcelain commodes. Two out of the three were broken into shards. A large thirty-gallon barrel of water rested against a wall below a window, and a smaller pail sat next to it. Luke had demonstrated to the men how to flush the badly stained working toilet by using the bucket.

"I know it looks a bit gross, but it beats going out back to the outhouse, especially in the dark," Alex explained.

On the counter sat two large plastic wash basins and tin pitchers filled with hot water. Next to the basins were two neatly stacked sets of towels with a fresh bar of soap on top of each. Another set of pitchers were resting atop a blazing wood stove. Luke told them to use as much water as they needed; the barrel would be refilled with snow during the next workers' rotation.

"I am sorry we cannot offer you a shower or a true bath," Alex said apologetically.

Brad smiled, "No, this is fantastic, warm water is a luxury we haven't experienced recently."

"Good. My uncle is searching through the stores, he will be bringing you sets of bedding to help you rest. Go ahead and get cleaned up, I'll meet you back at your room later," Alex said as he left the washroom, closing the door behind him.

Before the door had even completely closed Brad began stripping off his heavy coats and shirts. He let them fall to the floor behind him, then grabbed the pitcher with his right hand and poured the water over his left and let it flow over his hand and into the basin. After a moment he bent his head over the basin and poured the remainder of the pitcher onto his head. He reached out with his right hand and placed one of the towels over his head to hold in the warmth of the hot water.

Brad grabbed the towel with both hands and scrubbed his scalp vigorously before letting the towel fall around his shoulders. He let out a long sigh before opening his eyes and saying, "This is great, isn't it Sean."

"Hell yeah," he heard Sean say from behind him.

Brad slowly opened his eyes and looked over his shoulder. He saw Sean sitting buck naked on the toilet. "Aww man, what the hell Chief!" he shouted as he quickly turned back.

"Sorry brother, but I've been missing the ol' porcelain throne something fierce," Sean said.

"Well damn man, I coulda gave you some privacy." Brad walked to the window and opened it before he refilled the pitcher of water and swapped it with one on the stove.

"Don't mind me, I ain't shy."

"Yeah, ya think!" Brad said as he added hot water to the basin and began using the soap to build a lather on his hands. He added a wash rag to the basin and continued to wash himself as he heard Sean finish behind him. Sean joined him at the counter and filled his own basin as he began washing himself.

"Seriously, give me some warning next time, now I have that image burned into my memory," Brad laughed.

Sean let out a small chuckle. "I'll try but I can't make any promises buddy. So what do you think of our hosts?" he asked as he poured the remainder of the pitcher over his head.

"I'm not sure ... they seem like good people just trying to get by. I guess I have always been conditioned to think that the end of the world would come with social structures falling apart, instead of groups like this pulling together."

"Damn Brad, that's some deep thinking." Sean laughed again. "You're right though, I find it hard to trust them, guess it's in my nature."

"So what do we do?"

"Let's just take it easy, go along with it all, until they give us a reason to think otherwise. Even if these guys turn out to be shady, you saw as well as I did that they aren't well armed. Keep an eye on them, same as working with the Afghan army boys back in the sandbox," Sean said as he wrapped a towel around his waist and bundled up his clothing in his arms.

Brad gave a knowing grin, "Yeah, I can relate to that. Treat them like friends, but never turn your back to 'em."

"Exactly." Sean put his hand on the handle of the door. "I'll see you back at the room."

Brad used another pitcher of water to rinse off, removing the lather from his face and beard. He reached into his assault pack and removed an old and battered shaving kit, unzipping it and removing a break-proof mirror. Brad looked into the mirror and barely recognized himself. His hair had grown long and was hanging over his ears and neck, matching the patchy straggled beard that now covered his face. He considered using his small pair of scissors to remove the beard and trim his long unkempt hair. Smiling, he reconsidered, fully afraid of the possible results. In the end he stuffed the mirror back into the kit and gathered the rest of his things before heading out of the latrine.

Brad exited through the door and moved back into the larger space of the third floor. He could see down the long structure and towards the small storage room. The area he was standing in was dark and gloomy, old plank flooring was below his feet and dusty steel beams over his head. The walls were made up of old brick, the same as below. The building had the smell of an old musty barn, the smells of old wood and smoke being heavily present.

Brad moved along, following the wall down the long room. As he got closer, he saw David standing in the doorway with a bundle of heavy wool blankets under his arm. Sean was laughing and nodding his head, holding the door as he followed David into the storage room. Brad strolled up behind them and moved into the doorway, catching the attention of David.

"Aye ducky, you look a sight better, just bringing you lads some bedding. Hope it suits you," David said, tossing the pile to the dusty floor.

Brad nodded, moving past David and dropping his belongings on the floor, then taking a seat on his larger rucksack positioned against the wall. "I'm sure they will be fine, thank you."

Sean lifted a uniform blouse to his face and smelled it, giving a sour expression as he pulled it away. "David, I hate to impose anymore, but is there a place for us to launder our clothing?"

"Of course, don't worry about it, leave your clothing outside the door. Mary will send one of the boys up after it."

"That would be great," Sean said.

"Very well, if you need anything else, the boys are all set up at the end of the corridor. Feel free to move about but try to stay out of the family areas after dark. The husbands get a bit touchy once the sun goes down," David said.

"Yeah, I can imagine. Once again, thank you for all of your help," Sean said, reaching out for a handshake.

David returned the gesture and slowly

moved from the room before turning back. "The fires go out after dark so bundle up, it gets cold." Sean nodded in reply as David closed the door behind him.

Brad opened the straps on his large rucksack and dug for his cleanest dirty clothes. He found a dry shirt and a pair of clean underwear he had been saving for a special occasion. He left one set of uniforms out in case they needed to move in a hurry. The remainder of the soiled clothing he stuffed into a large netted sack he kept in his ruck, happy to finally get a chance to have them cleaned. He tossed the bag in Sean's direction.

Sean stared at the sack, amused. "I'm not sure about having our underwear touch, but guess I'll make an exception," he joked as he eagerly added his own set of uniforms and clothing to the sack and placed it outside the door. Sean then divided the bedding and tossed Brad a pair of heavy wool blankets and a worn white sheet. "Whoever they are, they seem to be very resourceful," he said, breaking the silence.

Brad pulled on the dry T-shirt and looked down at the wool blankets. "I know, right ... shelter, hot water, food, doing pretty well by most standards, gives ya hope, you know."

Sean folded the heavy blankets in half with the sheet on top. He then used a third field blanket from his own pack to complete his makeshift bed. He folded the heavy coat into the shape of a pillow. Next he pulled his .45 pistol and stuck it on top of his pack just inside of arm's reach. "I know, brother, I had some of the same thoughts," he said, laying back, resting his head on the coat.

Brad continued talking to Sean as he dug through his pack, sorting his belongings and taking inventory. Before long he noticed Sean snoring. "Damn, thanks for the company, Chief," he said in a low voice. He made a bed of his own, following Sean's example, and removed his own poncho liner to use as a blanket. He moved his heavy pack and placed it in front of the door. It wouldn't keep out an intruder, but it would slow them up.

Before Brad sat on his own bedroll, he removed the Sigma pistol from his body armor. He stared at the handgun silently, wondering how the weapon had managed its journey all this way without having fired a shot. Brad pressed the magazine release with his thumb and let the mag drop into his left palm. It was still fully loaded. He used his thumb to remove the top two rounds; he rolled them between his fingers before pressing them back into the magazine. Brad slowly pulled the slide on the pistol, ejecting the chambered round into his lap. He picked up the round, examining it before dropping it back into the chamber, cautiously letting the slide close on it. He then reinserted the magazine and placed the pistol on his own pack lying just behind him.

    Brad lay back and closed his eyes just as the window above his head began to lose the light. He didn't know what time it was, and at the moment he didn't care. Even though he didn't know the men outside the door, he felt at ease around them, and knew he would sleep better with them standing the watch. It sure beat the hell out of the last few days of running and gunning. He worried about Hahn lying downstairs alone. He debated in his mind, should he visit his friend? What if Hahn was to awaken alone in the room? Brad pulled the poncho liner over his chest, continuing the internal argument as he gave into exhaustion and drifted to sleep.

22.

He woke to the sounds of footfalls outside the door. The dull orange glow of daybreak was beginning to fill the space. Brad looked to his right and saw that Sean was already up and dressing, with one of the heavy blankets draped over his shoulders. He noticed Brad stirring on the floor. "That old man wasn't joking when he said they turn the heat off at night, son of a bitch it got cold in here—"

Sean was interrupted by a knock at the door. Somewhat startled, he moved to the entrance and slid Brad's pack out of the way. Sean posted his boot to prevent the door from being forced open; then unlatched the lock and slowly cracked the door revealing the smiling faces of Luke and Alex.

"Good morning boys, what brings you by?" Sean said as he opened the door wide.

"Thought you would like to know that breakfast is ready, down at the end there," Alex said, holding the laundry sack stuffed with folded laundry.

Sean took the bag, smiling. "Wow, thank your aunt for this!"

Alex chuckled, "Shoot, Luke is the one you should be thanking. He was washing yer clothes all night."

"Shut up Alex," Luke said, looking away. "Well hey, breakfast is ready, you should try and eat it while it's still hot."

Brad stood, pulling on his uniform trousers. "Great, I'm starving," he said, lifting his arms to stretch his back before pulling on his heavy thermal shirt.

Luke made a twisted face. "Don't get too excited, you haven't seen it yet."

"Don't mind Luke, he is a picky eater, it's really not so bad," Alex said. "Uncle says we should be ready to travel in a couple hours, we like to take advantage of the high points of the day."

"High points?" Brad asked.

"Yes, when the sun is brightest we see less of the smart ones then. The creepers don't seem to mind the sun as much anymore," Luke answered.

"Anymore?" Sean asked.

"Yeah you know, in the first days we didn't have creepers and things got quiet during the day … in the summer and fall … but since the winter has fallen, the creepers have shown up," Luke answered.

"Either way, have your stuff packed or ready to go," Alex said.

Sean gave a mock salute. "Will do … and Luke, thank you for washing my undies," he said sincerely, causing Luke to scowl.

The boys left the two men alone. They

quickly separated the laundry and dressed in fresh uniforms. Then they packed their bags, preparing for another day of travel. Brad put his M9 in the hip holster and tucked the Sigma into a pocket on the front of his heavy coat. He tightened the straps on his bags, attaching the smaller assault pack to the outside of his ruck. He then laid his heavy body armor on top of it before lifting the entire kit as one. Stepping out of the room, he followed Sean down the corridor to where they saw a gathering of men around a long plank table.

The table seated ten men and was crowded on both sides. Brad moved towards a wall and dropped his kit next to Sean's. As he turned around he took notice of the brothers Luke and Alex sitting across from one another at an end of the table. An older man that they recognized as the door guard, Robby, from the previous night jumped from his seat next to Luke with an empty tin plate. "Here you go friend, I was just finishing up, take me spot," Robby announced. Following his lead a second man also got up, offering his seat.

"Thank you," Brad said, taking Robby's seat next to Luke. Before he could ask, a tin plate stacked with strips of brown meat and kidney beans was slid in front of him by a middle-aged man dressed in a heavy dark red and black flannel shirt. Sean took the seat across from Brad and was also quickly served with a plate of food.

Brad lifted a piece of the meat to his mouth and took a cautious bite. He found the meat warm, tough, dry, and heavily salted. "Venison?" Brad asked as he continued to chew.

"It's moose," the man in the red flannel responded.

"It's good, did you take it?" Brad asked.

"Aye, two days ago, in the woods behind the factory. Not in season, but the game wardens don't seem to mind much these days," the man, said causing others around the table to laugh. "Are you a hunter?"

"I have been known to bag a white-tailed deer or two," Brad said.

The man laughed again, "Hell, you can't be all bad then. My name is Jorgensen," he said, outstretching a large hand. Brad returned the handshake, feeling the man's powerful grip.

Sean outstretched his own hand, introducing himself, "I'm Sean, I think we nearly met yesterday out by the fence?"

Jorgensen gave Sean a puzzled stare.

"We didn't meet per se, but I recognize the red flannel. Was it not you with the scoped rifle?"

"Well I'll be … you're good … I heard you were soldiers but didn't expect such talented ones," Jorgensen again laughed while taking Sean's hand. "Yes that was me, I spend a lot of time on the hillside. Watching for the Buhmann mostly, or observing traffic on the road." He paused, stroking his clean-shaven chin. "Hasn't been much friendly traffic lately."

"Friendly?" Sean asked, scooping a spoonful of beans into his mouth.

"Yeah, not everyone on the rock these days is friendly. Most of the bad ones have set up closer to the coast, we don't see much of them out here. Although they have a camp some thirty kilometers south—"

"We try to stay away from them," a boy Luke's age interrupted.

Brad turned to look at the boy, recognizing him as the passenger from the truck which had picked them up on the road.

"That's James. He's my cousin. Uncle Dave is his dad," Alex said quickly.

"I can speak for myself, Alex. But yeah, we *try* to keep our distance from strangers," James said. "You have been the exception, I would have left you all on the road."

Sean nodded. "It probably wouldn't have been a bad idea. I don't think I would have faulted you for it. But I appreciate you all stopping and helping my man. How is he, anyhow?"

The table suddenly grew quiet. "He's still with the doctor. We can see him after breakfast if you'd like," Alex said.

Brad, wanting to know more about the others, turned the conversation back towards the strangers. "What do you know about the people from the coast? What makes them unfriendly?"

Jorgensen moved a chair close to the table and took a seat. "They ain't from here. If I had to take a guess I'd say they come in on a freighter. A number of them beached up and took shelter here when the ports on the mainland turned them away.

"Most of 'em kept to themselves when they got here, isolated and under quarantine. After the lights went out, who knows what they would turn to … I ran into them a few times, always from afar, keeping my distance. I watched these fellas a bit, you know, when they came in to our valley.

"They used to come by here every now and again, quite often before the heavy snowfall, not so much anymore, but they still out there. Mostly rummaging through empty homes and what not. They travel in fancy sports cars, not useful things like trucks. Seem to be townies mostly, not much practical sense of things. I figure the snow has kept them closer to home nowadays."

"How do you know they aren't friendly?" Sean asked.

Jorgensen took a sip from the water glass he had been holding and gave a look as if he was pondering the answer. "Just speculation, I guess. I left a note on a pole where they wouldn't miss it. Trying to make contact, ya know. Offering to set up a means of communication. I watched them from far away. They saw the note alright they did. But a big man, he tore it down and read the paper then crumpled it. Tossed it to the ground and carried on as if it was a burden to him."

Brad turned to face Jorgensen, "Maybe they just keep to themselves as well?"

"There's more," James said, slamming a fist on the table.

Jorgensen continued to speak. "There was family further south. A man with his wife, a son and daughter each. We offered to bring them into the factory, but the man said they would make due. They had a nice place, back off the road and settled into the woods a bit. We made a habit of checking in on them, bringing goods to trade." Jorgensen laughed, "Even though that man never gave much in return. Still though, Mary always sent good things for the girls."

Jorgensen paused and looked down at the table, shaking his head, "That man was a fool."

James got up from the table angrily and stepped away. After a few paces he stopped and looked back. "More than a fool, he was reckless, and he had no right to make the decision for all of them. Dad should have made them move here."

Things fell uncomfortably quiet around the table. Sean placed his spoon on his empty plate and slid it to the center of the table. "I take it ... they were more than just strangers from up the road."

"Aye, the girl Molly, she was familiar with James, they were classmates." Jorgensen said.

"What happened to the family?" Brad asked.

"Can't be sure. Me and the boys ... we paid 'em a visit ... some two, 'bout maybe three weeks ago," Jorgensen said, pausing to search for the right words.

"They were dead," Luke blurted out.

"Primals ... ah ... the Buhmann?" Brad asked.

"No, not unless they have taken to binding wrists and ankles and burning their dead," Jorgensen said with his head down.

"You figuring it was the others then?" Sean asked.

"Can't confirm it, but whoever it was, they took the girls. We only found the old man and his boy. House was ransacked, all of their stores were emptied. There was no need for it, they were good people," Jorgensen said, finishing. He shook his head again before getting to his feet.

"If you want to see your man before we leave, we need to get moving," Jorgensen said as he turned and headed for the stairway.

They left the room and followed the boys down the stairs and back into the makeshift infirmary at the end of the second floor. A young girl in her twenties was sitting in a chair next to Hahn, removing the sweat from his brow with a damp cloth. Hahn was still unconscious in the bed, an IV bag still attached to his good arm. Brad looked and saw that his left arm had been amputated. "Jesus Christ, you took his arm!" he blurted out.

The girl quickly turned to face Brad, the sad expression on her face quickly disarming his anger. Brad stared at her speechless, then looked back at the stub just above where Hahn's elbow should be.

"The doctor wanted to tell you first, but we made him get some rest. He was up with your soldier all night," the girl said apologetically.

"Why, though? His arm?" Brad mumbled.

"We couldn't break his fever, even with the better meds. The doc said it had to go, we don't have the facilities to treat him here," she said, a tear forming below her eye.

Luke moved forward, walking between Brad and the girl and putting a hand on her shoulder. "It's okay Sara, we know the doc did his best," Luke said softly.

Brad moved away from the bed and took a seat on the bench. Sean moved to the bedside, looking Hahn over. "How is he now? The fever," Sean asked.

"We think he is getting better, but he still has a long way to go," Sara said.

"Where is the doctor?" Sean asked.

Sara looked at a watch on her wrist. "He should be downstairs by now, preparing for the trip."

"The trip? He still plans on going ... with Hahn in this condition?" Sean asked.

"The doctor said he would be back before dark, your friend will be fine in my care," Sara said.

Sean looked her dead in the eye. "Are you a doctor? A nurse?"

"Well no, but I have training," she answered.

"Explain," Sean blurted out.

"I worked as a veterinary assistant, and I grew up on farms."

"Good lord, I've had enough. Luke, lead me to the doctor please."

Brad got to his feet as Luke opened the door into the family area of the second floor. He stepped off quickly, with Alex and Sean close behind him. Brad had to walk fast to keep up with them. They moved through the family area and into the next stairwell. At the bottom landing they found another guard, a fresh face that Brad had not seen before. He said good morning to the boys and opened the door, allowing the men into the first floor office. They found David and Jorgensen sitting on a desk. The doctor was in the far corner leaning back on a chair. He was dressed in heavy khaki pants, with a leather bomber's jacket and fleece cap, as if he was preparing for a grand adventure.

Sean saw the doctor and headed directly in his direction. "Hey Indiana Jones, what the hell do you think you are doing cutting on my man without consulting me first!" he yelled.

"The wound was gangrenous and putting the man at risk for sepsis. He would have died, he still might, and the arm had to come off," Ericson said, getting right back into Sean's face, not backing down.

"That was my call to make!" Sean yelled back.

"If it had been a multiple choice problem I would have consulted you for your expert opinion, but turns out it wasn't. Your guidance was not required."

Sean stared at the doctor. "Well you have balls, I'll give you that."

"Like I said, I'm not interested in your opinions. Your man is resting well, I have him on the strongest course of antibiotics available. With a bit of luck he will pull through."

David clapped his hands loudly. "Please be to God!" he shouted. "Now if this most eloquent discussion be over, I could go about unlocking your weapons."

Sean moved away from the doctor and leaned against a wall. "Yeah, I suppose we're good. Doc, you sure Hahn will be okay with that girl you left him with?"

"Not much I can do for him, he needs rest. Sara will see to his needs," Ericson answered.

"Okay, then let's get a move on," Sean said.

David opened the safe and handed out the weapons to Sean and Brad, who quickly reassembled them. When they were ready they moved back out into the empty first floor of the building. James was beside the truck, refueling it with a large five-gallon can. He announced that the truck was nearly full and ready to go. There would be plenty for the trip north up the road and back again.

David went to the large overhead door and began raising it as Alex and Jorgensen leapt into the back. "Doc, you can ride up front with me and Luke," James shouted over the rumble of the overhead door. Doors opened and slammed shut as the truck's engine roared to life. Brad and Sean joined the other men in the back, and once the factory door was opened just enough to allow the truck to clear, they backed out of the large building.

James quickly maneuvered the truck around in a three-point turn and pulled up next to a waiting David. "Okay boys, get to the Murphys' road, and be sure and get back before dark, ya understand?"

"Yes, Father," they heard James answer from the cab.

David looked to Jorgensen in the bed of the truck and gave him a nod. Jorgensen responded with a nod of his own. The truck ground into gear and slowly crept back down the broken concrete drive. Brad looked at the surroundings. Unlike on the trip up when they were confined to the interior of the van, he could now clearly see the terrain. They were surrounded by a number of old abandoned buildings, many of them crumbling with nothing left but battered foundations. As Brad searched the area, he could see that the factory they had taken refuge in was just one of many, a perfect hiding spot.

23.

The truck moved steadily on the road heading north. The temperature was lower than the previous day but the skies were clear, giving no indication of foul weather. Brad watched as the forest again thinned and returned to the snow-covered rolling hills. There were no signs of creepers or primals in any direction. Brad put his head down, pulling his fleece cap low, and tried to relax as the truck rolled down the paved road.

Alex was sitting in a corner of the bed with his back resting against the cab of the truck. Like the first time they had met him, he was again holding the old and battered shotgun. Jorgensen was next to him cradling a heavy barreled, scoped bolt action .308 rifle. Sean looked up at Jorgensen and slapped the sole of his boot. "So what's your role on this trip?"

"Me? I'm just along to keep the doc safe and make sure the boys get home okay," Jorgensen answered.

Sean nodded. "Are you a professional bodyguard then?"

Jorgensen laughed. "No, more of a tour guide."

Sean didn't bother concealing his smile. "I'm thinking there is a bit more to that story,

Jorgensen."

"Please friend, call me George. Yeah, I have been a hunting guide on this isle for close to twenty years. Mostly rich folks from the mainland. Over my time I have camped or scouted nearly every inch of this rock."

"That's more like it, George. I'd say you have a valuable skill set."

"Some may think so, lately I have felt more like a babysitter than anything else."

Sean laughed. "Trust me brother, I know the feeling. So how did you get paired up with this group ... I'm sensing you're not family, or from the neighborhood."

"You have a keen sense, Sean, that you do," Jorgensen said. "I found David and his group a bit after things went dark. They were held up in the woods in a tidy little campsite some distance from here. David claims I saved them, I think they saved me."

"So you didn't know them at all, before I mean?"

"No. I usually work farther west. Taking out groups of three to four on week-long excursions. Was on a hunt when this all started. Brought my clients back to the city to try and get them a flight home. Airports were closed up by then, more planes were landing then going out."

"What did you do?"

"I had a mate that ran a charter fishing business. I thought we might be able to come to an agreement. In those days a lot of the fishermen were smuggling folks back and forth. We managed to make it to the marina. Never found my mate, things had begun to fall apart by then. Signs of infection had been encountered in the cities south and up some spots north. Most of the mainland was already going dark. Riots were starting, the military was putting up roadblocks restricting travel. I offered to take them back to the hunting grounds. I have equipment there, shelter, food. I figured we could hold out indefinitely."

"Sound decision-making. What happened?"

"All of this," Jorgensen said, raising his hands. "I waited too long."

"Your clients?"

"Don't rightly know friend, lost them in the chaos. We were at the marina behind the barricades when they hit. The things broke through … folks were panicking, trying to get to the boats, anything that floated to get away. Most of the water crafts were swamped. I made it to a roof top, tried to use my rifle to hold them off. It was no good, nothing I could do for them," Jorgensen said, putting both hands on his rifle and squeezing the handguards.

The truck slowed and pulled to the side of the road before its engine shut off. Alex and Jorgensen jumped from the bed as the cab doors opened and shut. "This is the spot," Luke said as he walked towards a gravel cut in the road that led further up the hill, perpendicular and away from the road. With the snowfall and overgrown grass, many would miss the turnoff if they didn't know it was there. Adding to the natural cover, several large boulders and sections of tree trunks had been placed across a section of the path.

Brad and Sean climbed from the truck bed to join the others on the ground. Brad carried his heavy pack with his left hand and walked around the truck to where the gravel path met the road. Looking up the drive and beyond the barrier, he could see nothing. The broken trail seemed to go on and on before disappearing into a tree line near the top of the hill. Casually searching the ground, he saw no footprints, no signs of life. Brad could see from the corner of his eye that Jorgensen was doing the same thing.

"You sure this is the correct spot, boys?" Brad asked.

"Oh yeah, this is the Murphys' place. I know it don't look like it, but up beyond those trees it opens up into some prime pasture. Been here plenty of times," Luke said.

"We should get going then boys, we don't want to waste the daylight. Luke, I'll be seeing you back here in about five hours. Keep an eye on your cousin there," Jorgensen said, smiling.

"You aren't all going?" Sean asked.

"No, sir, we need to make our rounds, we

have hides to visit and goods to retrieve," James answered. "Plus it ain't good to have this truck parked here, might draw suspicions to the road."

"Here Luke, take the shotgun," Alex said, tossing the old battered weapon to his brother.

Luke caught the gun one-handed and looked it over. "No, you better take it brother, I'll be okay in the truck, and if we see any trouble we will just come on back."

Brad listened to the discussion and looked down at his pack and the 870 shotgun strapped to the top. He hesitated for a moment before making the decision. He loosened the strap holding down the Remington and slid out the shotgun with the synthetic black stock. "Go ahead and take that gun Luke, I have something for your brother," Brad said, handing the shotgun off to Alex.

"Wow, you sure? This is a lot nicer than the one we got," Alex replied.

"Yeah I'm sure, just be careful with that thing. Works just like the one you got. There's already a round loaded in the pipe, and it's on safe. This isn't like TV where we wait until we see the bad guy to go racking a round to look cool. In real life we pop the safety and squeeze," Brad explained.

Jorgensen interrupted, "That's settled. Luke, James, hit the road, I don't want any excuses for why you didn't make it back here on time."

"Yes sir," Luke said, climbing into the truck beside his cousin. The engine started and the truck pulled away from the shoulder and continued tracking north away from them.

"Where are they headed?" Brad asked as he watched the truck fade from view.

"We all have our secrets, Sergeant," Jorgensen answered. "But they will be fine, if'in that's your concern."

They stayed in position, hiding by the concealed road entrance for another thirty minutes until they were sure they hadn't drawn the attention of any nearby primals. Brad had offered the doctor one of his handguns, but the doctor declined. Even in the interest of his own safety, he refused to arm himself. He convinced the others that he would be plenty protected with their company.

When it was time to move out, Sean asked Jorgensen to lead the way on point, keeping Alex close to him. He said it would make more sense for the Murphys to see a friendly face than those of strangers. Jorgensen politely accepted the suggestion, but Sean knew he suspected the real reason. Even though everyone was friendly, there was still tension in the group, and Sean didn't want the armed men having his back.

They walked the road in a traveling formation, two in the front, the doctor holding the center, followed up by Sean and Brad in the rear. As they traveled, Brad examined the surface and shoulders of the pockmarked drive. There was little to no evidence of the road being used recently. If it was in use, the owners had taken precautions to conceal it. No boot prints, no drag marks or tire tracks. Perhaps there was another trail leading in and out of the property.

Brad looked up and noticed that the doctor had slowed his pace and was now walking just in front of him. Ericson looked back at Brad. "I'm sorry about your friend … have you known him long?" he said.

"Keep it down, Doc, you'd be surprised how voices can travel out in the open like this," Brad said, seeing the immediate disappointment on the doctor's face. Brad took a few more steps and the doctor fell back to walk beside him.

"No, I only met him a few weeks ago, he's a good man though," Brad said, barely above a whisper.

The doctor spoke, still looking straight ahead. "I find it amazing that the man wasn't infected. Do you all have these bite shirts?"

Brad pulled down the collar of his jacket, showing the thick fabric to the doctor. "Yup, we all do."

"Amazing, something so simple yet so effective," Ericson whispered.

"Doc, exactly how much do you know about these things, the ones with the *primalis rabia?*" Brad asked.

"Actually, not a lot. I haven't had the opportunity to examine one. And either way, I'm not that type of doctor. To be honest, I have been fairly insulated from them since the first major attacks. I was lucky to have found my way to David and his family very early. Still, we were briefed at the hospital, but this wasn't like a flu pandemic, all hands on deck type of thing. This was more like nuclear fallout. By the time we were hit it was too late to respond. From the early medical bulletins, I understood it to be a sort of rage virus, perhaps rabies based," Ericson answered. "It fits the spectrum ... Rabies, for example, just by the simple symptoms alone ... aggression, light sensitivity, no social speech patterns, inability to reason. It is uncanny."

"But what about the creepers, the ones that stagger about as if ... like zombies."

"Scientifically speaking, there is more than one strain of the rabies virus. Not all animals that contract it go into a rage. Some just wither and die, or lose some motor function faster than others, or fall into a coma. I suspect the same things exist in this *primalis rabia* virus. Is that the phrase you used to describe it?"

"That's what the chief said they called it. He said it was weaponised and used against us."

"If this was modified in a laboratory, then all bets are off, my friend," Ericson whispered. "I would suspect they found a greater means of transmission, and a way to accelerate the incubation period, even to extend the life of the infected victim. Fascinating, really." Brad looked at the doctor with a puzzled expression. He was about to make a comment when Jorgensen stopped just where the road entered the tree line. He motioned for Sean to come to the front. Brad stopped and dropped to a knee, pulling the doctor down beside him. As Sean moved forward to join Jorgensen and Alex at the front, Brad saw a man exit the woods, walking towards them.

Not wanting to raise his rifle to use the optic, Brad squinted hard, trying to focus on the far-off figure. He watched as Sean changed into a ready stance, then relaxed his posture, lowering his weapon as he walked forward. He suddenly recognized the man as Brooks. Brad smiled. "Come on Doc, let's go, that's our man," he said, barely concealing his excitement.

Brad charged up the road with the doctor behind him struggling to keep up. As they got closer Brad saw more figures exit the tree line. They joined Sean and Brooks at the end of the drive. He recognized more of them, all of his friends. He saw Chelsea. She turned in his direction and recognized him at nearly the same time. Brad watched as she began running towards him down the path. He stopped and waited for her.

He began to speak just as she leapt at him,

catching him in a deep bear hug and planting a wet kiss on his lips. Brad took a step back, trying to catch his balance. He dropped his rifle and let it hang from the end of its sling. Failing to steady himself with the large pack on his back and Chelsea hanging onto him for dear life, he fell backwards onto the road, landing on the pack, with Chelsea still on top of him.

She lifted her head and looked at Brad and he saw tears in the corners of her eyes. "That was some welcome," he said, trying to hide the surprise in his voice.

"We thought you were dead. I promised myself if I ever saw you again ... well, you know," she said, her voice breaking. She buried her head in his chest, still hugging him tightly. Brad's arms now free of the rifle, he relaxed, lying back against his pack and wrapping his arms around her. He closed his eyes, feeling the weeks of frustration leaving him. He squeezed her tight, forgetting about everything that was happening, embracing the moment, letting down his guard. The sudden release of emotions caused his own eyes to tear up.

Brad opened his eyes and lifted his head. He saw that they were alone. The others were all at the top of the hill near the tree line. He laid back, exhausted, not wanting to get up, the cold winter air seemingly refreshing now. Brad closed his eyes again and rested his head back against his pack, enjoying the feel of Chelsea against him. He didn't want to think about anything, he just wanted to rest and take in the present moment.

"The others are leaving," he heard her whisper.

Brad sighed. "It's okay, everything is okay now," he said, not wanting to move and re-enter the real world.

"So much has happened, Brad," he heard her say as she pushed off of him and got back to her feet. She reached down and grabbed his hand, pulling. "Come on soldier, up and at 'em. The others will want to see you too," she joked.

Brad got to his feet. Chelsea took his arm and wrapped it around her shoulder, still gripping his gloved hand. All of the previous tension and awkwardness between them had vanished. It felt normal for him to be holding her, walking beside her on the gravel road. He didn't want to make it to the top of the hill, to rejoin the others. "Why can't things just go back to the way they were. I wish I could wake up from this nightmare," Brad said in a low voice.

"Like you said Brad, everything is okay now."

24.

When they reached the top of the hill and entered the tree line, Brad could see why the farm had been so hard for anyone to find. The thick row of trees were barely fifteen feet wide but they hung over and shadowed the gravel drive. The trees were full, and the drive curved through them just enough to conceal the large snow-covered pasture beyond them. Farther out across the rolling hills, Brad spotted the large fieldstone farm house. It was flanked by a large barn and several smaller outbuildings.

As they walked towards the farmhouse, Brooks and Parker came out to meet them. Brad shook both of their hands and embraced them with hugs. "It's good to see you Brad, I thought we lost you," Brooks said as he slapped him on the back. "Not this one though, she wouldn't stop talking about you, pressing me to go out and search every day," he said, looking at Chelsea.

Brad looked down, then back up at Brooks. "Honestly, I don't even know how long it's been … after the crash things just blurred together… Oh, how is Kelli? We brought a doctor."

"I just met him. Chief filled me in on what you all have been through, that's some crazy shit, brother… I wouldn't have sent you for the meds had I known."

"Yeah," Brad said, shaking his head, "I don't want to talk about that …"

"Yup the doc just headed off with Mrs. Murphy to take a look at our wounded. She will surely put him to work," Brooks said.

"Wait … *the wounded* … who else is hurt?" Brad asked.

Avoiding the question, Brooks slapped Brad on the back and pointed towards the large plank wood outbuilding. "Come on, let's get to the barn. The Murphys have been letting us hold up in there."

Brad followed them down the drive which wound past the large stone farmhouse. As they walked, he told them about how they had found Hahn and brought him to the factory. How the people there had taken them in, fed them and helped them find the farm.

The home sat three stories tall, big and square; the first story was comprised completely of fieldstone. Beyond that, the top two stories were made of overlapping thick blocks of timber. The windows were high off the ground and set into the stone, with more on the second and third stories. Along the front of the house wrapped a decorative covered front porch. From the design of the porch it looked to have been added to the farm house more recently.

As the drive widened, it flattened out into

a large lot, broken and rutted up, probably from hay wagons and tractors. It would have been extremely muddy in the spring, but now in the cold weather the soil was stiff and crumbled under his boots. The barn was tall and matched the design of the house with stone walls and a flat roof. It was sturdy and well built. It wasn't the type of barn he was used to on the dairy farms back in Michigan, but more closely resembled those he had seen in Germany and Ireland.

Brooks moved past the large sliding barn door and reached for a wooden handle on a smaller entryway. As they moved inside, Brad could smell the musty hay and livestock, a familiar smell, having grown up near similar rural farms. He looked about and saw that the first floor of the barn had been divided. A large aisle went down the center with livestock pens on either side. There was a loft covering the back half of the barn, and he could see his men up there. Brooks moved to a ladder and began climbing up. Parker urged Brad to go next and he took the heavy rungs in his hand and lifted himself and the weight of the pack up and onto the second floor of the barn.

He came up over the edge of the loft and was pulled forward by Brooks and quickly helped out of his rucksack. He finally saw everyone together. They were all there. This large area of the loft was arranged like a barracks, with the exception of cots, but individual sleep spaces and personal areas had been arranged with blankets and sleeping bags. Daniel Villegas was in a corner. Sean was talking to him, and from his body language Brad could tell that the conversation was not a pleasant one.

Brooks indicated Sean and Daniel. "Chief is ripping Danny a new one over the incident at the cabin. Those brothers have had it rough since they got here. Gunner already tore them up over it, and that was when we still thought Hahn was dead."

"Where are the wounded" Brad asked.

"Back here," Brooks said, indicating for Brad to follow him.

A section of the loft had been broken up and divided by heavy tarps. Four walls hung, made of fabric, with another providing overhead cover. Once inside the tarps one instantly got the feeling of being in an enclosed tent. A small kerosene stove burned in the center, providing significantly more warmth than outside the canvas partition.

A row of hasty beds were set up, running head to foot along the back wall of the partition. Kelli was leaned up against a set of large pillows resting, conscious, her bandaged legs outstretched and elevated. Gunner was sitting on a bunk with his shoulder heavily bandaged. Daniel Villegas was laid back on a rack. Ericson and the nurse were slowly unwrapping a set of stained bandages which covered his abdomen. Alex and Jorgensen were just behind them, nervously holding the bag of medical supplies and the doctor's medical kit.

"Wha ... what happened?" Brad stuttered. He was expecting to see Kelli convalescing, not half his team down.

Chelsea moved beside Brad and grabbed his hand. "We had trouble," she said.

Gunner looked up at Brad. "We had a bit more than that." He struggled to sit up and face the men, nursing his wounded shoulder, the effort seeming to take all of his wind. "Good to see you Brad, as you can see I'm a bit banged up."

"How?" Brad said, still unsure what to make of their situation.

"We went out looking for you two. After the rest of the team returned from the cabin empty-handed." Gunner waved a hand and shot a disgusted glare to the outside of the tent. They could just overhear the heated discussion between Joseph and Sean. "When they came back and told us how they abandoned you all in the field, and left Hahn to die …. Well we scrambled a team together."

"Hahn isn't dead," Brad said in a low voice, not changing his expression.

"Yeah, I heard," Gunner acknowledged. "They assumed the worst for him, seeing as they were sure he had been infected. Sean told us the story of how Hahn stayed behind. I guess leaving him was the right thing to do with the information they had." Gunner paused, looking frustrated, searching for the right words. "It's all in the past I guess … Anyhow, the brothers were eager to go out after you two, looking for redemption for fucking up and leading that herd back to the cabin, dumb fucks." Gunner was growing visibly agitated.

Brooks moved to Gunner's rack and sat next to him, "Like you said Gunner, it's in the past."

"Yeah, I know …" Gunner looked exhausted and leaned back, trying to get comfortable. "Those shitty painkillers you keep giving me make me tired."

"Yeah, it has nothing to do with the blood loss and that hole in your shoulder," Brooks said sarcastically.

Brooks continued for Gunner. "Anyhow, the next morning we formed up a small search party, moved out and patrolled the road, figuring that would be the best bet to find you. We searched all day until just before dark, turning up nothing but those slow primals. The next day we decided to cut south and patrol towards the cabin, sticking to the secondary roads.

"We put down a few of those things on the way, avoiding others when we could. Thought we would come up empty again, ready to turn back for the day, when we came upon a bunch of houses just off the road. Small places, nothing special. But there was a car parked in the road just in front of them. Damn thing was running, could see the hot exhaust rising in the cold air. Just sitting there idling quietly.

"We dug in and watched, planted ourselves in some heavy cover, saw two men. They were ferrying goods to the car from the house. They *were* armed," Brooks paused briefly to motion towards a corner of the tent where two Colt C7 rifles and an older scoped hunting rifle were leaning against a pack. "Their rifles were slung across their backs while they carried boxes of food and other things from the homes. We didn't have all day to scout them out. Gunner decided to move forward with the Villegases to approach them, while I stayed back in over watch with the long gun."

Gunner sat up and jumped back into the story. "Those cocksuckers ... They played it up real good, said they were sailors just looking for food, trying to get by. They weren't real clear on where the hell they were from, but they spoke with a Russian accent. Said they found the rifles at an abandoned checkpoint. They was real interested in how we got here. Wanted to know where we were staying, what provisions we had, if we *had women*.

"They got agitated when I wouldn't tell them. I said we were alone on the trail in search of a couple friends after we got separated in the storm. Everything I owned was on my back, I just wanted to know if they had seen two men. They were about as useless as a bent dick.

"Talk turned to how impressed they were with our weapons and equipment, and how much ammo did we have, would we be interested in a trade. I still didn't pick up on them being hostile … Shit, they had their rifles slung behind their backs …" Gunner shook his head, "We told them we didn't have anything to spare, and they seemed okay with the answer. Russian bastards … I took a round to the shoulder, put me on my ass before I even heard the shot.

"Second shot took Danny in the gut. Joey somehow made it to cover, he was able to get his rifle up before those two Russian fucks … he had em painted red before they could unsling their rifles. Brooks here put down the sniper."

Jorgensen, overhearing the conversation, stepped forward. "I know who they are. I'm sure it's the same group."

Brooks looked at Jorgensen. "Who is this?"

"His name is Jorgensen, he's a friend," Brad said.

Jorgensen moved closer and extended a hand, "Call me George. I have seen this same group of men. I believe they are responsible for other deaths near here."

Jorgensen retold the story of the others, and the missing and murdered families. The encounters on the road. How they had come in on freighters that were now sitting off the coast. The sailors seeking refuge during the outbreak. Jorgensen told how he had tried to get close to their camp near one of the port villages, but didn't want to risk being caught, or leading them back to the factory. For the most part they had just avoided the strangers, and kept their distance.

Brooks listened politely before asking questions. "George, this camp, could you show me?"

Jorgensen looked at him, puzzled. "Well sure, but ... We don't want trouble from them, I have families to protect, and not enough men or weapons to stand up against them. My people have already discussed this, it's better to keep our distance and stay out of sight."

Brooks looked at him seriously, "You do know that these types won't just stay down there on their side of the valley? Gangs like this are cancers, they will take everything. Once the low-hanging fruit is gone, they will come up this valley in force. Hell, they are already here patrolling, looking for easy targets. What happens when the stuff on the main roads is picked clean, and they start branching out?

"You said they had some local girls? I'm sure the girls have already told them about your camp. Those men are probably just waiting for spring to come and take what they want."

Jorgensen looked frustrated. "I'm sorry friend, like I said it was decided amongst my people to avoid them."

Gunner, growing agitated, leaned in towards Jorgensen. "George, we aren't asking for your permission. Just a little help in locating their camp. We won't need anything else. We can take care of the rest."

"And what will you do when you find them?"

Gunner smiled. "Think of us as your friendly neighborhood exterminators."

"I see," Jorgensen mumbled. "And if you fail, you poke the hornets' nest and they come for me and my people, then what?"

"Just tell them already," Alex blurted out, joining the conversation.

"We won't fail," Brooks said.

Jorgensen looked at Alex, shaking his head, "And when they kill these men, then what? Then they are in charge, then they come after us? Is that it?"

"Jorgensen!" Brad said loudly, getting the man's attention, "All we want is to get out of here. You said these men were sailors? They came in on ships, are they seaworthy?"

Jorgensen, thrown off guard by the outburst, looked back to Brad. "Well yes, they came here because they had no place else to go, they were not shipwrecked if that's what you mean."

"It's exactly what I mean. Could we use their vessels to get home?" Brad asked.

Ericson turned around from his patient and gave all of them a stern look. "Gentlemen, I must insist you get the hell out of my infirmary. I am sure you can find a more suitable place to discuss such things."

Gunner looked to the doctor and nodded his head. "You're right, Doc, sorry for the disruption," he said as he prepared to stand.

"Oh no, not you old man, not till I have had a chance to examine that wound," Ericson ordered.

Gunner slumped back onto his rack like a scorned child. "Go on ahead boys, you can fill me in later."

25.

Brad followed the men downstairs into the larger stable area of the barn. They turned and walked behind the ladder, following the middle aisle of the barn, passing the livestock pens filled with sheep, and into a larger workshop space located off the back. The room was annexed onto the rear of the barn and was also built from large pieces of carved fieldstone. A wood stove was glowing in the room with a kettle resting on top. Brad recognized Jeremiah, the man who'd come to them at the plane crash. He was resting in a chair, the stem of a pipe hanging from his lips.

He leaned forward in his chair and shook Brad and Sean's hands as they entered the room. "Good to see you men again," he said.

"Yes, took us a bit longer to get here than we'd planned," Sean answered.

"But still you are here now, that is something."

"Can't argue with that," Sean said.

"And who is this? I recognize Alex, but not this man," Jeremiah said, pointing the pipe at Jorgensen.

Jorgensen extended his hand to Jeremiah, "I am George, a friend of the boy's uncle."

"David? David is alive?" Jeremiah laughed. "Figures out of everyone … David would be the one to make it, and let me guess, that red-haired fool cousin of his … Francis as well?"

Alex smiled. "Yes sir, Uncle David and Francis are both well."

"And your father? How is he, I haven't seen him in quite some time?"

"Mom and Dad are gone," Alex said, looking down.

"That's a shame, your father was a good man, not like that uncle of yours," Jeremiah said.

Brooks moved past them and deeper into the workshop before taking a seat at a large workbench. The others took notice and followed him into the larger part of the workshop. Jeremiah sighed before getting to his feet and following them towards a large block wood table that sat in the middle of the room. He pulled a stool from against the wall and joined them at the table.

The table already had a large topographical map sitting in the center. Wooden blocks had been placed on it. One was in the approximate location of the farmhouse. Others marked the cabin and the crash site. A large circle was drawn around the village and the clinic. Several X's were marked, indicating places the team had searched or visited in the days prior.

Sean stood at the edge of the table and leaned over the map. "You all have been busy."

"You didn't think we were just gonna sit on our asses, did you? Once things quieted down we managed to remove most of the goods from the Antonov. We were able to recover Theo as well. With the help of Jeremiah and his boys, of course," Brooks said.

"Thank you for that, sir," Sean said.

Jeremiah acknowledged his comment with a nod. Sean turned his gaze back to Jorgensen. "Now on this map, can you tell me where their camp is located?"

Jorgensen paused, scratching his chin. "If I do this, you have to give me assurances that my people will be safe."

"They will be safer than they are now with them out there," Brooks said.

"I need more than that. We need weapons like those ones you had up there that you took from their dead," Jorgensen said.

Sean gave Jorgensen a hard stare. "I tell you what George, you take us to their camp, and I'll give you first choice of war souvenirs."

"Their camp may hold over a hundred men. I see here, what ... seven, maybe eight fighters? I'm sure you understand why it is hard for me to trust you."

"Leave that to us, just get us to the camp so we can see what we are dealing with," Sean said.

"And you promise you will arm and protect my people?"

"You have my word," Sean said.

"Do you have a pen?" Jorgensen asked.

Jeremiah reached into a trough that flanked the table and tossed Jorgensen a red grease marker. Jorgensen picked up the pen and stared at the map. He circled an elevated wooded area where two main roads intersected. "I saw their camp here," he said, then moved his finger down a long road towards a coastal area which was marked with objects identifying manmade structures. "I suspect the main body of their people are here, in this fishing village. I know from news reports before things went dark that several freighters had anchored in this bay. The village is protected by cliffs, but easily accessible by the road."

"You said there could be a hundred of them, how do you know this?" Brooks asked.

Jorgensen looked across the table to Brooks, then to Alex. "Alex, would you mind leaving the room? Could you join the doctor, please?"

"Why? The doctor is fine," Alex protested.

"Alex has seemed to handle himself pretty good, why not let him stay?" Brad asked.

"Some things you cannot un-see, and some things you cannot un-hear," Jorgensen mumbled.

Alex glared at him. "I watched my parents slaughtered, what could be worse?"

There was an uncomfortable silence in the room as Jorgensen stared at the map, contemplating his next words. Sean finally spoke, breaking the tension. "Please George, continue."

"Okay, but Alex, talk of this does not leave the room. Do you understand, boy?"

Alex nodded his head yes.

"I need to hear you speak it. If the people in the factory hear … They will be scared. We can't have that, Alex."

"I understand, I won't repeat it," Alex blurted out.

Jorgensen took in a deep breath and exhaled. "After we found the father and the boy dead, and the girls missing …" Jorgensen paused again, looking at Alex before continuing, "I decided to make another attempt at finding their camp, learning more about them. I left the factory. It is common for me to be gone days at a time on a hunt. No one is ever concerned as long as I return with fresh meat. This time was different. I followed the roads to here then crossed into the high grounds," Jorgensen said, tracing his route on the map.

"I made it to this point, just above the intersection and their camp," he pointed. "I arrived just before dark and I was afraid to move after the sun fell for fear of the Buhmann. I got my rest in the high branches of a pine tree. Occasionally I could see lights from their buildings when they would open doors, but they were quiet. I suspect they fear the Buhmann as much as we do.

"As the sun came up I found I had picked a perfect vantage point to view the intersection and the *camp*. But this is no camp."

"What are you saying?" Brad asked.

"They use this place to hold the road, looking like an official checkpoint. I watched them stop a car, a family. They pulled them from the vehicle and executed the males before dragging off the females to a waiting car that took them down the road to the coast. Some of them are dressed as policemen, others in military uniforms."

"How long did you stay?" Brooks asked.

"I watched them through the day. They stopped three cars, killing the occupants and taking their belongings. They piled the dead in a trench, stripping them of their clothing, and parking their vehicles in a lot.

"Many times one of their own cars would approach the barricade. They would leave with three to four men, presumably on their patrols to scavenge supplies. For the most part the vehicles went to the south and away from the factory. I counted at least fifty armed men between those in the vehicles and those working the gates."

"Why didn't you tell us?" Alex asked.

"Your uncle knows, and Francis too. They thought it best to keep it quiet until we had a solution. We didn't want the people to scatter and flee the safety of the factory."

Sean reached forward and placed a single .308 round on its end over the marked intersection on the map. "Well now you have a solution."

"But still you are only seven, and they are so many," Jorgensen said.

Brooks laughed. "We prefer target-rich environments."

Sean turned to Alex. "You will need to return the doctor to the factory, make sure he checks in on Hahn."

"No, I will go with you, to the camp," Alex said eagerly.

"No, not this time. Take the doctor. I need you to make sure he gets back safely. Parker, you go with him, I'm sure Hahn would be happy to see you," Sean said, looking across the table to the soldier who had remained silent.

"Roger, Chief," Parker answered.

"Jorgensen, we will travel at first light. Hope you packed extra underwear, because I will need you to stay over tonight. Brad, hate to pick on you, but I want you and Brooks to roll with me. I think four is the magic number for this little operation," Sean said.

"And what is the op exactly?" Brooks asked.

Sean looked across the table to Brooks and Brad. "Let's just get eyes on before we put anything in stone, but pack for a faceoff with the devil." Sean stood up from the table and walked towards the door. "That's all I've got, anyone want to show me where I can get some chow?"

Brad stayed behind, examining the map as the rest of them walked out of the workshop. He found himself alone with Chelsea. She walked around the table and stood next to him at the corner. "Brad, you just got back, why are you leaving again?" she asked, looking him in the eye.

"It's what we do, you heard George's story," Brad said.

"That's bullshit, this isn't what you do, and that's all behind you now. You don't have to do any of this, Brad. Stay here, stay with me."

"Not yet Chelsea, I can't quit on them yet," Brad said, looking away from her, not able to say it to her face.

"Then when, when does it all end?"

"Chelsea, if this works, we might find a ship. We could make it back to the States, we could get home."

"At what cost, Brad? There is no more home, it's all lost," she said, beginning to raise her voice.

Brad put his hands on the table and retrieved the .308 round Sean had placed there. He fumbled with the round, tumbling it in his fingers. "I have to find out, I want to see it for myself."

"Where does that leave me, Brad, am I just supposed to stay here on this farm while you go out and get yourself killed? What am I supposed to do?"

"I don't know."

"I thought maybe things would be different when you came back," Chelsea said, her voice cracking, a tear falling down her cheek.

"I'm sorry," Brad said, watching as Chelsea left the room, leaving him alone. He sat there silently for a while, trying to collect his thoughts. There were too many things happening at once, too many to comprehend. The last thing he wanted to do was to go back out into the cold, dark woods to face the primals again ... and even worse, the men who seemed to be terrorizing the roads to the south.

"Damn it!" he yelled, slamming his hand on the table. "Of course I don't want to go, fuck yeah I'd rather stay here. Why can't she understand that I don't have a choice?" he said to himself.

He couldn't leave Sean and Brooks to do this alone. He would have to push it all back, back to the furthest part of his brain. Time to shut down and get back on mission. Sean was making the calls now, and he was okay with that. Brad was content with being the good soldier and following orders for a bit longer, as long as they kept moving towards the goal of getting home.

26.

When Brad left the workshop he saw Doctor Ericson and Alex gathered at the bottom of the ladder with Specialist Parker and Mrs. Murphy. Ericson was giving last minute instructions to the nurse on the care of the men. He had promised to return the following day, and if Hahn was able to travel he would bring him to the farm so he could be with the rest of the men.

Jorgensen walked into the barn to tell them the truck was at the bottom of the hill and they needed to get moving. They all headed for the barn door. Alex stopped when he saw Brad at the back of the room and turned back towards him. He extended the unslung the 870 shotgun and went to hand it back. "Thank you for letting me carry this," Alex said.

"Keep it," Brad said, slapping the boy on the back.

"Wow, really? Thank you Brad. I'll be seeing you soon, okay?"

"Yeah, you betcha, Alex," Brad said, following them outside. He watched the party follow the drive back out and just into the trees, Jorgensen walking the group most of the way. Brad watched them exchange handshakes and hugs before Jorgensen turned and headed back towards Brad, who was waiting outside the barn.

"You ate?" Jorgensen asked.

"No, not yet, you?"

"Nope, was fixin' to, though. Care if I join you? Mrs. Murphy said there was food laid out in the main house."

"I'm following you, then," Brad said.

Brad followed Jorgensen through a back door in the farmhouse. They entered into an old plank mudroom, then down a hallway. They saw they were tracking in clods of dirt and snow so they stopped to strip their boots before continuing into the house. There were few lights burning in the house so they followed the low glow of oil lamps to lead them to the kitchen.

As promised, food was laid out on an antique kitchen table. Thomas Murphy and his younger brother William were standing over a kitchen island opening canned jars of vegetables. "Hey Thomas, was wondering where you were hiding," Brad said jokingly.

"Hey Brad, I was meaning to make it out to the barn to welcome you, been busy most of the day. Dad has us working pretty hard. It's not easy feeding so many," Thomas said.

"Well make sure the guys are doing their share," Brad said.

"Oh they been great, Nelson is getting pretty good with the animals too," William added.

"Good to hear. What's on the menu?"

"Nothing special, I'm afraid. It's a weekday ... I think? Anyhow, we tend to eat better on Sundays. Weekdays it's dried meats and canned potatoes," Thomas said.

"Well hell boys, turns out them be some of my favorite eats," Jorgensen said, lifting a plate. "Load me up, friends."

"Shit, who doesn't like meat and potatoes," Brad laughed, grabbing a plate of his own.

He found a spot at the table and quietly ate his dinner. William brought him a cup of warm tea and a glass of water. "You all are doing pretty well out here, aren't ya?" Brad said.

Thomas finished rinsing the jars and wiped his hands with a towel. He carried the oil lamp to the table and sat down, joining the rest of them. "We have done surprisingly well. These things are hard to explain. After the first days the wild unpredictable movement kinda ceased. We don't see them too far from the cities and villages now unless they are pursuing something."

William checked the window and pulled the curtains tight, ensuring they were closed. "Nighttime is the most critical. That's when the smart ones are moving. We don't burn fires, or venture out past dark."

"We share the same experiences, boys," Jorgensen said. "At the factory, we don't burn wood after dark. The dumb ones, the creepers, they don't seem to care at all about wood smoke. They are mostly attracted to sight and sounds. But the Buhmann, they are different. They will track you, they can smell you, and they can associate a wood fire with prey. Have to be careful with them ones."

Brad finished the rest of his food and placed his knife and fork on his plate. "Where did the others go?" he asked.

"Dad is in the attic, standing first watch. I'd imagine the rest are cleaning up ... readying to lock in for the night. Everyone else already ate. We go to bed early here, we have to be up with the sun to take advantage of the daylight hours," William said.

"I guess we should be moving to the barn as well then, don't ya think George?" Brad said.

"Aye, don't want to get locked out in the cold now do we," Jorgensen joked as he chugged the last of his tea.

"Thank you for the meal, boys, good night," Brad said.

"Wait a second," William said as he ran down a hall and then came back, carrying a pair of old sleeping bags. "Most of the others already had choice of Mom's good blankets and the nice bags, but you are welcome to these if you need one."

"I'd be most grateful," Jorgensen said, taking a bag and passing the other to Brad. "I wasn't planning for an overnight trip."

The two men made their way back to the barn just as the last of the daylight began to fade. Joseph was standing watch at the door when they arrived. He welcomed them inside but asked them to keep their voices low. They observed serious light and sound discipline once the sun went down. Brad nodded and moved towards the ladder to the loft.

He climbed to the top and found his pack where he had left it earlier. Looking around, he could see all of the others had turned in for the night. Their shapes covered the loft floor. Piles of clothing and boots lay next to their sleeping forms. A small crack of light bled from under the canvas shelter that made do as their infirmary. The soft glow of leaked light was the only light in the entire space. Brad watched as Jorgensen made his way into the infirmary tent. As he lifted the flap and passed inside, Brad caught a glimpse of Chelsea sitting on Kelli's bed. She didn't look up and probably wouldn't have seen him standing in the dark anyhow.

He moved about, looking for a spot on the floor to call his own. Nearly every inch of board was occupied. Brad moved closer to the tent and saw that there was a narrow gap of maybe three feet between the edge of the canvas wall and the barn wall itself. "Guess this will have to do," Brad whispered to himself as he moved into the narrow alley. He unrolled the sleeping bag, choosing to use it as a cushion rather than get inside.

Brad dug though his ruck, removing a heavy wool blanket he had procured from the factory as well as his poncho liner. He quietly spread them out in the dark, finally folding his coat as a pillow. Brad stripped out of his clothing, choosing to sleep in his shorts and undershirt. He felt safe in this elevated position surrounded by his men. He pulled the poncho liner over his shoulders and tried to find sleep.

He heard noise, the sounds of laughter. Brad struggled to open his eyes, finding his eyelids heavy. He could feel the sunlight on his face. He sat up in the bed. He was back in the house, in the middle of the village. He heard the laughter. He could smell bacon.

Brad smiled and got to his feet. He wasn't in his boots, no uniform. He was dressed in his boxers and a brown T-shirt. He stretched his arms and moved down the hallway and into the living room, admiring the family photos as he walked towards the kitchen.

As he moved through the living room he saw a man sitting at the head of the table, a young child next to him, smiling. They asked Brad to have a seat, it was time to eat. Brad moved to the table and sat with them. Listening to the child laugh, the father smiled proudly. In walked a woman holding a large tray of bacon and eggs. She smiled at Brad, offering him the first serving. Brad smiled and lifted his arm to take a large spoon.

When Brad raised his hand he was holding the

silenced MKII Pistol. "No!" Brad screamed, trying to let go of it, but had no control of his body. He screamed, fighting his own muscles as the pistol swung towards the face of the father. Brad couldn't control his movements. His finger depressed the trigger rapidly, and he watched in horror as the slide retracted back and forth, spitting spent brass from the receiver. Rounds impacted the man's face; he flew back and out of his chair.

"No!" Brad continued to scream as his arm swung left, now aiming the pistol into the laughing face of the mother. Again he felt the trigger pull as the pistol bucked, rounds hitting the woman over and over in the neck and head. The child continued to laugh as Brad's arm moved right, the pistol going in the child's direction. He couldn't control his actions. Brad screamed in agony, trying to override his muscles; he struggled to drop the pistol, to lower his arm.

Brad woke in the dark, his heart pounding. He felt pressure. His hand was being held softly and pushed back towards his body. Another hand touched his face and brushed his hair. He went to leap forward but heard a soft whisper. It was Chelsea, telling him it was okay. He relaxed and lay back, trying to breathe. She ran her fingers through his hair, then leaned over and kissed him softly on the forehead.

Chelsea lifted the blanket and crawled in next to him, placing her back against his chest. She pulled his arm over her hip, pressing her warm body close to him. Brad squeezed her hand and pulled her tight, pressing his face close against her shoulder, smelling her hair and listening to her breathe. He was relaxed, he felt safe and warm. He closed his eyes yet didn't want to sleep, instead wanting to stay in the moment, embracing the feelings of warmth and love that he had been without for so long.

27.

When he woke, she was gone. Brad rolled to his back, wondering if it had all been a dream. He sat up and dressed, pulling on his thermals and uniform. He folded the blankets and rolled up the sleeping bag, then reached for his rucksack, preparing to pack it for the coming patrol. Resting on the top was a single folded slip of paper. Brad grabbed it and unfolded it.

Find us a way home. When you return, I will be waiting.

Brad held the paper in his hand, reading it several times before folding it and placing it into the breast pocket of his shirt. He packed everything into the rucksack, checking his weapons and ammunition before moving back into the large space of the loft. The others were already up, cleaning their areas and preparing for the day. Brad walked to the infirmary tent, going inside and hoping to find Chelsea.

He found Kelli on her bunk. She smiled at him when he walked in. Daniel and Gunner were still asleep, Gunner snoring loudly. Brad walked to Kelli. "Have you seen Chelsea?" he asked her.

She smiled at him. "She's gone, Brad."

"Gone?" he asked.

"She went to help Mrs. Murphy in the

house. She said she couldn't watch you walk away again. Just make sure you come back, okay?"

Brad returned Kelli's smile. "I promise," he said.

"Brad," Kelli called out as he exited the tent, causing him to stop and look back.

"Thank you for what you did for me," she said. "You know I owe you one."

"Just take care of her, okay?" Brad said as he left the tent, grabbing his bag as he passed it.

He navigated the ladder and joined the others in the stable. He found the rest of his team suited up and ready to go. "'Bout time you joined us," Sean joked as Brad cleared the last rung of the ladder. "The boys brought us some sandwiches and filled some water bottles if you're interested." Sean pointed to a nearby table.

Brad acknowledged him by grabbing a sandwich and stuffing half of it in his mouth. He chewed heartily and washed it down with a huge gulp of water. "So George, how long is this walk today?"

"I have good news there, friend. Murphy has offered to loan us his car. I'd say we will be in position by late morning," Jorgensen said.

"Really? Things are looking up," Brad said, smiling.

Brooks laughed, "Don't get too excited, Thomas tells me it's a real piece of shit."

Sean lifted his heavy rucksack to his back. "You guys ready?" he said before heading to the door. Brad lifted his own pack and followed the rest of the men outside. Thomas was waiting for them by one of the other outbuildings. He swung open the door of an old-style pole building to reveal a four-door 1990's Renault Clio. "What the fuck is that?" Sean asked, looking at the tiny car.

Thomas grinned. "It's Mom's old car, she used to drive it when she worked at the clinic. Don't worry it still runs pretty good, we take it for rides every now and then."

Thomas opened the driver's door and put the car in neutral. Jeremiah and the other boys walked behind the car and pushed it out of the barn and onto the driveway. Jeremiah came out carrying a large bundle of rope. "There isn't much room inside. I'm afraid you'll have to lash your bags to the top."

"Fair enough, I s'pose," Jorgensen said as he hoisted his bag to the roof. The rest of the men stripped their bags of weapons, then lifted them onto the roof next to Jorgensen's. Brooks bundled the bags towards the center of the vehicle as Thomas and William tightly lashed them together.

Thomas held up the keys, and Sean took them. "You drive, George, I call shotgun," he said, tossing the keys to Jorgensen.

"It's all gassed up. You will have plenty

of fuel. You'll have to pop the clutch to get her started though," Jeremiah said. "Just bring it to the top of the hill, give us some time to remove the barricade, then you can be on your way."

Sean looked at all of them, "We ready?"

Brad opened the rear passenger door and squeezed into the back of the car. Brooks got in beside him with the other two men in front. Jorgensen put the key in the ignition and depressed the clutch. Jeremiah and his sons began to push the car down the drive. When it hit the hill it picked up speed. Jorgensen released the clutch. The Renault backfired then revved to life. Jorgensen drove the car past the house then up the far side of the hill as he had been asked. He then put the car in neutral, nursing the throttle, making sure the small car didn't stall out.

They watched the boys run past them and down the hill. Quickly they dragged the large trees away from the entrance to the road, then rolled away the boulders. Thomas shot a thumbs up to his father waiting at the top of the hill. Jeremiah walked back to the car and wished the men good luck as he slapped the roof. Once again the Renault was put into gear and they were again rolling down the driveway. Jorgensen slowed, turned onto the main road and accelerated.

Jorgensen navigated the car down the paved road. It had been days since snow had fallen so much of the road was clear, or only slightly marked with the melting snow. He drove cautiously, avoiding the deeper banks of snow that had accumulated and frozen in low spots as the snow melted. For the first leg of the trip and until they reached the turn off to the factory, they followed the tracks of the pickup truck. Jorgensen said they would have another thirty kilometers until they neared the camp.

The trees had grown thick as they got closer to the coast. The road began to twist following the rolls of the hilly terrain. Occasionally they would pass a house, or a cluster of buildings, all of them showing signs of forced entry: kicked-open doors or broken windows. It was obvious the gang had traveled here. As they continued to get closer to the camp, the tension in the vehicle rose. The men readied their weapons and checked their magazines. Jorgensen slowed as they drove past a burnt-down home. The house itself wasn't unusual. Several homes had burnt since the fall. What was different was the five bodies lying face down in the driveway in front of the home. Brad clenched his jaw, watching the bodies as the car slowly rolled past.

"How much farther?" Brooks asked impatiently.

Jorgensen looked at Brooks in the rearview mirror. "Not much further, there is a place up ahead where we can hide the car. We will travel the rest of the distance on foot."

The car moved on, following another very long bend in the road. As the car pulled out of the curve, Jorgensen slowed then turned off on to a barely visible side road that cut up and away from the main road. The side road was composed of loose gravel that was covered in snow and ice. Quickly the car began to slip and the wheels spun, losing traction. Jorgensen put the small car into reverse and used the slope of the hill to turn it around. Then he eased it to the side of the narrow road before cutting the engine and applying the parking brake.

"End of the road, friends," Jorgensen said as he removed the keys from the ignition and stowed them in the glove box.

The team quickly exited the vehicle and removed their gear. They gathered brush from nearby and hastily camouflaged the Renault. It wouldn't do much good on close inspection. But the brush would at least cover the glare from the paint and windshield from reflecting down to the main road below them. Sean made a quick walk-around inspection of the vehicle before signaling to Jorgensen to lead the way.

They continued following the road up the hill until it ended at a small overlook. There was a small parking area here, with trash cans and picnic tables. It looked to have been a park at one time, but it was empty now with no signs of life. They followed Jorgensen diagonally across the parking lot and to a small foot-trail that continued up the high hill.

"There is another overlook at the top. That is where we will be able to see the intersection," Jorgensen said.

"How far is it from the top of the hill to the intersection?" Sean asked as they walked.

"I didn't pace it out, but I'd guess twelve to sixteen hundred meters. Somewhat out of reach of your rifles if that is what you are wondering. But there are plenty of firing positions," Jorgensen said.

"Are you a sniper, George?" Brooks asked.

"I am a hunter," Jorgensen muttered as he continued trekking up the trail.

It took them another thirty minutes before the trail leveled out and again traveled to the south. Jorgensen continued leading the way, walking point. Being an experienced hunting guide had served him well. He moved along the trail slowly as if stalking a deer, pausing often to check the trail and to look back as if checking on his clients. He moved quickly and quietly, feeling very comfortable in the forest.

At a sharp corner in the trail Jorgensen stopped and took a knee, signaling for the rest of them to come forward. "This is the spot."

Sean looked around them in a 360 before shaking his head no. "See if you can get us closer," he whispered.

Without speaking, Jorgensen indicated a narrow path through heavy brush. Just beyond the brush you could see bright light coming through the leaves where a break in the forest started. He mimicked with his hands for them to crawl and follow behind him.

It didn't take long. Just beyond the heavy brush more signs of a hiker's path developed, with flattened dirt and even an occasional piece of litter or names carved into a stump. Jorgensen moved down the path, crawling on his belly to keep himself concealed among the high grass that surrounded the trail. Again he stopped at a large wall made of dry, stacked stone. He scooted then turned so that he was sitting with his back against the rock wall.

It looked to have been a popular picnic site for hikers. Brad could see how the path moved in and next to the wall. Names had been written on it in paint; stumps and logs were carved into rustic benches. Jorgensen used his hands to call them all together. Again he used his rudimentary sign language to tell them to slowly peek over the wall. Sean first lifted his head. The grass was high here, and even with his head above the wall he had to use his hands to part the vegetation to see the intersection below.

Sean looked, pivoting his head from side to side before dropping back into the cover of the wall. He brought his hands in towards his body, signaling for the others to come closer.

"You did good George," Sean whispered. He looked at Brad and Brooks. "We're going to spread out along the wall and observe for a while. George, you're with me. Brooks, take Brad that way and find a good observation point."

Brooks punched Brad on the shoulder before he rolled back to the prone and began crawling farther down the stone fence. He moved slowly, making it easy for Brad to stay just behind his heels. They moved beyond the wall and created at least fifty feet of separation from the others before they settled into heavy grass in search of a hide. Brooks lay with his head facing the road and pushed backwards, being careful not to disturb the high grass in front of him.

They crawled back until they found a downed tree. It was large and solid and would provide a safe firing position. Quietly they rolled over the log and into the depression behind it. Brooks pulled a shoulder release on the strap of his pack and let it drop beside him. Brad did the same and settled up next to the large tree trunk. They sat silently listening, trying to adjust to the sounds of their environment, hearing the winds blow through the trees above and behind them. Birds chirped intermittently.

It was still early in the day, maybe late morning. The sun hadn't hit the top of its arch yet. As they sat, they heard the sound of a car engine. It got louder until it seemed to be just below them. The engine stopped and a car door creaked open and slammed shut. They heard the vague sounds of voices on the winds; they couldn't make out the words. There was another noise. A squeaky door opening followed by the slamming shut of another, or possibly the same one.

Brooks tapped Brad and moved his head close. "Okay, let's take a peek," he whispered.

Brad let his rifle lay against the pack, turned over and got his knees beneath him. Slowly he raised up until his head was level with the stump. Then a bit higher until they were above the tall grass. Even with the sounds echoing up, Brad was shocked to see how close they were. He had imagined they were farther away.

The hill gradually fell away from them for maybe thirty feet before it quickly dropped to the ground below. A wide blacktop road ran along the bottom of the hill, traveling left to right. Immediately below them and on the far side of the road sat a large paved parking lot. There was a long steel building located at the back of the lot. It was close, maybe four football fields from their current position.

Several cars were parked in front of the building. Looking to the right you could see the main north/south road. Here a barricade had been positioned. Two police cars painted white with a number of saw horse barriers blocked the road. Behind them sat a parked Canadian Army G-Wagon. The armored military vehicle built on a Mercedes G-class platform was painted in dark olive green holding a mounted machine gun.

They heard a door open and focused on the building across the street. Four men exited, two of them in police uniforms, C7's slung over their shoulders. The other two were in civilian clothing, wearing heavy coats. They all walked towards a car, laughing. The two dressed as civilians entered the car and drove off. The two uniformed men strolled towards the road block. One of them pulled himself to the hood of the G-Wagon and fished a package of cigarettes from his pocket.

The man offered a cigarette to his comrade and they sat quietly, smoking. There were other sounds of a car approaching. The men casually looked up as a larger four-door sedan drove up the road from the left towards the barricade. The uniformed men approached the vehicle and joked with the occupants before lifting the barricade and allowing the vehicle to pass to the south.

"Must be on their way to rape and pillage," Brooks whispered.

A door at the building opened and more men came out. They also laughed and joked, loitering around the parking lot. Most of these new men were also in uniform, but in mixed varieties: police, military, even a couple in firefighters' jackets. They seemed to have no purpose other than to man the barricade. Brad counted eleven of them, all armed with rifles or sidearms.

They watched through the rest of the morning and into the afternoon. Vehicles left and sometimes returned. Late in the day the large four-door sedan returned to the barricade. A man exited the driver's door excitedly. He approached one of the gate guards, laughing. Quickly they talked and two of the guards followed the man to the back of the car. The driver opened the trunk and removed two tied and gagged individuals. They were young, maybe in their teens.

Brad watched them intensely through the scope of his rifle. From their dress he couldn't identify them as male or female, only that they were young and afraid. The driver seemed to be proud of his find. He pushed the kids around in front of him, boasting to the guards before stuffing the two back into the trunk of the car. The driver walked back towards the front of the vehicle and entered the vehicle, slamming the door behind him. The guards lifted the barricade and allowed the sedan to pass through and back down the road to the left.

After a few minutes Sean crawled up on them from down the trail. They got back low behind the log. "I've seen enough, it's time to act," Sean whispered.

"What's the plan?" Brooks asked.

"We're going to ruin their day."

28.

The team rallied back under the cover of the stone wall. Sean sketched a rough layout of the road and buildings on the mud surface of the trail. He placed pebbles along a line that symbolized his men along the ridge, then drew in the intersection and marked X's where the building and barricade sat. "I was really hoping we could hold off, possibly do this tomorrow with a couple more shooters," Sean whispered.

"Then why don't we?" Brad asked.

"No time, these guys have run loose long enough, done too much damage. It's time we let them know that they are not the big dogs anymore. We're going to send a message that the baddest motherfuckers in the valley have arrived, and they have plenty to fear," Sean said.

"How do you propose we make this grand gesture? Without getting ourselves killed?" Jorgensen whispered skeptically.

"Here," Sean whispered back, pointing at the sketch in the dirt. "There are only eleven of them, they aren't tactical, and they mostly cluster in and around this building's entrance. They think they are smart but the fools put themselves in a low spot where two valleys converge. We hold the high ground. Sure, the uphill terrain, the choke point, it all makes sense for holding off primals, but we are going to use it against them tonight. This isn't a video game where they can hit reset and try again. By the time they realize what's going on they'll be bleeding out."

Sean moved the stick across the sketch. "I will be far on the right flank just below you. Brooks, you have far left. Brad, you'll take up a one-man skirmish line all along the wall. Jorgensen, I trust you are handy with that rifle … I'm gonna sit you at the end of the rock wall." Sean pointed his stick at every point where he wanted a man located.

"Brooks, you and I will stay whisper quiet on the flanks. Angels of death. Pop them when nobody is watching. Hit the ones hanging back so the others don't know where the fire is coming from. Shoot to wound."

Brooks squinted at the comment. "Wounding kinda goes against the book, don't it?"

"Not this book. I want to fuck these guys up, leave them wounded and screaming, the more chaos and panic the better.

"George, you have one job, and one job only. I want you to find a tidy little hole in the wall where you can stay in cover, yet still keep your scope on that gun truck by the barricade. Your only responsibility is to kill anyone who tries to get on that gun. No matter what you think may be going on around you, glue your cross hair to that turret, we can't afford to get pinned down.

"Brad, you have the fun work, you will go loud, I want the primals to know there's a party going on. Direct aimed fire from the wall, get their attention and harass them. One to two shots then move, don't pop up twice from the same location. I want these fucktards thinking we have one rookie gunman up here. Let them get cocky and run outside. I want them looking at the wall while Brooks and I put them down.

"Once they are all on the ground, back in cover, licking their wounds, I have a surprise for them," Sean said, pulling two parachute flares from his pack. "These are my last two, you know what happens when they go off."

Brad nodded, "It's a primal dinner bell."

"Exactly. If all goes well, these guys will panic, they will be bloodied and maimed. In no shape to fight. I'm hoping they crawl back to their base with the horde in fast pursuit," Sean said. "These primals are going to make for one hell of a force multiplier. Once the primals come on scene, go quiet, dig in and enjoy the show."

Jorgensen still looked skeptical. "These men, these raiders, they have been here a while. I'm sure they are prepared for the Buhmann. Even if a horde does go to the port, they will know how to fight them."

Sean nodded in agreement. "I'm counting on that. They should have some sort of defense against them by now. I don't want their main camp overrun, or any civilian hostages killed. My hope is the longer we can keep them focused on the Prim— Buhmann, the easier we will find it to get closer to the main camp without being detected.

"Any more questions?" Sean asked.

The men looked down at the crude drawing thoughtfully before looking up and shaking their heads.

"Good, get into position. Brad, you get to light the candles. I want this party kicked off in thirty minutes ... that will be just before sunset when these guys are planning to go silent for the night."

They broke up the huddle. Sean and Brooks crawled off in opposite directions, headed for their assigned flanks. Brad stayed low against the stone wall, allowing the others time to get into position. He had set the timer on his digital watch. He stared as the seconds slowly counted off.

Jorgensen was still on the ground in front of him. He had rolled to his hip and was pulling rounds from his pack, placing them in his coat pocket so he would have easy access to them. Then he began silently moving the rocks in front of him to provide for a concealed firing position. He put his pack in front of him then rested his rifle so that he had a clear view of the G-Wagon's turret.

"You going to be okay with this George? Living men aren't the same as a deer," Brad whispered.

Jorgensen looked back at him. "Friend, I have more regard for a deer than I do those animals down there."

Brad stared at him silently for a moment. "Okay then, good luck," he whispered as he crawled off towards the far end of the wall. He took his time, making sure he made no noise. He didn't want to do anything wrong and blow the assault. As he crawled he felt his heart rate increase. Regardless of how much he tried to relax, it continued to thump.

Even though there was a stiff chill in the air, he began to sweat. He was feeling his muscles twitch; the pre-mission jitters were back. Brad grinned and shook his head. He was back doing what he'd been trained for. To hunt and kill the enemy. It was what he was good at. The men below him would pay a high price for the crimes they had committed in this valley. Brad steeled his mind as he crawled another ten meters, then rolled back against the wall.

He pushed in tight and looked down at his watch: less than three minutes to go. Brad double-checked his weapon. He cautiously pulled the charging handle, just enough so that he could see brass. He let the bolt go forward, then tapped the forward assist the way he had done hundreds of times before. He pushed the magazine release and let the thirty-round mag slide into his gloved hand. He pressed on the top rounds, feeling the resistance, pushing them back with his thumb, ensuring they were properly seated. Thirty-round capacity, but he only loaded twenty-eight, cautious not to put too much strain on the springs. Brad reseated the magazine and pulled down, making sure it was secure.

He checked his watch: sixty seconds. Brad got to his knees and pressed his non-firing shoulder against the wall. He raised his body, bringing his rifle up and over the wall in a fluid motion. It was time to start the ambush. He aimed down range toward the enemy. Quickly his eyes scanned right to left, prioritizing targets. Four men positioned by the barricade, more standing by the parked cars. The distance was long for his M4, but he would get them moving. Brad glanced at his watch.

"Time to say goodnight, boys," Brad whispered as he flipped the selector switch from safe to semi and focused on a man standing just in front of the barricade. He aimed high, above center mass to compensate for the range. He squeezed the trigger and felt the response from the rifle and the sound of the buffer spring doing its work. Brad didn't wait to see if he had a hit. Instead he rolled back to the ground and began crawling further to the left towards Brooks.

He pressed in tight to the wall. He heard

the yelling below, someone shouting orders. The yells were quickly answered by the barely audible clack of Brooks's suppressed rifle. Sporadic gunfire started below, scared men firing rounds off into the tree lines. Then the loud crack of Jorgensen's rifle. Someone must have gone for the mounted gun. Bad move. Panicked shouts, pain-filled screams and calls for help filled the valley floor.

Brad again pushed his shoulder to the wall and popped up. Just in front of the door to the building, three men had run out. Their C7 rifles were up and aiming for the barricade. They hadn't identified the source of the fire yet. A silenced round knocked down the man standing to the left with a hit low to the abdomen. Brad focused on the man in the middle. He had just looked over to watch his comrade stumble. Brad lined up on him and pulled the trigger. Again he dropped and rolled to the ground without confirming his hit. He quickly crawled back to the right towards Jorgensen. When he was within three meters of his friend he popped up again and searched for targets.

Searching left to right, he was finding nothing worth killing. Men were on the ground screaming in agony, having been maimed by the snipers's well-placed shots. Brad continued scanning for threats. Most of the guard force was down and bleeding, some were firing blindly over the barricade, or up at the face of the hill.

An occasional round skipped off the earth high above Brad's head. He saw a man in his peripheral rise from the far side of the G-Wagon. He fired blindly then opened the door of the gun truck.

Brad pivoted in that direction just as the man disappeared into the cab of the vehicle. He watched as the man climbed up into the turret. He went to rack the heavy machine gun, but before he could begin to move the charging handle a loud crack from Jorgensen's rifle dropped him back into the crew compartment.

Brad spotted a man in a policeman's uniform kneeling near a parked car at the far end of the lot. The man appeared to think he was well-hidden, cowering at the corner of the hood. Brad clicked the selector switch another notch and took aim, firing a three-round burst. This time he stayed in position, watching rounds tear through the hood of the vehicle and into his intended target. Brad dropped back to the ground, crawling closer to Jorgensen.

As he moved, he could hear the men's screams intensify, pleading for help. He heard a car engine start followed by a loud *twang, twang* as suppressed rounds tore into the vehicle's engine. The desperation fire from the ground picked up as men fired wildly in all directions, hoping to make the killing stop. Brad was ready to pop up again when he began to hear the first of the primal moans. Instead of rising up he crawled to Jorgensen's position, nestling in behind him.

Bread reached out with his hand and slapped Jorgensen's boot so he would know that he was there. Jorgensen looked back at him. Brad continued crawling until he was alongside him, then Jorgensen took his right arm and slapped Brad on the back. "The Buhmann has arrived," he said, not needing to whisper with the sounds of the sporadic fire from below covering his voice.

Brad slowly lifted his head so that he could see over the wall. As Sean had predicted, the Buhmann and several creepers had responded to the noise. They were coming up the road from the south in force. A wall of creepers had formed and were pouring over the barricade. Occasionally a faster primal would rush through the mob, moaning in rage as it tackled a wounded man. Brad looked down at them, still frightened at seeing them en masse.

The screaming men on the ground hobbled and crawled, fleeing back down the road, headed towards the port and the main camp. Some turned and fought the primals. One made a desperate run for the mounted machine gun, but he was quickly dropped by a suppressed rifle before he cleared half the distance. Brad watched as the man was cut down, his momentum causing him to roll into the waiting hands of the creepers.

The sun's light was fading from the valley. The orange glow of the setting sun blanketed the scene below; bright muzzle flashes from the desperate men threw creepy shadows over the slow-moving mob. Sean's flare popped and launched high in the air, the bright burning light hanging from a parachute. The slow floating star drifting towards the ground infuriated the primals. Brad watched them arch their backs and scream into the night sky. More had surrounded the barricade as they slowly came out of the woods. Alphas that had held back initially now showed themselves, joining the fight.

Brad watched as the primals swarmed over the wounded men, removing limbs and ripping their torsos open. Men that were able, struggled to their feet and tried to run, leaving the more badly wounded behind. Soon the shooting and the last of the screams had stopped. Only the moans remained.

"Where do they all come from?" Brad whispered as he watched hundreds of them pour over the barricade and march towards the port.

"These things are everywhere. Because we do not see them, we assume they are gone. I believe many of them lie dormant in homes, just waiting for a reason to attack, a reason like this," Jorgensen said.

"I won't lie George ... that is some scary

shit."

Brad heard a rustling in the brush and turned in time to see Sean crawling through the high grass, rejoining them at the wall. "Well gentlemen, I would consider that a success."

"So what now?" Brad asked.

"Now we lay low and rest. Let these things pass through the valley and do their thing. Tomorrow after the sun comes up, we push forward," Sean whispered.

29.

The primals flowed through the intersection and down the road towards the port's main camp. As the mass bled through the valley, their broken feet slapped the cold pavement. They would snarl and growl at each other as smaller packs met and mixed together. The snarling and moaning echoed up the walls as they moved down the now dark road. If the team closed their eyes and tried to sleep the sounds worked into their dreams, causing them to be startled awake.

Brad was sitting with his back against the wall, his poncho liner wrapped around his shoulders. Jorgensen was next to him. Jorgensen had pulled a sleeping bag up to his waist but kept his upper body free. Brad searched down the stone wall and could just make out Sean's form guarding the right flank. Brooks was on the other side, leaning with his back to the hill watching forward, keeping vigil over the mob below. Brad tried to mentally plan his escape if the primals somehow made it up the steep hillside.

He would have no place to run but up, back towards the hilltop overlook. He didn't want to think about what would happen if they managed to get behind them, or somehow came at one of the flanks. To be surrounded with no hard shelter would mean death. Those scenarios were not likely. From experience the primals didn't like traveling uphill. That's what had kept the factory and the farms, both located on high ground, safe during the fall. The only exception was when they were in pursuit. If they made contact they would follow until their prey fell, or managed to break away.

As the night slowly dragged on, they began to hear gunfire coming from far down the road. The primals had reached the raiders' main camp. The firing was heavy and steady. The sounds reminded Brad of the prolonged engagements he had heard on deployments to Iraq and Afghanistan. The steady reports of automatic weapons and large caliber rifles were only interrupted by the occasional explosion. Sometimes a scream would reach them carried on the wind. It had become difficult to distinguish between human agony and primal rage.

As dawn approached, the gunfire ceased. Looking towards the coast they could see billowing clouds of black smoke rising above them and blowing to the south. Brad raised up so that he could take in the view below. The road was littered with the dead. Corpses of both the primals and the defenders were intermixed. There were no signs of life in the once-bustling intersection.

The smell of pungent smoke and primal death lingered in the air. Jorgensen was still huddled beside Brad, and both men had wrapped scarves over their noses. Brooks had moved closer once the sun came up; he was now leaning against his pack feasting on an MRE.

Brad looked at him with a scowl. "How can you eat man, with that stink?" he asked.

Brooks shrugged his shoulders as he crammed a mouthful of brisket into his mouth. "Food is fuel, brother," he mumbled after swallowing.

There was a rustling of brush and grass behind them. Both Brooks and Brad went for their weapons as Sean emerged from the thick trees to their rear. He looked up at the men he had startled.

"Sorry fellas, nature called," Sean said. "You guys ready to move out? I haven't seen anything moving in over an hour."

Jorgensen began pulling himself from the bag. "I would like nothing more than to leave this place."

"Good, everyone gather your shit, we'll move out in five. I found a break near the spot I had set up in last night, we should be able to follow it down," Sean said before turning to gather his belongings at the end of the wall.

They quickly got to their feet and organized their equipment. By the time Brad had his pack strapped to his shoulders, Sean was making his way back from his hiding spot. He had his long gun in his hands. He looked them over quickly, then nodded. "Brooks, would you mind hanging back a bit in over watch while we do some recon?"

"Got you covered, Boss," Brooks answered.

Sean moved out, keeping Jorgensen behind him and within arm's reach. Brad let them move a few paces ahead before following them back into the heavy underbrush. It was only a short distance to the path Sean had found. It was narrow, but the cut of the angle made the drop down the face of the hill manageable. Brad took his time navigating the path, not wanting to lose his balance carrying a rifle and the heavy load on his back.

When he reached the bottom, he joined the other two men at the edge of the road. There was a large depression that skirted the shoulder of the road. Sean had gone prone and crawled to the very edge of the pavement. Jorgensen held back and was kneeling in the heavy snow-covered vegetation. Brad turned to look behind him, searching for Brooks. He was nowhere to be found. The man had faded into the hillside. Well hidden, he would be their safety net.

Sean got to his feet, and without looking back raised his hand signaling for the others to move forward. He held his rifle just below his eye, swiveling left to right as he walked directly towards the roadblock. Brad joined them on the road, keeping Jorgensen to his left while he followed, sweeping his barrel to the right and stopping to look behind him every few steps.

Sean posted himself near the left rear panel of the G-Wagon. The turret still held the C6 machine gun, although several attempted gunners lay dead below the mount. When Brad moved towards the back of the vehicle to join the others, Sean gave instructions for them to defend the road while he moved forward to clear the truck.

Brad took up a position on the back right of the truck near the bumper. He held his rifle so that he could observe past the barricade yet still cover Sean as he searched. Sean moved to the front of the G-Wagon and opened the unlocked driver's side doors. He swept inside, clearing the compartment, before moving around the vehicle and opening the passenger doors. He reached inside and grabbed the back of a man's uniform shirt and pulled him out of the vehicle and onto the pavement. He did this twice more before declaring the vehicle clear.

Sean reached down and grabbed a C7 rifle from the road. He locked the bolt to the rear and dropped the magazine. He placed the mag in his drop pouch then tossed the rifle onto the back seat of the truck. "Any rifles you find, clear them and put 'em back here," he said. "Like I promised George, these weapons and this truck

... if it runs ... will go home with you."

George nodded and lifted a rifle lying near his feet. Following Sean's example, he placed it on the rear seat. Brad lowered his weapon and walked around to the front of the truck, looking down the long road towards the parking lot and steel building. "What's next?" he asked.

"Let's search these bodies and check out that structure," Sean said before turning to look at Jorgensen. "George, you hang back, cover the intersection for us."

"Alone?" Jorgensen asked.

"You're not alone, buddy," Sean said, looking up at the hillside.

Sean and Brad patrolled forward. They separated themselves, Sean eight paces ahead on the right side of the road, and Brad on the left. Whenever they approached a body they would halt, one man providing watch while the other searched it for weapons and intel. Most of the dead raiders were found outside, close to the barriers. They were easy to separate from the primals because their bodies had been mauled and torn apart.

Brad found a middle-aged man with a full beard. He was wearing a parka with the camouflage pattern of a Canadian soldier. Brad felt through the man's pockets, careful to avoid bodily fluids. In a shirt pocket he found a small bundle wrapped in a leather cloth. Brad untied it and laid it on the ground. Inside was a red passport with gold writing, several personal photos, and an identification card from what appeared to be a shipping company. Brad lifted the passport and flipped through it before tossing it to Sean.

Sean held the passport in one hand, examining it. "Lithuanian. Guy is a long way from home."

"Aren't we all? What makes a guy like this go bad?" Brad said, looking at the photo of the man in happier times, standing beside a woman holding an infant.

"All about opportunity, he probably had it in him all along," Sean mumbled.

Brad tucked the papers and photos back into the man's parka before rolling over a nearby primal body, a large adult male dressed in a khaki jacket and jeans. He had gaping neck wounds with powder burns on his face. Most of the primals were hit at close range, probably as they rushed their prey with disregard for their own safety. Brad looked at them. A good amount had been taken down, easily a four to one ratio. The raiders had managed to take several primals with them. It was a valiant yet failed effort. The primals had overtaken the men with force, overwhelming them, then ripping them apart. It was hard for Brad to find pity for the men that had died here. They deserved the savage death the primals had brought them.

Sean moved to where the pavement met the snow-covered asphalt parking lot. Several cars were parked in front of the steel building. He waved for Brad to walk forward to join him. Brad finished searching the primal body and walked across the road to Sean. There was a familiar *zip* through the air, followed by a loud *ping*. Brad paused and ducked low, knowing the sound of a high velocity projectile cutting across his path.

Another *zip*, and another *ping*. "Oh shit, targets front!" Sean shouted as he brought up his rifle, firing quick suppressed shots as he stepped back. Sean's 7.62 rounds cut through the advancing primals and pinged against the steel building behind them. From around the far corner of the structure a number of the crazies had shown themselves. Brooks and Sean managed to drop the first few as soon as they came into view, but more had quickly rounded and headed towards the team. "Fuckers must have been held up in the woods," Sean yelled as more of them rounded the corner and began filling the lot.

Now screaming and moaning, they poured from the woods on the right side of the road, moving slowly but picking up speed as they caught sight of the men. Brad raised his rifle, taking quick shots. For every one he knocked down, two more would take its place. He planted his feet and fired rapidly, dropping those closest to him. "I'm dry," Brad yelled, scrambling to reload. He could hear the rapid *zip, zip, zip* of rounds flying over his head, Brooks doing his best to cover them.

"Fall back to the hill!" Sean screamed as he drew his pistol.

Brad took a last look. There were too many, they would be running today, he thought just as the air over his head filled with tracers. Brad dove to the ground, the rapid firing of a heavy machine gun cutting through the primals. Brad looked back over his shoulder and saw that Jorgensen had climbed into the G-Wagon. He had mounted the gun and put it into action, quickly cutting down the creepers. Jorgensen fired until the weapon was dry. Brad lifted his head to survey the damage and saw that the entire herd was now on the ground, dead or dying.

Brad climbed to his feet and jogged towards the G-Wagon. Jorgensen was standing through the roof of the truck. He had replaced a box of linked ammo and was quickly loading another belt of 7.62 rounds into the C6 machine gun. When Jorgensen finished he angled the weapon up in its mount and left the vehicle. "We need to get out of here, more will be coming," Jorgensen yelled as he climbed down from the roof of the vehicle.

Sean approached the G-Wagon from the front and laid his rifle on the hood as he dug through his pack and began reloading magazines. "Nice shooting George, where'd you learn to operate a C6?"

"I'm Danish, mate, we all learn to fight as boys," Jorgensen said.

Brad smiled as he flashed Jorgensen a mock salute. "You never told us you served, George."

"You never bothered to ask, friend," Jorgensen answered.

Sean pointed to the hilltop then waved a finger in the air, signaling for Brooks to join them. Then he opened the front door of the G-Wagon and got in the driver's seat. After a short protest the turbo diesel engine came to life. Sean stayed in the seat until he was sure it was idling soundly, then exited, closing the door behind him. "Well at least something is going our way," he said as he moved back towards Brad and Jorgensen. He saw Brooks enter the road from the heavy vegetation.

"Change of plans, guys," Sean said.

"I'm listening," Brooks said as he joined them by the vehicle.

"George, take the truck and rifles back to the factory. I need you to get volunteers, arm them with these weapons," Sean said, pointing to the back seat that now held several C7 rifles. "Meet up with the rest of my team at the farm, they will have ammo for you."

"Then what?" Jorgensen asked

suspiciously.

Sean moved back to the hood of the truck, signaling for the others to follow him. He pulled a folded map from his thigh pocket and carefully unfolded it. "My guys will lead you out here on foot. Stay out of sight, patrol to the raiders' camp sticking to the left side of the road and keep to the highest ground," Sean said, tracing a route on the map.

Jorgensen shook his head. "I told you before, friend, the men at the factory are not soldiers."

"George, the people that did this shit are not soldiers either," Sean said, pointing to the row of executed bodies lying in a ditch that ran alongside the road. Piles of discarded luggage and belongings were thrown on top of them. "I'm sure if we enter that building we will find more evidence of the things they have done here. It's time to stop hiding behind brick walls and take back what's yours."

"They won't listen," Jorgensen said.

"We're running out of time here, George. Get me what you can. Either way, tell my men to join us where I showed you on the map. I need them there by tomorrow night, before the sun goes down."

"And what will you do until then?" Jorgensen asked.

"We are going to make life miserable for those bastards on the coast. Now go and get me those men," Sean ordered.

30.

They took off at a full jog, wanting to clear the area of the intersection as quickly as possible. Even though Jorgensen had ended the assault with the use of the mounted machine gun, the noise was sure to gather attention. Sean was concerned that more of the raiders may venture up the road looking for survivors of their party, but at a minimum, it would attract more creepers.

Sean led them back up the hill to the stone wall. From there they backtracked to the hilltop overlook. Sean placed the map on the ground and used his compass to quickly orient himself. Brad chugged the contents of a bottle of water and stuffed the empty in his cargo pocket. Sean folded the map and put it back in his thigh packet. He ordered Brad to hold the middle while Brooks took the rear.

They moved fast, avoiding trails now, instead opting for unbroken ground and heavy vegetation. Brad tried to keep track of his pace count as they traveled, trying to estimate the distance. He found it impossible with the way they were constantly having to backtrack and loop around impassable bits of terrain. The elevation increased as they patrolled closer to the coast. Soon they had lost sight of the road below. The ground was steep; the higher they moved the more snow they found.

Most of the snow here was untouched, with only a few animal tracks here and there. After several hours of marching, Sean moved them into a bunching of tall pine trees. The smoke had gotten thicker here. Whatever was burning at the raiders' camp had not been extinguished. Sean pulled away several large branches from a fat pine, making a hollow space beneath it. The men crowded in and dropped their packs. Sean immediately went for the map, trying to estimate their position relative to the coast.

"I plot the camp to be a mile east of here," Sean whispered. "The road twists around and should run right into it."

Sean had the map laid out on the ground in front of them. He pointed to where he thought their current position was. Sliding his finger, he showed how the terrain would peak, then drop sharply to the road below and eventually the coastline. The camp, if Jorgensen was correct, would be in the vicinity of a small coastal village. The map identified a small marina built up in a natural harbor. Surrounded by cliffs, and sheltered by the water, it would be a suitable position to hold off the primals.

"They would have ..." Sean grinned, "should have heard the gunfire earlier. That should give suspicions that someone is out here. Hopefully they think some of their buddies survived last night."

"Hopefully?" Brad asked.

"Anything that keeps them looking for us," Brooks added.

Sean folded the map and placed it back in his pocket. "Exactly. From here on out we go slow and quiet. I want to get eyes on that encampment before mid-day." He moved his pack towards the trunk of the tree and dug out a can of kidney beans and a small can opener. "Get some chow, we'll be moving in thirty."

Brad pushed his pack in front of him and sat back on crossed legs. He found one of the last of his MRE packets and stared at, debating if he should eat it now, or save it. "Dig in buddy, never know when you'll have another chance," Brooks whispered to him.

Brad looked at Brooks knowingly and pulled the tab at the top of the foil package. He had lost his MRE spoon so he squeezed the cold mix directly into his mouth. "Food is fuel," he said to Brooks, trying not to laugh. He ate as quickly as he could, then finished off the mix with a bottle of water. Then he took his time refilling the bottle with snow, slowly packing it into the plastic container before placing the bottle back into his pack.

"How we looking on ammo, guys?" Sean whispered.

Brooks pulled a flap on the front of his vest, showing two empty mags for his MP5.

"I've been short of 9mm since we got here. Still have a couple hundred or so for the M14, got a brick of .22 and three mags of .45."

Brad checked the pouches on his vest, then reached into a cargo pocket on his pack. He had two fifty-round boxes of 9mm rounds and six full magazines. He took the boxes from his pack and set them on the ground in front of him. "I'm just short of a combat load for the M4, probably got another hundred or so in a bandoleer in my pack. Six M9 mags, two more on my belt, one in the gun and another in the sigma. Brooks, take these boxes, I'm heavy on 9."

"I'll take one of those boxes if you don't mind," Sean said. "I'm under on MP5 myself. I was able to scrounge up some feed for my long gun at the farm. I'm light on handgun. Brooks, you mind consolidating and splitting .45 and .22 with me?"

Brad packed away his gear as he waited for Sean and Brooks to split their ammo and load magazines. He buried his empty MRE pouch under the pine needles, then hefted his pack to his shoulders. "I'm going to take a leak, guys," he whispered before stepping out of the cover of the tree. He walked only a few paces and relieved himself on some brush. Brad looked around him. They were in the middle of a high country pine forest. There were patches of snow everywhere but the ground was not entirely covered.

He looked up at the blue sky. They had been lucky, since the storm that brought them here the weather had been favorable. Brad lifted his rifle to use the optics to check their back trail. The ground was rough and uneven; heavy boulders and rock formations were scattered in all directions. Brad turned as Brooks and Sean exited the base of the tree. Sean lifted his pack and swung it over his shoulders. "Brad, you hang back with me, Brooks will have point now," Sean whispered.

Brooks finished putting freshly filled mags in the front of his tactical vest, then lifted his own pack. He looked back at them and nodded, turned forward and began slowly stalking the ground in front of them. Sean let Brooks get a good twenty paces before he tapped Brad on the shoulder. Brad stepped off, mimicking the SEAL's movements, walking slowly and trying to maintain his distance from Brooks. Sean followed closer behind him. As they moved he slowly stepped off to his right, keeping his weapon pointed in the direction where the road should be.

They kept an extremely slow pace. Brooks stopped often, taking a knee or sometimes dropping into the prone before crawling next to a tree trunk. Every time Brooks stopped, Brad would slowly lower himself to a knee. If they were halted more than thirty seconds, Brad would drop to his belly and try and take up a hasty fighting position while he waited for Brooks to signal the all clear. As they got closer to the coast, the smoke got thicker and they could occasionally hear the clanging of metal on metal.

Brad felt the tension rise in his body the closer he got to the encampment. He squeezed the pistol grip of his M4, his thumb constantly checking the selector switch, making sure his rifle was on safe. Brooks's hand shot into the air as he dropped down and out of sight. Brad paused and lowered himself behind a large downed tree. He glanced off to his right and saw that Sean had also taken efforts to conceal himself. Brad looked forward with his rifle pointed off and to the left, occasionally looking behind him to make sure they weren't being followed.

He watched Brooks rise up and signal for them to move forward before dropping back to a kneeling position. Brad let Sean cross in front of him, then he got to his own feet and followed him forward. Sean stepped slowly till he was alongside Brooks, then dropped in next to him. Brad took up a kneeling position just behind them, facing to the rear with his profile hidden by a tree. Brooks pointed to a break in the trees ahead. In the distance Brad could see the ocean through openings in the thick black smoke.

Sean whispered for them to drop their packs and low crawl forward. It was unlikely that they would be seen high in their current position, but they had traveled too far to get sloppy. They hid their gear under the branches of a thick bush. Sean led the way with the others close behind. It didn't take long for them to reach a high vantage point. They were now on a high peak with the terrain around them swiftly dropping towards the coast.

They were still over a hundred yards from the cliffs that were indicated on the maps. Brad crawled in close behind Sean and Brooks, then crept up alongside them. The sun was bright and there was a clear blue sky. The black smoke was still rising in plumes that were barely moving on the calm winds. From his position Brad could now clearly see the ocean and the opening of the harbor. The land formed a natural bay with high ground on all sides.

Even though Brad couldn't see it from his current position, it was obvious the road must spill into this bay. Sean signaled for them to move forward so they could get a better view of the village below. Carefully they began sliding forward on their bellies, leaving the cover of the thick trees. As they moved closer the village and harbor slowly came into view. It wasn't much of a harbor as the map depicted it, it should be described as more of a bay, or even a cove. The cliffs wrapped the terrain securely leaving a small strip of land along a narrow coastline.

There was one street traveling along the

shoreline with several buildings lining it. The ocean side of the street was bare and gradually went down to the waterline. The shore was littered with remnants of old fishing vessels and smaller sailboats. Farther out to sea sat a flotilla of larger vessels, half a dozen freighters and a couple of smaller boats. At least one was marked in red and white, possibly Coast Guard. Off to the right down the beach they could see the makings of an ancient pier. A breakwater really, it traveled out into the sea and formed a right angle running parallel to the village street.

"You can see why the Canadian Coasties would have directed the merchant ships here. This sheltered cove, one channel in by sea and one road out by land. Coast Guard and local authorities would have had an easy time of keeping an eye on them," Brooks whispered.

"Did the boys a favor, gave them prime terrain for survival, nice beachhead position at the end of a valley run. High ground on all sides, probably saved their worthless lives," Sean grunted. "Until now anyway, because that wall ain't keeping us out."

The people had built a rudimentary barricade from the shells of boats, cars, and earth. There was a bright yellow bulldozer sitting behind a large earthen berm. Along the outside face of the berm burnt a bright orange and black fire. "There's the source of the black smoke," Sean whispered.

"That was smart of them, if they get rushed, ignite the tires ... look at the burnt bodies, must have had a hell of a primal BBQ last night," Brooks responded. "Way this valley backs up, and the bottle neck here at the end ... I can just see them. The primals, bunching up on those burning tires, the crazies in the back pushing the ones up front into the flames." Brooks sat staring at the fire for a moment before closing his eyes and shaking his head.

Brad stretched to see the burning barrier. It was at fifteen feet high and fifty feet wide and ran hundreds of yards, entirely choking the road that ran through the valley. "Where the hell would they get so many tires?"

"Looking at what's down there, I'm guessing one of those boats must be full of 'em, the pile there looks to be made up of brand new rubber," Sean said as he ran his spotting scope across the village. "Here, have a look," he said, handing the scope to Brad.

Brad took the glass from Sean and let his eye adjust to the magnification. Aiming towards the barricade, he could see the bright burning flames. Parts of primal bodies were scattered all along the barricade. As Brad looked closer he could see a small work party lifting bodies and throwing them into the fire. The men doing the work were being closely observed by a pair of men with rifles. Whoever they were, they were efficient against the primals. There were piles of them on the road being fed into the flames.

Brad looked beyond the barricade and saw a group of women rolling more tires towards an already high stack. Just as Sean had said, the tires looked new, some still with white stickers on their sides. Brad followed the trail of people back towards the end of a pier where they were unloading tires and other equipment from a smaller boat under the supervision of armed men. More uniformed raiders walked about casually with rifles in their hands, while others sat huddled together on the ground. Brad watched as a guard with a rifle approached a man sitting on a container. The guard quickly punched him in the back of the head, causing the man to collapse to the ground. The man with the rifle then turned to another guard and leaned back, roaring with laughter.

"What the hell is going on down there?" Brad asked, handing back the scope.

Brooks lowered his binoculars, having seen enough. "Looks like some sort of prison camp, or slaves. That red and white ship out there looks to be Coast Guard. I bet I could get it running."

"Yeah I saw that too. It's a solid option, get that operational we could take it all the way to Boston," Sean said.

"What about the camp, how do we get past them?" Brad asked.

"Hmm, I figure we will get to softening

them up pretty soon here, let's move back up top," Sean answered.

31.

Sean moved them farther into the thick woods. As before, they moved the inner limbs of a large pine tree, making shelter beneath of it. Once inside the thick cover of the pine boughs, Brad got a false sense of security. The thick bed of needles and soft earth padded the ground under his bed roll. They made an early camp, trying to rest up for what would make out to be another long night.

Brad had the first watch. His pack was pressed against the trunk of the tree. He was leaning against it with his poncho liner around his legs. Sean was behind him with Brooks just to his left. His two friends were in similar positions, sleeping soundly in the shelter of the tree. It wasn't much of a watch, as there was little Brad could see, but the longer they sat the noisier the surrounding woods became.

He picked up on the subtle sounds of wind in the trees. Looking up he could see the gentle sway of the limbs far above him. Birds chirped in the distance, and the branches of trees clacked together. He heard the crashing of dry leaves. The sound at first startled him, but concentrating and ducking his head Brad was able to locate the source of the noise. A pair of red foxes were jumping and wrestling in the thick leaves. He adjusted his position for a better view and allowed the pair to entertain him. The sight of the wild life relaxed him; he knew that the foxes wouldn't let their guard down in the presence of danger.

Brooks lifted his head and looked at his watch. Brad watched him sleepily dig through his pack for a bottle of water and drink thirstily. He looked to Brad and pointed at his watch, indicating that he was taking the watch. Brad nodded and looked back ahead towards the pair of foxes. He pulled his fleece skull cap down over his eyes and rested his head against the tree. Pulling in his knees and wrapping himself tightly in the poncho liner, he relaxed to the sounds of the wind. It was hard to imagine it was the end of the world here in the lively forest. He closed his eyes and easily found sleep.

He woke to the sounds of Brooks and Sean crawling out of the cover of the tree. It was nearly dusk, the blue sky having transformed into shades of orange and purple. Brad saw that the others had left their large packs, so he stuffed his bedding into the top of his rucksack and followed them out into the open. Sean and Brooks were positioned just feet apart laying still and listening to the surrounds. When they were convinced they were still alone in the forest, Sean got to his feet and moved back towards the tree.

Brooks joined them but kept his face

towards the open woods as he listened. Sean pulled his map from his pocket and turned it over to the clean white back. With a black felt tip pen he quickly sketched out the encampment and sheltered cove from memory. Then he drew a line representing the valley and the roads, and finally added a dashed line representing the path they had taken to get to this point. He sat the finished sketch on the ground in front of him.

"How are you all doing on juice for your NVGs?" he asked them quietly.

"I have plenty," Brad whispered back. Brooks nodded his head in agreement.

"Good, we're doing some night hunting, you'll need them," Sean said.

Sean told them to pack light, only their weapons and essential gear. They would be doing a movement to contact tonight. His plan was to take out the night guards; he wanted to let the raiders know they were no longer alone, and that the primals should be the least of their concerns. He wanted the camp's defenses in disarray. He wanted them on the defensive and locked down or all dead by the time his men arrived on the following night.

"But won't that make them harder to attack, losing the surprise I mean?" Brad asked.

Sean looked at Brad, then at Brooks who grinned. "We aren't attacking anyone."

Brad gave him a puzzled look. "I don't

understand."

Brooks put his finger on the map. "We don't have to attack. We hold the high ground, we can toy with them for days if that's what it takes. Why risk our people for a frontal attack against a dug-in force? And besides, we have friends on the ground," he said, smiling.

Sean nodded. "Either way the raiders will not leave this cove."

Brad still looked at them with a confused expression. Sean smiled and slapped him on the shoulder. "Don't worry brother, you'll catch up as it all comes together. Let's move back to the cliffs."

Sean led them back to their hide at the edge of the cliffs above the village. The fires were all but out now, just a trail of smoke as the ring of tires and bodies cooled. The sun had completely fallen now, leaving the camp in darkness. Brad looked around. Even with the full moon his team was completely hidden in the tall grass on the incline above the cliff's face. Looking out into the cove he could see dim navigation lights on the vessels anchored and tied together. Below, people were still moving about. He saw a set of guards walking the perimeter, and another man was standing at a high spot atop the berm wall.

Brad searched the street front and the surrounding buildings. A few had small leaks of light coming through thick drapes. Most though had been completely blacked out. He saw a row of aged and rusted shipping containers. There were people sitting on the ground in front of them around a small fire. Brad focused on the group, watching their movements. He saw a woman venture out of the container, holding an infant child. She walked near the fire and a man stood, handing her a container he had filled from a larger pot on the fire.

Brad watched as the roving guards made their way past the containers. He could hear them shouting, kicking dirt and gravel on the fire as they rushed the prisoners into the containers. One of the prisoners appeared to argue with them. This man was grabbed by his shirt collar and pulled to the ground as the others were locked into the container. The defiant prisoner made to stand but was quickly struck in the head with the stock of a rifle, then dragged across the gravel to a large ship's mast where his hands were bound to it. Brad watched as the guards laughed, leaving the beaten prisoner unconscious and tied to the pole.

"I think we found volunteers for tonight's activities," Sean whispered.

Brad looked up from his scope and realized Sean and Brooks had watched the same scene unfold. "What do you need me to do?" Brad whispered with a hint of anger in his voice.

"Just stay put and observe, Brooks and I will do the dirty work tonight. We are going to have to get in close so don't expect us back for a while," Sean whispered.

"I can do that," Brad answered, not turning to look.

"If things go south on us, and I mean really sideway, fire off a mag then pop this and move out," Sean whispered, putting the last remaining flare in Brad's hand. "We should be back here before dawn. If not, wait for us at the hide. If we don't make it there by late afternoon, meet up with the others and fall back to the barricade."

"Then what?" Brad asked.

"Whatever you want, 'cause you'll be in charge if you don't see us by then," Sean chuckled.

"You sure about this plan, Chief?"

Sean nodded and shot Brad a thumbs up. He looked to Brooks who had his goggles down over his eyes. Sean made the motion of a man walking with his fingers and Brooks began crawling in the direction of the valley road, moving parallel to the cliff face. "Remember Brad, only use the flare if all hell breaks loose, controlled chaos is still in our favor," Sean whispered as he turned and crawled after Brooks.

Brad sat still, watching the others fade from his view. He was alone on the incline now. He looked around, trying to find a better position, something with more cover. Just to the left of him the ground was more broken and elevated. He could see where a tree had come down and fallen into the clearing, its large root ball upheaved and exposed. Brad slowly crept for the space. The trunk was weathered and stripped of bark, the vegetation long gone. He found a spot where he could rest in cover yet still have an expansive view of the encampment.

Brad flipped up the night vision from his eyes to allow them to adjust to the moonlight. He checked his rifle's optics and powered up the scope. After doing a quick scan of his surroundings, he shut off the device and let the barrel of his rifle rest against the tree trunk. Brad removed his assault pack and let it rest on the ground behind him. He settled in, pushing his back against the trunk, getting into a body position where he could make minimal movements but still have an expansive view.

As his eyes adjusted he could see more activity in the camp. More men moved around in the dark without the aid of lights. A guard quietly paced the pier that led out to the moored boat. Brad watched as more men walked towards a makeshift latrine. One man held rifles and lit a cigarette as another entered the latrine. Even though they were amateurs, Brad was impressed at their organization. Being sailors probably helped, they would already be used to splitting work and performing various watches. Being commercial sailors they'd probably had military experience as well.

Brad watched the man come out of the latrine. He took the rifles from the first man and lit a cigarette of his own, using his partner's. The now empty-handed man turned and walked into the latrine. Brad watched the second man sling one of the rifles over his back and put another over his shoulder. He then walked farther away before leaning against an old battered fiberglass boat. He reached into his pocket, searching for something. Brad saw him pull out a white folded paper.

A distant *crack* filled the air. Not as loud as an unsuppressed gunshot, but louder than a slamming door. Brad quickly scanned the area then back to the man by the fiberglass boat. The man had slumped over, still leaning against the boat, the paper fallen from his hands. The first man walked from the latrine and looked around. Seeing his friend against the boats, he threw his hands in the air in an exaggerated expression as he walked towards him, smiling. The man moved three paces, then another *crack*. Brad watched as the guard's leg lifted to move forward. The man froze then collapsed heavily to the ground.

Once it started, things happened fast. Brad scanned the surroundings, trying to keep pace with his shooters. *Crack*. He looked left and right, and saw the pair still roving the perimeter, another still pacing the pier. Brad turned and looked far to his right with his binoculars where the guard had been atop the berm. He was gone now. Brad searched again. He could see the second guard still standing below the barrier on the inside. *Crack.* The barrier guard fell forward, hitting the hard ground. Brad looked back to the top of the berm and saw that the top guard was in fact down, he had fallen and rolled down the barrier near the smoldering ring of burnt tires.

Brad turned back, searching for the roving guards. They had paused and were looking around, having finally taken notice of the suppressed gunshots. The guards lifted their heads, intently listening but hearing nothing. They seemed to joke and one of them pointed off to the center of the camp where they had bound the prisoner. They stepped off, walking towards the mast at a brisk pace. As they neared, a guard stopped and picked up a rock, tossing it at the man. Brad watched the bound man struggle and kick his feet towards them.

In the silence of the night, he could just make out their voices. Not the words but the exchange of angry tones. One of the guards picked up another stone and threw it at the prisoner, this time causing the bound man to cry out. The guards laughed, one handing the other his rifle as he reached down to gather another stone. *Crack.* Brad watched as a round tore through the chest of the guard holding the rifles; he fell sideways, spinning as he dropped at the feet of the bound man. The second guard dropped the stones and jumped back to his feet.

He looked down at his dead comrade, the weapons within reach of the bound prisoner. The guard took a hasty step forward, reaching for a rifle. *Crack*. The guard's neck exploded, spraying the prisoner with a mist of fluids. The prisoner covered his face with his free hand then slowly lowered it, searching in all directions. He used his feet to grab and drag a dead guard closer to himself. Brad watched as he dug a knife from the guard's pocket and cut his bindings. With his hands free, he stood looking in all directions. He lifted a rifle from the dead guard, then took another in his free hand.

He crouched and ran towards the shipping containers. He dropped the rifles at his feet, lifted a metal latch and swung the door open with a metallic screech. The man stooped to retrieve the rifles then disappeared inside. After a tense moment the man came back into the moonlight with a second man by his side. They stepped out and ran back towards the ship's mast. The prisoner showed the new man the bodies of the guards, then held up a finger and pointed to the hillsides.

A light shone across the rocky beach as a door opened on one of the wooden buildings that ran along the street. Brad couldn't see the front of the building from his vantage point, but knew something was happening by the way the prisoners crouched down and took cover behind the mast. Someone called out but the men stayed hidden behind the mast. There was more shouting and the man that had been patrolling the pier took notice. The pier guard started moving in the direction of the building.

The prisoners on the ground slowly stood with the rifles in their arms, just as the man from the building hurriedly walked into Brad's view. He was pointing and yelling, still trying to figure out what was happening. When he saw the bodies of the fallen guards he froze and attempted to pull a holstered pistol. It was too late. The raider's forward movement towards the prisoner had taken him out of the blind spot provided by the building and back into the SEALs' line of sight. *Crack*. The man froze and fell into the dirt. This time the shot did not go unnoticed; the man from the pier lifted his rifle to fire on the prisoners. *Crack*. The pier guard spun around, firing a blind, unsuppressed shot off into the gravel as he dropped.

Lights came on in the row of buildings below. The prisoners were caught and trapped in the open. Men moved out into the street. Brad could clearly see them, but they were far out of range for his rifle. A bright flashlight shone across the gravel beach, lighting the faces of the prisoners. The light moved past the body of the dead men. The light stopped on the man. *Crack*. The light dropped to the surface of the road and rolled.

The prisoners raised their rifles and fired at the men wildly, muzzle flashes lighting them in a strobe. The guards fired back. Brad watched a prisoner fall with hits to the chest. Brad raised his rifle and considered firing. Knowing it was unlikely he would hit the guards at the extended range, he took his finger from the trigger. Brooks's and Sean's fire intensified, giving the remaining prisoner an opportunity to run back to the cover of the containers.

Men yelled in panic on the ground. Some ran back towards the buildings. Others mistakenly ran towards the body of the man with the pistol. Three guards all armed with long rifles ran directly to the downed man and rolled him over, seeing the blood on his shirt. A man turned to look up at the hillside ... *Crack*. The man's head snapped back. His comrades dropped onto the stony surface of the beach. One crawled behind a body, using it for cover as he squeezed off several shots into the night.

The man fired, pivoting to change directions as he swept the hillside. The man's gunfire provided cover for the suppressed round that took off the top of his head. The remaining member of the trio, seeing his two friends killed, tried to run back to the shelter of the building. As he sprinted there was another *crack*. The man fell with a round through his pelvis, causing him to tumble and roll to the surface of the street.

The man screamed and called out for help, the foreign words now easily reaching Brad's ears.

No one came for him. The man continued to scream. He finally rolled to his stomach and began to crawl towards the building. *Crack.* The man's elbow exploded and he rolled to his back, screaming in agony. The man rolled again, screaming, pleading for help. No one came for him. *Crack.* The man's head snapped back, silencing him.

Yelling and shouting for orders came from the row of buildings. A ship in the harbor blasted its horn loudly. Brad looked out into the bay and watched as the ship flashed its navigation lights. Probably sending some sort of prearranged signal. A door opened at the rear of one of the buildings. Four men crept out of a back door and along a wooden boardwalk, moving to the end of the long row of buildings. The man in the lead stopped at the corner. He turned back to face the men behind him, whispering instructions.

Crack. A round ripped through the forehead of the leader and into the face of the man in front of him. The remaining men fired their rifles in panic, again at the hillside in all directions, not able to determine the direction of the enemy. A man jerked into a wall as he dropped his weapon and reached for his shoulder. The final man took a hit high in the chest and fell to the boardwalk. The man with

the shoulder wound stood silently, holding his upper arm and looking up at the hill. He held his good hand over his head as if to surrender.
Crack.

The ship in the bay blasted its horn again and flashed its lights. A spotlight came on, searching the water and trying to reach the coast. A small boat began approaching with a smaller spotlight of its own searching the pier and shoreline. Brad watched as the prisoner broke cover from the container; he opened the door, shouting inside. A group of three women and two men stepped out. They followed the armed prisoners, running towards the pier. One of the women stopped, seeing the dead man near the fiberglass boat. She saw the rifles and lifted them, taking one and handing off the other. They ran past the dead pier guard, also stripping him of his weapon before dropping behind a large stack of car tires near the pier.

Brad watched them squat behind the tires as the small boat drew closer. It headed directly for the pier, sweeping its spotlight across the water and the pier. The boat stopped forward movement as it bobbed in the water, its engine still idling softly. Two men were on the bow, both holding assault rifles. At least one more was in the cabin at the controls while another was on the stern manning the spotlight. The light panned from the end of the pier to the beach then completely down the shoreline.

The large ship in the water gave a blast of its horn, and the small boat replied with a blast of its own. The boat's engine changed pitch as it rode closer to the pier with its bow pointed towards the shore. When it was within a hundred feet, the motor again idled and the boat bobbed in the water. A man on the bow of the ship called out several times. After getting no reply, he moved back towards the cabin and leaned into an open window. He returned with a set of binoculars.

The man on the forward deck searched the shoreline with the binoculars. The spotlight continued to search the pier and beach as the boat slowly drifted towards the shore. There was a single unsuppressed gunshot as the cabin window exploded, dropping the man at the controls. Energized by the sound of the shot, the prisoners behind the tires rose up and unleashed a salvo at the small boat. Most of the rounds went wide or fell short, but the wild shots and noise provided more cover for the snipers on the hillside. In quick succession the man at the spotlight and the one with the binos fell into the water.

As the remaining man ran back towards the cabin, the prisoners found their aim and fired rapidly, rounds tearing into him, knocking him into the water. The prisoners cheered before being hushed by one of them, then dropped back into cover. There was another loud blast from the ship's horn. This time the blast wasn't answered as the small boat drifted towards the shore. The ship let out a long blast, again with no response. The small boat bounced then slapped against the pier.

A male prisoner looked over the tires, then got to his feet and ran down the pier followed by a woman. The man slowed as he approached the bouncing boat. He tried to visually inspect the vessel then took a running start as he leapt to the rear deck. The man disappeared into the cabin. The engine cut off and the man returned and tossed a length of line to the female. The woman pulled the boat in close to the pier and tied it off. The man ran to the bow and jumped back to the pier before pulling in and securing the front of the craft.

When the small boat was secure, the pair ran back, joining the others at the tires. Brad watched as they hugged each other and shook hands. Brad lifted his binoculars and again searched the entire area. Slowly he watched more people leave the confines of the containers. Most just huddled around the entrance, afraid to move any further. Some walked completely out, and the prisoners by the tires, spotting them, moved in their direction.

The large ship blasted its horn over and over, not getting a response from the shore. The prisoners seemed to ignore the horn now, overwhelmed with their new freedom. A few of them walked towards the row of buildings carrying rifles. Brad heard doors open and close and an occasional gunshot as they entered and cleared building after building. They relit the fire on the beach and huddled around it. People brought containers of food from the buildings and cooked it over the fire.

Brad watched as children left the confines of the container and joined the others. He heard a noise behind him and searched the top of the cliff. Seeing nothing, he dropped his night vision over his eyes and continued to search the hill and the tree line. He saw a bright IR strobe. Brad reached up to his own goggles and switched his IR headlight on and off. He watched as Sean and Brooks came into view and walked across the incline towards him. Brad got to his feet and walked to join his friends.

32.

They spent the rest of the night in the high position guarding the civilians below. Sean was concerned primals may make their way up the road drawn in by the gunfire, but they never came. The cove was indeed sheltered and secluded. Brad stayed in over watch on the cliff as Brooks and Sean retrieved their rucksacks. Even though they weren't ready to approach the civilians, they didn't want to take their eyes off of them.

They had retrieved their heavy packs under the cover of darkness and returned to the sides of the cliff. It was still predawn but there was plenty of activity on the beach. Brad sat and observed the people below. The ship blasted its horn several more times, causing the trio to look up. The ship now had all of its navigation lights and spotlights on.

"Might as well give up on that shit," Brooks said as he sat back against his pack, eating a tin of fruit. "Ain't nobody gonna reply to that horn."

"We going down there?" Brad asked.

Sean looked up from his breakfast, "Yeah, as soon as the sun comes up. I don't want to spook anyone and get shot in the dark."

The freighter's horn blared long and

steady, giving a solid blast. The freighter began to drift, then moved backwards and farther away.

"Something's happening," Brooks said, lifting his binoculars to look at the freighter. "Looks like they're pulling anchor."

"What about that ship? Do we go after it?" Brad said.

"It'll work itself out," Sean said, finishing his meal. "Looks like they all took to the single freighter, I never saw movement on the other vessels."

"Yeah, me either," Brooks added. "By my count we brought down twenty last night, and another ten or so at the roadblock. Who knows what kind of damage the primals did to 'em."

Sean stood, straightening his jacket. "Yeah, we will have to see what answers the civilians can give us. To be honest, I'm happy not having to take down a freighter with just the three of us."

He stood and prepared his pack as the first glimpses of the sun peeked out over the water. Brad and Brooks took cues off what he was doing and readied their own gear. They put on their packs and walked closer to the cliff's face. Looking down, they could see that more of the civilians were up and moving around now. They had stacked the dead guards in a row along the street. Others were moving around the small boat, searching it and removing gear.

"Figure it's time to say hello," Sean said.

He walked closer to the cliff face and cupped his hands around his mouth before letting out a loud yell. At first no one noticed so he tried again, this time getting the attention of a group of children standing near the buildings. They ran excitedly towards the beach, grabbing a man by the arm then pointing towards the cliffs. Sean raised his hands in the air and waved them. The man on the ground waved back and signaled for them to come down.

"Okay guys, follow me. We'll follow the same path as last night, just be careful around these folks, they might be skittish," Sean said as he stepped off, walking in the direction of the valley road. Walking upright and casually it took them less than thirty minutes to reach the valley that sloped down to the road. The valley was steep, but there was plenty of evidence of people having hiked these hills in the past.

They followed a steep broken dirt path down, grabbing trees and vegetation often so that they didn't fall. As they got closer, the stench overwhelmed them. Brad stepped into a trench that skirted the road, then onto the paved surface itself. Looking left and right, he could see that the road was still littered with bloated primals' bodies. He stepped over one and into the middle of the road. Sean and Brooks moved up beside him. "They need to do something about this, gonna fuck up property values," Sean said, looking disgusted.

"Yeah, it was your idea to send the horde after them two nights ago," Brooks said.

Sean grunted. "Point taken, but it did its job. And on the plus side, I bet this attack cut down on the numbers in the area."

Brooks stopped and looked up and down the road, "Yeah, enough here to make up a small town. So much death," he said, shaking his head sadly.

"They were already dead, this just put them to rest," Sean said, looking at the decaying corpses. "Okay fellas, weapons down and follow me, let's make ourselves known," he ordered.

The trio walked in line, arm's length apart as they rounded a bend in the road. As they got closer to the berm, the primal bodies thinned out. Brad could see drag marks where the bodies had been moved and thrown into fires. He had witnessed that on the first day of their arrival. He looked at the top of the earthen barrier and could see that it was now lined with the civilians. A man Brad recognized as the one who had been beaten and tied to the mast came forward and walked down the barrier through a break in the tire wall.

He was armed as the others but his rifle was slung over his shoulder. Sean stopped and the others stopped with him. They waited for the civilian to approach them. As he got closer, Sean waved but the man's face remained stone solid.

He gave no indication whether he was friend or foe. The stranger stopped a good ten paces away and looked at them apprehensively.

"You the ones that helped us last night?" the man asked.

Sean smiled and stepped forward with his hand extended. "Sean Rogers, U.S. Navy, or used to be," he said, introducing himself.

The man gave Sean a puzzled look and Sean lowered his hand. "Were you expecting someone else, friend?"

The man looked at Brad, then at Brooks before turning back to Sean. "Where are the rest?" he said in a confused voice.

"Don't worry pal, there are more of us, they'll be here tonight."

The man smiled then closed the distance and extended his own hand, shaking Sean's. "I'm sorry, so much has happened. Please, please, come and meet the rest of us."

The man introduced himself as Johnathon. He wasn't from the area. He and his wife had been taken at the roadblock. It was rare for the raiders to take men, but they had manual labor to do that day and he got lucky, if you could call it that. Johnathon had been at the camp for over three weeks. He had lost count after they started locking them in the containers at night. That was where he had spent days and nights locked away with his wife and infant child. Johnathon guided them through the barriers and over the berm where they were quickly greeted and welcomed by the other survivors.

Brad was grabbed and hugged deeply by a man and a woman, and several children grabbed at his jacket sleeves and pants. Quickly they were guided across the stony beach and to the small fire pit near the shipping containers. They were ushered to sit and eat. Men were preparing more food on the fire. Johnathon explained how they had been nearly starved by their captors. Their keepers had plenty of food but rarely shared it with them.

"Who were they?" Brad asked as he was served a bowl of stew filled with bits of thick vegetables and seafood.

"They came from all over, but most of them came from that ship, the one that left." Johnathon spit and gave a sour look as he stared where the large freighter had been.

A woman who had remained silent now stepped forward towards the fire. "Eastern Europe but mostly Russian, one of them … Mika," she said, causing others to shake their heads and look towards the pile of bodies. "Yes, Mika, he talked of home often, he was the devil."

Johnathon looked to the woman, then back to Brad and the others. "Mika was one of the worst, not the leader, but he acted like it."

"How many are left?" Sean asked.

Johnathon answered. "Not many now …

less than five. The captain and his officers rarely left the ship. At one time there were twice as many sailors, but they didn't all agree with the way Mika's crew had taken over, especially with the killing. Some ships left after the Coast Guard vanished, other crews were murdered."

"Wait ... what about the Coast Guard, what do you mean vanished?" Brooks asked.

Johnathon looked over his shoulder at the Coast Guard ship. "They were gone long before I arrived."

The woman spoke again, "Mika's men killed them, the Coast Guard sailors."

"I'm sorry," Johnathon said. "This is Jane, she is from here, the village, she has been here since the beginning."

Sean nodded to her. "Jane, what do you know about them?"

"It doesn't matter who they were now. They were brought here when the quarantines started. The Coast Guard put their boats in a row and left them there. Men from the government arrived. They built a road block, it was small at first. They just wanted to keep people away from the village, keep them from seeing the boats.

"When the attacks started most of the policemen and military went up the valley to defend the other roadblocks. Things got worse. Some of those people, the sick ones, managed to get by them, to get this far. They attacked the village. Mika and his men, they saved us. We thought. They came forward with the Coast Guard captain. They cleared out the village, the beach, and built the berm. Mika's ship had tires and mechanical stuff for the barricade, others had food.

"Mika ... he wanted more, he wanted to leave the village and move up the road. The Coast Guard had orders to hold the village. They argued over it for several days. In the meantime we could hear the fighting from the valley, the shooting. Occasionally a creature would manage to make it to our barrier. But Mika's people always dealt with them.

"One morning the Coast Guard was gone. Mika said they left, but no one believed him. Mika and his people started going up the road. They would return with vehicles, new weapons. They started wearing uniforms. Then ..." Jane paused and looked down. Another woman moved and sat beside her.

Jane looked back up at Sean and the others. "Mika's men returned with several new people, captives. Women, and young girls ... they did things to them. The other sailors argued, they confronted Mika. But he was too strong by then, he killed them, anyone who disagreed. He killed my husband and most of the villagers, sparing only a select few of us. He imprisoned us, worked us, and discarded us when we failed to obey," Jane's voice began to break as she buried her hands in her face.

Johnathon got to his feet. "It's over now. We don't have to fear them anymore."

Sean walked away from the fire having heard enough. He looked towards the ships anchored in the cove. Brad and Brooks moved across the stone-covered beach to join him. The civilians had stayed by the fire, letting their saviors have a moment. "What are you thinking Sean?" Brooks asked.

"I'm thinking I don't want to stick around."

"Really, we just got here," Brad halfheartedly joked.

"We need to check out that Coast Guard boat, get on the radios. Put out to sea before the weather turns on us."

33.

Sean sent Brad and Brooks back up to the high ground to find the others. They walked through the forest, this time sticking to visible trails. After a distance they found a flat spot with long views and lay in position, waiting for Jorgensen and the rest of the team. Sean had chosen to stay back with Johnathon and the others. He was planning to give them instructions on using the weapons and training on how to split up watches and defend the walls. Brad didn't want to leave Sean alone, but he was anxious to see the rest of the men.

They didn't have to wait on the trail for long. Hours before sundown, they saw Joseph Vilegas moving down the path slowly. He stopped often, crouching down or taking cover. Others were behind him, following far off. Brooks didn't want to spook Joseph into a firefight so he called out when they were still far away.

As Brooks yelled Joseph's name, they watched as the man dropped into the prone and out of sight. Brooks called out again, then watched Joey get back to his feet and step out into the open. Brad and Brooks stood up and waved to him. They approached each other on the trail and exchanged handshakes as the rest of the patrol filed forward. Jorgensen had come through. Brad recognized several faces from the factory as well as Jeremiah Murphy.

Brad looked back to Joseph, "You can relax a bit, the village ahead is clear for the most part."

Joseph nodded and slung his rifle. He was quieter than usual.

"How's your brother?" Brooks asked.

Joseph didn't speak. Instead he shook his head.

"I'm sorry to hear that, Joey," Brad said somberly. Joseph still didn't say a word and walked further up the trail.

Jorgensen walked towards the front of the patrol with Parker and Alex close behind him. Chelsea smiled and walked up next to Brad. Luke and Alex and their cousin had also joined them on the trail. All of the factory boys now carried the Canadian versions of M4s, except for Alex who had held onto the Remington shotgun.

Jeremiah Murphy had moved next to Brooks. He was wearing an old set of camouflage fatigues with a Canadian flag on the sleeve and held his rifle naturally like a trained soldier. "So what the hell are we standing around for?" Jeremiah asked Brooks.

Brooks shrugged his shoulders and laughed, "Well, you heard the man, let's get moving."

The civilians from the village eagerly

greeted the members of the factory. Even though none of them knew each other personally, they were excited to find other survivors. Luke and the other boys told them about the factory and the farm, and how they were able to sneak past the creepers and avoid the Buhmann. Their stories gave them all hope, hope that they could still find a future on the island.

Brad was exhausted from the past days' work. He was resting on a bench near the road, silently watching all of the activity. He smiled as he watched the boys talk and lighten the mood of the survivors. He saw Chelsea helping children gather their things. Many of them would be moving to the factory. Others would stay here at the cove to rebuild. Chelsea took notice of Brad looking at her; she returned his smile. He watched as she hugged the children then left them to join him.

She walked across the small road and took the seat next to him, sitting close. Brad leaned back and made an exaggerated stretching gesture before putting his arm around her, causing her to laugh. Chelsea smiled and grabbed his fingers, pulling his arm down and around her. "I'll admit it ... Sean was right to come here," Chelsea said, watching the families interact.

Brad pulled her close to him, not giving a response, knowing how things could have easily been different. Once again they had gotten lucky. Many things could have gone wrong, if the gang had been better prepared to face an armed force and not just the occasional civilian. As it turned out they were weak and arrogant. They had never prepared for any defense other than those that worked against the primals.

Their arrogance, or lack of respect for other survivors, caused them to ignore the fact that they themselves may become targets of a greater predator. Sean's plan to take them by surprise while they slept, while their guard was down, had worked. Only a small crew had been able to escape. This group would be stronger now, and better able to defend themselves against primals or raiders.

"Not much for talking right now, are ya," Chelsea said.

"I'm just taking it all in. Sometimes ... if you try really hard, you can imagine things the way they used to be." Brad sighed, squeezing her hand and watching the waves roll up and splash on the beach where hours earlier the raider bodies had been stacked.

Chelsea nodded, then spoke, changing the subject. "Kelli is doing well. She took to the antibiotics you found. The doctor says her leg is mending great and she should be walking soon. It will never be the same though, she will probably need a cane from now on. He says he would recommend surgery if a place existed today."

"She's a tough girl. Any word on Hahn?"

Chelsea let out a small laugh, "Some. Mrs. Murphy says he has fallen for that nurse, the one from the factory."

"Sara?" Brad asked in a surprised voice.

"Yeah, that's the one. Jeremiah and Parker traveled to the factory and offered to bring him to the farm. He said he didn't want to leave, he said he needed to stay closer to the doctor," Chelsea laughed again. "Alex told me that Sara hasn't left his side, and he has gotten very protective of her and the others at the factory."

Brad laughed, "Figures, even missing an arm Hahn is a badass and pulls the ladies."

They sat, quietly watching the people on the beach. Sean was talking to a group of the recently liberated men. With Joseph and Parker's help they were instructing them how to load and clear the C7 assault rifles. The civilians had taken to the training, excited to be able to protect their own. Brad watched as they went through firing positions and basic drills. Joseph was out front, shouting orders like a seasoned drill sergeant.

"How is Joey doing? I mean about his brother?" Brad asked.

Chelsea looked down for a moment. "He doesn't talk about it to me. I overheard him speaking to Gunner. He said it was his fault ... if they hadn't led the group back to the cabin. If they had waited and walked in like Sean told them to. The cabin never would have been attacked, they never would have been out searching for you all, and Daniel never would have been hurt.

"You know that he isn't right, he's angry, he might even be a little crazy. I think he's going to snap, and when he does someone is going to get hurt."

"We all have our ghosts, Chelsea., I don't think we can count anyone out right now," Brad said.

"That's what Gunner said. He knows them all better than anyone, I guess."

"Why isn't Gunner here now?" Brad asked.

"Oh, he wanted to go, he was really pissed off that we kept him at the farm. Mrs. Murphy wouldn't hear it though, she said he needs to stay put until that shoulder heals."

"Damn, I'd have liked to see that one," Brad laughed before leaning back into the bench, stretching his legs to be warmed in the welcome sun.

"You know we could stay here," she whispered, changing the subject. "Things are getting better, they would welcome our help."

Brad didn't say anything. He liked the idea, but couldn't get the thought of his stranded men out of his head. They were counting on him to bring them home. As long as he still had the means, he would continue his mission. He didn't know how his men in the desert were getting by, or if they were even still alive. It really didn't matter to him. He'd made a promise and he intended to keep it. There were times when he wanted to quit and give up, but it was the quiet moments like this that gave him the energy to continue.

Chelsea put her head on Brad's shoulder and closed her eyes. They sat quietly on the bench, blocking out the movement around them. Trying to pretend things were normal for a while. They stayed on the bench until the dinner fires had been lit. Children came to them and asked that they join the families. Brad smiled and let a small boy pull him to his feet. He then turned and held Chelsea's hand as she walked beside him.

Walking to the fire pit, they heard the small boat's horn. Brad turned to see Sean waving and calling him to the pier. Brooks and the rest of the team were with him. Brad let out a long sigh. "Well, so much for that," he said. "Maybe I could just ignore them."

"Yeah right, we know that isn't going to happen," Chelsea said, turning and pulling Brad towards the pier.

Epilogue.

Days and nights were spent preparing the Coast Guard ship for voyage. Unlike most military vessels, they found this one to be an unarmed fishery research vessel. Sean was somewhat disappointed by the discovery. He was hoping for a well-armed surface ship that they could take to the shores of the United States. Still, this craft was filled with high tech equipment that would come in very handy once they figured out how to use it.

The ship was the perfect size for their crew, and it came equipped with its own Zodiac. At barely twenty-five meters, it was short and fat, resembling a tug boat more than a military craft. Brooks had quickly taken on the assignment of getting the ship ready for its maiden voyage. As on their last maritime adventure, Brooks quickly leveraged the expertise of Nelson and Chelsea to help with the ship's systems. Jonathon had kept his word, and they worked quickly to make sure the ship was loaded with food and fuel.

Kelli and Gunner joined them at the village. Kelli's expertise as a pilot and naval officer had paid off well in using many of the ship's navigation instruments. She readily took on the position of captain, eager to earn a place back on the crew. Gunner's shoulder continued to plague him but was healing. He had to keep it in a sling, and had lost a great deal of range of motion from the gunshot wound. Even with all of that, Gunner refused to take a back seat to Sean. Together the two had become a formidable team.

Hahn never joined them at the beach. Brad had made several visits to the factory to speak with him, but he had lost his passion for the fight and the return home. He had found something new with the people at the factory and in the woman, Sara. He had asked Gunner's permission to stay behind, and Gunner granted his request. Gunner explained that their mission was entirely voluntary. He wouldn't ask anyone to go along with them unless they were committed to the goal.

The ship sailed early on the fourth morning, setting a course for the eastern coast of the United States. None of them were familiar with the waters, and even after extensive lectures and hearing countless stories from the sailors at the village they still felt unprepared. The winter weather had come in and the seas were as rough as you would expect for the season. Most of the crew had little experience on seagoing vessels and found themselves sick as soon as they hit open water.

Kelli, Brooks, Sean, and Gunner were all experienced sailors, but the rest of them had a hard time in the rough seas. Brad found himself spending most of his time on the bow of the ship trying to let the cool sea air calm his stomach and ease his headaches. The waters raged and slapped the sides of the ship. When Brad had first seen it in the cove, he'd thought it was huge, but now in the endless ocean it felt like a toy being tossed about in the large waves.

They maintained a constant radio watch, broadcasting several times an hour. No word was received. At one time they picked up an automated broadcast from a far-off tower near Halifax. Instead of a welcome, it was a warning to stay away from their shores. All were dead, and there would be no rescue. They continued to try. Kelli had figured out some of the research equipment and managed to boost the radio's reception capabilities, but they still garnered no response.

As they neared the shores of Massachusetts, they picked up radar anomalies. Unknown objects in the water. Kelli approached close enough to one of them to be able to see it through binoculars. A small tanker ship, drifting dead. The 'Yellow Jack' – the plague flag – was flying high off its mast, providing a warning for others not to approach. Kelli steered clear of the ghost ship and continued their course towards Boston.

On the morning of the fourth day they caught sight of the Brewster Islands off the coast of Boston. Kelli brought the ship in close, holding out hope that survivors may have sought refuge there. They cruised slow and close to the islands, blowing the ship's horn and making calls on the radio. There were no signs of life. The ship continued on into the greater harbor. They hoped to hear sirens, or even gunshots, but they found nothing but a cold and quiet skyline.

They kept the ship far off shore, using the scopes and radars to search. At night they used the spotlights to signal to survivors. They received no signals back, no manmade lights; instead the shorelines were filled with primals howling and screaming at the light. Thousands of them flocked to the shores, their moans and screams filling the night air. The sounds terrified and discouraged them. How could they ever leave the ship and go ashore?

They pulled anchor at first light and carefully navigated their way out of the harbor. They moved south, hugging the coastline, passing Cape Cod and around the island of Nantucket. Every time they stopped and moved towards shore to sound their horn they were greeted by the primals. They sailed west towards New York, growing desperate, knowing they didn't have indefinite stores of fuel, yet wanting to find a safe port. As they passed the Hamptons they saw signs of burnt homes and destroyed cottages.

They dropped anchor off the coast of a

State Park, preserving fuel and using their radios to continue to call for help. The ship when topped off had enough for fourteen days; as they approached the halfway point their goals began to change. Instead of finding safe harbor, they began to search for sources of fuel. They debated taking the Zodiac to do an inland patrol, to search for survivors, or even find small ships they could board and salvage, but in the end it was decided it would be too dangerous.

The next morning they patrolled closer to New York and around Breezy Point. Kelli again cut the engines and let the ship drift the entire afternoon. By late day they had come close, within easy view of Brighton Beach. Brad had traveled to Coney Island with his family as a boy. He recognized some of the familiar sights. The boardwalk was empty of pedestrians; the attractions and rides stood idle. They used binoculars to scan the long sandy beach, finding it completely void of life.

A number of boats were tied to the pier. Kelli let them drift closer before powering up the engines and slowly maneuvering near the moored vessels. As they patrolled in, they saw the primals emerge from the shadows. Quickly they rushed the boardwalk and filled the beach. Within minutes the pier itself was crammed with the screaming and moaning crazies. The sounds filled the air and easily drowned out the rumble of the ship's engines. Gunner ordered Kelli to turn them around and head southeast into open waters.

Brad moved below decks as the ship traveled away from New York. The boat was small and only designed for a permanent crew of six, although there was plenty of room for their current crew of nine. They paired up, sharing the four berthing compartments. Since Kelli and Chelsea were the only females, and Kelli the only officer, they took the captain's berthing. Brad had seen enough for one day, and moved into the ship's small mess area.

He moved through the dining room and into the galley, finding a large pot of coffee. He put his hand to the metal skin to find it was barely warm. Still, coffee wasn't something to be thrown out these days, so he poured himself a cup and moved towards a far seat at the countertop. He had finally gotten over his sea sickness. It helped that the waters had calmed as they moved farther south. The lights were off in the galley. Many of the ship's non-essential breakers had been cut to conserve power, especially while they drifted.

Brad sat watching through a porthole window. He could barely see the tan and greens of the far away coastline. He didn't enjoy sailing, but had to admit it was nice enjoying the comforts of a floating hotel. Even though far from luxurious, the accommodations of a water plant and hot showers were better than humping it out on shore. Brad heard a noise and looked behind him to see Brooks enter the galley.

Brooks poured himself a cup of coffee and made a scowl as he sipped the cold liquid. "Kelli cut the power to the galley again I see," Brooks muttered as he moved across the room and took a seat next to Brad.

"Cold coffee beats no coffee," Brad said. "Anything new up top?"

Brooks took another sip of his coffee then got up to dig through the cupboards, finding a tin of crackers. He opened the container and grabbed a handful, then offered the can to Brad. "Nelson thinks he may have heard a ping on some of the sonar equipment."

"Ping? What, like from another ship?" Brad asked.

Brooks chewed the crackers and took another gulp of the cold coffee. "Yeah I guess, who knows if the kid even knows how to work that shit. He says he made an active sonar, he's been running it day and night. So much scientific gear in that lab to mess with. The little geek likes to tinker though, I'll give him that."

"Whatever keeps him out of trouble," Brad joked.

Brooks finished his coffee and moved out of the galley. Brad really had nothing to do as they moved into warmer waters. He decided to make his way to the back deck of the vessel. He walked onto the open deck in time to see

Chelsea moving towards the rail with a fishing pole. Some of the crew had taken up fishing as the boat slowly crawled to the south. Sean had beginner's luck, but the rest of them had struck out. Brad took a seat near a bundle of supplies and watched Chelsea cast the line far to the side of the ship and slowly reel it back in.

The weather had turned favorable as they moved down the East Coast. Brad lay back and let the bright sunlight warm him, using his hat to cover his eyes while he rested. Fading in and out of sleep, Brad was startled by the slamming of a hatch behind him. Nelson was yelling and running to the ladder that led towards the upper decks. Brad lifted his head and sat up. Chelsea had pulled in the line and dropped the pole behind the rail, moving in the direction of the ladder.

"What did he say?" Brad asked Chelsea.

Chelsea gave him an excited look. "He said we're being pinged," she shouted as she grabbed the ladder and climbed to the top.

Brad tiredly climbed to his feet and walked to the side rail of the ship. They were traveling slowly now, under five knots. The blue waters slapped at the side as the ship cut through the swells. Brad heard the engines cut again as Kelli powered down and allowed the boat to drift. He could hear them talking excitedly on the top decks. Brad looked towards the distant shore miles away. They were void of city skylines now, just open greens cut by sandy cliffs.

He looked down at the calm blue waters. Occasionally a sea bird would fly overhead, circling the boat before landing in the swells alongside. Brad climbed the ladder to the upper decks. He avoided the chaos in the control room and headed directly to the bow. He could still hear them shouting behind him. Brad leaned over the bow and watched the water. Suddenly the team behind him grew quiet. Brad could hear the rapid beeping coming over a speaker in the control room as Kelli tuned in the ping.

Brad turned to see the crew gathered around a console, staring at it intently. Brad heard a loud breaking of water behind him. He turned to see the ocean surface turn to foam far off the bow. Quickly the black hulk of a submarine's sail came vertically straight out of the blue water, white foam rolling off its sides. Brad stepped back in shock as the rest of the large submarine, at least a hundred meters long, came into view. He stumbled forward and placed both hands on the bow rail as the rest of the crew rushed forward and joined him.

They watched as the submarine floated silently hundreds of meters off of their bow. He could hear Kelli shouting behind him, calling them on the radio, flipping channels and hailing over and over with no response. Brad watched as men in yellow and orange jackets came into view atop the sail. Chelsea moved beside him and placed her hand on his. The men on the sail moved back and forth before hoisting a British flag atop a tall mast.

Thank You for Reading
If you have an opportunity
Please leave a review on Amazon
Walking In the Shadow of Death.
Lundy W. J. (2014-05-01).
Whiskey Tango Foxtrot: Volume IV
Visit W.J. Lundy on Facebook
Volume I Whiskey Tango Foxtrot. Kindle Edition.
Volume II Tales of the Forgotten. Kindle Edition.
Volume III Only the Dead Live Forever. Kindle Edition.

Book five in the Series
In progress

Printed in Great Britain
by Amazon